MURDER AT DONWELL ABBEY

Books by Vanessa Kelly

MURDER IN HIGHBURY

MURDER AT DONWELL ABBEY

Published by Kensington Publishing Corp.

MURDER AT DONWELL ABBEY

VANESSA KELLY

KENSINGTON
PUBLISHING CORP.
kensingtonbooks.com

This book is a work of fiction. Names, characters, businesses, organizations, places, events, and incidents either are the product of the author's imagination or are used fictitiously. Any resemblance to actual persons, living or dead, events, or locales is entirely coincidental.

To the extent that the image or images on the cover of this book depict a person or persons, such person or persons are merely models, and are not intended to portray any character or characters featured in the book.

KENSINGTON BOOKS are published by

Kensington Publishing Corp.
900 Third Avenue
New York, NY 10022

Copyright © 2025 by Vanessa Kelly

All rights reserved. No part of this book may be reproduced in any form or by any means without the prior written consent of the Publisher, excepting brief quotes used in reviews.

Without limiting the author's and publisher's exclusive rights, any unauthorized use of this publication to train generative artificial intelligence (AI) technologies is expressly prohibited.

All Kensington titles, imprints, and distributed lines are available at special quantity discounts for bulk purchases for sales promotion, premiums, fundraising, educational, or institutional use.

Special book excerpts or customized printings can also be created to fit specific needs. For details, write or phone the office of the Kensington Special Sales Manager: Attn. Special Sales Department, Kensington Publishing Corp., 900 Third Avenue, New York, NY 10022. Phone: 1-800-221-2647.

KENSINGTON and the K with book logo Reg. US Pat. & TM Off.

Library of Congress Card Catalogue Number: 2025940689

ISBN: 978-1-4967-4600-9
First Kensington Hardcover Edition: December 2025

ISBN: 978-1-4967-4602-3 (ebook)

10 9 8 7 6 5 4 3 2 1

Printed in the United States of America

The authorized representative in the EU for product safety and compliance
is eucomply OU, Parnu mnt 139b-14, Apt 123
Tallinn, Berlin 11317, hello@eucompliancepartner.com

To my dear readers, who followed along on this new writing adventure—I appreciate you more than you'll ever know. Thank you!

Acknowledgments

To take on a project that attempts to emulate the great Jane Austen—or is even Austen-adjacent—is quite mad. Therefore, it is one that requires considerable support from very skilled and knowledgeable people. I'm so grateful to John Scognamiglio and Alex Nicolajsen, who have been true champions of my work at Kensington. Larissa Ackerman's support has gone above and beyond, and I would be sunk in a promotional morass without her nimble assistance. In fact, the entire Kensington promotional and marketing team has performed miracles with this series, and I'm so grateful to them. A thousand thank-yous!

As always, I owe my agent, Evan Marshall, a debt of gratitude for his help and support over the years. I'm also deeply grateful to Louisa Cornell and Laurel Ann Nattress for helping me up my Austen game.

To my friends and family—thank you! A special call-out must go to Laurie Lynd, Moze Mossanen, Allison Van Diepen, Digby Ricci, Minerva Spencer, and Debbie Mazzuca for their friendship, advice, and support. The publishing/entertainment business can be, ahem, challenging at times, and I've been blessed to have excellent friends to help carry me through the heavy bits. To my nephew, Nick Rudman—you're the best, and may both our futures be bright! To my family, especially Trish, Anne, Philip, Brian, Liz, and Wendy and Joe . . . I love you and am so grateful for your kindness and support.

And to my dear husband, Randy, I couldn't do it without you. I love you the most, and am forever grateful for you.

Chapter 1

Hartfield
January 1816

Emma Knightley had encountered her share of vexing moments in life. Stumbling across the body of a murder victim last year was certainly one of them. But nothing could have prepared her for *this* moment. For a few seconds, she wondered if she'd misheard her father's shocking statement.

Her family had been enjoying a cup of tea, ensconced in Hartfield's drawing room for their final evening together before the holiday season ended. George had been chatting with John, his brother, while Isabella, Emma's older sister as well as John's wife, had been expressing regret that they must return to London after such a charming visit to Highbury with their children. Naturally, their home in London beckoned, as did John's work at the Inns of Court.

At that point, Father had abruptly made his announcement, one that landed with the force of a cannonball crashing into the drawing room.

Emma finally gathered her wits. "I beg your pardon, Father. I don't think I heard you—"

"What the devil do you mean you're going to marry Miss Bates?" John blustered. "Surely you cannot be serious. The woman's a—"

Emma ruthlessly interrupted her brother-in-law. "What John means, Father, is that perhaps we misunderstood you. You cannot mean that you truly wish to . . ." She found the words almost too hideous to utter. "You know."

Father graced her with a beatific smile. "To take that dear lady as my wife? Yes, I certainly do. Miss Bates and I have discussed the matter at great length. Given the nature of our friendship, we feel that marriage is the proper course of action."

Since Emma found herself unwilling to contemplate what her father meant by *the nature* of their friendship, she cast a pleading gaze at her husband. George, however, was still regarding his father-in-law with his jaw agape.

Emma cleared her throat to catch his attention before tapping a finger under her jaw. George blinked, and then snapped his mouth shut.

"But, Father," Isabella plaintively said. "You always maintained that you never wished to marry again. You said no one could ever replace Mama in your heart."

"No one will ever replace you blessed mother's memory, my dear girl," Father gently said. "Indeed, I had quite the job persuading Miss Bates to accept my hand, because she feared she could never measure up to such a fine woman's legacy."

"I should think not," exclaimed John. "Miss Bates is a kind woman, but she's a blasted chatterbox, not to mention—ouch!"

He glared at George, who was sitting next to him on the sofa. Most likely George had just forcefully jabbed his brother in the leg.

Emma refocused her attention. "Father, I know you and Miss Bates have been a great comfort to each other through difficult times, but is this decision not a trifle . . . well, impetuous? After all, you know how much you hate change." She got a flash of inspiration. "And what of Mrs. Bates? Surely Miss Bates would not wish to leave her mother."

Mrs. Bates was the widow of one of Highbury's former vicars, and well advanced in years. She and her daughter had lived in a small set of apartments in the village ever since the death of Mr. Bates.

Father nodded. "It's kind of you to be worried about Mrs. Bates, but such anxieties are unnecessary. She will be moving to Hartfield with Miss Bates."

Emma swallowed a whimper, while George pressed a finger to his lips. He seemed to have recovered from his shock and was now looking rather amused. She supposed she couldn't blame him, since the idea of her father marrying Miss Bates was absurd. From a certain point of view, one might even call it comical. But that point of view didn't happen to be hers.

Then another thought struck with terrible force. Miss Bates would not only become her father's wife, she would become Emma's stepmother.

Heaven help me.

Isabella rose and went to their father, taking his hand. "Are you sure, Father? Such a drastic change might greatly affect your health. You and I are not robust, and I cannot fathom what I would do without John to look after me, providing me with everything necessary to my comfort. We go on so quietly in Brunswick Square, with nothing changing from one day to the next—just as you do with Emma and George."

Although John did take excellent care of his wife, Isabella's life was hardly quiet. Not as the mother of five young children.

"I understand, my dear," Father replied. "But Miss Bates and I will take care of each other."

Emma blinked, rather stung by that statement. "I take care of you, Father. George and I both do so, gladly."

"You do indeed, my dear. Still, I am such a burden, with all my little oddities. It does weigh on me, on occasion."

"Nonsense, sir," said George in a bracing tone. "You are never a burden. Emma loves you, as do I."

"And why cannot you and Miss Bates simply go on as you have, as the best of friends and companions?" Emma was now a trifle desperate. "She visits almost every day as it is."

"But that's just it," her father replied in a gentle but unyielding tone. "As one gets older, one wishes for companionship with someone of like mind. Miss Bates and I take great comfort in each other's company, and that is nothing to be sneezed at when one reaches my years."

Emma sighed. As sweet-tempered as her father was, he had a stubborn streak. It usually manifested in harmless ways, such as his strict admonitions against cake or his never-ending battle against drafts. But experience had taught her that when Father made up his mind, it was all but impossible to change it.

She mustered a smile that likely looked more like a grimace. "I know how her friendship has been a comfort to you."

He nodded. "Especially in this year past, when life has been so fraught."

This was an obvious reference to the murder of Mrs. Elton, one of Highbury's leading citizens. Both Miss Bates and Father had been greatly affected by that dreadful event, and it had drawn them even closer together.

If the poor woman hadn't come to such an unfortunate end, Emma could almost be cross with Mrs. Elton for having set in motion this domestic cataclysm that was erupting at Hartfield months later.

"And you and George are always so busy—you with Hartfield and your charitable work, and George with Donwell Abbey," her father added. "But now I will have Miss Bates to keep me company. She will also be a great aid to you in managing Hartfield. Miss Bates is a fine housekeeper in her own right, and can relieve you of much of that burden."

The notion of Miss Bates taking over the management of Hartfield was so ghastly that Emma was again stunned into silence.

John snorted. "Miss Bates managing Hartfield? That's the most—"

"I'm sure Miss Bates is more than up to the task," George firmly cut in. "Especially with Emma's help." He cast her a mildly challenging glance. "Is that not so, my dear?"

"Er, yes. Of course," she managed. "If Father is *really* sure about this."

"I am," Father replied with quiet dignity.

George nodded. "Then please accept my congratulations, sir. We're very happy for you."

Emma bit back a sigh. Once George gave his approval, there was no point in prolonging the battle.

She dredged up a smile and rose. "Of course we want you to be happy, dearest. If Miss Bates makes you happy, then I am pleased for you."

"I'm not," muttered John.

Emma bent down to give her father a hug. Isabella pulled a slight grimace, but did the same.

"Ridiculous," John groused.

Emma ignored her dratted brother-in-law as she and Isabella resumed their seats. One frequently had to ignore John's outbursts.

"Have you and Miss Bates decided on a date?" George asked.

"No," her father replied. "We must think of Jane and Frank. They must travel a great distance for the wedding, and one would not wish them to do so at such an inclement time of year. Jane is still recovering from her lying-in."

Good Lord, Jane and Frank!

Emma had not even thought of how the Churchills might react to this unsettling news.

Jane, formerly Jane Fairfax, was the granddaughter of Mrs. Bates and the niece of Miss Bates. Orphaned at an early age, she had been lovingly cared for by the two of them. Jane had eventually gone to live with a school friend whose well-to-do parents had raised her as a second daughter. When she finally returned to Highbury, her intention had been to find a position as a governess. Before that unpleasant prospect had come to fruition, she'd fallen in love with the wealthy Frank Churchill and he with her. They were married a few months before Emma and George, and now resided on the Churchill family estate in Yorkshire.

"Do Jane and Frank know about your plans?" she asked.

Father shook his silver-haired head. "Miss Bates intends to send an express post to Jane first thing in the morning."

"Then I take it the Westons aren't privy to the news, either," said George.

Frank was Mr. Weston's son by his first wife. Unable to care for his little boy after his wife died, Mr. Weston had made the difficult decision to allow Frank to be adopted and raised by her wealthy relatives, the Churchills. Frank and Mr. Weston, however, now enjoyed an excellent filial relationship.

"Not yet." Father smiled at Emma. "I was hoping you could tell the Westons the happy news, my dear. I thought you would enjoy doing so. Perhaps first thing in the morning?"

John let out a snort, while George actually had to smother a laugh.

After casting her husband a warning glare, Emma nodded at her father. "Of course."

If nothing else, Mrs. Weston would provide a sympathetic ear. Having lived for many years at Hartfield as Emma's governess, she was well aware of her former employer's disposition. Mrs. Weston would be astounded by this turn of events.

Father beamed at her. "Then it's all settled. Miss Bates will be so pleased."

"I'm only sorry John and I won't be here to give Miss Bates our best wishes, since we leave tomorrow," Isabella said, making a game attempt at sounding sincere.

Father wrinkled his brow. "I was hoping I could prevail upon you and the children to stay an extra week or so. I know John must get back to London, but surely you will not want to miss the party."

Isabella and Emma exchanged a perplexed glance.

"What party are you referring to?" Emma asked.

"Did I fail to mention the party?" Father chuckled. "How like me. I'm referring to our betrothal party, naturally. Miss Bates insisted on it, and I didn't have the heart to deny her. But there mustn't be any cake, Emma. I hold the line on that point, at least."

For her father to suggest any sort of large social gathering was unheard of. In fact, it took a great deal of coaxing to persuade him to go even as far as the Westons' home, Randalls, for a holiday party, or for an outing at Donwell on a sunny day.

"Do you mean something like a dinner party at Hartfield?" she cautiously asked. "I'm sure we can—"

"No, my dear. I mean a *proper* party, something along the lines of a dance or a ball."

George's eyebrows practically shot up into his hairline. "Are you certain you heard Miss Bates correctly, sir? She knows your preferences. Would you not find a dance or a large party inconvenient?"

"I confess that I cannot view such an event without trepidation, but Miss Bates insists on making it a festive occasion. She says it will be a great treat for Highbury after the difficult year we've all had." He fluttered a hand. "With Mrs. Elton, you know. Most distressing for everyone."

"Especially Mrs. Elton," John sardonically replied. "But where will you hold this grand event? Surely you don't wish for all of Highbury to be tromping about Hartfield, dirtying the carpets and causing a grand fuss."

Emma felt herself go cold at the very idea. "Perhaps you're thinking of the Crown Inn for a ball? Though I cannot think you would like that very well."

Father looked horrified. "Emma, inns are such unhealthy, drafty places, especially at this time of year."

She breathed a sigh of relief. "I so agree. That being the case, I think a nice dinner party at Hartfield—"

"I suppose we could hold a dance at the abbey," George said, almost to himself.

"What?" Emma exclaimed.

Isabella winced. "Emma, that was right in my ear."

"I apologize, dear." Emma glared at her husband. "I was merely surprised."

"I suppose you could hold it at Donwell," commented John. "From what George told me, you did manage Mrs. Elton's funeral reception with quite a large crowd. Smashing success, apparently."

Emma gazed at him with disbelief. "Funeral receptions are not intended to be smashing successes. And it was a mob scene and an exceedingly troublesome event."

George smiled at her. "John is correct, though. You managed that affair with great aplomb."

"Emma, I think George's idea has great merit," Father said. "I feel certain Miss Bates would be thrilled with a party at Donwell Abbey."

"Then we shall be happy to comply." George gave Emma a pointed look. "Is that not right, my dear?"

Emma took in her father's hopeful expression. For so many years, the old darling had mourned his wife's death, retiring from the world to fret about his health and his loved ones. There was no doubt he'd changed in this past year, and for the better. That was obviously down to Miss Bates.

Mentally sighing, she capitulated. "George and I would be happy to host a party for you and Miss Bates at Donwell. When would you like to have it?"

"I thought Saturday, my dear. That should give you ample time to prepare. And that way Isabella will still be here to attend."

Emma gaped him. "That gives us but six days, and in the middle of winter, too!"

"I'm sure we can manage," George smoothly interjected. "The roads have been dry, so we can import from Leatherhead any supplies not available in Highbury. It will be fine, my dear."

With George so obviously in favor of the whole demented project, Emma realized she might as well rip off the bandage and get on with it.

"I'll call on Miss Bates tomorrow to discuss the arrangements," she said.

Her father beamed. "There's no need, since Miss Bates will be visiting Hartfield first thing in the morning. You can have a nice, cozy chat then and make all the plans you like." He gave Isabella a tentative smile. "And you as well, my dear. I do hope we can persuade you to stay."

Isabella was spared the need to reply when the clock on the mantle chimed out the hour.

Emma was surprised at the late hour. "Goodness, Father, I really do think you must retire now. Mr. Perry will be cross if you wear yourself out."

At the alarming prospect of incurring his apothecary's disapproval, her father responded with alacrity. "Very true, my dear. We should all be abed."

Emma rose, rang the bell, and then went to her father. "Let me help you up."

She escorted him to the corridor where Simon, their senior footman, hovered by the door.

"Are you ready to retire, Mr. Woodhouse?" the young man asked.

"I am." Father gave Emma a smile. "Good night, my dear. Don't stay up too late."

After handing her father off to the faithful Simon, she rejoined the group and flopped down in his vacated chair. "This was certainly not how I was expecting the evening to end."

John crossed to the drinks trolley. "How could you allow this to happen, Emma? Miss Bates as mistress of Hartfield? It's simply deranged."

"It's not as if I planned it," she defensively replied. "I'd no idea they were anything more than very good friends."

"And yet, from what George tells me, your father has been giving Miss Bates a singular degree of notice for some months now."

"But George never suggested that something like this could happen!"

Her husband shrugged. "It never struck me that your father could possibly be amenable to so drastic a change. After all, this is the man who still refers to Mrs. Weston as Miss Taylor."

John returned to his seat. "I for one do not relish the thought of spending our visits at Hartfield with Miss Bates in charge of domestic matters. It's a blasted uncomfortable prospect."

Isabella sighed. "I must agree. In fact, I find it all very daunting. However will we manage it?"

"You'll manage by staying at Donwell Abbey," George calmly said.

Startled, Emma peered at him. "We can hardly expect them to stay at the abbey while the rest of us are at Hartfield. It's in no condition to host anyone."

"But it will be, once we take up residence there," he replied.

Her mind couldn't seem to absorb the words. "I beg your pardon?"

John laughed. "So that's how it's to be. Good plan, old man. Surprised I didn't think of it myself."

"What are you two talking about?" asked Isabella.

"It's obvious. Now that your father has Miss Bates to look

after him and keep him busy, George and Emma can finally move to Donwell. It's the silver lining to an otherwise ridiculous situation."

"Hmm," Emma muttered.

When she and George became betrothed, she'd made it clear that she couldn't leave her father. He'd always dreaded the prospect of losing her even to a house less than a mile away and to a man he loved as a son. Nor could her father have borne a move from his beloved Hartfield, the only place he truly felt safe.

Thankfully, George had solved the problem by proposing that he and Emma live at Hartfield for as long as necessary. Although getting on in years, her father was no antique nor was he as frail as he supposed himself to be. He could easily live for many more years, which had meant that Hartfield would remain their home for the foreseeable future—or so, at least, Emma had thought.

Her husband cocked an inquiring eyebrow. "What do you think, my dear?"

"I suppose that makes sense," she cautiously replied. "I'm not sure Miss Bates is up to running Hartfield, but I can easily help her from Donwell."

Isabella rested a gentle hand on Emma's knee. "Are you sure, Emma? Donwell is a very fine house, but you've resided at Hartfield your entire life."

Emma smiled at her sister. "As you know, in the natural order of things wives usually move in with their husbands. Besides, I love Donwell, and it's past time it receive the attention it deserves."

She truly did love the gracious old abbey. It wouldn't be easy to whip it into proper shape, but she would relish the challenge.

John regarded her with a sardonic eye. "Even better, you'll escape having to live with Miss Bates."

She wrinkled her nose at him, half in reprimand and half in agreement.

"I suppose that settles it," Isabella said with a sigh. "Goodness, what an evening!"

Emma held up hand. "There's one more thing I'd like to discuss."

"What now?" John groaned.

"This party . . . ball . . . or dance that we're supposed to organize in six days. I don't see how I can do it without help."

George frowned. "Emma, you will have my help."

"Of course, but it's not the same thing." She cast a pleading eye at her sister. "It requires a woman's touch."

And talents.

Her sister gave her a rueful smile. "You wish me to stay."

"Yes, please. Besides, you know how much Father would enjoy having you and the children at Hartfield for another week. He never wishes you to leave."

"And what about my wishes?" asked John. "Don't they enter into it?"

"Of course they do, my love," Isabella replied in a gentle voice. "But these are very unusual circumstances. Father and Emma need me, and it will only be for another week or so."

John blew out an exasperated sigh. "Very well, but *only* a week. Not a day more."

Isabella simply shrugged.

John stared at her for a few moments before switching his attention to Emma. "Is there anything else? Are we *now* allowed to retire? I must be on the road, first thing."

Emma managed a smile. "Of course."

"Goodness," she said, after John and Isabella left the room. "What has come over our family? I hardly recognize anyone."

"Words fail me," George dryly replied. "You must admit, though, that life has suddenly become quite interesting. One can only imagine how Highbury will react to the news of your father's betrothal."

Ugh.

"The gossip will be utterly gruesome," she said.

It seemed their welcome spell of peace and quiet was coming to a close.

Chapter 2

Emma surveyed Donwell Abbey's large supper room, where spare tables had been commandeered and dressed in crisp linens, then set with long-unused silver and glassware. The crystal glittered in the candlelight, platters were piled high with delicacies, and guests milled about, happily chatting and eating. No one would have guessed that the hosts' frantic preparations had been completed a mere hour before the first arrivals.

Mrs. Hodges, Donwell's inestimable housekeeper, studied the room with an anxious gaze. "I hope we don't run out of punch."

"I shouldn't think so. We're halfway through the evening and still seem to have plenty of it."

"Wait till that lot dancing in the great hall come in," Mrs. Hodges sourly noted. "A plague of locusts, they'll be."

Mrs. Hodges's alarmist tendency helped make her an excellent housekeeper. She made sure to prepare for any eventuality, including organizing large parties in less than a week.

"As long as we don't run out of cider," said Emma. "It's been very popular with the gentlemen."

"Mr. Larkins says we're in good trim. He held back three half ankers, just in case."

"Where is Larkins, by the by? I haven't seen him in over an hour."

Donwell's manager was as valuable to the smooth running of the estate as Mrs. Hodges was to the household. Larkins was unflappable, and once set to a task never left it undone. Emma couldn't think how they'd ever get on without him.

"Mr. Larkins went to the stables to check on the arrangements with the carriages. Then he was going to go back to his cottage. He said he'll return before the end of the party to help with the cleanup—or if he's needed before, I'm to send the kitchen boy down to fetch him."

Larkins dwelled in the steward's cottage, just outside the gates of the abbey. The separation from the big house suited him, since he had a tendency to prefer solitude. Work was his life, and he only rarely socialized. As far as Emma knew, he'd never once asked George for a holiday to visit friends or family. Even convincing the man to take a day off was something of a chore.

"I envy his peace and quiet," Emma wryly replied as a gaggle of teachers from Mrs. Goddard's school squeezed by them, heading for the great hall.

"I do hope Mr. Woodhouse and Miss Bates are pleased, ma'am. Everyone seems to be enjoying themselves."

"My father would faint dead away if he saw this mob. Thankfully, Donwell's library is far enough away that the noise shouldn't bother him."

Emma had wanted her father safely ensconced and out of the way in the abbey's comfortable library. There, he could spend most of the evening with Isabella, who also disliked noisy affairs. Mrs. Bates had joined them, and was very likely having a snooze by the cozy, crackling fire.

"I had Prudence bring Mr. Woodhouse and Mrs. Knightley

a tray of stewed chicken and biscuits, along with some of Serle's custards," said Mrs. Hodges. "Prudence said Mrs. Weston was there as well, keeping them company."

That was just like dear Mrs. Weston, Emma's former governess. For her, the comfort of the Woodhouse family would always be a priority.

"It seems that Prudence is working out very well," Emma commented, referring to the chambermaid. "She helped me dress for the party."

"That girl has been a godsend, ma'am. Very hardworking and with the sweetest temper—I wish we could hire three more like her."

Prudence Parr had been hired only three months ago, after the previous maid had moved on to another establishment. If the girl continued to work out so well, Emma thought to promote her to lady's maid after she and George moved to Donwell.

Mrs. Hodges ran another gaze over the refreshment tables. "Looks like the punch bowl needs refilling. Where is that dratted Harry when you need him?"

Harry Trotman, Donwell's sole footman, was the bane of Mrs. Hodges's existence. Though he seemed a pleasant fellow to Emma and George liked him, their housekeeper was not so generous. She rated the young man as only a step or two above lazy.

"I will let you get back to your work, Mrs. Hodges," Emma said.

The housekeeper sketched a curtsey. "Of course, ma'am."

Emma smiled. "And if I see Harry, I'll send him your way."

Mrs. Hodges huffed and departed for the back of the house.

Emma strolled through the supper room, chatting with guests and receiving well wishes on her father's behalf—some delivered with an understandable air of incredulity.

George awaited her at the refreshment tables, where he was

conversing with Highbury's curate, Mr. Barlowe, and a nattily dressed young man whom she didn't recognize.

"There you are, my dear," said George. "I hope all is well?"

"Apparently so, according to Mrs. Hodges."

"Mrs. Hodges is a most estimable woman," Mr. Barlowe earnestly commented. "Only a few days ago, she sent your footman to the vicarage with a bag of potatoes. And they are excellent potatoes, Mr. Knightley, truly excellent. That you manage to keep them in such prime condition during the winter must be counted a miracle. I cannot think how you do it."

"My dear fellow, I'm sure Mr. Knightley knows his potatoes very well," said the other man in a humorous tone. "No need to rave on about them."

Mr. Barlowe flushed at the good-natured jibe and turned an apologetic glance on George. "Forgive me, sir. I only meant to show my appreciation. You and Mrs. Knightley have been exceedingly kind since my arrival."

Alan Barlowe had come to Highbury but four months previous, as their new clergyman. A slight man of equally slight means, he struck Emma as suffering from a nervous disposition. He fulfilled his duties well enough, but he was not a social person and occasionally blurted out awkward comments. As for his sermons, he droned his way through them as if they were a highly unpleasant exercise. But he seemed diligent, determined to do his duties no matter his personal afflictions.

Emma smiled at the curate. "You can never offend my husband by complimenting anything to do with Donwell. Given half the chance, he will be happy to tell you exactly how he manages to keep his potatoes so fresh."

"I suspect Mr. Knightley could make even that subject interesting," said the other young man, giving George a slight bow. "My father speaks very highly of you, sir, and says that your knowledge of estate management is second to none. I wouldn't know, of course, since I'm utterly hopeless when it comes to such matters."

That was certainly blunt speaking.

"George, I don't believe I've met this gentleman," Emma said. "Perhaps you might introduce me?"

Her husband winced. "Forgive me, Emma. I thought you were acquainted with Mr. Plumtree."

Ah. Now she knew who the man was.

"You're Squire Plumtree's son," she said with a smile. "I've met your father on a few occasions, and have heard him speak of you."

The young man gave another slight bow and cast her a charmingly crooked grin. "It's a great pleasure, Mrs. Knightley. But I confess I'd rather not hear what my father has to say about me. I'm afraid I'm something of a trial to the poor fellow."

It seemed an odd thing to say to a stranger, but perhaps she was too harsh. Mr. Plumtree was a good-looking young man with an obviously light-hearted manner. Also in his favor was the fact that he was correctly if very fashionably attired for an evening party.

"We hoped to see Squire Plumtree at our party tonight," she said.

"He sends his regrets, ma'am. His business, unfortunately, has kept him in London."

Emma rummaged in her brain. "Your father is a wool merchant, is he not?"

"Indeed." His smile turned self-deprecating. "It might seem odd for him to be in trade, given that our family has resided at Plumtree Manor for many generations. But my father had an opportunity to invest in the wool industry some years ago and became quite taken with it. He spends much of his time in London, as a result."

"Many a family now finds it prudent to invest in trade," George kindly replied. "The wars on the Continent provided ample opportunity to do so."

"So my father says. I must admit that I'm woefully ignorant in that regard, as well. I'm afraid I don't share my father's enthusiasm for trade."

Mr. Barlowe gave him a sympathetic grimace. "One can hardly blame you. Many of those involved in trade can be quite vulgar in their mannerisms." He flushed bright red a moment later. "Excepting your father, of course. I'm sure he's not in the least bit vulgar."

Mr. Plumtree responded with a polite smile. "Just as you say, dear fellow."

In the painful silence that followed, Emma became acutely aware of the cheerful din of chatter around them.

"Mr. Plumtree, do you reside at Plumtree Manor?" she asked, trying to rescue the conversation.

"I do, ma'am. I've lived at Plumtree my entire life."

"I imagine your father must be grateful to have a son there in his absence."

Her comment produced an outright grin from him. "That observation would certainly make my father laugh, since I'm as hopeless at estate management as I am at trade. My dear papa, however, still holds out hope for my eventual reform."

While it was a cynical statement, he said it with such good humor that it was hard not to feel some charity for him.

"I'm sure you underestimate your talents," she protested.

His eyes gleamed with amusement. "You must be sure to ask my father about that when next you meet him."

"Plumtree, you must stop teasing Mrs. Knightley," Mr. Barlowe admonished. "She won't know what to think."

"Mrs. Knightley thinks she will ask her husband for a glass of wine," Emma humorously replied. She glanced at the curate's half-empty glass. "Mr. Barlowe, would you like more punch?"

"Thank you, ma'am, but I thought to visit the great hall now to listen to the music and see the dancing." He gave an admonishing glance to his companion. "I think that would be just the thing."

Plumtree affected great astonishment. "You astound me, Barlowe. Are you sure such pleasures don't fall under the category of inappropriate behavior? Or are you gathering material for your Sunday sermon?"

"Now you're talking nonsense," the curate replied in a cross tone.

Plumtree laughed. "I am, indeed, which is most unfair of me. I will do my best to atone for my behavior by finding you a partner. You're one of the few eligible men in the village, so there must be at least one young lady who will be eager to dance with you."

After sketching bows to Emma and George, he led the blushing curate away.

"What an interesting young man," she said, watching them go.

"Which one," George dryly replied.

She laughed. "They do seem a mismatched pair. Mr. Barlowe is so terribly shy, while Mr. Plumtree is . . ."

"An impertinent puppy."

"But a charming one, nevertheless. I wonder what his story is?"

"You must be sure to ask his father when next you see him."

Emma regarded her beloved with a degree of disfavor. "Now who's impertinent? And heaven knows this village could use a few more eligible gentlemen like Mr. Plumtree. I'm afraid Mr. Barlowe hardly counts in that respect."

Her husband adopted an expression of mock alarm. "Emma, your words strike fear into my heart. I was under the impression that your matchmaking days were over."

"Dearest, I'm simply stating facts. Besides, Mr. Plumtree is quite an attractive young man. I'm sure he needs no help from me in that regard."

Well . . . perhaps just a little.

George's knowing expression suggested that he'd surmised

what she was thinking—not that she had any intention of admitting to the truth of it. And, really, her matchmaking efforts, such as they were, had ended with her marriage. Still, one couldn't help but feel for the young ladies of Highbury, who stood in dire need of a new crop of eligible bachelors.

"I stand corrected, my Emma," her husband wryly replied. "Now, shall I fetch you a glass of wine?"

She glanced over to the doorway. "Later, perhaps. I see Mrs. Weston is waving to me from across the room."

"And I see Dr. Hughes. He wished to buttonhole me about some matter of business, although I cannot imagine what."

The village's physician, who also served as coroner, was pontificating to a resigned-looked Mr. Cox, Highbury's resident solicitor, over by the fireplace.

"You have my sympathies, dearest."

An amused snort was his only reply. Emma wended her way to the doorway of the room where Mrs. Weston chatted with Mrs. Cole, one of Highbury's leading residents.

"There you are, my dear," said Mrs. Weston. "Your father has been wondering what's become of you."

"I'll visit him as soon as I check on the great hall."

"Mrs. Knightley, what a splendid occasion," enthused Mrs. Cole. "Only imagine—Mr. Woodhouse and Miss Bates to be married!"

"Yes, it was quite the surprise," Emma replied. "A happy one, naturally."

"I would be thrilled to host a dinner party for them in a few weeks' time. Both Miss Bates and your father deserve some well-earned fussing."

Father would no doubt think one party was quite enough fussing. "That's very kind of you, but we cannot ask you to put yourself out, ma'am."

The always-cheerful woman—sometimes a bit *too* cheerful—beamed at her. "Nonsense. Now if you'll excuse me, I see Mrs.

Cox." She glanced around, looking conspiratorial. "Young William is in his cups and causing quite a bit of a commotion in the great hall. I thought to drop a word in his mother's ear."

Emma sighed as Mrs. Cole bustled off. "Is it possible to hold an event at Donwell without one of the Cox children behaving badly? I suppose I must go and assess the damage."

"I'm sure it's not as bad as Mrs. Cole suggested," Mrs. Weston replied. "William is with his sisters, after all."

"Oh, joy. My cup overflows."

While both sisters could be annoying, the eldest, Miss Anne Cox, was surely the most impertinent girl in Highbury—if not the county.

Mrs. Weston laughed. "I'll come with you. We'll have a chat along the way."

"I feel as if we've barely exchanged a word in a week," Emma replied as she linked arms with her friend.

After the death of Emma's mother, Mrs. Weston—then Miss Taylor—had taken up residence at Hartfield as governess, handling the care of two grief-stricken girls. She'd managed Emma and Isabella with tender affection, becoming almost a second mother to them. Once Isabella married John, Emma and Miss Taylor had grown ever closer. And although it had been a day of great joy when her beloved governess became Mrs. Weston, there was sorrow, too. Emma had lost her anchor and for some months she'd floated adrift.

Thankfully, she'd found her course in time. Falling in love with George, and having that love so generously returned, had brought Emma to safe harbor.

"You must forgive me. I've been so busy with my daughter."

"How is little Anna?" Emma asked. "It sounded like she had a dreadful cold."

"Mr. Perry says she is well on the mend, even though Mr. Weston is inclined to doubt him."

"Then Mr. Weston should have another chat with our good apothecary tonight to assuage his worries. Mr. Perry has been here all evening. Father insisted he come early to oversee the refreshments, so as to ascertain that nothing harmful would be served."

"I hope you had the foresight to hide the cakes."

"Mrs. Hodges was—"

She broke off when Prudence Parr hurried toward them from the great hall. The girl looked terribly flustered, with her mobcap askew and her normally rosy cheeks bleached white. She almost rushed past them until Emma put out a hand.

"Prudence! Is everything all right?"

The maid jerked to a halt. "Oh, Mrs. Knightley... excuse me, madam, I didn't see you there. Or you, Mrs. Weston. Forgive me."

She bobbed an off-kilter curtsy. Her eyes were red-rimmed, and she clutched one hand into the starched fabric of her apron, wrinkling it. Her entire attitude suggested one of considerable distress.

"My dear child," Mrs. Weston kindly said, "whatever is the matter?"

"I... oh, nothing," she stammered.

A thought darted into Emma's head. "Has someone been pestering you, Prudence?"

Like William Cox?

It was entirely possible that William, in his cups, might have importuned Prudence. Some males, especially in these social settings, were notorious for their shabby treatment of female servants. It was a state of affairs Emma had always despised.

Prudence's gaze slid sideways. "No, nothing like that, Mrs. Knightley. I'm... it's just the migraine. I'm very prone to them. Mrs. Hodges said I should go up to my room and lie down until it passes."

Emma had never heard mention of Prudence suffering from migraines. Still, the girl looked quite ill. "Yes, you should. I'm sorry you're not well."

Prudence wrung her hands in her apron. "I apologize, Mrs. Knightley, and with so much work to be done tonight."

Emma patted her shoulder. "We have more than enough staff for tonight. Take as much time as you need."

The girl heaved a grateful sigh. "Thank you, madam. It's very kind of you."

Then she picked up her skirts and all but fled in the direction of the back stairs.

Mrs. Weston grimaced. "I hope Prudence is not coming down with something worse than a headache. She was waiting on your father and Mrs. Bates earlier in the evening."

"Which we will *not* mention to Father. But I'll ask Mrs. Hodges to check on Prudence later."

As they approached the hall, the chatter of voices and the gay notes of a country-dance loudly swelled.

"What a din," exclaimed Mrs. Weston.

"Understandable, since most of the—"

Another young woman burst into the corridor and rushed toward them.

Mrs. Weston sighed. "Susan Cox appears upset, too."

"Her dratted brother, no doubt."

Susan came to a halt, looking rattled but possessing enough sense to dip a shallow curtsy.

"How are you, Susan?" Mrs. Weston asked.

"Fine, ma'am," she nervously replied. "It's ever so nice a party, Mrs. Knightley. Anne was just saying that the dancing is quite good—although not as good as the dancing at Mr. Weston's ball last year."

Emma refrained from rolling her eyes. "Is something wrong, Miss Cox? You seem discomposed."

"I . . . I'm going to fetch my mother. William isn't feeling well, and Mama will know what to do with him."

"I surmise that your brother has become inebriated," Emma dryly replied.

The girl hesitated, and then gloomily nodded. Of all the Cox children, she was the least annoying. One also had to remember that she was the youngest and of course under the influence of her unfortunate siblings.

"Where is your brother now?" Emma asked.

"One of the footmen was helping Anne take him to the long gallery." She wrinkled her nose. "And help clean him up. William tripped and fell into one of the tables."

Give me patience, Lord.

"Which table?"

"The one with the punch bowl. But the bowl was almost empty," Susan hastily added. "So it didn't make much of a mess, except on William."

"There's justice, I suppose," said Emma. "All right, go find your mother. And I would suggest it might be time to take William home."

"Thank you, Mrs. Knightley," she said, flinging the words over her shoulder as she fled.

"Disgraceful," Emma huffed. "It is beyond me how a respectable couple like the Coxes managed to produce such unpleasant children."

"Should we go check on William and Anne?"

"Only if you wish to see me box their ears."

Mrs. Weston choked on a laugh.

They turned toward the great hall. At the massive stone arch that framed the entrance, they paused to observe the merriment.

"You've made a splendid job of it, Emma," Mrs. Weston commented. "How clever to place the musicians up in the balcony and out of the way."

A reminder of Donwell's antique origins, the great hall boasted a timbered ceiling and a carved wooden screen beneath the balcony. Normally a space imbued with a rarified sense of peace, the hall currently resembled a packed assembly room at a public ball.

The cacophony of voices threatened to overwhelm the music.

Although most of the floor had been cleared for dancing, trestle tables, benches, and chairs ringed the perimeter of the room. It seemed that every seated person was engaged in a shouting match to be heard over the music.

The refreshment tables near the front entrance of the hall were staffed by two of Hartfield's footmen. Off to the side stood a smaller table for the punch bowl. The abbey's groom, seconded to work the party, was setting up a new punch bowl with Mr. Weston's cheerful assistance.

Mrs. Weston smiled. "How fortunate that my husband happened to be in the hall when the accident occurred."

"Indeed. There is nothing more satisfying than an excellent husband."

Her friend cast her an amused glance. "I obviously agree."

"Mr. Weston is a splendid man, and I will always take a great deal of pleasure in the triumph of promoting your match."

Her friend twinkled at her. "He would have found his way there eventually, but your assistance was appreciated nonetheless."

"As is right and proper. But look at Mr. Hughes, who is almost as boring as his cousin, and he's trapped poor Mr. Weston behind the table. Don't you think you should rescue your husband? Dr. Hughes is bound to appear at any moment and join them, and then Mr. Weston will become desperate."

Mrs. Weston laughed. "Emma, Dr. Hughes is a very good man—if a trifle pompous. It was kind of you to invite him."

"Miss Bates was in charge of the invitations, with the predictable result that almost everyone within a five-mile radius of Highbury has descended upon us like marauding Saxons. Now, go rescue your husband."

For the next half hour, Emma circled the room, checking on the partygoers and even managing a cup of punch and a pleasant chat with Mrs. Goddard. Now, though, it was past time to check on her father and Isabella.

Slipping into the relative quiet of the long gallery—thankfully absent of Coxes—she turned toward the library. The noise of the party faded, and she found herself enjoying the welcome peace of the old stone building after enduring the commotion of the hall.

She'd almost reached the library when the door flew open and Miss Bates burst forth in a frantic flurry of skirts. The spinster all but skidded to a halt in front of her.

"Miss Bates," Emma exclaimed. "Whatever is the matter?"

The little spinster flapped her arms like a duck about to take flight. "Oh, Mrs. Knightley, you must come! There's been a terrible accident!"

Chapter 3

Emma's mind cast up a terrifying image. "Is it Father? Is he ill?"

Miss Bates grabbed her arm, tugging her through the door. "It's not your father. It's . . . oh, Mrs. Knightley, please come. It's the most dreadful thing I've ever seen."

Emma allowed Miss Bates to propel her into the room—a room even chillier than the old stone corridors of the abbey. The doors to the terrace were wide open, their thick velvet curtains flapping in the gusty night air.

She darted a glance toward the fireplace, where she'd settled her father and the ladies earlier in the evening. Father had flung off his lap blanket and come to his feet, supporting a wide-awake and obviously distressed Mrs. Bates.

"Dearest," Emma exclaimed. "Why are you and Mrs. Bates standing about with the doors open? It's freezing in here."

She took the elderly woman by the arm to steer her back to her wingback, but her father waved her away.

"Emma, you must go outside and look! It is too dreadful for words."

"I will, just as soon as I get Mrs. Bates settled. And you must also sit under your blanket."

Miss Bates appeared at her side. "Let me take care of Mother and your father. You go outside."

Emma glanced at her with some surprise. The spinster had always reminded her of a little sparrow, flitting here and there with great cheer but prone to bouts of nerves during moments of great upset. Now, though, she seemed to have recovered her equanimity as she took her mother's arm and helped her to resume her seat in front of the marble-topped fireplace.

When Father sank into his chair and took up the lap blanket in trembling hands, a grim premonition seized Emma. She drew in a slow, calming breath, and then she strode toward the open doors.

"Wait." Miss Bates snatched a wool shawl draped over the back of a chair—it looked like Isabella's—and rushed to give it to her. "You'll perish in that light gown, Mrs. Knightley."

Emma wrapped the shawl around her shoulders and picked up a lamp from one of the side tables. "All right. Now, let us go see."

They stepped onto the wide stone terrace that faced the back gardens.

The garden furniture was stored away until spring, so the terrace was bare. In the fitful light of the lamp, a thin layer of frost glittered on the gray stones. The garden looked as it always did at this time of year—the trees with their leafless branches reaching like spindly arms to the sky, and the flower beds empty save for the boxwoods and the rose bushes cut back for winter.

All was silent but for the faint drift of music from the other end of the abbey.

Emma held the lamp up higher. The light dazzled her, but once her vision adjusted she saw nothing but the inkblot lawn stretching away into the darkness.

"Miss Bates, what am I supposed to see?"

Wordlessly, the spinster pointed over to the left.

Emma turned and almost dropped the lamp. The body of a woman lay on the stones, limbs splayed out in a terrible fashion.

"Good God!" she gasped.

The gruesome image swam before her eyes in a wave of vertigo. Emma felt herself sway, sending the lamplight wildly flickering.

"Mrs. Knightley," the spinster cried. "Are you all right?"

Emma forced past the nauseating wave. "Yes."

She took a few steps forward and held out the lamp so as to illuminate the entire body. A sickening sorrow tightened her chest.

"She is dead, isn't she?" whispered Miss Bates.

"There can be no doubt of that."

The unnatural attitude of the limbs, the pool of blood spreading outward from beneath the head... there was no need to feel for a pulse to recognize that the poor girl had expired.

"It is Prudence, isn't it?" asked Miss Bates. "The maid."

"I'm afraid it is."

"But we saw her only two hours ago! She brought us supper and was so terribly sweet. You should have seen her with Mother, Mrs. Knightley. Prudence was so good with her. How could this possibly be?"

Emma stepped back a few paces and looked upward, already quite sure of what she would see—an open casement window on the top floor of the abbey, light faintly issuing forth. While that floor housed the servants' quarters, how in heaven's name could Prudence manage to fall out the window? Indeed, why was the window even open on such a cold night?

On that thought, a shiver racked through her, as the immediate shock of seeing the body began to fade. She glanced over at Miss Bates, whose shoulders were drawn up around her ears, her thick shawl wrapped tightly around her body. The poor woman looked frozen and miserable.

Emma put a hand on her shoulder. "Come, we must go back inside before you freeze to death."

Miss Bates startled under her touch. "Oh, yes, whatever you say, Mrs. Knightley. But shouldn't we do something about the body. . . ." She swallowed. "Cover her with something? It's so dreadfully cold out here."

"The cold won't bother her now."

When the other woman's gaze leapt to hers, Emma winced. What a *dreadfully* inappropriate thing to say. Perhaps the night air was freezing her brain.

She took Miss Bates and guided her back to the open doors. "We must leave the body exactly as is until Mr. Knightley has viewed it. And Dr. Hughes as well, I imagine."

Emma closed the doors firmly behind them. No need to keep them open, at this point.

"I'm the one who discovered the body," the spinster said in a miserable tone. "I don't think Dr. Hughes will be very pleased with me."

"I'm sure he won't give it a second thought."

He will absolutely give it a second thought.

In last summer's investigation into Mrs. Elton's death, Miss Bates had inadvertently locked horns with Highbury's coroner on more than one occasion. Then again, Emma had also locked horns with him, deliberately so. It was likely that Dr. Hughes would be more annoyed to see Emma than Miss Bates.

At least it's not murder.

Prudence had somehow tragically fallen to her death from the top floor of the abbey.

"Miss Bates, how did you come to discover the body?"

"Because I heard a tremendous thud coming from the terrace. We were all sitting by the fire, having a comfortable chat, although Mother had dozed off, I think. We were talking about Jane and Frank, and wondering when they might be able to come to Highbury. The baby, you know, and Jane's health." She frowned. "Yes, Mother had definitely dozed off, so it was just Mr. Woodhouse and I who were chatting then."

Miss Bates had a tendency to rattle on when she was, well, rattled. Emma had learned that trying to hurry her rarely achieved the desired results.

"So you were all sitting by the fire. What happened next?"

"Forgive me, Mrs. Knightley. As I said, your father and I were chatting. Your sister had left us several minutes before...." She seized Emma's arm. "Thank goodness she was not in the room! I'm so grateful she was spared this terrible shock."

"Miss Bates, Emma," her father called from across the library. "What is happening?"

"Just a minute, Father." Emma refocused on Miss Bates. "So you heard the thud. Then what?"

"It was quite loud, Mrs. Knightley. At first I thought a bird—an owl or a hawk, perhaps—had flown into the doorframe. They do that sometimes, you know. They are drawn to the light and grow confused. Your father didn't think that could possibly be right, so I decided to look. While he wanted me to ring for a footman, I didn't wish to bother anyone. Now I wish I had." She ended on an unhappy note.

"It was very brave of you," Emma said in a comforting tone. "So, you went to investigate this noise, and . . ."

"I opened the door and looked out. At first I saw nothing. So I opened the doors wide and looked all around. That's . . . that's when I saw . . . saw Prudence. Although of course I didn't realize it was she, at first. I could only tell it was a body."

Emma thought for a moment. "You didn't hear anything else before the thud? A cry, perhaps?"

"No. I think that's why I was so . . . so brave as to go out and look in the first place. It never occurred to me that it would be so horrible. Oh, Mrs. Knightley, what are we to do?"

"Ring for help." She glanced over at her father and Mrs. Bates, huddled under lap blankets and shawls. "But first let me build up the fire."

She crossed the room, Miss Bates scurrying in her wake.

"Emma, what are we to do?" Father plaintively asked.

She retrieved the tongs from the firebox. "I'm going to get help, dear."

"But that poor girl! We mustn't leave her out in that perishing cold."

"A few more minutes won't make a difference. Please don't worry."

"I cannot help but worry," he replied as she placed the log into the flames. "You and Miss Bates were out on the terrace for such a long time. We grew quite afraid, didn't we, Mrs. Bates? What if you and Miss Bates were to come down with a putrid fever as a result?"

"We were both wearing very warm shawls. We'll be fine."

Miss Bates, who had been attending to her mother, glanced over her shoulder. "There is no need to worry about me, sir. I am quite robust. And Mrs. Knightley never gets sick, you know."

Will wonders never cease?

Miss Bates was showing uncommon fortitude. Under the circumstances, it was a welcome development.

Once she got the fire going strong, Emma slipped behind her husband's desk to yank the bellpull. "Father, someone will arrive soon to stay with you. Once they do, I should go find George."

He reached out a hand. "Please don't leave, Emma. What if Isabella were to return? Anyone could come into the library at any moment."

The Bates ladies also fastened pleading gazes on her. Emma longed to find George and pass this burden over to him, but heaven only knew what Miss Bates or her father would say if a guest wandered in to chat. This situation needed careful handling.

"Then I'll stay right here with you," she said. "In the meantime, I think you could all do with a glass of sherry to warm you up. How would that be?"

She spoke in a normal voice, hoping to inject a note of calm. It seemed to work, because her father gave her a tentative smile.

"That would be most welcome," he said. "For Miss Bates as well, I imagine."

"And me," added Mrs. Bates in her quavering voice.

Mrs. Bates, who was *very* elderly, rarely touched anything but the occasional thimbleful of ratafia. Then again, it wasn't every day that one heard a body crashing to its death outside the window.

Emma poured three small wineglasses of sherry from the drinks trolley. Since each of them would no doubt be required to give a witness statement, it wouldn't do for them to get tipsy.

She carried a silver tray with the drinks back to the little group huddled around the fire. After handing them out, she watched with astonishment as Mrs. Bates downed her sherry in one go.

"Gracious," Miss Bates said in a faint tone.

The elderly woman handed her glass back to Emma.

"Er... would you like another, Mrs. Bates?" she asked.

"If you wouldn't mind, Mrs. Knightley."

"Mother!" Miss Bates exclaimed. "Do you think that's wise?"

Mrs. Bates narrowed her rheumy eyes behind her spectacles. "There's no need to fuss, Hetty. I am perfectly capable of holding my drink. And tonight's events certainly warrant a bit of Dutch courage."

"Goodness me," said Father. "I am in awe of your fortitude."

"Mr. Woodhouse, to still be alive at my age requires a good deal of fortitude."

Emma had to bite back a smile as she went to refill the lady's glass.

As she did so, the door opened and Harry, Donwell's lone footman, entered the room.

"Did you ring, Mrs. Knightley?" he asked. "It's so noisy in the kitchen that we wasn't sure we actually heard a ring. But Mrs. Hodges insisted I come up and check."

"Yes. Harry, I need you to find Mr. Knightley and bring him to the library. Immediately."

The footman peered at her with his usual befuddled expression. "Is everything all right, Mrs. Knightley?"

Outwardly, Harry was the perfect footman. He was tall and well built, possessing a fine head of hair and handsome features. Unfortunately, he did not appear to be the sharpest pin in the pincushion.

"No, young man, everything is *not* all right," Emma's father huffed. "In fact, there's been—"

Miss Bates jumped to her feet. "Dear Mr. Woodhouse, let me fetch you another sherry. It will be just the thing."

Harry looked utterly confused. "Mrs. Knightley?"

"It's fine," said Emma. "Just go find Mr. Knightley and tell him that there's been a... small incident. And don't speak to anyone else."

"Yes, Mrs. Knightley, right away."

He hurried out.

Emma eyed the drinks trolley, but then decided against a medicinal brandy. Someone needed to keep a clear head.

"Here is your sherry, Mr. Woodhouse," Miss Bates said. "It's all very upsetting, but Mr. Knightley will know exactly what to do. He's a very fine magistrate, you know."

Emma mustered a smile. "That's right. George will take care of everything."

"I hope so," Father plaintively said. "To sit here in such

dreadful circumstances is intolerable. I wonder if we will ever get home."

Thankfully, the door opened in the next moment and George strode in.

Emma hurried to him. "Thank goodness. I thought Harry would have to search the house for you."

"I was already on my way to the library to see you when he waylaid me. He said there had been some kind of incident."

"A terrible incident!" Father exclaimed. "Too terrible for words."

George cast him a startled glance. "What's happened?"

Emma took him by the hand and began to draw him toward the terrace doors.

"My dear, your fingers are ice-cold," he said with a frown.

"It's no matter. There's been a dreadful accident outside."

He let go her hand and strode to the doors. Emma retrieved her lamp from the side table and followed him out.

"To the left," she said.

George turned and then froze in his tracks.

"It's Prudence," Emma said in a quiet voice.

Her husband gazed down at the girl for several long moments. Emma closed the terrace doors and went to him.

"I know," she said. "It's appalling."

George crouched beside the body. Emma saw in the fitful light of the lamp that it was clear Prudence must have perished instantaneously. The injury to her head was ghastly.

"How can this be?" Disbelief echoed in his voice. "I saw her earlier in the evening, and she seemed fine."

"Actually, she became ill with the headache some time ago, so Mrs. Hodges sent her to her room. As to what happened after that, I cannot say."

He straightened up, his face a grim mask in the flickering light. To George, this would be more than simply a tragic accident. Anyone who lived or worked at the abbey or on his farms was part of the Donwell family. He felt responsible for them, from the lowliest stable boy to a prosperous tenant farmer like Robert Martin.

"I'm so sorry, George. She was such a sweet girl."

"Yes, it's beyond dreadful." He took the lamp and held it high over the body, inspecting it. "Who found her?"

"Miss Bates. They all heard the fall, though. Or, I should say, the . . . impact." Emma felt her gorge start to rise, but she forced it back down. "Miss Bates came out to investigate."

George grimaced. "She must have been greatly upset."

"She was, although I must say she's done an excellent job of keeping Father and Mrs. Bates relatively calm."

"Then I'm grateful to her. And grateful that you were close by when the accident occurred."

He stepped back as she had done and peered up at the open window above them.

"I'm assuming the height is great enough that she would have died immediately," Emma said.

"I should think so, given the condition of her skull."

She shivered and drew her shawl more tightly around her shoulders.

George took her arm and led her back to the terrace doors. "There is no need for you to stand around in this cold. I'm going to check a few more things, and then I'll be right in."

"What else can I do?"

"I told Harry to wait outside the library door. Have him fetch Mrs. Hodges, and also tell him to find Dr. Hughes. We cannot move the body until he sees it."

Emma felt another nasty premonition well up. "George, you don't think she was . . ."

The awful word hung between them.

He shook his head. "It certainly seems to have been an accident, but the coroner needs to make that determination."

"All right. I'll ask Harry to fetch Mrs. Hodges, and then go look for Dr. Hughes myself."

"Quietly, though. We must go quietly."

"I understand."

She slipped back into the room.

"Emma, must you keep going outside?" her father exclaimed. "You'll catch a chill!"

"I'm perfectly well. George will come inside in a few minutes, and then—"

Isabella suddenly burst into the room. "Emma, what is happening here? Why is the footman guarding the door? He didn't wish to let me in."

Harry hovered in the doorway. "Begging your pardon, Mrs. Knightley." He glanced at Isabella. "Er, and Mrs. Knightley. But Mr. Knightley told me to stand outside the door and wait for him. So I was just doing what he said."

"It's fine," said Emma. "I'll speak to you—"

"I insist you tell me what's wrong!" Isabella's gaze darted to their father. "Is Father unwell? Should we fetch Mr. Perry?"

"Father is perfectly fine, but—"

"I am not perfectly fine," Father huffed. "And neither is anyone else, especially that poor, dead girl on the terrace."

Harry went bug-eyed, while Isabella pressed a hand to her bodice. "Emma, what is Father talking about?"

"It's Prudence, the maid," said Miss Bates. "She fell out the window and killed herself."

"What?" Her sister's shriek made Emma wince.

"Isabella, please. We don't yet fully know what has happened. We must be calm."

"How can we be calm?" Father dramatically pronounced. "There's a dead girl on the terrace, and Emma and Miss Bates have caught a terrible chill going out to look at her. We shall *all* come down with fevers, I know it!"

Isabella gazed at him in horror, and then burst into tears.

Emma sighed as she once more crossed to the drinks trolley, this time to fetch a sherry for her sister. She couldn't help thinking of all the family occasions that had ended on a similar note of panic—sans a dead body, of course.

Sadly, she knew the evening would only get worse.

Chapter 4

"How inconvenient that Dr. Hughes has left the party," Emma said to George as she leaned against his desk. "Normally, one cannot get rid of the man."

Her husband was jotting notes in his diary—his observations about the body, no doubt. "He had an early appointment tomorrow and did not wish to wear himself out with the evening's revelries."

She couldn't hold back a strangled laugh. "He actually said that?"

"He did indeed. By the by, Dr. Hughes was very impressed by your hospitality."

"I suspect that good grace will not survive our current situation."

She glanced at the small casement clock on the desk. Almost an hour had passed since Miss Bates discovered the body. It now was beginning to feel like they were kicking up their heels, waiting for something to happen.

Of course, it had taken some time to soothe Father's anxieties and Isabella's hysterics. Thankfully, Mr. Perry had been called in to help. The solicitous apothecary had administered a calming draught to both Father and Isabella, and even now sat with them, supplying a steady stream of medical reassurance.

"Mr. Perry, at least, has not abandoned us in our time of need," Emma commented.

George closed his diary. "I suspect Dr. Hughes will be displeased to see Perry. He might see it as a challenge to his authority."

She rolled her eyes. "Dr. Hughes should be grateful to Perry. Otherwise, he'd be dealing with a room full of hysterical witnesses."

Miss Bates hurried over to join them. "Mr. Knightley, I do hate to bother, but how much longer do you think we must wait? Mr. Woodhouse is fretful, and I fear my mother is tiring."

"I apologize, Miss Bates," said George. "But Dr. Hughes should be here very soon."

"What if Isabella took Mrs. Bates home in our carriage?" Emma suggested. "Mrs. Bates didn't truly hear anything, and Isabella wasn't even in the room. The carriage can then return for Father and Miss Bates. Surely Dr. Hughes will be finished interviewing them by that point."

Miss Bates clasped her hands. "Mrs. Knightley, I would be ever so grateful."

Emma lifted her brows. "Well, George? What do your magisterial instincts suggest? Will we upset the proper course of justice if Isabella and Mrs. Bates return home?"

"My magisterial instincts cede to your good sense, my dear. In fact, it might make the process run more smoothly if we have fewer people involved."

"Thank you," she replied. "Perhaps Harry can run out to the stables—"

George shook his head. "Harry is upstairs guarding Prudence's room."

Emma grimaced. "I'd forgotten that."

Shortly after George inspected the body, he'd begun issuing orders—one of which was to send Harry upstairs. George had wanted Prudence's room to remain untouched until Dr. Hughes arrived.

"Mrs. Hodges can send one of our footman to the stables."

"Perhaps I'd best go to the great hall and wait for Dr. Hughes," said Emma. "Mr. and Mrs. Weston have been manning the barricades, but I'm sure people are wondering where we've all disappeared to."

Emma had managed to briefly slip out to alert the Westons to their burgeoning crisis. They'd risen to the occasion as always, promising to oversee the party.

"You might keep an eye out for Constable Sharpe," George replied. "I sent the stable boy with a note requesting his presence."

Ugh.

"I suppose you thought that was necessary."

He shrugged. "I'm sure his presence will be a mere formality."

"Mere? As far as Constable Sharpe is concerned, he's always the hero of any drama. Besides, I'm the last person he'll wish to see."

In general, the constable didn't approve of women. In particular, he didn't approve of Emma.

"Perhaps, but you'd best be on your way," George replied. "The sooner this evening is concluded, the better."

After giving her husband a fleeting kiss on the cheek, Emma hurried from the room. Thankfully, she immediately encountered Mrs. Hodges in the corridor.

"Mrs. Knightley, do you need anything?"

Emma took her arm and turned her back the other way. "Yes, please. I need you to send word to James, our coachman. My sister is going to take Mrs. Bates home."

"Poor Mrs. Bates. She must be plumb frazzled out."

"Everyone is feeling the strain."

Mrs. Hodges let out a weary sigh. "Indeed, Mrs. Knightley."

Emma mentally scolded herself. She'd failed to recognize how deeply the housekeeper would be affected by Prudence's death. Surely it would be more than for anyone else in the household, since she'd worked with the girl every day.

"Mrs. Hodges, please forgive me. I know this has been a terrible blow."

"I won't deny it, ma'am. Prudence was a sweet girl and so full of life. It's hard to imagine—" She stopped and bit her lip.

Emma pressed her arm. "I understand completely."

"It's her father I can't help thinking about. He was so proud to see Prudence working in such a fine house." Mrs. Hodges grimaced. "Who will tell him?"

"Mr. Knightley will take care of it. Now, if you'll find James . . ."

The woman gathered herself. "Forgive me, ma'am."

"There's nothing to forgive. It's been a dreadful night."

As they entered the long gallery, Emma paused. "Mrs. Hodges, have you seen Larkins? I assumed he'd be back at the abbey by now."

"I'm afraid not. I sent the kitchen maid down to his cottage, but he wasn't there. I expect now it's going on eleven, he'll be back any moment." She grimaced again. "He'll be that shook up, he will. He was terribly fond of Prudence."

Emma mentally blinked. That seemed rather strange since Larkins was a man who rarely interacted on a personal level with the other servants, save for Mrs. Hodges. He even preferred to take his meals in his cottage.

"When Larkins returns, please send him straight to Mr. Knightley for instructions."

"Yes, ma'am."

The housekeeper departed for the kitchen, while Emma made her way to the great hall. Thankfully, all was quiet but for the low murmur of voices from the remaining guests. Peeking around the doorframe, she saw the room was now devoid of all but a few families. Up in the gallery, the musicians were stowing their instruments.

Steeling herself, Emma entered the hall.

Mrs. Weston was talking to Mrs. Cole, who was donning her pelisse and preparing to leave. Catching sight of Emma, Mrs. Weston smiled with evident relief and waved, bidding her to join them.

Drat and double drat.

While a kind woman, Mrs. Cole was a terrible gossip.

"Mrs. Knightley, there you are," exclaimed Mrs. Cole. "Such a shame you and Mr. Knightley had to miss so much of your own party. I do hope your father is feeling more the thing."

Emma darted a glance at Mrs. Weston, who gave a slight nod. It was an excellent excuse, since everyone in Highbury knew Father's little foibles.

"Yes, thank goodness," she replied. "Mr. Perry was able to work his usual magic."

Mrs. Cole clucked with sympathy. "Poor Mr. Woodhouse. Overcome with all the excitement, most likely."

You have no idea.

"Indeed. He is unused to these large affairs."

"And here are the ladies," Mr. Weston exclaimed as he joined them. "Mrs. Cole, I bring notice that your conveyance awaits." He nodded toward the front entrance, where Mr. Cole stood with the Gilberts. "The others are ready to depart."

"How excellent," Emma enthusiastically declared.

When Mrs. Cole cast her a startled glance, she realized she'd been a bit *too* enthusiastic.

"What I meant to say is that it's a blessing to have a nice, warm carriage waiting to take one home on a cold night," she added. "As one generally does in the winter."

Oh, Lord. She sounded like a henwit.

Mr. Weston came to her rescue. "Come along, Mrs. Cole. Don't want to keep the horses standing about."

He all but marched the poor woman to the door, while Emma and Mrs. Weston trailed behind them.

"I think you managed to pull it off, my dear," Mrs. Weston said in a low voice. "Mr. Weston was rather vague when a few of the gentlemen inquired about Mr. Knightley. Something about a problem in the stables that required his attention."

"George and I are both so grateful to you," Emma replied. "And I hope we have managed to—"

Just at that moment Constable Sharpe stomped through the front door, his usual dour self. He ignored the Gilberts and the Coles and fastened his gaze directly on Emma.

"Mrs. Knightley," he said with a scowl. "What's this I hear about a dead body?"

"What?" Mrs. Cole and Mrs. Gilbert screeched in perfect tandem.

Mr. Cole leveled an astonished gaze on the constable. "Good God, man. This is a party, not a crime scene. There are no dead bodies here."

Emma pinched the bridge of her nose. It was bad luck that Constable Sharpe had appeared on the scene before the final guests had departed, but to announce the existence of a dead body in front of two of Highbury's biggest gossips?

Fatal.

Arriving like a second harbinger of ill fortune, Dr. Hughes then walked in, looking most aggrieved.

"That's where you're wrong, Mr. Cole," Sharpe frostily replied. "There is definitely a dead body at Donwell Abbey."

"There's no need to make a general announcement," Dr. Hughes admonished. "You will distress the ladies."

The constable harrumphed. "Dead bodies cannot be hidden or pretended away." He then pointedly stared at Emma. "Although I imagine *some* might prefer it."

"No one wishes to hide anything, *Mr.* Sharpe," she frostily replied. "We were waiting for Dr. Hughes, so as to know exactly how to proceed."

"Very proper," the coroner said. "Mr. Knightley always knows exactly how things should be done."

Emma mentally rolled her eyes. Dr. Hughes had a marked tendency to believe that a woman's delicate emotions rendered them incapable of acting sensibly in a crisis.

The physician turned to the Gilberts and the Coles. "I apologize for any upset, ladies. There has been an incident at Donwell Abbey, but as yet nothing is clear. Therefore, I would ask that you disregard the constable's comments and refrain from any discussion on the matter, for now."

Mrs. Gilbert and Mrs. Cole exchanged a swift glance, agog with barely repressed excitement.

"Of course, sir," Mrs. Cole replied. "We won't say a word to anyone."

They will absolutely say a word to everyone.

By dawn, every household in Highbury would know a dead body had been discovered at Donwell.

Mr. Weston, with a surprisingly firm manner, steered the Coles and the Gilberts outside. They were actually in the middle of saying their farewells when he slammed the wide oak doors in their faces.

"Oh dear," said Mrs. Weston with a sigh.

Meanwhile, the coroner and the constable were standing in the middle of the hall, glaring at each other like bantam cocks about to employ their spurs.

The two officers of the law could not be more unlike. While Dr. Hughes was a large, portly man who moved and spoke with ponderous dignity, Constable Sharpe lived up to his name. He was all sharp angles and elbows, with a tendency to bark his way through every situation. He reminded Emma of a badly trained terrier, darting here and there, making a fuss.

To be fair, both men did take their jobs seriously and tried to execute their duties with diligence. Unfortunately, neither possessed a superior intellect, and both were prone to jumping to ridiculous conclusions. And while Dr. Hughes always exercised a degree of courtesy toward Emma because of her station, it was obvious that both men resented her.

She supposed she couldn't blame them, since she'd been the one to solve Mrs. Elton's murder, not they. Constable Sharpe had been particularly offended, while Dr. Hughes had been mostly shocked by what he saw as an unseemly involvement in matters violating female decorum.

Hoping to disrupt the glaring match, Emma cleared her throat. "Gentlemen, I'll escort you to the library."

"Is that the scene of the crime?" the constable barked.

Just like a terrier.

Mr. Weston tactfully intervened. "Emma, do you wish us to stay? We should be happy to lend any assistance."

She flashed him a grateful smile. "No, you must get home to little Anna. George and I cannot thank you enough."

Mrs. Weston enveloped her in a hug. For a moment, Emma clung to her, taking comfort in the familiar embrace.

After making her farewells, Emma led Dr. Hughes and the constable into the long gallery. As the little group turned into the east corridor, they encountered Isabella and Mrs. Bates under the solicitous escort of Mrs. Hodges.

"Oh, Emma," Isabella woefully said. "Father is in a terrible fret. I wish John were here. He would know exactly what to do."

Dr. Hughes gave Isabella and Mrs. Bates a courtly bow. "A distressing ending to the evening, to be sure."

"Indeed," Isabella replied. "I hope you won't keep my father any longer than necessary, Dr. Hughes. This is very taxing to his health."

"We will do our best—"

"And who might you be?" Constable Sharpe abruptly interrupted.

Isabella blinked, but Mrs. Bates glared at him, her expression conveying the desire to brain him with her walking stick.

"This is my sister, Constable Sharpe," Emma said. "Mrs. John Knightley. She has been staying with us at Hartfield."

"Why is she leaving? I might need to take a witness statement from her."

"My sister was not in the library when the incident occurred," Emma said in a cool tone. "Mrs. Bates was asleep. She heard nothing and saw nothing."

"Still, they ought to—"

Dr. Hughes held up an imperious hand. "If Mrs. Knightley says there is no need to detain the ladies, I am satisfied. This waiting about cannot be good for Mrs. Bates."

Mrs. Bates gave a dignified nod. "Thank you, Dr. Hughes. This has been a particularly difficult evening for my daughter, as well."

Sharpe registered a degree of alarm. "What does Miss Bates have to do with this?"

Might as well get it over with.

"Miss Bates discovered the body," Emma said.

Dr. Hughes stared at her over his too-small spectacles. Perched halfway down his nose, they gave him the appearance of a perpetually surprised, albeit large, insect.

"Miss Bates discovered the body?" he asked with a degree foreboding.

His tone was understandable. Miss Bates had been one of several witnesses Dr. Hughes had questioned in the course of Mrs. Elton's murder investigation last summer. It had been a frustrating experience for both of them.

"Yes, although my father was also in the room with her."

When the constable muttered under his breath, Emma repressed a sigh. Father had developed an unfortunate animosity toward both Constable Sharpe and Dr. Hughes, and had never hesitated to make his opinion known. That had led to several awkward encounters last summer, and it looked like they were due for a few more.

Isabella made an impatient noise. "Emma, I must see Mrs. Bates home and get back to the children. It's growing late."

Emma nodded. "Once James has taken you both home, send him back for Father and Miss Bates."

"Promise you'll send Father home as soon as possible."

"I promise."

After exchanging a glower with Constable Sharpe, Isabella ushered Mrs. Bates toward the great hall.

After having a short word with Mrs. Hodges, Emma gestured for the men to follow her to the library.

"I've asked Mrs. Hodges to bring up tea, which I hope will make you more comfortable," Emma said. "It's quite dreadful to be dragged out into the cold night."

Dr. Hughes nodded, his temper somewhat restored. "Your graciousness is greatly appreciated, madam. But as I witnessed earlier this evening, you are a most accomplished hostess. For your sake, I sincerely regret that such a convivial affair has ended on so unfortunate a note."

"Yes. Very unfortunate."

"Crime never sleeps, Mrs. Knightley," the constable interjected. "It cares not for a party or the weather, as experience has taught me over the years."

Emma tried not to clench her teeth. "There's no evidence of a crime, sir."

"No evidence, yet," he retorted.

Praying for patience, she ushered the men into the library—just in time to see George and Mr. Perry coming in from the terrace.

"I agree with you completely, sir," Perry was saying. "There can be no doubt in my mind."

Dr. Hughes stopped dead at the sight of Highbury's apothecary. "Mr. Knightley! I hope you haven't permitted Mr. Perry to view the body. Amateurs should not be involving themselves in these matters, as you *well* know."

Mr. Perry, an exceptionally mild-mannered person, simply crinkled his brow in perplexity.

Not so Emma's father. He rose from his chair, the picture of mortal offense. "Dr. Hughes, if it's your intention to insult our dear Perry, then I must *greatly* object. I hold his opinion in all medical matters to be above reproach. Unlike that of *some* in Highbury."

Emma and George exchanged an exasperated glance. This horrible evening was fast careening downward to the level of gruesome farce.

Chapter 5

Emma hurried over to her father, hoping to forestall further outbursts. "Father, there's no need to—"

He shot up a hand. "I will not countenance Dr. Hughes insulting my good friend. George simply asked for his opinion, and Perry was happy to comply. Perry might not be a coroner, although one may indeed wonder why a man of his talents is not in that position. But he is certainly capable of giving trustworthy observations when asked to do so."

By the end of this discourse, Highbury's actual coroner appeared on the verge of an apoplectic fit.

"Mr. Woodhouse," he said in freezing tones, "the law dictates that *I* make the appropriate determination regarding cause of death, and I alone."

Mr. Perry held up his hands. "I have no wish to cause trouble, sir. I was simply providing Mr. Knightley an opinion on a very particular question, at *his* request."

"Very true," said George. "And if—"

Dr. Hughes interrupted him. "Mr. Knightley, I must object to this breach in protocol. Frankly, I would not have believed it of you, given your normally firm command of the law."

Emma's irritation had swelled in proportion to the doctor's speech. "Dr. Hughes, not only is my husband the magistrate, but this is his estate. That surely gives him the authority to make certain decisions in your absence."

"That is a very salient point," said Father with approval. "If a similar tragic event were to occur at Hartfield, I can assure you that the first person I would ask to examine the body—after George, of course—would be our dear Perry."

Miss Bates let out a little shriek. "Oh, Mr. Woodhouse, I couldn't bear to think of such a thing happening at Hartfield. Such a lovely, elegant house could not possibly be the scene of so dreadful an occurrence."

George held up a hand. "If I may—"

"If you ask me," Sharpe interjected, "the opposite is true. If the incident occurred at the house of the magistrate, then it seems that said magistrate should be the *last* person in charge of any investigation."

Father looked aghast. "Emma, you should not let that dreadful Sharpe person speak to George in so rude a fashion!"

"Constable Sharpe is frequently in the habit of making rude statements, Father. It's best to simply ignore him."

Her husband shot her an incredulous glance. "Really?"

"It's ridiculous to think that you would ever act inappropriately," she replied, feeling a trifle defensive.

"I find I must agree with Mrs. Knightley," Dr. Hughes announced, unexpectedly entering the fray on her side. "Mr. Knightley could never be guilty of any sort of improper conduct, although I must admit that our good magistrate's judgment was perhaps temporarily deficient when he allowed Mr. Perry to view the body. However," he added, holding up his arms as if to confer a benediction on the room, "even our estimable Mr. Knightley's judgment cannot always be perfect, so we must make allowances for the very rare error."

"Thank you," George said in a long-suffering tone. "Now, if we could just return to the subject at hand?"

Miss Bates frowned. "I'm afraid I don't remember what that was."

"It was Dr. Hughes insulting Perry," responded Emma's father. "And that Sharpe person calling George's judgment into question, which was very rude."

"Now see here, sir," snapped Constable Sharpe. "You'd best—"

Emma chopped down her hand. "Gentlemen, if we go on much longer, that poor girl's body will be a block of ice. And then no one will be able to examine anything unless we bring her inside and thaw her out. I cannot imagine that would be a pleasant exercise for anyone."

A startled silence filled the room while everyone stared at her with varying degrees of disbelief.

Oh dear.

George cleared his throat. "Thank you, my dear. Your point is well taken." He turned to the coroner. "And I take your point as well, Dr. Hughes. Mr. Perry did not examine the body. I merely asked him to render an opinion on a matter where I believed time was of the essence."

Dr. Hughes unbent a bit. "I would be grateful if you explained the circumstances."

"While waiting for you and Constable Sharpe, I went outside to place a shawl over the body. The weather had begun to flurry, so it seemed a sensible precaution to preserve evidence. While placing the shawl over Miss Parr, I detected what I thought was the odor of spirits. Initially, I hadn't noticed it."

Emma frowned. "I don't remember smelling spirits, either."

"I smelled them," said Miss Bates.

George cast her a startled glance. "You did?"

The spinster nodded.

"As did I," Perry quietly confirmed. "It was quite strong."

"Very well," said Dr. Hughes. "Mr. Knightley, if you would be so good as to show us the body, I will begin my examination."

"*We* will begin our examination," Sharpe put in.

It was going to be a long night.

George led Dr. Hughes and the constable to the terrace doors. Emma made to go with them, but her husband gave her a look of very clear intent.

Stay inside.

She blew out an exasperated breath but acquiesced. Heaven forbid a woman should ever ruffle any official's masculine sense of superiority.

"Mrs. Knightley, if there is no further need for me, I'll be on my way," said Mr. Perry.

Emma forced a smile. "You've been a great help to all of us tonight. I'm only sorry that you were exposed to such a discourteous reception."

The apothecary gave her a slight bow. "Please don't worry, madam. And don't hesitate to send for me if my services are required. These are extraordinary circumstances, and I would not wish your father or Miss Bates to suffer additional anxieties."

Exchanging mutual assurances, Emma escorted him out to the hall and bade him farewell.

Returning to the library, she leaned against the door and closed her eyes, taking a moment to gather herself. Her eyes felt gritty, and fatigue was beginning to drag on her muscles. She shook it off and rejoined her father and Miss Bates.

"Poor Mrs. Knightley," said Miss Bates with concern. "You must sit and rest a minute."

"I'm fine."

She'd just sunk down into one of the overstuffed armchairs when the library door opened. Mrs. Hodges entered, holding a crisply folded linen sheet. Following her was Larkins and one of the abbey's grooms.

Emma rose with a relieved smile. "Mr. Larkins, there you are."

Donwell's steward had the physique and complexion of someone who spent most of his time outdoors and hard at work. A sober fellow, he was a few years older than George and had been a fixture at the estate for many years. Emma knew he loved Donwell Abbey almost as much as his master did, which spoke of the man's loyal nature. George greatly depended on him and gave Larkins substantial credit for Donwell's continuing prosperity.

"I apologize for my absence, Mrs. Knightley," he said. "I supped at the Crown tonight, and I stayed for a pint. I'll not be forgiving myself for failing to be here to help the master, or to . . . to help Prudence."

Emma heard more than a hint of the Irish brogue in his voice. Larkins's family emigrated from Galway when he was a boy, settling in a village just outside London. Usually, there was little trace of an accent in his well-modulated speech, but for when he was upset.

Tonight, he was obviously very upset.

"You have nothing to apologize for, Mr. Larkins," she replied. "No one could have anticipated this tragedy."

Larkins's expression was so bereft that it left Emma wondering about the exact nature of his feelings for Prudence. Was it simply the reaction of a good, kindly man who felt responsible for the staff under his care? Or could there have possibly been some stronger emotion he'd felt for the young woman?

"Mrs. Knightley," said Mrs. Hodges, "once the gentlemen are finished, we'll take Prudence up to the green bedroom, as you instructed."

"Thank you. Mr. Larkins, will you see to the other arrangements?" Emma asked.

He nodded. "I'll go into the village first thing in the morning, ma'am."

It would be necessary to commission a carpenter in Highbury to build a coffin. Emma wasn't quite sure what would happen after that. Presumably, George was already thinking through next steps.

"Mrs. Hodges, where do Prudence's family live?" she asked.

"Leatherhead, ma'am. Her father and brothers are blacksmiths."

Larkins breathed out a fractured sigh. "They'll be that torn apart, Mrs. Hodges."

The housekeeper made an effort to compose herself. "We have to bear up for their sake and take care of the poor girl."

In other words, mourning would have to wait. Any death, even a tragic one, demanded a number of practical details. Emotions must be held at bay until those details were addressed.

The men reentered the room, bringing a blast of cold air with them. George's expression lightened with relief as he spotted his estate steward.

Larkins stepped forward. "Begging your pardon, sir. I should have been here."

"There is no fault on your part, nor anyone else's," George replied.

"We'll see about that," Constable Sharpe muttered.

Larkins shot him a startled look, and some of the color drained from the steward's face. Given his red hair and ruddy complexion, it was quite noticeable.

Then he gathered himself. "What do you need from me now, Mr. Knightley?"

"You may take Prudence up to . . ." George looked at Emma.

"The green bedroom. Mrs. Hodges has prepared it."

George nodded before turning to Emma's father and Miss

Bates. "While outside, I took it upon myself to explain to Dr. Hughes and Constable Sharpe what you both heard and saw. Dr. Hughes is of the opinion that you needn't stay any longer, as it has been such a long night."

"Perry said as much at least a half hour ago," Father replied in a lofty tone. "It's a great shame we didn't listen to him."

When the coroner started to bristle, Emma hastily stepped in. "Thank you, Dr. Hughes. That's so kind. I'm sure James is already here to take my father and Miss Bates home."

"He is," said Mrs. Hodges. "The carriage is out front, so whenever Mr. Woodhouse is ready."

"Emma, we must not keep the horses standing about," her father exclaimed with alarm. "It is very bad for them."

"The horses will be fine, dear." She glanced at her husband. "George, is there anything you need?"

He shook his head. "I'm about to take Dr. Hughes and the constable up to servants' quarters."

"Very well. Once Father and Miss Bates are safely off, I'll join you upstairs."

Constable Sharpe scowled at her, no doubt wishing her to perdition, but Emma ignored him. After all, Donwell was her house as well, and she *had* been at the scene of the accident immediately after its occurrence.

Keeping up a soothing patter of reassurance, Emma bustled her father and Miss Bates from the room. She managed to get them to the great hall and garbed in coats, hats, shawls, and gloves without too much fuss. Simon, Hartfield's senior footman, had accompanied James back to Donwell and solicitously handed the pair into the carriage. After Emma gave him a few additional instructions, they were finally off.

She stood outside for a few moments, watching the carriage lights fade into the night. The chilly air was invigorating and a bracing antidote to her growing fatigue.

"Thank you, Donny," she said to the stable boy, serving as doorman. "I'm sorry you've been kept up so late. I know it's been a difficult evening."

Servants were thin on the ground at the moment. They'd all been rushing to and fro, dealing with both Prudence's death and the aftermath of the party.

The lad grimaced. "Poor Miss Prudence was a regular goer. Right bobbish she was, with everyone. Can't believe she's really gone."

Emma was no expert in cant, but the lad's meaning was clear. Everyone in the household had nothing but warm feelings for Prudence.

"Yes, it's dreadful." She turned back to the house. "Don't stay up too much longer, Donny. It's very late."

"Yes, ma'am."

Emma made her way through the hall to the stairs off the long gallery. She stopped for a moment, gathering her composure and her wits. Although part of her longed for answers, another part recoiled at what must happen next. George, Constable Sharpe, and Dr. Hughes would be searching Prudence's room, rummaging through her life for clues that might illuminate her death. It was a dreadful invasion of the poor girl's privacy, and who knew what secrets might be revealed. Nonetheless, it was unavoidable.

She put a hand on the banister and started to climb.

By the time Emma made it to the top floor of the abbey, she was regretting the second piece of Savoy cake she'd had after supper. The climb also gave her a renewed sympathy for the lives of the servants who had to continually traverse long hallways and numerous stairs in the course of their duties.

At the end of the corridor, Harry stood outside the open door of Prudence's room.

The footman respectfully bobbed his head. "Mrs. Knightley."

"How are you, Harry? We've given you an unpleasant task, standing up here all this time."

"I'm fine, ma'am. It's just . . ." He pressed his lips together, as if having difficulty holding his emotions in check.

"I'm sure you were all very fond of Prudence."

"She was like a sunbeam, she was," he quietly replied. "A very kind and good person to have about the place."

"So I understand."

She stood there feeling awkward, while Harry stared at her with a hangdog expression. But since there was nothing more to be said, she gave him a nod and proceeded inside.

The space was tucked up under a sharply pitched roof, forcing the men in the room to cluster about a round table in the center. All the basic necessaries were present, with some additional comforts. Aside from the bed and table, there were two cane-backed chairs with cushioned seats, a small chest of drawers holding a pitcher and washbasin, a drying rack tucked into the corner, and what looked like new Dutch matting covering the floor. The bed was dressed with a pristinely white coverlet and thick wool blanket, and a nice set of dimity curtains framed the casement window.

The life of a servant, never an easy one, was sometimes nothing less than miserable if a miserly master held the reins. Such was not the case with George. While certainly not given to extravagance, her husband would always be attentive to the comfort of others, including servants who were so often invisible to those they served.

Right now, the room was freezing. The casement window was still open, and the pretty cotton curtains whipped to and fro in a stiff breeze.

George glanced over. "Ah, there you are. I'm sorry the room is so cold. We should be able to close the window soon."

"Only after we finish with our investigations, sir," Constable Sharpe admonished. "You know better than anyone that we can't jump to conclusions without all the facts."

Given some of the foolish conclusions the constable had jumped to only six months ago, that was *quite* an outrageous assertion.

Dr. Hughes blessed her with a patronizing smile. "My dear Mrs. Knightley, there's really no need for you to be here. This entire evening has been an affront to your delicate sensibilities. You've undergone a great shock and should be resting."

Pulling her shawl more tightly around her shoulders, Emma edged her way over to George. She had no intention of leaving and every intention of supporting her husband. He'd adopted his usual calm demeanor, but she sensed the strain on him. As both master of Donwell *and* the local magistrate, he was in a difficult position. Constable Sharpe might again try to take advantage of that, and she had no intention of allowing such impertinence.

"Thank you for your consideration, Dr. Hughes. But as mistress of Donwell, I feel it only right to be here to support my husband and the servants, especially Mrs. Hodges."

Dr. Hughes nodded a grudging acquiescence. "Your diligence does your credit, ma'am. But if at any time you feel the need to leave, please don't hesitate to do so. A situation such as this can be most distressing."

"Especially for poor Miss Parr," she politely replied.

He looked disconcerted by her response but carried on. "Mr. Knightley, it would seem that you were correct in drawing your conclusion about the odor of spirits on Miss Parr's body. The presence of the decanter and glass would confirm that the deceased was imbibing spirits before her unfortunate fall."

For the first time since entering the room, Emma focused on the small table. It held a half-empty decanter and a glass—and not just any old decanter and glass, but ones from a set of Donwell's best crystal. It was jarring to see them there, and disturbing to speculate why they were.

"George," she said, "those were part of the crystal service in the drawing room for the party. I cannot imagine why they're here."

"I should think it obvious, ma'am," said Constable Sharpe. "Your girl filched them. From the looks of it, she took a hefty dose of the stuff, too."

George had no objection to his employees having a pint of ale or a glass of wine with their dinner, but he would frown on the servants keeping quantities of alcohol in their quarters. Mrs. Hodges had a bottle of sherry in her rooms, but she was the most senior of the household staff and had certain privileges.

"We cannot be sure of that," said George. "It's entirely possible that the decanter was almost half-empty when it was brought up here. Also, please note that she apparently spilled a quantity on her clothing."

"Mayhap because she was tipsy and had no control over herself?" the constable responded. "And who else would bring the decanter up here? The evidence suggests it was the girl herself."

From everything Emma knew about Prudence, Sharpe's conclusions simply didn't square.

"Perhaps someone else brought up the decanter and glass," she suggested. "Prudence wasn't feeling well, and one of the other servants might have thought she needed a restorative."

George waggled a hand. "I can certainly understand bringing her a small glass of wine, but to bring one of the good decanters up from the drawing room during a party? That makes no sense."

"You're right, it doesn't," she replied with a sigh. "What sort of drink is it?"

"Sherry," her husband replied.

Emma glanced at Harry, standing in the door. "Harry, do you know if Prudence drank sherry?"

He opened his mouth to reply but was forestalled by the appearance of Mrs. Hodges.

"I can answer that question." The housekeeper darted an irritated glance at the footman. "Harry, you're blocking the doorway."

"Sorry, Mrs. Hodges," he replied with a grimace. "Sometimes I forget how big I am."

As he stepped aside, the housekeeper muttered something that sounded suspiciously like *great oaf*.

"Prudence did not drink sherry," said Mrs. Hodges. "She was never one for spirits."

The constable scoffed. "The presence of a half-empty decanter would suggest otherwise. As would the smell of said spirits on her body."

Mrs. Hodges darted a questioning glance at Emma. There was no point in denying Sharpe's statement, so she simply nodded in reply.

The housekeeper was clearly distressed by that information. "I can only say that Prudence was not fond of strong drink, nor would she take one of the good decanters, not during a party or at any other time."

"But if she wasn't feeling well," Harry suddenly put in, "mayhap she thought a nice glass of sherry would help her feel better. My ma always gave us sherry or port whenever we had the toothache, when we was little."

No one seemed to know quite how to respond to that rather startling and uncalled-for admission.

"But that is more than one glass," Dr. Hughes finally observed.

Harry shrugged. "Maybe Mr. Knightley has the right of it, and it was half-empty when she brought it up."

Mrs. Hodges glared at him. "It's not something she would have done. Besides, Prudence had the migraine. I was going to send up headache powders when I got the chance."

"Mrs. Hodges," said George, "is it possible one of the staff brought up the decanter?"

She shook her head. "We were all well nigh rushed off our feet. Besides, I don't think anyone else but me knew that Prudence was feeling poorly."

Emma held up a hand. "I saw her as she was going up to her room. She did look quite distressed, but simply said her head was troubling her."

"Then are we to assume," said Dr. Hughes, "that only Mrs. Knightley and Mrs. Hodges knew the girl wasn't feeling well?"

"Mrs. Weston, who was with me at the time, also did. Other than that, I don't believe so," Emma replied.

Harry suddenly coughed. When Emma glanced at him, the young man was staring down at his feet, looking vastly uncomfortable.

"Did you wish to say something else?" asked George.

The footman hesitated. "I don't wish to get no one in trouble, sir."

"My good fellow, the girl is dead," exclaimed Dr. Hughes. "You can hardly get her in trouble."

"And this is an official investigation," the constable barked. "If you know anything, speak up now."

The footman rolled his eyes in George's direction, clearly alarmed.

"It's all right, Harry," George said. "Just tell us what you know."

"Well," he replied, drawing out the word. "I saw Prudence heading for the back stairs. I was bringing some dirty glasses to the kitchen when I spotted her."

He fell silent, frowning down at his shoes again.

"And?" George prompted.

"Pru looked—I mean, Prudence looked mighty upset. I think she was crying. When I asked what was wrong, she just shook her head and ran up the stairs. I thought about going after her, but I had to get them glasses back to the kitchen."

Mrs. Hodges made an exasperated noise. "Why didn't you tell me the poor girl was crying?"

Harry's expression was one of genuine dismay. "I guess I just forgot, Mrs. Hodges. What with all the commotion from the party."

"So, you didn't bring her the decanter?" the constable asked.

Harry frowned. "Why would I do that?"

Dr. Hughes tapped the crystal topper of the decanter, his brow creased in thought. "So, it would seem that although Miss Parr claimed to simply have a headache, it is quite possible she was also distressed about some matter." He looked to Mrs. Hodges. "And you have no idea what that might be?"

"I can only say she did look poorly."

"Something set her off," Harry said. "That was as plain as day, even to the likes of me," he added with a self-deprecating grimace.

Again unbidden, an image of an inebriated and obnoxious William Cox popped into Emma's brain. Could he have been importuning the poor girl after all? Was that why she was upset?

Still, Emma could hardly throw around such an accusation—even speculate on it—without some sort of evidence.

"So the girl was upset about something, filched the sherry decanter from the party, and then tried to drink her troubles away," Constable Sharpe proclaimed in a self-satisfied voice.

Emma pointed out the obvious. "But no one saw her with the decanter. Certainly Harry did not, and he was the last person to see her go upstairs."

"That's right. She wasn't carrying anything," Harry confirmed.

The constable waved a dismissive hand. "No doubt she snuck back down and took it later."

Now Emma tsked. "Without being seen? Doubtful."

Dr. Hughes held up a hand. "We can only ascertain that by interviewing the other guests."

That gave her pause. What if there *had* been someone else? What if it was a guest . . . a guest like William Cox, intending no good?

She glanced over at the bed. Slightly ruffled, the girl could perhaps have reclined on top of the coverlet. But the rest of the room showed no evidence of any sort of struggle or the presence of another person.

"As to how the decanter got up here," said George, "that is a question yet to be answered. But I think we can assume that Prudence had at least one glass of sherry. The question then becomes, why did she open the window and what caused her to fall out?"

Dr. Hughes nodded. "I suggest we inspect the window for any clues as to how the accident occurred."

"If it *was* an accident," said Constable Sharpe.

Botheration.

Emma couldn't help feeling annoyed that she was thinking along the same lines as the constable.

George ignored Sharpe and began to inspect the window. The constable followed closely behind, clearly intending to assert his authority.

Emma eyed the long but rather narrow casement window. "It's not very wide, is it?"

"No," her husband replied. "But it's wide enough for a slender girl like Prudence to fall through."

"True, but not easily, though."

George suddenly leaned in, peering at a particular spot on the window frame. "Dr. Hughes, what do you make of this?"

The coroner stepped over to the window. He glowered at Sharpe, who already had his nose a mere inch from the window frame.

"Constable Sharpe," Dr. Hughes huffily said. "You are blocking my way."

Sharpe ignored him. "That looks mighty suspicious, Mr. Knightley. What do you make of it?"

George stepped aside, making room for the coroner. "I would prefer to hear the doctor's opinion before stating my own."

After examining the spot for several long seconds, Dr. Hughes turned, his expression solemn. "That is definitely blood on the window frame, as well as a small amount of hair."

As Mrs. Hodges let out a quiet moan, Emma's stomach pitched sideways. She had to suck in a breath to quell both the sensation and the memory of Prudence's broken body on the terrace.

"Emma," George said, "please hand me that lamp."

She fetched the lamp from the dresser. He took it from her and brought it close to the window frame so that it could cast its light on the wood.

"Blond hair," he noted.

"I take it Miss Parr had blond hair?" asked the constable.

"Yes," George replied.

Dr. Hughes stepped away from the window. "Then the likely conclusion is that Miss Parr had a quantity of sherry, sufficient enough to make her woozy. She then opened the window, lost her balance, hit her head, and tragically fell four stories to the terrace."

George tapped his chin. Emma recognized that gesture. It meant he wasn't entirely convinced.

"She would have needed to be very off balance to fall out," he said. "As my wife noted, the window is quite narrow."

"It depends on how much she had to drink, Mr. Knightley," the coroner replied. "It's also possible that the wind gusted just as she opened it, pulling her even further off balance. The wind is quite strong tonight, and she was, as you say, a rather slight girl."

"But why would she open the window in the first place?" asked Emma. "It's freezing out."

"When one drinks a substantial quantity of alcohol," responded Dr. Hughes, "one can often feel overheated. The girl likely desired fresh air."

Emma supposed that made sense. She rarely had more than a glass of wine herself or the *very* occasional brandy when life proved particularly challenging, so she couldn't really speak to the doctor's broad assertion about the effects of alcohol. But she did live with a parent who insisted on roaring fires and overheated rooms, so she could understand the desire to open a window.

Still, there was no fireplace in this room, so one would think it rarely became overheated in the winter months.

"There's another possible explanation," said the constable.

The coroner peered over his spectacles, not bothering to hide his skepticism. "And what might that be?"

"She threw herself out the window." Constable Sharpe paused for gruesome effect. "Deliberately."

Silence reigned, except for a small, horrified gasp from Mrs. Hodges. George, who rarely allowed himself to be discomposed, stared at the constable in disbelief.

Emma felt more than disbelief. She felt the sudden urge to box Sharpe's ears for floating such a hideous accusation.

Harry broke the silence first. "Our Prudence would never do such a thing! She was the goodest girl you'd ever want to meet."

The constable sniffed, clearly unimpressed by the opinion of a mere servant. "She was a chambermaid, and those girls get up to all sorts of things. Everyone knows that."

Mrs. Hodges's scowl was ferocious. "Prudence was a sweet,

biddable girl, and a churchgoing one at that. She would never commit such a heinous sin, and would never cause such a scandal for her father."

George directed a coldly lethal gaze at the constable. "That is an exceedingly damning accusation to make, Constable. I would ask you to explain yourself."

Literally damning in the case of suicide. If proven, Prudence would be denied a Christian burial. Such a death would be a scandal that followed her loved ones for the rest of their lives.

The constable gestured at Emma. "For one, I'm taking up on Mrs. Knightley's point."

"I never suggested anything of the sort!" she protested.

"You pointed out that the window is not that easy to tumble out of by accident. I agree. Therefore, it makes sense to consider the alternative, one that *does* fit the rest of the evidence."

Emma had always known that the constable's intellect failed to live up to his name, but this particular accusation was beyond offensive.

"What evidence?" she snapped. "You haven't given us any."

George's eyebrows ticked up at her tone. Generally speaking, he did not approve of her tangling with Highbury's law officers, but in this case she found herself unable to remain silent.

"Well, Constable Sharpe?" she demanded. "What evidence do you have to support that outrageous assertion?"

"Begging pardon, Mrs. Knightley, but I don't answer to you," Sharpe disdainfully replied. "Ordinary folk have no business mucking about in the law or offering opinions on criminal matters."

Before she could open her mouth to retort, George intervened. "You may not answer to Mrs. Knightley, Constable Sharpe, but you *do* answer to me. And I expect you to answer my wife's question. What credible evidence do you have to support a conclusion of suicide?"

Constable Sharpe seemed to struggle with himself but then grudgingly replied, "The girl was obviously upset about something. Mayhap she had a falling-out with a sweetheart or was abandoned by him."

George looked to Mrs. Hodges. "Did Prudence have a sweetheart?"

The housekeeper hesitated for a few moments before replying. "No. At least not to my knowledge."

That caveat made Emma blink. Why did Mrs. Hodges seem reluctant to answer the question? Harry also looked uncomfortable, intently studying his shoes again.

"Constable Sharpe, young girls generally do not throw themselves out of windows because of quarrels with sweethearts," opined Dr. Hughes. "We are not living in a Shakespearian tragedy, after all."

"That's all well and good," Sharpe retorted. "I'm just saying we need to look at all the angles of the thing. The girl's dead, and it's my job to find out why."

Dr. Hughes held up an imperious hand. "I have heard and seen enough. What is clear is that Miss Parr was either upset or unwell. That state led her to drink a portion of sherry, a drink to which she was unaccustomed. She then opened the window, likely wishing to get some fresh air. Most unfortunately, she lost her balance, hit her head on the side of the frame, and tumbled to her death. As Highbury's coroner, that is my official determination."

George nodded. "I agree. Miss Parr's death was a tragic accident. There is certainly no need to inflict harm on her reputation with needless speculation that fails to hold up under scrutiny."

Under such withering fire, Constable Sharpe had no choice but to give in. He silently fumed for a few seconds, but then nodded.

"Then we are in agreement," said George. "Dr. Hughes, I will be happy to meet to discuss any legal necessities in a day or two. Before that, I must be off to Leatherhead in the morning to break the news to Miss Parr's family and help them make necessary arrangements."

"A heavy burden indeed, Mr. Knightley," replied the coroner. "Please convey my sympathies to Miss Parr's family."

George nodded. "Of course. Allow me to escort you and the constable downstairs."

Muttering under his breath, Constable Sharpe stomped out of the room, forcing Harry to scuttle aside. With a cluck of disapproval, Dr. Hughes followed at a more sedate pace.

George took Emma's hand. "Shall we, my dear?"

She shrugged. "I suppose there's nothing more to be done up here, is there?"

"I'll clean the window frame, Mr. Knightley," Mrs. Hodges quietly said. "That way we can lock the door and leave the rest of the room undisturbed."

George grimaced. "I'm sorry to leave you with such an unpleasant task."

"It's best if I do it, sir. I'll make sure everything is rightly taken care of."

"I'll help, Mrs. Hodges," Harry quietly said.

The sadness in their voices made Emma's heart ache.

Still, she couldn't help but notice the swift, almost furtive glance the servants exchanged. Emma had the distinct feeling that both were holding something back—presumably something about Prudence.

As George led her from the room, questions nipped at her heels. How *did* the decanter get up to the room? What was Prudence so upset about? Did she have a sweetheart, after all? Both Mrs. Hodges and Harry had evoked discomfort with that last question.

Although Emma was vastly relieved that Dr. Hughes had decisively ruled against suicide, and although it appeared that the fall *had* been an accident, there was nonetheless a mystery at the heart of the girl's death.

Those who knew Prudence best—the loyal staff of Donwell Abbey—might well be the keepers of that mystery.

Chapter 6

Emma was up early, shortly after George departed for Leatherhead. Despite his affectionate admonition to stay in bed and rest, a thousand questions bedeviled her, including how to manage Father and matters at Hartfield while she and George attended to the fraught situation at Donwell.

After dismissing the maid, Emma made her way downstairs, smiling faintly at the voices coming from the guest bedrooms. She heard giggles and teasing from her nieces and nephews, as well as the soothing tones of the nursemaid's voice as she responded to the cries of little Emma, the youngest of John and Isabella's children.

At the bottom of the stairs, she encountered Simon, their head footman.

"Good morning, Mrs. Knightley," he said. "You'll find a fresh pot of coffee and just-baked orange scones waiting for you. I can also fetch you some coddled eggs, and I'm about to bring up some gruel."

A slight spasm crossed his face at the mention of Serle's hideous gruel, the bane of Emma's childhood. Only Father willingly ate it, claiming it contained healthful benefits for sundry ailments.

"Is my father up already?" she asked, somewhat surprised.

"Not yet, ma'am. The gruel is for Mrs. Isabella Knightley."

Emma sighed. She'd forgotten that Isabella also ate the occasional bowl of gruel when she was feeling particularly frazzled.

"I'm surprised my sister is already in the breakfast parlor," she replied.

Even with five children, Isabella tended to be a late riser. Or perhaps it was *because* she had five children. Everyone needed a little peace now and again, and her sister's children, while charming, were the opposite of peaceful.

"Mrs. Knightley wishes to return to Brunswick Square this afternoon, and so is making an early start to the day," Simon replied.

Drat. I need her.

"Thank you, Simon. I'll make do with coffee and scones."

"Very good, madam."

Entering the breakfast parlor, Emma smiled to see Henry, Isabella's oldest child. He was kind and sensitive like his mamma but without her fretful anxieties. In fact, he greatly resembled his Uncle George, possessing a quiet dignity unusual and appealing in one so young.

"Good morning," she cheerfully said as she joined mother and son at the table.

Henry looked up from his honey-slathered scone. "Good morning, Auntie Emma. I hope you slept well."

"We returned home from Donwell quite late. I hope we didn't disturb you."

Isabella sighed. "It wouldn't matter if you did. I could barely sleep a wink for worrying about Father's health. And that poor girl, Emma! It's so terribly sad."

Emma directed a meaningful glance at Henry. "I wonder if we should be discussing this particular topic at . . . breakfast."

"I already heard our nursemaid talking to one of the footmen," Henry said around a mouthful of scone. "He said one of Donwell's maids fell out the window."

Emma couldn't be surprised at the gossip, since several of Hartfield's staff had been seconded to Donwell to assist with the party.

"I think you mean you *over*heard," she replied.

The boy shrugged. "How else am I supposed to find things out? It's not like adults will tell you anything."

Isabella looked perturbed. "Little boys are not to know such things. From now on, you're not to eavesdrop on adult conversations, Henry."

"Yes, Mamma," he politely replied.

When Emma lifted her eyebrows at him, Henry fought back a grin. He had no intention of obeying his mother's directive. Emma knew it, and he knew she knew it.

Repressing an answering smile, she addressed her sister instead. "Isabella, I understand you wish to depart for London, but there's no need to rush off. Father and I should be happy for you to stay."

Isabella shook her head. "You and George will be so busy these next days, I'm sure. I don't want to add to the commotion. It's not good for Father."

"As to that—"

The door opened and their father entered, wearing a colorful banyan and a cap on his head for extra warmth.

Emma jumped up to greet him. "Good morning, Father. I hope you were able to get some sleep."

"Some, my dear," he replied as she helped him to his seat. "I promised Miss Bates I wouldn't lie awake fretting about that poor girl, but I woke up quite early and couldn't stop thinking about it."

Emma patted his shoulder. "I know, dear. It was very distressing."

He sighed. "I do hope we won't have a repeat of the awful events of last summer when Mrs. Elton died. I don't think I could bear it."

"I wish I'd been here last summer," Henry stoutly said. "I could have helped Auntie Emma and Uncle George catch the killer."

Isabella gasped. "Henry Knightley, how could you wish for such a thing? It gives me palpitations just to think of it."

"Dear boy, you mustn't give your mother palpitations," Father exclaimed. "Palpitations are very bad for one's health."

"Yes, sir," Harry replied in the long-suffering tone of a child well used to the anxieties of his fretful relatives.

Fortunately, Simon entered with a dish of coddled eggs and the gruel, providing a timely diversion.

"Here's your breakfast, Father," Emma said in a bright tone. "Serle's eggs will set you up splendidly."

Her father morosely eyed his plate. "Perhaps I should have gruel, just in case. What do you think our dear Perry would suggest after such a harrowing evening?"

Emma resumed her seat and poured herself another cup of coffee. "Mr. Perry is firmly of the belief that none of us will suffer any lasting harm from last night's events. But I can send round a note asking him to stop by later, if that would ease your mind."

Father smiled. "That would be a great relief."

"Of course. Then we may all rest easy."

"Except for George," he replied. "Riding all the way to Leatherhead in this cold. I do not approve, Emma. That constable person should have gone to inform the unfortunate girl's family of her demise."

"It was more appropriate for George to go, Father. To help with the necessary arrangements."

Isabella pushed aside her bowl of untouched gruel. "Then the sooner we can be off, the better. The children and I will only be in your way."

Father stared at her, aghast. "Goodness, Isabella, I felt sure that you would stay for at least another week. Emma will need you."

"I only promised to stay for the party, Father. Besides, John will be missing the children."

"But John gets to see the children all the time," he plaintively replied. "And you."

It was a fact that John and Isabella could barely stand to be separated for more than a day. But he would simply have to survive another week without his family. Right now, Isabella was necessary for their father's comfort.

"Isabella, it would be a great help to me if you stayed," Emma coaxed.

Her sister frowned. "I don't see how."

"George and I need to spend more time at Donwell. The staff is most unsettled and would greatly benefit from having us in residence. It would be best if we stayed at Donwell for the next week or so, until we can sort through the various legal and personal matters."

Her father regarded her with dismay. "You mean you will stay overnight at Donwell?"

"Yes, Father. We've done it before, you know."

"But never for more than one night! What will I do if you're there all the time?"

"That's why I want Isabella to stay for another week. The children can keep you company, and Isabella can ensure that everything at Hartfield runs as it always does."

Isabella hesitated for a few seconds. "I don't know if John will approve of that."

"I'm sure John will understand," said Emma, "once you explain the reason. Or, you could ask him to return to Highbury and stay with you."

Isabella emphatically shook her head. "He couldn't possibly do that. He's very busy at the office with a particularly important case that takes up much of his time."

"Then I imagine he won't be home a great deal, will he?"

"An excellent point," Father said. "Why sit home waiting on John when you can be comfortable here at Hartfield? And the air is so much healthier in Highbury, you know. The children will surely benefit by remaining here."

Isabella began to waver. "Well, I don't—"

Henry, who'd been closely watching their conversation, tapped her arm to interrupt.

"Yes, dear?" Isabella said in a distracted tone.

"I heard Bella sneeze this morning," he casually stated. "At least twice."

Bella was the middle child of the Knightley brood, and the one most prone to sniffles.

His mother twisted in her chair to stare at him. "Are you sure?"

"Maybe even three times."

Father threw down his napkin. "Isabella, you cannot possibly travel if Bella is coming down with a cold. She must stay here, and you must allow Perry to treat her."

Isabella quickly stood. "Yes, of course. I'll go check on her. Emma, could you send for Perry immediately? He *must* see her before this develops into an infectious complaint."

Emma bit back a smile. "I'll send a boy around right away."

Isabella rushed from the room without bothering to reply.

"This is very bad," Father said, greatly perturbed. "What if all the children come down with a cold?"

She studied her nephew, who'd calmly moved on to his third scone. "Henry, did you really hear Bella sneeze three times?"

He waggled a hand. "Maybe she sneezed once."

Father peered at his grandson. "Are you saying that Bella is not sick?"

"It would seem that Henry was colluding with us to persuade his mother to remain at Hartfield," Emma replied with amusement.

Father's brow cleared. "Very clever, Henry." Then he held up a minatory hand. "But in general, one should not tell lies to one's parents."

"Unless it's for a good cause," Emma quipped.

Henry shrugged. "Bella won't mind, because Mamma will pay lots of attention to her."

"And I take it you're happy to stay at Hartfield for another week?"

The boy hesitated. "Actually, I was hoping I could stay at Donwell Abbey. It's fun over there, and I like spending time with you and Uncle George."

"But won't you miss your mother?" Father asked. "And your brothers and sisters?"

The boy rolled his eyes. "I won't miss baby Emma crying all the time, and John *always* wants me to play with him, even when I want to read."

Emma stifled a smile. "I'll have to ask your mother, but I for one would be happy for your company."

Henry beamed at her. "I think I can help you, too. I know you have lots to do at Donwell, because you're going to live there all the time once Grandfather and Miss Bates get married."

That reminder gave Emma a little jolt. There was indeed a great deal of work to be accomplished at Donwell before they made their permanent move.

But even more pressing was getting to the bottom of last night's tragic events. After sleeping on it—or tossing and turning on it—Emma was more convinced than ever that Donwell's servants knew more about Prudence's strange fall than they'd thus far revealed.

She glanced at the clock and rose to her feet, the vague outline of a plan forming in her mind. "Henry, you'd best run upstairs and have Nurse pack you some clothes. We leave for Donwell right after tea."

Chapter 7

When Emma entered the library, George put aside his book.

"I take it that Henry is settled for the night?" he asked.

She joined him on the sofa in front of the fireplace. A fire blazed merrily in the grate and the room had been returned to its habitual state of comfort, all traces of last night's events removed. The thick velvet drapes had been drawn over all the windows, closing off any view of the terrace and its tragic reminders.

"Happily settled," Emma replied. "I put him in the bedroom two doors down from us. It's cozier than the other rooms on our floor. They're much too grand, and I don't think he'd feel very comfortable."

When he put an arm around her, she nestled against him.

"I'm glad you didn't put him on the nursery floor," he replied.

"George, the nursery floor hasn't been used in decades. Frankly, I'm amazed it's not covered in cobwebs *and* haunted."

"You know I don't approve of ghosts, my dear. They spend all their time frightening the servants and generally misbehaving. I refuse to allow them at Donwell."

She poked him in the side. "Now you're being silly."

"Indeed. But I will also admit that a great deal of work needs to be done before we can make a permanent move. It will be a bother for you, I'm afraid."

She wriggled out of his embrace and reached for the silver teapot on the low table in front of them.

"It will be an interesting challenge," she said, pouring him a cup. "For now, though, it's just us, and everything is perfectly comfortable."

"As comfortable as it can be, under the circumstances," he dryly replied.

She sighed. "I know. I can't help wondering what would have happened to Prudence if we hadn't held that dratted party. Would she have died anyway?"

These last twenty-four hours, guilt had weighed more heavily on her than she cared to admit.

"We can never know," George replied. "Any such speculation in that regard could lead to nothing but pointless recriminations."

"True. If this last year has taught me anything, it's that we can never remake the past, no matter how hard we might try. Still, I can't help but think there must have been something we could have done to help Prudence."

"We can at least help her family."

She shifted to face him. "I would very much like to do that. I cannot imagine how dreadful it must have been for them to receive such shocking news—how dreadful for you to be the bearer of that news. I'm sorry, dearest."

"I don't know when I've ever seen a family so grieved. Prudence's mother died some years back. The poor girl was the only daughter, so her family was very protective of her. Her brothers opposed her taking the Donwell job in the first place, but her father agreed it was a good opportunity." He shook his head. "You can imagine how the poor man feels now."

Emma's heart wrung with pity. "What a terrible burden to carry." She hesitated. "I do hope he wasn't angry with you."

"One of the brothers was inclined to be angry with me. But when I tried to apologize, Mr. Parr would hear none of that." George put his teacup on the table. "He's a remarkably charitable man. In fact, he was inclined to apologize to *me* for bringing such trouble onto my household. Naturally, I told him that such was not the case, and that Prudence was greatly esteemed by everyone who worked at Donwell."

Emma propped her chin on the back of her hands, frowning absently at the fire. "I can't help wondering why Prudence wished to take employment in service. Mrs. Hodges told me that the Parrs' blacksmithing business does quite well. It employs her brothers too, does it not?"

"It does, and it seems prosperous. Leatherhead is large enough to support more than one smithy."

"It's a very respectable sort of business, too. One would think there would be a number of eligible tradesmen in Leatherhead who would be happy to court a pretty girl from a good family."

"That was apparently the very reason her brothers wished her to remain at home."

Emma toed off her slippers and pulled her feet up onto the sofa, getting comfortable. George snagged a lap blanket from the chair next to them and draped it over her legs.

"We cannot have you catching a chill," he wryly said. "Your father would never allow you to leave Hartfield again."

"A fate worse than death, once he marries Miss Bates."

"Now, Emma," he gently chided.

"I apologize, dearest. So, Prudence's brothers wished her to remain in Leatherhead, but her father allowed her to come to Donwell. Because he saw it as a good opportunity?"

"According to Mr. Parr, Prudence had ambitions to be a lady's maid. She found Leatherhead stifling—that was the word he used. She wished to find employment in a large household in London at some point."

"Then she certainly chose the wrong village. Leatherhead is a bustling metropolis compared with Highbury, and we never go anywhere."

"This position was a compromise. Her father allowed her to start at Donwell precisely because it is so quiet and because the distance from home was not great." He paused for a moment, glancing down at his hands. "Mr. Parr thought she would be safe in Highbury."

Emma pressed a hand to his knee. "I'm so sorry, George. But none of this is your fault. I suppose all we can do now is help her family as best we can. Did you mean with the funeral arrangements?"

"The Parrs are well able to manage that. In fact, they were quite offended when I offered. The funeral is the day after tomorrow, by the way. I will, of course, be attending."

"Another unhappy day for you, I'm afraid. Perhaps Larkins can accompany you."

"Any of the staff who wish to go are certainly welcome to do so."

"Then if we cannot help them with the funeral arrangements, how do we assist them?"

When he hesitated, Emma knew that he was about to pick his words very carefully.

"The Parrs have questions," he replied. "Unfortunately, at this point they seem impossible to answer."

"What sort of questions?"

He gave her a knowing look. "The same ones you had—and still have, I imagine."

"Ah. Such as, was she drinking spirits when she apparently never touched them. And how she managed to fall out the window."

"Correct. Mr. Parr was adamant that his daughter never drank spirits. Moreover, he and her brothers agreed that she would never jeopardize her employment by essentially stealing a decanter of expensive sherry."

Emma nodded. "Our staff would agree. Which raises the question as to how the decanter got to her room. Did you also tell him that something seemed to be troubling the girl?"

George rose and wandered over to the fireplace, where he stared intently into the flames before turning and propping a shoulder against the mantelpiece. "I did. But we must not forget she also complained of the headache, which might also explain her distress."

"I'm inclined to think that such was *not* the case. From what Mrs. Hodges and Harry said—and from what I observed myself—it's much more likely that some external situation disturbed her."

"It's true that one generally doesn't drink spirits to cure a headache. The opposite result is likely to occur."

Emma widened her eyes. "And you know this from personal experience, dearest?"

"Unfortunately, yes," he admitted. "When I was under the illusion that you were in love with Frank Churchill, I may have imbibed more than is my usual want on one or two occasions. A thundering headache was the result."

"Oh dear," she replied, trying to smother a laugh. "How . . . how unfortunate."

He scoffed. "Something tells me that your sympathy is less than genuine."

"Don't be silly, George. I'm terribly saddened to hear you had such a difficult time." Then she grew serious again. "But enough of *us* being silly. Did Mr. Parr have any thoughts as to why Prudence might have been troubled?"

George returned to the sofa. "He did. Prudence returned

home for a short visit a few weeks before her death. Both Mr. Parr and her brothers felt she was not herself, but Prudence was curiously reluctant to speak about it. Mr. Parr said he got the sense that she might have a beau, or at the very least an admirer."

Now *that* was interesting. Emma's own theory began to sharpen around the edges.

"Yet," George continued, "Mrs. Hodges and Harry both stated that no such beau existed."

Emma waggled a hand. "Not unequivocally, though. I thought they were dodging the issue somewhat."

He frowned. "Nevertheless, her brothers were adamant that even a disappointment in love wouldn't drive her to behave so rashly. She was too sensible to jeopardize her position at Donwell, for one thing."

"A mysterious beau is not the sort of thing a girl is likely to share with protective older brothers," she dryly replied.

"True. But we would certainly know if she had a beau here at Donwell, or one from the staff in a neighboring household. Nor would I have any objection as long as the relationship was conducted in an appropriate manner."

"But what if the beau—or admirer—wasn't a servant?" Emma cautiously said.

"Are you suggesting she might have been involved with someone from the village?"

"Not involved, necessarily."

"What exactly are you suggesting then, my dear?"

She hesitated for just a moment. "For the sake of argument, let's say Prudence had an admirer in Highbury. She was a very pretty girl, after all, and it would be reasonable that a young man would take an interest in her."

"Do you have a particular young man in mind?"

"Perhaps William Cox?"

Her husband's dark brows practically rose up to his hairline. "I cannot imagine his parents would look favorably on such a liaison."

"Dearest, I suspect there are any number of young men who are undeterred by parental disapproval in such matters."

He snorted. "I take your point. Still, William hardly seems the type to court a serving girl, even a very pretty one. And the Parrs are hardly on the same social level as the Coxes."

She rounded her eyes at him. "Have you met Anne Cox and her sister?"

He ignored that. "Mr. Cox is a solicitor from a very respectable family. Besides, when would William even have a chance to see Prudence, much less converse with her?"

"You don't keep the servants locked up, George. And Prudence went to church every Sunday, as do the Cox family."

Of course, William generally dozed during the services, which, in Emma's mind, certainly pointed to a deficiency in character.

"That, my dear, is hardly proof of anything."

"I know. As theories go, it's rather a muddle in my own head. But there *is* more. William Cox became inebriated at our party and made quite a spectacle. I was forced to order his sisters to remove him from the great hall."

George grimaced. "I didn't know that. I'm sorry, Emma. I wish I could have spared you such an unpleasant encounter."

"It was a trifle in comparison to later events."

"But clearly you think the two incidents might be connected. But how?"

"What if William Cox was attracted to Prudence? And in his inebriated state he tried to act on it, and she rebuffed him? I'm sure that sort of awful behavior happens to female servants more than we know."

George looked momentarily startled. "True, and if I ever heard of such a thing at Donwell I would immediately put a stop to it."

"Of course you would. But you'd have to *hear* about it first."

He fell silent. Emma patiently waited, letting him sift through the implications.

"All right," he finally said. "Let's say that William importuned Prudence and she rejected him. Then what?"

"It would stand to reason that an inebriated William could be angry enough that he might have followed Prudence up to her room to . . . to try to importune her again."

"That is a grim thought, my dear."

"Yes, it turns one's stomach," she quietly replied.

He briefly cupped her cheek. "I understand. Are you also suggesting it was he who took the sherry decanter up with him?"

"He was certainly in a condition to do something that stupid. Perhaps he thought to ply her with drink, but Prudence rebuffed him again." She hesitated for a moment. "There might even have been a struggle, which led to . . . her fall."

George blinked, clearly startled. "Are you suggesting he murdered her?"

She wavered. "Well . . . no. An accident, I think, not deliberate."

"Yet, if you recall, there were no signs of struggle. And Mrs. Hodges confirmed that nothing was out of place."

"Perhaps he took the time to straighten the room. Of course he would wish to hide any sign of a struggle."

George's expression was openly skeptical. "That kind of cool, calculated action would seem remarkable in a man so thoroughly drunk. And why would he leave the decanter and wineglass in her room if he was determined to clean it up?"

Ah, she had him on that one. "He wished it to seem that she'd been drinking, to reinforce the appearance that it was an accident of her own making."

"If William were sober, I might be inclined to agree with you. I find it difficult, however, to believe that a heavily intoxicated man would likely act with such forethought." He tilted an eyebrow at her. "Especially so foolish a young man as William."

And he had her on that one. "Well . . . I don't think he went up there with the goal of murdering her."

"All right, but if she was drinking with him, where was the other glass?"

"Obviously he took that one down with him."

"Perhaps. But you'll recall that I sent Harry up to secure Prudence's room almost on the heels of the discovery of her body. I doubt there was enough time for William—or anyone else—to clean up signs of what likely would have been a desperate struggle."

Emma blew out a frustrated sigh. Her husband was making perfect sense, but some deep instinct rebelled against the too-neat conclusion that Prudence was responsible for her own death.

George took her hands in a comforting grip. "I think we must accept the coroner's verdict that it was simply an exceedingly tragic accident. Let us be thankful, at least, that he ruled it such instead of a suicide."

"I am, but everyone who knew Prudence confirmed her distaste for spirits as well as her loyalty to Donwell. Why then would a dutiful servant like her essentially steal an expensive crystal decanter and take it up to her room? To drink away some vague sorrows?" She shook her head. "Given everything we know of her, it makes no sense."

George ruffled a hand through his hair, suddenly looking quite tired. It had been a difficult day for him, and this would be the last thing he would wish to talk about.

"I'm sorry, dearest," she said ruefully. "I shouldn't be pestering you with my theories. I have to accept that Prudence's death was most likely an accident. It certainly appears so on the basis of the evidence."

Still...

She remained convinced that both Mrs. Hodges and Harry were hiding something about Prudence. Perhaps something that might cast her in a bad light? In their own way, were they trying to protect the girl of whom they were clearly so fond?

"Emma, what is it?" George asked.

She dredged up a smile. "I suppose I just loathe not knowing what upset the poor girl so much that she would act in so impetuous a manner."

"We have yet to go through Prudence's belongings, which I will do tomorrow with Mrs. Hodges. Perhaps that might provide a clue as to her state of mind."

He didn't sound terribly convinced, nor was she.

"Perhaps," she doubtfully echoed.

George rose and tugged her to her feet. "We've both had a long day, and I suspect tomorrow will be much the same. I confess to being all but asleep on my feet."

She felt a pang of guilt. "Of course, dearest. We both need a good night's rest."

Emma earnestly hoped that her poor husband *would* sleep well. She, however, would likely lie awake, with an unanswered question spinning relentlessly in her brain.

What had upset Prudence so greatly that it had ultimately led to her death?

Chapter 8

The stone steps down to Donwell's old kitchen had been worn smooth and to a slight slope over the centuries, first by the monks and then by generations of servants. Emma worried that the steps one day would cause someone to slip while carrying a heavy tray of food or a tureen of soup. It would be just like Harry, for instance, to fall and bash his head, which would be terribly inconvenient for the poor fellow.

That was but one of the problems she needed to solve about the house's old kitchen. Besides the slippery steps, the dining room was so far away from the kitchen that most of their food often arrived in a tepid or wilted state. As a bachelor living alone amongst Donwell's ancient splendors, George, though, had barely noticed such things, satisfied with a plate of cold meats and cheeses instead of a proper meal.

Those days were now gone, and bringing the abbey up to snuff was going to be a challenge. Emma looked forward to tackling it—after she dealt with the challenge of Prudence Parr's tragic death. She remained convinced there had to be something more to the story, a buried secret or a mystery to be solved.

Getting to the bottom of it wouldn't bring the girl back, but it might provide her grieving family with answers and also give George some well-needed peace of mind.

Emma hadn't known Prudence that well, but by all accounts she was an excellent young woman. For the last word on her short life to be so tawdry was simply unacceptable.

The kitchen was a long, narrow room with a fairly low ceiling, though it was surprisingly bright thanks to windows set high in the walls, facing both west and south. When the weather was pleasant, the door to the kitchen gardens and stable yard was left open to bring in fresh air and more light. An enormous stone fireplace, original to the abbey, served as the hub, where most of the cooking took place. A large wooden table occupied the center of the room, and crockery and gleaming cookware filled neatly arranged shelves. Despite the antique nature of the kitchen, it radiated cleanliness and order, which was a tribute to Mrs. Hodges's ferocious efficiency.

"Good morning, Mrs. Hodges," Emma cheerfully announced.

The housekeeper, who'd been seated in a cane-back chair with her back to the stairs, jumped to her feet and spun around.

"Mrs. Knightley! I apologize, ma'am. I didn't hear you come down the stairs."

That was understandable, because Emma thought she might have been delivering a scold to Harry, in what was apparently a regular occurrence. Now, the footman simply stared at Emma with a morose expression.

The housekeeper shot an irritated glance at him. "Harry, stop gaping and fetch Mrs. Knightley a chair."

Harry shook off his momentary paralysis, much like a spaniel shook off the rain coming indoors. He fetched another cane-back chair tucked behind the pantry door and carried it around the table, almost knocking over Mrs. Hodges's chair in the process. The housekeeper let out an aggrieved sigh but declined further chastisement.

From what Emma had been able to observe, it wouldn't do much good anyway. Harry seemed to be naturally clumsy, something not usually found in a footman. It was fortunate that he had an excellent, tolerant employer in George, since she doubted he would last very long anywhere else.

"Can I get you a cup of tea, ma'am?" asked Mrs. Hodges. "I just made a fresh pot for Mr. Larkins, since I expect him in from the stables any time."

"A cup of tea sounds lovely," she replied, taking her seat.

The servants began to bustle about the kitchen. Well, Mrs. Hodges bustled, while Harry mostly stood about looking awkward, darting uneasy glances at Emma. Perhaps he hadn't been on the working end of a scold, after all. Perhaps he and Mrs. Hodges had been discussing something that made them both uncomfortable—something like Prudence's death.

"If you won't be needing me, Mrs. Hodges," he finally said, "I can get back upstairs to finish up the dusting."

Obviously he'd already had to take on some of Prudence's tasks. That left Emma somewhat alarmed for the delicate knickknacks that adorned the drawing room and library.

"There's no need to rush off, Harry," she said. "I'd like to speak to both you and Mrs. Hodges."

As she deposited the tea tray in front of her, the housekeeper shot Emma a startled frown. But then she recovered her composure and began preparing the tea.

"Of course, Mrs. Knightley," she said, stacking macaroons on a blue floral plate. "What can Harry and I do for you?"

"Please make yourself a cup of tea and have a seat, Mrs. Hodges. You as well, Harry."

His eyes went almost as round as the plate. "No, thank you, madam. I mean, ma'am, I mean Mrs. Knightley. I'll just stand here against the wall, if you don't mind."

He was no doubt shocked by her sudden appearance, wishing to have a cup of tea with the servants in the kitchen. Emma hoped that in treating them in such an informal manner they might be thrown slightly off-balance, and as a result be more forthcoming in sharing what they knew about Prudence.

Mrs. Hodges looked askance at Harry before returning her attention to Emma. "How can we help you, Mrs. Knightley?"

"I would like to discuss the necessary changes that will facilitate our permanent move back to Donwell Abbey," she replied.

Mrs. Hodges's features eased into a smile. "Of course, ma'am. But wouldn't you be more comfortable in the library?" Her glance slid sideways to Harry. "I'd be happy to bring the tea tray up there."

"I want to discuss improvements to the kitchen as well, so it would make sense to stay here while we go over them."

"I'm not sure how I could help with that, Mrs. Knightley," Harry stated in a doubtful tone.

Emma hesitated. "Well . . . before we get to that, I'd like to discuss something else first."

Mrs. Hodges stilled for a moment before breathing out a sigh. "I expect you mean Prudence. I thought you might have a few questions."

Aha!

"So, my assumption the other night was correct," replied Emma. "You didn't wish to speak frankly in front of Dr. Hughes and Constable Sharpe."

Harry grimaced. "Can you blame us, ma'am? That bottle-headed constable, saying them nasty things about our Prudence."

"That's enough, Harry," Mrs. Hodges rapped out. "You're not to be talking to the mistress in that way."

Harry shuffled his feet. "Sorry, Mrs. Knightley. But that constable . . . well, he made me right angry saying those things."

"We were all dismayed by Constable Sharpe's unjust accusations, Harry. However," Emma added, belatedly realizing that she shouldn't criticize Highbury's lawman in front of the servants, "Constable Sharpe was only doing his duty."

"Not very well," Mrs. Hodges muttered.

"Too right, Mrs. H," Harry muttered back.

The housekeeper sighed. "Harry, how many times must I ask you *not* to call me Mrs. H?"

"Sorry, Mrs. H. I mean, Mrs. Hodges."

Emma did her best to ignore the rather comical exchange. "Mrs. Hodges, where are the other kitchen staff?"

At this point, it wouldn't be appropriate to discuss Prudence's situation with the junior staff.

"I sent Molly and Leah off to the market, ma'am. Leah lives in the village but comes to help with the work in the kitchen." Mrs. Hodges cast her a shrewd look. "You may be sure they won't be gossiping about what we discuss today."

Emma nodded. "Thank you."

"How then can we help you, ma'am?"

"I know you said that Prudence complained of a headache."

The housekeeper nodded. "That's what she told me."

Emma rubbed a casual fingertip over the wooden tabletop, worn smooth by decades of diligent scrubbing. "But I think we know there was more to it than that."

The housekeeper seemed to consider her words before replying. "At first, I thought she might just have a sore head. Except Prudence never had headaches before, and the poor girl was near tears. Something had rattled her, and I made a point of saying so."

"Did she tell you anything about it?"

When Mrs. Hodges and Harry exchanged a furtive glance, Emma knew she was on the right path.

"It's a bit delicate, ma'am," said the housekeeper. "I didn't want anyone to be thinking . . ."

"Thinking that Prudence had behaved inappropriately." Emma nodded. "I understand. Correct me if I'm wrong, but did Prudence's distress have something to do with William Cox?"

Mrs. Hodges's mouth gaped for a moment, before she recovered. "How did you know?"

"Prudence admitted such to you?" Emma said instead of answering the question.

She nodded. "Yes, after a bit. Prudence said he was in his cups and was pestering her. He even followed her back to the long gallery, flirting and carrying on something terrible."

Emma had to force back a flare of anger. If William Cox had been standing in front of her at this moment, she likely would have smashed the teapot over his head.

"How very unfortunate," she tersely replied.

"Begging your pardon, Mrs. Knightley," said Harry, "but how *did* you know?"

"I observed his condition in the great hall. At the time, of course, I didn't realize he was bothering Prudence. Mrs. Hodges, what did you do after she told you about William?"

"I offered to go straight to Mr. Knightley, but Prudence begged me not to. She said he was just a stupid fellow, and she didn't want to make a fuss about it." The housekeeper sighed. "I wish I'd made a fuss. She might still be alive."

"There's no way to know that," Emma calmly replied. "I can well imagine that Prudence was distressed by the incident. Still, I find it hard to believe that she would then drink herself into such a state that she would accidentally fall out of her window. She was too sensible for that."

Harry cleared his throat, his gaze firmly fixed on his shoes. His expression suggested he was torn about something.

"Harry, is there something you'd like to say?" Emma asked.

He looked at her and then at Mrs. Hodges, who regarded him through a narrowed gaze.

"Mayhap it's not my place to say," he said.

"Then perhaps it's best you keep it to yourself," Mrs. Hodges crisply replied.

Emma held up a hand. "No, I want to hear it. Harry, did you know that William Cox was pestering Prudence?"

"Not until later, ma'am, when Mrs. Hodges told me. But I don't know if he was pestering her so much as . . ." He trailed off with a grimace.

"Yes?" Emma prompted after a few moments.

"I think Prudence may have been sweet on Mr. Cox," he suddenly burst out. "And she wasn't upset that he was pestering her, she was upset that he *wasn't*."

"Good heavens," exclaimed Mrs. Hodges. "What are you going on about now?"

"I knew you wouldn't like it," he morosely replied.

Emma leaned forward. "So, you're suggesting Prudence had feelings for William, and possibly even saw him as a beau?"

He shrugged. "I'm fair sure there was someone she was sweet on. It makes sense it would be Mr. Cox, if she was upset about him."

Emma frowned. "I don't follow."

"If she was sweet on him and then found out that he was only flirting with her, she'd be upset," he explained. "But men like that don't take up with the likes of us, do they? Servants, I mean."

Mrs. Hodges made an exasperated noise. "Prudence would know that. She was a practical girl."

Even practical girls fell in love with men above their station. Harriet, for instance, had once developed strong feelings for Mr. Elton—and even for George. Emma supposed it wasn't out of the question that Prudence might think herself an eligible match for William Cox, especially since her father was a respectable blacksmith with a good trade.

"So you think that Prudence was upset because William Cox rejected her?" she asked Harry.

He nodded. "That's why she had a tipple to make herself feel better."

Mrs. Hodges emphatically shook her head. "Prudence would no more steal a decanter of sherry than she would fall in love with William Cox."

"Prudence's family feels the same," Emma said. "They insisted she would never do anything to jeopardize her position at Donwell."

"That's true, Mrs. Knightley." The housekeeper directed a glare at Harry. "And you are not to spread that tale around. It's sheer nonsense, and I don't believe it for a minute."

Harry's shoulders went up around his ears. "Prudence *was* sweet on someone, though. I'd bet half a bob on that."

Emma expected the housekeeper to refute that statement, too. Instead, she clamped her lips shut and looked as uncomfortable as Harry had a few minutes ago. Emma couldn't help but recall that Mr. Parr had also suspected his daughter might be in love with someone.

"Mrs. Hodges, do *you* think Prudence had a beau?" she asked.

The housekeeper made a helpless gesture. "I cannot be sure. The only thing I *can* be sure about is that Prudence denied having a sweetheart."

Emma lifted her eyebrows. "You asked her directly?"

"I did, ma'am."

"May I ask why?"

"Starting about a month ago she was . . . well, not her usual self. She seemed distracted. I asked about a beau more in jest than anything else, but she blushed and looked mighty unhappy about the question. I'll admit that gave me a worry. I'm responsible for the girls in the house, ma'am. I don't want them getting themselves into trouble or being taken advantage of."

"The servants are fortunate to have you looking after them, Mrs. Hodges."

Harry muttered something inaudible.

"Do you have something to say?" Mrs. Hodges tartly asked him.

Emma hastily intervened. "Prudence denied having a sweetheart, you said."

The housekeeper nodded.

Another thought occurred. Harry certainly wasn't the sharpest pin in the box, but he was a big, strapping fellow who most girls would consider attractive.

"Harry, what about you?" Emma asked. "Do you think Prudence had feelings for you?"

He stared for several long moments, and then burst into a loud guffaw.

Mrs. Hodges bristled. "You sound like a bellowing ox, Harry. Control yourself."

The footman choked as he tried to stifle his laughter. "S . . . sorry, Mrs. Knightley. But Prudence would never look at a fellow like me. Too clever for me, she was."

At least he knew his limitations. "I assume, then, that you didn't harbor any feelings for her?"

"I have a girl back in Hampstead. We've been sweethearts since we was kids." He perked up. "Mr. Hodges said you'll be hiring more staff, so mayhap you'll have a word with Mr. Knightley. Daisy would be ever so thrilled to work at Donwell Abbey."

Mrs. Hodges jumped in. "Is there anything else we can help you with, ma'am?"

"I suppose none of the other servants would have any idea about how the decanter got up to Prudence's room?" Emma asked.

"They do not."

That brought Emma right back to William Cox. Despite Harry's theory, it struck her as much more likely that William *had* been forward with Prudence, and had pursued her up to her room—with the decanter.

When Mrs. Hodges glanced at the watch pinned to her waist, Emma realized that the morning was getting on.

She stood. "I won't keep you any longer, Mrs. Hodges. Perhaps we can speak tomorrow about the necessary changes—"

She stopped when the door to the stable yard opened and William Larkins strode into the kitchen, bringing in a blast of cold air. If he was surprised to see her, he didn't show it.

"Good morning, Mrs. Knightley."

"Actually, almost afternoon," she humorously replied. "How are you, Mr. Larkins?"

"I'm tolerable, ma'am. Thank you for asking."

In fact, he looked terrible. His normally ruddy features were drawn and pale, and he seemed to have aged overnight.

"Can I get you a cup of tea, Mr. Larkins?" asked Mrs. Hodges.

"No, I'm fine." He glanced at Emma. "Can I be of any assistance, Mrs. Knightley?"

She thought to ask him about Prudence but decided against it. Larkins was a very private man and would no doubt be mortified to be questioned about the girl.

Then again . . .

"Yes, actually," she said with a smile. "My nephew wishes to walk to Hartfield. I was going to take him, but I have an errand I must attend to. Are you by any chance going into the village today?"

Larkins nodded. "I am, and I'll be happy to walk the boy to Hartfield."

"I can do it if you're busy," Harry piped up.

Larkins gave him a somewhat dismissive glance. "I'm sure Mrs. Hodges needs your help around the house."

"Indeed I do," the housekeeper said. "Harry, you need to finish your dusting."

The footman sighed. "Yes, Mrs. Hodges."

Emma smiled at Larkins. "I'll get Henry ready to go. In ten minutes, shall we say?"

"Very good, Mrs. Knightley."
Excellent.

With her nephew sorted for the afternoon, Emma could pursue the question of William Cox. And she knew just the person to ask.

Chapter 9

A chill breeze whipped among the hedgerows and rattled the empty branches of the trees. Thankfully, the walk from Donwell to Randalls was a mere ten minutes, especially if one took the footpath that ran directly from the abbey to fetch up behind Randalls.

As Emma cut across the back lawn, the frost-covered grass crunched under her feet. By the time she circled around to the front door, she was more than ready for a hot cup of tea and a chat with her oldest friend. Although not a gossip herself, Mrs. Weston was married to a man who collected information from the locals as readily as a sponge drew up water. Mr. Weston was the easiest man in the world to talk to, and talk to him the villagers certainly did. Even better, he was dreadful at keeping confidences. That made him the perfect source of information, which he invariably shared with his wife.

Hannah, one of the housemaids, admitted her into the entrance hall.

"Good afternoon, Mrs. Knightley." The girl eyed Emma's boots. "It's right nasty out there, ma'am. You should have asked my father to drive you over instead of tramping out in this cold. It's not good for your lungs."

Hannah's father was James, Hartfield's ever-loyal coachman.

Emma smiled at her. "I'm sure he would have, but Mr. Knightley and I are at Donwell for the present."

Hannah folded Emma's pelisse over her arm. "Mrs. Hodges will be grateful to have you there, what with all the sad goings-on."

"Did you know Prudence?"

"Not well, but I'd see her in the village on occasion, and at church. I know Mrs. Hodges thought the world of her, as did Mr. Larkins. I expect they're both terrible cut up about it."

This wasn't the first time someone had mentioned that Larkins would be upset by Prudence's death. As estate steward, he would of course feel responsible for Donwell's staff, but he would have little contact with servants like a chambermaid.

"Mrs. Weston is in the parlor with Miss Bates," Hannah added. "I was just going to fetch the tea tray when you rang."

Drat.

Emma had hoped that her conversation with Mrs. Weston would be private, since the subject required a degree of delicacy and discretion. Although Miss Bates was a kind and sensitive soul, discretion was by no means her forte.

Not that Emma had any intention of directly accusing William Cox of assault, or even murder. What she was hoping to gain was a greater knowledge of his character and of any recent changes in his behavior. Since they generally moved in different social circles, Emma had little opportunity to observe William or his sisters.

Then again, Miss Bates was both friendly with Mrs. Cox *and* one of Highbury's most notable gossips. Unlike Mr. Weston, whose reliability in that regard was sometimes a trifle wobbly, Emma's future stepmother was a surprisingly accurate source of information about anything affecting their little village.

"Don't let me keep you, Hannah," Emma said. "I know the way."

She headed down the corridor toward the back of the house, where the family parlor was situated.

"There you are," exclaimed Mrs. Weston as Emma entered the room. "We saw you through the window. But Emma, you must be chilled to the bone."

"You must be careful, Mrs. Knightley," Miss Bates earnestly said. "Mr. Woodhouse would be quite distraught to hear you caught a chill."

Emma smiled. "I wrapped up very warmly, I assure you. The walk did me good."

Miss Bates looked much struck by her reply. "You will hardly believe it, Mrs. Knightley, but I said just the same thing to your father. I was visiting Hartfield before I came to see Mrs. Weston, and your father insisted that I take his carriage. He said that James and the horses wouldn't mind in the least. But I refused, of course, since I walk all the time. There is nothing more healthful than a brisk walk. In fact, I said to your father—"

"And how is my father today?" Emma smoothly interjected into the usual torrent of words.

"Oh, your father," said Miss Bates, properly distracted. "He's so happy to have Isabella and the children at Hartfield. The little ones are such a delightful diversion. Why, I don't know when I've met better children. Except for my niece Jane, of course. And you. I believe you and Jane were the best children I ever knew."

Emma repressed a smile. "Jane was always much better behaved than I was. Mrs. Weston can certainly attest to that."

"You were a delightful child," her former governess said. "If a trifle headstrong at times."

Emma shot her a sly grin. "Only a trifle?"

Mrs. Weston took her arm. "Come sit by the fire, dear. Hannah is fetching the tea tray. I'm sure we will all be happy for a cup on such a chilly day."

Miss Bates bustled in their wake. "Dear me, yes. There is nothing better than a cup of hot tea on a cold winter's day. And Randalls serves quite the best tea in Highbury. I always say that to mother—although Hartfield also serves excellent tea. No one puts a tea tray together like Serle. I made that point just the other day to your dear father, Mrs. Knightley."

Emma gratefully sank onto the sofa in front of the fireplace. Nestling into the overstuffed cushions, she extended her feet toward the crackling fire in the grate. She always enjoyed her visits to Randalls, especially when she could have a quiet chat with Mrs. Weston. Sadly, that was not to be the case today. Still, she was determined to make the best of it—for the greater good, of course.

Hannah entered, bearing the tea tray.

"And speaking of tea," said Mrs. Weston.

Emma pulled herself upright. "Excellent. I'm famished."

Her former governess frowned. "Emma, when was the last time you ate?"

"I had cup of tea earlier, but I haven't eaten anything since breakfast."

"Mr. Woodhouse would be very distressed to think of you not having enough to eat," said Miss Bates, looking worried.

Emma lifted an eyebrow. "Let's not mention it to him then, shall we?"

"I'm sure Miss Bates will do no such thing," said Mrs. Weston. "Especially since I'm going to make you a nice plate, and you're going to eat everything on it."

Her former governess filled a plate with macaroons, a scone with jam and clotted cream, and a large slice of date cake.

Emma eyed the plate. "That's quite a lot of food."

"And you're to eat all of it."

She took the plate with a shrug because she could, in fact, eat all of it.

They chatted about innocuous topics, including the children's health and the shocking state of the chimney in Donwell's east drawing room. After they'd exhausted those subjects, Emma thought it time to turn the discussion in the appropriate direction.

"Will we be seeing Mr. Weston this afternoon?"

Mrs. Weston shot her a perplexed look. "He went to Leatherhead for Miss Parr's funeral. Do you not remember? He wished to lend Mr. Knightley whatever assistance he needed."

Emma grimaced. "I had forgotten, but I'm grateful for Mr. Weston's kindness, else George would have travelled alone."

"Did Larkins not go with him, also?" Mrs. Weston asked. "I thought he surely would."

"None of the Donwell staff went to the funeral," Emma slowly replied.

Leatherhead was some miles distant, so it made sense that the servants wouldn't attend. But of course Larkins should have been there. As estate steward, one would have expected him to both represent the staff and support his employer.

The fact that Larkins hadn't gone with George made her feel oddly uneasy.

She shook it off and forced a smile. "Then I am doubly grateful that Mr. Weston was so kind as to accompany George. I hated the notion of him going alone."

Naturally, Emma would have been happy to accompany him. But women did not generally attend funerals, particularly women of a certain social standing.

Miss Bates breathed a doleful sigh. "I will never forget the sight of that sweet girl coming to such a dreadful end. And her poor father . . . how will he ever survive it, Mrs. Knightley?"

Emma felt a twinge of guilt. It had been a terrible shock for all of them, but doubly so for Miss Bates.

"We can only be grateful that Mr. Parr has his sons to support him. But how are you, ma'am? This event has put a strain on you, as well."

Miss Bates pressed a feeling hand to her chest. "You are so good to think of me, Mrs. Knightley. But I am determined to recover from the shock for Mr. Woodhouse's sake. It won't do for him to dwell on such an unhappy subject, and so I must try to turn my mind in happier directions as well."

As she had on the night of Prudence's fall, Miss Bates continued to surprise Emma with her unexpected fortitude.

"Very sensible," Emma said with an encouraging smile.

"I am determined to be as strong as I can be," Miss Bates stoutly replied. "Not simply for Mr. Woodhouse, but also for you and for Mrs. Isabella Knightley."

Emma was almost afraid to ask. "And how is my sister these last few days?"

Rather than rattling off her usual somewhat garbled reply, Miss Bates thoughtfully frowned.

"Ma'am?" Emma prompted.

"She's well enough, I think, although she seems quite distracted. Why, I spoke to her three times this morning, and she failed to hear me."

Emma had to repress a smile. Isabella had a remarkable ability to ignore those with whom she did not wish to converse, and do it without giving offense.

"I expect Isabella is also feeling the strain of this week's events," Mrs. Weston tactfully said. "And missing John, no doubt."

"We're all feeling it," Emma said. "The staff at Donwell are quite distraught—not only about the death itself but the manner of it as well."

Mrs. Weston grimaced. "We can only hope the memory of this tragic accident will begin to fade, and life will soon return to normal at Donwell."

"I'm not so sure about that," Emma replied. "There are aspects of Prudence's death that can only be described as perplexing."

Miss Bates looked puzzled, but Mrs. Weston's expression began to transform into one of foreboding.

Her former governess knew her too well.

"Whatever can you mean, Mrs. Knightley?" asked Miss Bates.

Emma ran her finger around the rim of her teacup. "It seems that Prudence might have been keeping secrets."

Miss Bates tilted her head, looking like an inquisitive sparrow. "What sort of secrets? And what would they have to do with—" She twirled a hand. "You know."

"I'm not sure yet."

Mrs. Weston let out an exasperated sigh. "Miss Parr's death was simply an unfortunate accident. Dr. Hughes ruled it so, did he not?"

"Yes, but there was initially some question about that."

"Are you referring to Constable Sharpe's ridiculous theory that Miss Parr killed herself?" Mrs. Weston dryly asked.

Miss Bates clapped her hands to her cheeks. "Never say so! I cannot believe such a dreadful thing of that sweet girl."

"She did no such thing, I assure you." Emma frowned at her governess. "How did you hear about that nonsense?"

"As I understand it, there were servants in the room when this discussion occurred," her friend replied.

"Mrs. Hodges would never—" Emma broke off with an exasperated sigh. "Harry."

She was beginning to grasp what a nuisance the fellow could be. Still, she felt sure that Harry wasn't engaging in malicious gossip for the sake of it. He was merely a dolt.

"I'll have to speak with him," she added. "Spreading that sort of tale will not do."

"Perhaps it's best if the entire subject is best avoided in the future," said Mrs. Weston, giving her *the* look.

Emma had always called it *the governess gaze*, and it had generally been employed when the former Miss Taylor thought Emma was sticking her nose where it didn't belong.

"But Mrs. Knightley said there were questions," Miss Bates said in a hesitant tone. "And if Mrs. Knightley is concerned, then surely we should all be concerned."

"I think Mrs. Knightley should discuss these questions with Mr. Knightley," Mrs. Weston responded.

Emma rolled her eyes. "Mrs. Knightley already has."

"And?"

"Let's just say new evidence has come to light."

"My dear—"

Emma put up her hands. "Just hear me out."

"But why bring this to me?" Mrs. Weston glanced at Miss Bates. "To us?"

"Because you know most everyone, and you know everything that goes on in Highbury."

She couldn't help eyeing Miss Bates, though. Mrs. Weston's discretion was assured, but her future stepmother's? Not so much.

"It's quite a delicate situation," Emma added. "Someone's reputation might be at stake."

Miss Bates shook her head. "How could Miss Parr's reputation be damaged any more than it already has been?"

"It's not Prudence I'm speaking of."

The spinster's eyes went wide. "You're speaking of someone who's not dead! A not-dead person's reputation."

Emma had to repress an impulse to laugh. "That's one way to put it. And since this person is . . . not dead, we must be careful not to besmirch his . . . their reputation if we . . . I arrive at the wrong conclusion."

Good Lord. She was beginning to sound like Miss Bates.

"Then, Emma, are you perfectly sure you wish to discuss this now?" Mrs. Weston cast a meaningful glance at Miss Bates.

The spinster, unfortunately, caught the exchange of glances.

"You mustn't worry about me, Mrs. Weston," Miss Bates earnestly said. "If Mrs. Knightley wishes this information to be confidential, I assure you that my lips will be sealed—as well sealed as any of the letters I send to Jane. And I put a *great* deal of sealing wax on them, you know."

"Of course, but I'm also not fond of keeping secrets from my husband," Mrs. Weston said.

"I trust you understand that necessity, however," Emma wryly replied.

Her friend huffed out a breath. "Very well. What, precisely, are you worried about?"

"Prudence's manner of death, for one thing. I don't know if you're aware that the casement windows on that floor are quite narrow."

"How observant of you," Miss Bates said with admiration. "Of course, one is simply struck by the general beauty of Donwell, not necessarily the particulars."

Mrs. Weston frowned. "Now that you mention it, I am aware that they're long but narrow."

"It wouldn't be easy to fall out of one," Emma said. "Even if someone was . . . unwell."

Mrs. Weston looked blank for a few seconds and then let out a gasp. "Are you suggesting someone was in the room with Prudence?"

"Heavens!" cried Miss Bates.

Emma held up her hands again. "I'm not entirely sure what I'm suggesting. But it has come to my attention that someone was bothering Prudence that evening. In fact, behaving quite inappropriately."

"How did you acquire this information?" Mrs. Weston asked.

"From Mrs. Hodges and Harry. It was clear to me that they were concerned about something but were reluctant to speak in front of Constable Sharpe and Dr. Hughes."

Miss Bates crinkled her face, making her spectacles go lopsided. "I can certainly sympathize. Constable Sharpe can be quite intimidating."

"For a nincompoop," Emma couldn't help but add.

Mrs. Weston tsked at her.

"In any event," Emma continued, "this person was very forward with Prudence, which caused her to be quite upset. He was inebriated as well."

"Are you referring to William Cox?" asked Miss Bates.

Emma blinked. "How did you know?"

"Mrs. Goddard told me." She frowned. "I don't quite remember when, although I do know it was before I went to sit with Mr. Woodhouse."

Now *that* was interesting. "What did Mrs. Goddard tell you?"

"She said William had consumed a copious amount of ale and was making a nuisance of himself in the great hall. Mrs. Goddard was quite shocked because he was apparently flirting with one of her teachers."

That was an unexpected revelation. "Do you know which one?"

Miss Bates shook her head. "No, but I'm sure she'd tell me if I asked."

"I don't think that would be a good idea," Mrs. Weston dubiously noted.

"But if William was flirting with someone else, why did he then pursue Prudence?" Emma murmured, mostly to herself.

"Mrs. Goddard was very displeased with him," Miss Bates added. "She gave William a sharp scold and frightened him quite off."

"That doesn't seem to have stopped him, if he then went on to make himself a nuisance with Prudence," said Mrs. Weston.

Rather more than a nuisance, but how to prove it?

"Miss Bates, please try to remember as precisely as possible when William was behaving so badly," asked Emma.

Miss Bates tapped her cheeks. "Let me see . . . not more than midway through the evening, I believe. His sisters were terribly embarrassed by his behavior."

"I rarely cross paths with William Cox," said Emma. "Is he in the habit of behaving so poorly?"

Mrs. Weston hesitated. "I never noticed so in the past."

"Hmm," muttered Miss Bates.

Emma raised an eyebrow at the spinster. "Ma'am?"

Her future stepmother looked apologetic. "Naturally, one doesn't like to gossip about these things."

Now Miss Bates was having qualms about gossiping?

"It's for Prudence, though," Emma said.

"Of course, Mrs. Knightley. You're absolutely right," the spinster replied. "I must not allow myself to become squeamish."

Emma gave her an encouraging smile. "I think justice demands a stout response."

Mrs. Weston sighed.

"Well," said Miss Bates, leaning forward, "Mrs. Cox has expressed her concern for William. She's afraid he's fallen in with bad company and grown rather wild."

Emma and Mrs. Weston exchanged a startled glance.

"In Highbury? What sort of bad company might that be?" Emma asked.

Miss Bates shook her head. "I don't know that, but I *do* know that Mrs. Cox thought to discuss the matter with the curate. She hoped Mr. Barlowe could talk some sense into William."

Emma found it hard to imagine the timid Mr. Barlowe making an impression on anyone, much less an obnoxious young man like William Cox. Still . . .

"I wonder if he did ever speak to William," she murmured.

If so, the curate might be able to shed some light on the current state of William's temperament, if nothing else.

"We could ask him," Miss Bates innocently suggested.

Mrs. Weston looked startled. "I hardly think that would be appropriate."

Emma flapped a hand. "I wouldn't ask Mr. Barlowe directly. I would simply find a way to express my concern. After seeing the way William behaved at the party, that is."

Mrs. Weston scoffed. "Yes, I can see that working very well. Emma—"

"Mrs. Knightley is correct," interjected Miss Bates. "If William had anything to do with that poor girl's death, we should do all in our power to find out."

Emma stared at her, astonished. "Really? You agree with me?"

Mrs. Weston gripped her hands in her lap. "Emma, surely you cannot think that William Cox had anything to do with Miss Parr's death. That would be . . ."

Murder.

The word seemed to hover in the air.

"I wouldn't go that far," Emma replied. "But I think it's possible something happened between them."

"Then we should find out," said Miss Bates. "I saw Mr. Barlowe returning to the vicarage on my way here. We can go there right now, Mrs. Knightley."

This was certainly an unexpected twist. "That's very kind of you, Miss Bates. However, I think it's best that I speak with Mr. Barlowe alone."

Miss Bates decisively shook her head. "I wouldn't dream of letting you take on such an unpleasant task by yourself, Mrs. Knightley. Besides, as the daughter of a vicar, I know just how to talk to curates. They tend to be rather skittish. Why, I even thought to marry one of my father's curates at one point. But he was quite a nervous man and never worked up the fortitude to propose, even though I was very encouraging at the time."

Emma and Mrs. Weston exchanged a dumbfounded glance at that astonishing glimpse into the spinster's past.

Miss Bates all but jumped to her feet. "Shall we, Mrs. Knightley?"

It would seem that Emma had just acquired a highly unlikely partner in her inquiries.

Chapter 10

The wind had kicked up and gray clouds scudded across the sky, playing hide-and-seek with the sun. Emma slid a glance at her companion marching by her side.

"Miss Bates, are you sure you wish to do this?" she asked.

"I would never abandon you to such an unpleasant task," the spinster earnestly replied. "What would Mr. Knightley think?"

Emma had a fairly good idea how her husband would react to this excursion, and it would have little to do with Miss Bates.

"That's very kind, ma'am, but I wonder if Mr. Barlowe might feel more comfortable talking to only one person about such a delicate matter. Since William's unfortunate conduct occurred at Donwell, it makes sense that I raise the issue with him, particularly as I am the wife of the local magistrate."

Emma hoped that pulling rank would produce the desired result on the impecunious curate. Besides, as accomplices went, Miss Bates left something to be desired. She tended to rattle on about inconsequential matters, which would surely confuse the situation.

Her companion seemed struck by Emma's comments. "I see

your point entirely, Mrs. Knightley. Your position in Highbury is second to none, as mistress of both Hartfield *and* Donwell Abbey. Mr. Barlowe will no doubt wish to give you as much assistance as he can."

Emma rewarded her with a smile. "Excellent. Then I suggest—"

Miss Bates held up a gloved hand. "But Mr. Barlowe is shy, and I suspect he'll find your presence intimidating. Not that *you* are an intimidating person, Mrs. Knightley. Quite the opposite, in fact. No one could be kinder than you. But as I mentioned over tea—and such an excellent tea it was, I must say—I have a great deal of experience in dealing with timid curates. Mr. Barlowe is quite comfortable with me, you know. He calls on us once a week for tea and to hear the latest news from Jane and Frank. His interest is rather remarkable, I must say. Always so attentive to everything Jane has to say in her letters."

Emma rather suspected that Mr. Barlowe's interest in Jane had more to do the fact that her uncle-in-law was a wealthy landowner who held the patronage of a tidy church on his estate.

"I'm sure you and Mr. Barlowe get along splendidly," Emma started. "However—"

Miss Bates rested a gentle hand on Emma's arm.

"Mrs. Knightley, I know I can be a dreadful nuisance sometimes, and you are so very kind to put up with me, especially given that Mother and I will soon be foisting ourselves on you at Hartfield. But I do want to help you in any way I can. *Please* let me help."

The spinster gazed up at her with a terribly earnest expression, her bespectacled gaze silently pleading. And, yes, the sweet, odd little woman could be rather a nuisance at times, which might be more a reflection on Emma's lack of patience and charity than anything else.

Besides, Miss Bates *was* going to marry her father, so they would soon be on equal footing—a rather alarming concept Emma had yet to fully grapple with. George would rightly tell her that it was time to accept reality and act accordingly.

Emma pressed the gloved hand on her arm. "I shall be glad of your help. I simply didn't wish to put you in an awkward position."

While not quite the truth, it sounded reasonable.

Miss Bates shrugged. "I don't imagine it will be any less awkward for you than it will be for me. Goodness, what isn't awkward about this situation, starting with Prudence falling out of the window? I cannot imagine anything more awkward in my life."

It took Emma a moment to recover from that observation. "Indeed, ma'am."

"And I do feel a sense of responsibility to the poor girl. After all, I was the first person to find her in that terrible state. You will think me foolish, but there it is."

"Actually, I felt the same way about Mrs. Elton after Harriet and I stumbled upon her lying dead in the church," Emma admitted.

Miss Bates beamed at her. "I knew you would understand, Mrs. Knightley. You're so clever about these things." Her gaze darted off to the side, and she suddenly looked shy. "I count myself so very fortunate that I will soon be a member of your family."

And wasn't that a dagger to the heart? Here she was trying to bull the poor woman out of her way, when all Miss Bates wished to do was help her.

Emma gave her a wry smile. "Then don't you think it's time you began referring to me by my given name? After all, you're going to be my stepmother."

The spinster's startled gaze flew to hers. "I don't possibly think I could do so, Mrs. Knightley. Why, I don't know how I'm going to call your father anything but Mr. Woodhouse, even though he insists I refer to him as Henry."

A gust of wind swirled up, hitting them both in the face. Emma took her companion's arm and started her forward. "Come. If we stand about much longer, we'll both be frozen."

They hurried along the high street. There were few villagers out and about, and those that were all passed by with little more than a tip of the hat or a quick greeting.

When they arrived at their destination, they paused to catch their breath and shake the dust from their pelisses.

The vicarage was an old and not especially good house. The previous occupants had embarked on a number of improvements, but they would likely be the end of such endeavors. Mr. Barlowe would find it a challenge simply to manage the upkeep of the place on a curate's salary.

Emma knocked on the door. The hollow sound echoed inside the house, and then a prolonged silence followed.

"Perhaps no one is home," said Miss Bates.

"You'd think one of the servants would be."

Emma tried again and was rewarded by the muffled sound of footsteps. The door swung open and Mr. Barlowe stood before them, a befuddled expression on his thin features.

"Good afternoon, sir," Emma said with a warm smile.

When he peered back at her, wordless, she exchanged a puzzled glance with Miss Bates.

"Mr. Barlowe," said the spinster, "Mrs. Knightley and I were out for a walk and thought to stop by for a visit."

"Just to see how you get on," Emma added.

"How . . . how kind," he hesitantly responded. "Though it's entirely unnecessary."

"Is this a bad time, sir?" Miss Bates asked a trifle anxiously.

"Actually—"

"We won't stay for long," Emma jumped in, forestalling any attempt to put them off. "There are a few matters Miss Bates and I would like to discuss with you. In your role as Highbury's curate, that is."

He stared for a few moments longer before moving aside. "Of course. Do forgive me. I was writing my sermon, and I confess to being rather absent-minded while wrestling with the Good Lord's word."

Miss Bates fluttered a hand. "Dear sir, as the daughter of a vicar, I perfectly understand. And your sermons do you *great* credit. Mother and I truly enjoyed your disquisition last Sunday on the Parable of the Wise Virgins. Indeed, it was as full of wisdom as those most excellent virgins and their lamps. It's always so important to keep one's lamps properly trimmed, something I say to Mother all the time. An untrimmed wick or an empty lamp is simply disastrous, as your sermon so finely illustrated."

Emma bit the inside her cheek to keep from laughing, since Mr. Barlowe was now looking vaguely alarmed.

"Ah... would you ladies care to step into the drawing room?" he finally said.

He ushered them through to the formal drawing room. Thanks to its previous occupants, the room was excessively stylish. Mrs. Elton had outfitted it with bright yellow wallpaper, red velvet furniture and draperies, and a great deal of trim. It was an absurd room for a country vicarage, and Mr. Barlowe looked completely out of place in such surroundings. From the fine layer of dust on the tables and the stale atmosphere in the room, Emma deduced that he wasn't much in the habit of entertaining.

As they took a seat on the sofa, Mr. Barlowe remained standing, eyeing them with a degree of trepidation. She couldn't help but wonder why he seemed so nervous.

"Would you like some tea?" he asked.

"That won't be—"

Miss Bates interrupted her. "We'd love tea, thank you. It's terribly raw outside, and tea will be most welcome."

He nodded. "I will just step back to the kitchen. Cook was about to bring tea to my study, so it should be ready in only a few minutes."

"Thank you, sir," Emma politely replied.

After he'd departed, Miss Bates shook her head. "He's so very shy. I thought if we gave him something to do it might make him more comfortable."

Emma had to admit her reasoning made sense. "I don't think he entertains very much."

"The life of a curate is a difficult one, Mrs. Knightley. I suspect he cannot afford it."

That was undoubtedly true, as curates were at the beck and call of the clergymen or bishop who held the living. They did much of the work with little financial reward and an uncertain future.

As they waited, Emma let her gaze wander about the room. There was only the smallest of fires in the grate, which wasn't surprising. What *was* surprising was the impressive collection of wine bottles and decanters on the sideboard. That was hardly what one would expect in a bachelor-curate's modest household.

"Do you know how many servants Mr. Barlowe keeps?" she asked.

"Two, I believe," replied Miss Bates. "A cook and a manservant."

That was sparse living, indeed.

The door opened and Mr. Barlowe entered, followed by a grizzled-looking manservant of indeterminate years who carried the tea tray. The man thumped it down on the table in front of them before shuffling back out of the room and slamming the door behind him.

Mr. Barlowe looked embarrassed. "Please forgive Victor, ladies. I'm afraid his rheumatics bother him. I did offer to carry the tea tray myself, but he wouldn't hear of it." He dredged up a weak smile. "He likes to be useful, you see."

"As do we all," Emma replied. "Did he come with you from your last position?"

"Quite."

After another awkward silence, she offered to pour the tea. Miss Bates stepped into the conversational breach with a patter of inconsequential questions and statements. Her flow of words was strangely relaxing, and Mr. Barlowe finally seemed to unbend.

"It is kind of you to visit me," he said with a tentative smile. "I know you both must be so busy, what with the unfortunate events of the other night."

Ah, just the opening we were looking for.

"Indeed," replied Miss Bates. "We were all required to give statements to Constable Sharpe. It was very shocking and sad to think of it all over again." She gave a visible shudder. "Not that I will ever forget that night."

Emma handed the curate his teacup. "Were you required to make a statement, Mr. Barlowe?"

He accepted the cup with a frown. "No. Was there any reason I should have?"

"Only if you saw or heard something that might shed light on the event."

He took a sip of tea before replying. "I believe I was in the great hall at the time of . . . of the accident. The hall was very noisy. But very cheerful," he hastily added. "Quite a party, Mrs. Knightley. Not that I am generally one for such affairs, but Miss Bates was so kind as to invite me. I could hardly refuse her gracious offer. And you and Mr. Knightley are always so hospitable. Still, even though I was present at Donwell Abbey at the time of Miss Parr's death, I remained completely unaware of what happened until the next morning."

Mr. Barlowe hardly seemed the sort to babble, but he was babbling now.

Emma took a sip of her tea and got another surprise. The tea was a high-quality Congou tea, if she wasn't mistaken, and was quite expensive. Could he truly afford it on a curate's salary?

"This is an excellent cup of tea," she said.

Miss Bates smiled at the curate. "Indeed, it's almost as good as that of Hartfield. Not that anything could equal tea at Hartfield, Mrs. Knightley, not even tea at the Coles. Certainly Mrs. Cole serves an excellent tea, but this is most enjoyable, too."

Emma would have been annoyed at the notion of Mrs. Cole's tea compared favorably with that of Hartfield if Mr. Barlowe hadn't just flushed so red that his cheeks all but burned.

"I can hardly take credit," he replied. "The pantry was well stocked with tea and other goods when I arrived, which was certainly a blessing."

If that was the case, why was he so embarrassed?

What does it matter?

"How fortunate for you," Emma said, putting the mystery of the tea out of her mind. "Now, to return to the subject of Miss Parr's death, I'm wondering if you can help me with a certain matter."

He paused with the teacup halfway to his lips. "If I can."

"I was wondering how well you knew Prudence?"

Mr. Barlowe's expression betrayed puzzlement. "Not well at all. Still, Miss Parr was always kind enough to compliment my sermons after Sunday services."

Miss Bates sighed. "That poor girl. She was obviously so sweet. And she was very observant, as well, since your sermons *are* excellent."

"Thank you," the curate replied. "I'm afraid I cannot tell you much more than that. Miss Parr appeared to be a pleasant, good sort of girl. But other than seeing her at Sunday services with Mrs. Hodges, we had no other interactions."

Emma tried again. "So Prudence never came to you to discuss problems of a personal nature?"

Mr. Barlowe accidentally slopped some tea into the dish. "Oh, bother."

He put the offending teacup on the table, picked up a napkin, and wiped a few drops of liquid from his hand.

"Mr. Barlowe?" Emma prompted.

"What? Did Miss Parr ever come speak to me about a personal matter? Not that I recall, and I don't know why she would."

His reply was chippy to the point of rudeness.

Emma swallowed her irritation. "It's not surprising that she—or any parishioner—would come to her local clergyman if troubled." She smiled at him. "Especially to a sympathetic person such as yourself."

"The villagers were always coming to speak to my father about their various troubles," Miss Bates piped in. "Father always saw it as a very important part of his duties, helping people as best he could."

"As I said, Miss Parr never spoke to me about any problems she might have been having," Mr. Barlowe all but ground out.

Clearly, gentle handling was not advancing their cause, so perhaps a more direct approach was in order.

"It's just that her fellow servants had a sense that Prudence was troubled about something these last few weeks," Emma said. "I thought—"

"Mrs. Knightley," he interrupted. "Are you saying Miss Parr had personal problems that may have contributed to her death? Are you saying that she may have taken..." He trailed off, looking immensely shocked.

Emma flapped a hand. "No, it's not like that. Dr. Hughes declared her death an accident."

"Then I truly don't know what you want from me," he replied. "Since I didn't know the girl and I don't know anything about her death, I'm not sure why we're even discussing the matter."

Well, really. For a clergyman, he certainly wasn't very sympathetic.

"I understand," she replied. "It was just a thought, nothing more."

"Then if that is all, ma'am," he said. "I'm afraid that—"

"There is one more thing," Miss Bates blurted out. "And I *do* think this is something you can help us with."

Mr. Barlowe had been rising from his chair, but now subsided with an aggrieved sigh. "Yes?"

Miss Bates cast Emma an imploring glance, as if having blundered into the topic she didn't know how to next proceed.

"It's a rather delicate situation," Emma said.

"And?" the curate asked in a long-suffering tone.

For a man of the cloth, he had *quite* a dreadful manner.

Miss Bates, recovering her footing, barged back into taking the lead. "It's about William Cox. He seems to be getting into quite a lot of trouble, which is terribly worrisome for his dear mother."

The color slowly drained from Mr. Barlowe's face. Even though he was a pale-complexioned man to begin with, the change was noticeable, despite the rather dim light of the parlor.

"I . . . I'm not sure I should be discussing my parishioners with you," he stammered.

It was a valid point, but Emma batted it aside. "We ask because William was behaving inappropriately during the party at Donwell Abbey. He was in his cups and making a bother of himself with some of the young ladies."

Miss Bates shook her head. "Very naughty of him. One is quite shocked."

The curate began to fidget with his collar. "I must admit I observed that Mr. Cox was a trifle disguised that night. Still, I'm not sure what you expect of me."

Emma speared him with her gaze. "It's my understanding that Mrs. Cox was desirous that you speak to William about his behavior." She held up a hand to forestall his objection. "And in case you're wondering, it's common knowledge that Mrs. Cox is distressed about her son. Mrs. Cole, for one, communicated that to me along with her own concerns for the young man's behavior."

"And Mrs. Cox told me herself that she wanted you to speak to William," Miss Bates added. "So it's not exactly a secret."

"Neither is William's behavior," Emma dryly added.

Miss Bates shook her head. "Poor Mrs. Cox. One wishes to help as best one can, of course."

Emma flashed her an approving smile. "Exactly, ma'am. Stronger measures can certainly be taken, if necessary. But we were hoping that you, Mr. Barlowe, would be able to talk some sense into William."

Now the curate was looking positively alarmed. "I . . . I . . ."

"Of course, if you're not comfortable discussing it with us," Emma smoothly interjected, "I can bring the matter to my husband's attention. While he's very busy as you might imagine, we cannot allow William to go about making a pest of himself to Highbury's young ladies, can we?"

Mr. Barlowe withered under the combined assault. "Very well. Mrs. Cox did speak to me about William the day after your party. I confess I've not yet had the chance to speak to the young man. But I assure you that I'll be doing so very soon." He frowned. "It's odd, though. Mrs. Cox didn't express any concerns about her son's behavior toward young ladies.

Rather, she felt he'd fallen into rough company, which was having a deleterious effect on his temperament."

Emma shook her head. "Rough company in Highbury? That doesn't make much sense."

"From what Mrs. Cox told me, William's new companions were not from Highbury. She mentioned Leatherhead."

Leatherhead! Where Prudence was from.

Miss Bates frowned. "Isn't that where—"

"Thank you, Mr. Barlowe," Emma said, cutting her off. "You've been very helpful."

If her as-yet-unsubstantiated theory about Prudence and William were to begin circulating around Highbury, George would have her head. And her husband was the person with whom she truly needed to share this development. It certainly pointed to a possible connection between Prudence and William.

She rose. "We know you're busy, sir, so now we'll thank you for the excellent tea and be on our way."

Mr. Barlowe stood. "You're welcome."

"Dear sir," said Miss Bates, "I hope you'll be able to talk some sense into William."

"I'll try my best, ma'am."

Miss Bates pointed a finger at him. "You must be very firm. My father always said it was a fool's errand to beat around the bush with naughty young men. You must point out the error of his ways in no uncertain terms."

Mr. Barlowe looked unenthused at the prospect. William—a boisterous young man—would probably laugh in his face.

"As I said, I shall do my best," he gloomily replied.

He showed them to the door with a certain amount of haste, practically slamming it shut behind them.

"I don't think Mr. Barlowe appreciated our visit," Emma dryly commented.

Miss Bates grimaced. "He seemed so very nervous. Perhaps Mr. Perry can prescribe him some calming powders."

"He's certainly an odd little man."

In fact, everything about their visit had been odd, including Mr. Barlowe's reaction to their questions about William. Even the quality of his tea was odd for a curate.

Still, their visit had yielded a very interesting clue, and Emma fully intended to pursue it.

Chapter 11

Emma firmly shut the drawing room door behind her. Donwell had many beauties and many benefits, but cold stone hallways in the winter were not among them.

George, comfortably ensconced in a wing chair by the fireplace, glanced up with a smile and put aside his book.

"Your nose is looking a trifle red, my love," he said as he stood. "Come warm yourself by the fire."

She playfully swatted his arm. "I'm sure it's quite red, but how rude of you to notice."

He kissed the tip of her nose. "I'm very fond of your nose. And red is a charming color on you."

"You're too kind, sir."

She sank onto the plump cushions of the giltwood sofa and extended her feet toward the crackling flames in the hearth. George angled the painted fire screen to moderate the outpouring of heat before joining her, wrapping his arm snugly about her shoulders.

The yellow drawing room was quite her favorite room in the old abbey, and for a few minutes she simply enjoyed its quiet tranquility and the security of her husband's embrace. The walls were hung with striped silk wallpaper in a beautiful shade of pale lemon, and comfortable, overstuffed chairs were arranged in cozy groupings that were perfect for conversation, reading, or viewing Donwell's excellent collection of antiques, books, and curiosities. It was a peaceful retreat, and she was determined to transform the rest of the house into a similar haven of beauty and comfort.

Of course, those changes would have to wait behind more practical matters. While beautiful rooms and an ancient patrimony were excellent things, so were modern stoves, chimneys that didn't smoke, and food that arrived from the kitchen at the correct temperature. Emma had a few traditions of her own, including the habit of eating foods that were either properly hot or properly cold.

"Henry is safely tucked away in his room?" George asked.

"With extra blankets and a lamp by the bed so he can read. I asked Mrs. Hodges to check in on him shortly to make sure he doesn't fall asleep with the lamp still burning."

George frowned. "It's Harry's job to make sure candles and lamps are safely extinguished after the family retires to bed."

"I know, but I couldn't find him, which is apparently a fairly common occurrence."

"You're used to Hartfield's excellent standards, my dear. We at Donwell must make do with what we have."

She scoffed. "While I agree that Hartfield is *the* standard of excellence in Highbury, Harry is a rather low bar to set."

"True. Still, up till now he's adequately served our needs. Having said that, I'm sure you'll whip him into shape."

"Even Mrs. Hodges can't whip him into shape."

"We'll be hiring more staff soon enough." He sighed. "When I can find a minute to sit down and discuss it with Larkins and Mrs. Hodges."

Emma winced with guilt. "Here I am nattering on, when you've had a dreadfully difficult day. I'm sorry, dearest."

George pressed a quick kiss to the top of her head. "Thankfully, I was able to return home to a quiet evening with my wife and my favorite nephew."

"Thank goodness. But Prudence's poor family, especially Mr. Parr. I cannot imagine how cut up he must be feeling."

"His grief was difficult to witness," George quietly replied.

Emma turned and pressed a hand to his chest. "I know how this has affected you, and how greatly you must feel for the family."

His expression was somber. "I wish I could do more for them. As it was, I had little comfort to give."

"Did Mr. Parr have more questions?"

"I only spoke to him to offer my condolences. But Prudence's older brother again expressed his dismay over the coroner's conclusions, specifically regarding the statement that she'd been drinking."

"I can understand his dismay."

"Yes. Young Mr. Parr was not best pleased with me," he dryly said.

"How unfortunate. Then I'm doubly glad Mr. Weston was there to support you."

"I appreciated his company."

She frowned, suddenly remembering a niggling question. "George, why didn't Larkins go with you? I thought he planned to do that."

"He did, but then he asked this morning to be excused. Stomach troubles, apparently."

Larkins had seemed perfectly fine when she'd spoken to him in the kitchen earlier in the day. Still . . .

"Perhaps he simply couldn't face it," she said. "When I spoke to Mrs. Hodges and Harry this morning, they were still very upset—and perplexed, quite honestly. They have questions as well."

George tilted his head to get a better look at her. "You spoke to them about the accident, did you?"

She recognized *that* tone of voice.

"Well, yes. I had a few concerns about what happened that night, and I thought Mrs. Hodges and Harry might be able to address them."

He sighed. "Emma..."

She patted his chest. "Please hear me out, George. I think it might be important."

He closed his eyes and muttered something under his breath that sounded suspiciously like *not again*.

She gave him a nudge. "Dearest?"

"Very well, but let me replenish the fire first. Something tells me that we might be here for a while."

Part of her felt guilty to be raising these issues with him after such a difficult day, but there was little point in delay. Not only was George the person she trusted most in the world, he was the local magistrate. If there was anything suspicious in Prudence's death, he should be informed of it as soon as possible.

And if occasionally—very occasionally—she let her imagination run just a tiny bit ahead of the facts, George would invariably point that out, too.

As he built up the fire, Emma took a few moments to indulge in admiration of his masculine physique. George had a plethora of excellent qualities—one of which was a splendid set of shoulders.

"All right," he said, rejoining her. "Tell me why you felt the need to discuss Prudence's accident with the staff."

She settled under his arm. "When we were in Prudence's room the night of the accident, it seemed to me that both Mrs. Hodges and Harry were holding something back. I sensed that they had more to say but were intimidated by the presence of Constable Sharpe and Dr. Hughes."

George frowned, obviously thinking over her words. Emma loved that about him. Even when he disagreed with her—sometimes vociferously in the days before their marriage—he never brushed aside her concerns and opinions.

"While I did sense their discomfort," he finally replied, "I assumed it had to do with their shock over Prudence's death."

"They were shocked, of course. But a few times I caught them exchanging what I can only describe as furtive glances." She held up a hand. "And, no. It wasn't my imagination."

"So, what do you think they were holding back?"

"For one thing, Mrs. Hodges admitted that Prudence had more than a headache — she was also distressed. You'll recall we did have a discussion that night, somewhat to that effect."

"With Constable Sharpe arriving at the unfortunate conclusion that she'd killed herself," he replied.

Emma scoffed. "That man is truly a dolt. As it turns out, though, Prudence had reason to be upset. William Cox *had* been harassing her, as I suspected, and she found his attentions most unwelcome."

George jerked his head around to stare at her. "Mrs. Hodges confirmed that?"

"Yes."

He muttered an oath under his breath. "I wish I'd known. I would have tossed the bounder into the nearest rosebush."

"George, there's no need to punish our poor rosebushes for William Cox's repellant behavior."

He frowned again, deep in thought, then cast her a sideways glance.

Emma patted his thigh. "Just say it, dearest. You won't shock me, I promise."

"Did Mrs. Hodges detail the nature of William's harassment?"

"Prudence didn't give her any specifics."

"And no one else saw it?"

"Apparently not. And it was only after Mrs. Hodges pressed her that Prudence admitted what had happened. She said she also didn't wish Mrs. Hodges to pester you about it."

George grimaced. "Unfortunate. Are we to assume, then, that Prudence was so upset by this incident that she felt compelled to find solace in spirits? That would suggest she did indeed filch the decanter from the drawing room."

Emma waggled a hand. "Perhaps, though Harry proposed a different theory."

"Which is?"

"He thought Prudence was sweet on William, and was distraught to learn he was only dallying with her."

George scoffed. "While I can certainly see William making a fool of himself at the party, I cannot see him dallying with chambermaids. As I said the other day, his parents wouldn't stand for it."

"And you still think he would share such exploits with his parents?"

"Emma—"

She patted his cheek. "I know it's hard to imagine, because you never acted that way, even in your wild salad days."

"I never *had* wild salad days."

"Because you were too busy lecturing me on my various faults and recommending dreary improving books for me to read."

He ignored her little dig. "What did Mrs. Hodges think of this theory?"

"She thought it nonsense." Emma held up a restraining hand. "But, she's also fairly convinced that Prudence had a secret beau."

George raised his eyebrows. "That sounds rather dramatic."

"Girls of Prudence's age are often dramatic."

"True enough, yet as we have previously discussed, there is no evidence to suggest that William was ever in Prudence's room."

Again, she waggled her hand.

He sighed. "There's more, isn't there?"

"I'm afraid so."

He listened with a resigned expression as she explained her discussion with Mrs. Weston and Miss Bates.

"Emma, gossip is rarely accurate," he commented when she'd finished.

"Surprisingly, it is when it comes to Miss Bates. In fact, it was her suggestion that we speak with Mr. Barlowe."

George frowned. "Why would Miss Bates suggest such a thing?"

"Mrs. Cox asked Mr. Barlowe to confront William about his poor behavior. Unfortunately, Mr. Barlowe has yet to grab the bull by the horns."

"How do you—" His gaze turned sardonic. "Of course. You went and spoke to Mr. Barlowe."

"As I said, it was Miss Bates's suggestion."

"Emma—"

She fluttered a hand. "It was fine, George. And very interesting, I might add."

"And Miss Bates accompanied you?"

"Yes."

"Good Lord," he muttered.

"Miss Bates was oddly helpful," she replied, feeling slightly defensive of her future stepmother. "And I was surprised by her determination. She simply wouldn't take no for an answer."

"It would seem your habits are starting to rub off on her. I wonder how your father will react to this change in his betrothed's temperament?"

"He'll be thrilled, because she'll be more like me. Now, be serious, George. This *is* serious."

"Very well. What was the upshot of your joint interrogation of poor Mr. Barlowe?"

When she stuck her tongue out at him, he chuckled.

"All right," he said. "I'll be serious. Did you learn anything of interest?"

"Apparently, William has fallen in with a rough crowd." She gave him a significant look. "And he met these people in Leatherhead."

He blinked. "Leatherhead."

"A strange coincidence, don't you think?"

"Did Mrs. Cox indicate any other... concerns about William's behavior?"

She guessed what he was really asking. "You mean with young women? She raised no concerns in that regard. But I don't think that's definitive. William may very well have met Prudence in Leatherhead before she came to work at Donwell."

George thought for a few moments. "I presume William has been ostensibly meeting with these new friends in taverns or pubs?"

"I would assume so."

"I'll admit it's an interesting coincidence. Still, I think it unlikely that William and Prudence met in Leatherhead. For one thing, she would not be frequenting taverns or pubs."

Emma raised her eyebrows. "Even Harriet occasionally has a meal with Robert at the Crown Inn, on market day."

"There's quite a difference between a respectable coaching inn and a tavern frequented by rough men. Prudence's father would never allow her to step foot in such places."

"Then she might have met William somewhere else. Perhaps his horse lost a shoe, and he came to her father's shop to get a new one."

George shifted to face her. "My darling, why are you determined to make William Cox the villain in this? I grant you that his behavior was disgraceful, but there's no evidence that he had anything to do with Prudence's death."

Emma blew out a frustrated sigh. "Because what we know doesn't seem to fit what happened. Prudence disliked spirits, yet there was a decanter of sherry in her room. She falls out a window that was not particularly easy to fall out of. And we *know* she was upset about something—or someone. That someone might very well be William Cox."

He studied her for a few moments. "Emma, do you truly believe William killed Prudence?"

At this point, she was reluctant to make so bold a claim. George was right about the lack of evidence. "It could have been an accident, at least in the sense that he didn't mean to kill her. Perhaps the window wasn't latched correctly and she fell against it in their struggle. Or it was already open. At the very least, you must admit the possibility."

"I probably would, if we hadn't secured the room so quickly after her fall. As we discussed before, there were no signs of a struggle. If your theory was correct, there most certainly would have been some such signs."

That, of course, was the immensely frustrating rub. "I know."

He took her hand. "Emma, please know that I'm not trying to dismiss you or your concerns out of hand. Was William's behavior toward Prudence highly inappropriate? Yes, and be sure that I will deal with that. But we cannot accuse him of murder when there's no evidence to back up such a bold claim."

"I do realize that, which is why I brought the matter to you," she replied, trying not to sound *too* grumpy.

His momentary smile was wry. "Thank you. And as I said, I'll address your concerns about William, certainly regarding his conduct at our party. I'll also try to find out more about those dodgy characters from Leatherhead—for his parents' sake, if nothing else."

She squeezed his hand. "Thank you, George. And thank you for listening. It's been a dreadful day for you, and this is a dreadful topic to be forced to think about."

"My darling, I will *always* listen to you. Never fear that I won't."

Emma poked a gentle finger into his cravat. "I will hold you to that promise, husband."

"Please do. And speaking of promises, I would ask that you bring any further rumors you might hear on this matter directly to me." He raised his eyebrows. "Not to Mrs. Weston, and certainly not to Miss Bates."

She widened her eyes, trying to look innocent. "I'll do my best, dearest, I promise."

With a long-suffering sigh, her husband took her hand and led her off to bed.

Chapter 12

For the second time in a just a few minutes, Larkins failed to respond to Emma's question. From the gloomy frown that marked his countenance, whatever mental paths he was wandering along were not happy ones.

She exchanged a worried glance with Mrs. Hodges, who was seated next to Larkins on the other side of George's desk. Since George was out at a vestry meeting, Emma had commandeered his library to meet with the senior staff to discuss the upcoming changes at Donwell.

So far, it had been something of a slog.

"Mr. Larkins, what do you think of Mrs. Hodges's suggestion?"

He slowly raised his head, as if coming out of a trance. Then his gaze sharpened, and he dredged up a travesty of a smile. The poor man looked quite worn down. His gaze was shadowed and his normally ruddy complexion had turned pallid.

"Forgive me, Mrs. Knightley. What was the suggestion again?"

"We were discussing the possibility of renovating the old butler's room and using it as an office for Mrs. Knightley," Mrs. Hodges patiently replied.

Larkins nodded. "It's a convenient location, close to the kitchen and service rooms. It's rather small, though, Mrs. Knightley. The old family breakfast parlor might do nicely instead, since it's also near the service rooms. There's a bit of wood rot so it'll need some work, but nothing that can't be fixed."

Emma shook her head. "I fully intend to convert that parlor into the family dining room. Then the servants won't be required to traverse half the house with our meals. Mr. Knightley might be indifferent to properly heated food, but I find myself strangely attached to the notion of hot soup."

Her comment finally won her a reluctant smile from Larkins. "That's a fine idea, Mrs. Knightley. It's well situated for that purpose."

"The butler's room will do nicely for me as an office. As long as the fireplace doesn't smoke, I shall be quite satisfied."

Larkins nodded. "I'll discuss plans with the village carpenter first thing tomorrow. Do you want me to draw up some plans for the parlor, as well?"

"Yes, please. The sooner the better."

Aside from the tepid soup, Emma was growing rather tired of Donwell's meals in general. Mrs. Hodges did her best with the one kitchen maid, but it was time to hire a proper cook. Emma made a note in her pocketbook, and then perused the rest of her list. While there was much work to be done to properly fit up the house, the cellars, the service rooms, and the pantries took priority.

"I think that's all for now," she said, glancing up from her list. "I do want to have a good look at the cellars and the attics. Mr. Knightley tells me that they've been rather neglected, so I think it makes sense to start there."

Especially since she intended to use them to store some of the rather ghastly and outdated furniture that populated several rooms in the abbey. Though they were part of Donwell's history, there was no reason to put up with a creaky, moth-eaten bed that family lore suggested had once been slept in by Queen Anne.

Larkins frowned. "I wouldn't recommend spending time in those old cellars, ma'am. Very cold they are at this time of year, and they can be quite damp at times."

She found that surprising. "I had hoped to expand their use for cold storage for food. I understand they were originally used as such."

"Not since the old master's time," said Mrs. Hodges. "Seeing as the household has been so much smaller for years, there's been no need for them."

"That seems a great waste," Emma replied.

"They can be restored to their original purpose with some work, ma'am," said Larkins. "Just tell me what needs doing, and I'll see to it."

Emma nodded. "I will—once I've inspected them for myself."

She was determined to familiarize herself with the abbey from top to bottom. It was her home now, and she wanted to know everything there was about the old place.

Larkins shook his head. "It'll not be pleasant for you, ma'am. You might catch your death from the cold, and then what would Mr. Knightley say?"

Goodness, the man could be stubborn. Then again, it was an adjustment for all the servants to have a mistress in the house again. Emma would do her best to accommodate them, but it was also necessary that they understood who was now in charge of domestic matters.

"I will be perfectly fine, Mr. Larkins. You are welcome to inspect them with me. I should be happy for your input."

He looked slightly obstreperous before nodding. "I'm at your disposal, ma'am."

"Thank you."

Emma tapped her pencil on the list's final item. This one was a bit trickier to deal with, given recent events.

"As we all know, we're quite shorthanded in the house. With Mr. Knightley and me back in residence, along with my nephew, the lack of adequate staff is a burden on all of you. We must think about finding a new maid as soon as possible, even temporarily. Perhaps someone from the village might be willing to take on the work until we can find a permanent replacement for Prudence."

Mrs. Hodges sighed. "I'll ask around the village, ma'am. It won't be easy to replace someone like Prudence on short notice, I'm afraid."

Emma crinkled her nose in sympathy. "Mr. Knightley will soon be advertising for more staff, so just do your best in the meantime."

Larkins had gone silent again, staring down at his lap. If his expression was any indication, he was struggling to contain his emotions. Emma was again surprised at his reaction to Prudence's death. It spoke of more than just a general fondness—like something that cut deeply to the bone. She found it mystifying, given his temperament and the fact that he was so much older than Prudence had been.

"Mr. Larkins, I know all the staff are deeply troubled by what happened to Prudence," she hesitantly said. "And I know there are questions regarding the manner of her death. Do you have any concerns you wish to share about what happened?"

When he jerked up his head, looking almost distraught, Emma's breath caught in her throat.

"You can also bring any concerns directly to Mr. Knightley, of course," she hastily added.

He seemed to struggle for a few moments before finding his voice. "It wasn't right what happened to her. It makes no sense, either."

Emma decided to follow her instincts. "Mr. Larkins, did you ever get a sense that Prudence was troubled by anything? Or anyone?"

He frowned. "I . . . I'm not sure what you mean, Mrs. Knightley."

His reply left Emma at a loss.

Fortunately, Mrs. Hodges quickly responded. "I think Mrs. Knightley wants to know if you heard tell of anyone pestering Prudence. Even before that night, something seemed to be on the poor girl's mind, something that mayhap troubled her."

Larkins peered at her. "Who would bother that sweet lass?" Then understanding seemed to dawn, and a sudden fury ignited his gaze. "Do you mean a man was bothering her? You just tell me who it was, Mrs. Hodges, and I'll take care of the bas—I'll take care of him, I will."

Emma almost gaped at him. The man had gone from perplexed to murderous from one breath to the next. If she even hinted about what they knew regarding William Cox, Larkins would probably storm into the village and throttle the man with his bare hands.

"It was a general question on my part," Emma replied. "We're simply trying to understand what happened."

He shoved to his feet so forcefully that he almost knocked over his chair. "You'll have to excuse me, Mrs. Knightley. I don't know anything about what might have been bothering Prudence. If I had, I would have—"

He broke off, his hand curling into a fist. He made a visible effort to bring his emotions under control. "I beg your pardon, Mrs. Knightley. Is there anything else you're needing from me at the moment?"

"No, I think we're done for—"

"Then you'll be excusing me. I have work to attend to."

He turned on his heel and strode from the room. Emma and Mrs. Hodges exchanged an astonished glance.

"What just happened?" Emma asked.

"I've never seen the man so upset, excepting the night Prudence died. I'm sorry, Mrs. Knightley. Larkins is a good man, but he should know better than to snap at you like that."

"There's no need to apologize. And I'm going to assume that he doesn't know about William Cox?"

"He doesn't." The housekeeper tapped the tabletop. "And I'd best tell that Harry to keep his mouth shut about it. If he were to blab it to Mr. Larkins, heaven only knows what would happen."

"Mrs. Hodges, I know all the staff were fond of Prudence, but Mr. Larkins truly seems to be grief-stricken."

Mrs. Hodges seemed to hold a small debate with herself before answering. "The fact is, ma'am, Mr. Larkins was in love with Prudence. That's why he's so despondent."

It took Emma a moment to recover from her astonishment at such a revelation. "That's really quite surprising. I thought him a confirmed bachelor, devoted to Donwell and nothing else. I used to tease Mr. Knightley that he spent more time with Larkins than with me."

That Larkins, a middle-aged, taciturn man, would fall in love with a girl so young and so unlike him was indeed hard to fathom. Then again, she'd fallen in love with George, also a quiet man some years older than she was.

Mrs. Hodges shifted with discomfort. "I shouldn't have said anything. The poor fellow would be mortified that I told anyone, much less the mistress."

Emma held up a hand. "Believe me, I wouldn't dream of violating the poor man's privacy. My lips are forever sealed."

The housekeeper flashed her a relieved smile. "Thank you, ma'am."

"Was Prudence aware of how he felt?"

Mrs. Hodges emphatically shook her head. "He was always careful and correct in his conduct toward her. I think she saw him more like an uncle. She was always very easy and open with him, which I think was part of the problem."

Emma lifted an eyebrow. "In what way?"

The housekeeper hesitated, as if trying to find the right words.

"It's just that Prudence was such a charmer—not that the girl was a flirt, or carried on with teasing a man. She was just so sweet and funny. And being away from home for the first time, I think Mr. Larkins made her feel safe. He watched out for her, you see."

Emma nodded. "I think I understand. Her looks and sweet nature would make her rather irresistible."

Mrs. Hodges sighed again. "That's it, Mrs. Knightley. I'm certain Mr. Larkins wasn't expecting to have feelings for the girl. But she seemed to draw him out of himself, if you know what I mean."

"I do."

"Not that he ever expected anything from Prudence," Mrs. Hodges hastily added. "He knew the girl would never feel for him like that. Given their difference in age, and . . ."

"And the fact that he's Irish Catholic?" Emma guessed.

The housekeeper made a face. "No one at Donwell gives a fig about that. Still, you know how some people are, Mrs. Knightley."

Emma remembered some of the mutterings and mean-spirited comments when George had hired an Irishman—and a Catholic at that. Eventually, the locals had come to realize that Larkins was a fine man, and as dedicated to Donwell and its people as its owner was.

"Mrs. Hodges, are you the only person who knows how he felt about Prudence?"

"Yes, I'm certain of that."

"Did you ever ask him about it?"

"Once, after I suspected how he was feeling. I'm responsible for the girls who work in the household, so I felt duty bound to ask him—for his sake as much for hers."

Emma took in the rueful expression on the housekeeper's face. "I'm guessing that went down a treat."

"He told me I was daft if I thought he'd pester the girl, or think he was good enough for someone like her. He swore me never to say a word to Prudence or anyone else." She sighed. "And here I am breaking my word, poor man."

"Again, I won't breathe a word to another soul, not even to my husband."

"I'm obliged to you, ma'am."

Now that Emma understood their estate steward's odd behavior since the girl's death, there was no need to draw further attention to it. What the poor man required now was peace and the time to recover from such a devastating blow.

"Mrs. Hodges, I think at this point the less said about Prudence, the better. You and Mr. Larkins would never engage in idle gossip, but we must be sure none of the other servants do, either. It would be most unfortunate if rumors were to originate here and then filter down to Highbury."

The evolving situation, however, did make things a bit tricky for Emma, since any further investigations into Prudence's death required both discretion and tact. Thank goodness she possessed a surfeit of both.

"Yes, ma'am," said Mrs. Hodges. "The poor girl doesn't deserve to have her good name bandied about, nor should anyone's grief be made sport of."

"And thank you for your honesty with me. It's much appreciated."

"Of course, ma'am. I'm always—"

The door suddenly opened, revealing Harry the footman. He hesitated, and then knocked tentatively on the door.

"Harry, you knock *before* you open the door, not after," said an exasperated Mrs. Hodges.

"Sorry, Mrs. H. Sorry to interrupt Mrs. Knightley, but Mrs. Martin has come to call."

Emma nodded. "Thank you, Harry. Where is she?"

"In the great hall, ma'am."

Emma could all but hear Mrs. Hodges grinding her teeth.

"Mrs. Knightley's friends are not to be left waiting in the hall," the housekeeper said. "You should always show them to the drawing room."

"Sorry, Mrs. H."

Since Mrs. Hodges looked ready to deliver yet another Harry-scold, Emma forestalled her by standing.

"I'll go right now," she said. "Harry, have you seen my nephew?"

"Up in the great hall with Mrs. Martin, as it happens."

"*Master Henry is in the great hall with Mrs. Martin, ma'am.* That is the appropriate response, Harry," Mrs. Hodges corrected. "Mrs. Knightley, will you be wanting the tea tray sent up?"

"Yes, please."

As she went by him, Harry gave her a mournful smile. "I'm sorry for being such a dolt, Mrs. Knightley. I'm still at sixes and sevens because of Miss Prudence."

"I understand completely."

Despite his protestations the other day, Emma couldn't help but wonder if Harry *had* harbored tender feelings for Prudence. Clearly, her effect on all the servants at Donwell had been profound.

Despite Donwell's ancient and storied history, no ghosts had ever walked the vaulted halls and stone of the abbey. Now, though, a spirit did seem to linger over the household—one that spoke of sadness and a quiet grief.

Accompanying that sorrowful spirit were too many haunting questions that begged for answers.

Chapter 13

"Auntie Emma, can I have another piece of plum cake?"

Emma raised her eyebrows. "That would be your third piece, dear."

"But I'm still hungry," he protested. "Don't forget I walked all the way to Hartfield and back."

"That's quite the hike," said Harriet with a smile. "Surely Henry has earned another piece of cake. And after all, it *is* excellent. I didn't realize Mrs. Hodges was such a good baker."

"Serle baked it," Emma dryly replied. "We've been getting supplies from Hartfield on a regular basis. My father is convinced we're starving over here."

Henry adopted a doleful expression. "Well, I'm starving."

Emma relented. "All right, you may have another piece."

Truthfully, she thought Henry too thin. The boy had a nervous energy about him, never seeming to settle. Emma certainly hoped he would inherit his mother's loving disposition, but without Isabella's anxious tendencies.

"If you don't mind," said Henry, "may I read my book while I eat my cake?"

Emma smiled at his earnest expression. The boy read well in advance of his years, and he'd been ecstatic to be let loose in Donwell's library.

"Of course. You've been very kind to sit with us when I'm sure we've been terribly boring."

"I like listening to you and Mrs. Martin," Henry replied. "You make me laugh, Auntie Emma, especially when you poke fun at people you don't like."

Oh dear.

"I would advise you not follow my example in that regard, Henry. I don't think your mother would be terribly pleased."

"You're not nearly as bad as my father. He makes fun of everyone."

With that trenchant and too-accurate assessment, he departed for the other side of the drawing room, where he settled into an oversized armchair to read.

Emma made a comical face at Harriet. "I'm clearly a dreadful influence on my nephew."

"Henry is a dear child but seems quite solemn to me. It's wonderful that you make him laugh, because there's nothing better than a child's laughter. It's the happiest sound in the world."

Emma replenished her friend's teacup. "Soon you'll have your own child, who will no doubt give you a great deal of laughter and joy."

Harriet's hand flitted down to her burgeoning stomach. "It's hard not to worry, though. It's terribly exciting to think about having a baby, but first I have to go through . . . well, what if something were to go wrong?"

Emma took her hand. "You're a very healthy person, dear, and your pregnancy has gone exceedingly well. You have a very capable midwife and an excellent mother-in-law. Mrs. Martin will take care of you, never fear."

Harriet flashed her a grateful smile. "Thank you, Mrs. Knightley. You always know just the right thing to say."

"Of course I do. Now, I feel like I haven't seen you in an age. Not since before that dreadful party. I hope all is well at Abbey Mill Farm."

"Yes, thank you. We've been ever so worried about you and Mr. Knightley, though, and about everyone here at Donwell." Harriet grimaced. "It still feels impossible to believe. To fall out a window . . . it all seems so strange."

This was the opening Emma had been looking for. Like Miss Bates, Harriet often found herself in possession of all sorts of interesting information. Her kind and cheerful nature was just the sort that encouraged others to confide in her.

"Speaking of that horrible party," Emma said, "I was wondering if you'd heard anything about William Cox of late. He made a spectacle of himself, and I understand his mother is quite worried about him."

Harriet quickly glanced at Henry, then cast Emma a furtive look.

"As a matter of fact, I have," she whispered. "William has been behaving in *quite* a naughty fashion."

"Don't worry. Henry is completely ignoring us. Now, what do you mean by *naughty*?"

"Mrs. Cox told Mrs. Gilbert that she was worried about William, then Mrs. Gilbert told me when I was at Mrs. Ford's picking up a piece of flannel to make a waistcoat for Robert." She twirled a hand. "Not that Robert actually wants me to make him a flannel waistcoat. He says it makes him sound like an old man with rheumatics, but I insisted on it. He's outside all day in the cold and damp, you know."

Emma dearly loved her friend, but she had a tendency to get distracted by the mundane. "Very sensible of you. What, exactly, did Mrs. Gilbert tell you about William?"

"She said William had fallen in with some very low people. Not that Mrs. Cox has met any of William's new friends . . ." She frowned. "At least I suppose that's what you would call them. Anyway, she's not met any of them, because none live in Highbury."

"Did she mention where he met them? Perhaps in Leatherhead? It's just the sort of place one might meet low companions."

"I don't recall her mentioning Leatherhead," Harriet replied. "Apparently, though, there are nights when William doesn't return home at all. Mrs. Gilbert said that when Mr. Cox demanded that William account for his whereabouts, William grew angry and stormed out of the house. I found that very odd. William always had such a good relationship with his father."

"Did she say how long this odd behavior has been occurring?"

"For a few months, perhaps." Harriet shrugged. "She wasn't really sure."

Prudence had moved to Donwell three months ago. William's odd disappearances and behavior would have to have predated Prudence's arrival in Highbury for there to be any credence to the notion that he met her in Leatherhead.

"William's sisters are also quite worried and vexed," added Harriet. "They think his bad behavior might damage their reputations."

Emma scoffed. "That horse has already bolted the barn."

Harriet tried and failed to smother a grin. Anne Cox was rather her nemesis, since the dratted girl flirted with Harriet's husband whenever she had the chance.

"I do think Susan *tries* to be nice," said Harriet. "And I know the girls were very embarrassed by William's behavior at Donwell's party. He was making quite a pest of himself, from what I could see."

Startled, Emma leaned forward a bit. "You actually observed him pestering girls, then? Anyone in particular?"

"He spent half the night following Miss Nash about the hall. When he wouldn't leave her alone, I went to her and made her come away with me."

Emma frowned. "Miss Nash?"

"Yes. William was making quite a fool of himself over her."

That was an unexpected and rather deflating revelation. Miss Nash was a schoolteacher at Mrs. Goddard's establishment and a friend of Harriet's. If William was so taken with Miss Nash, why then did he go on to bother Prudence?

Emma mulled that over for a few moments. "Did you see William bother any other girls that night?"

Perhaps after his intentions with Miss Nash had been thwarted, William had become frustrated and chosen an even more vulnerable woman to harass.

Harriet shook her head. "No. As I said, I made Miss Nash come away with me to the drawing room, so I didn't see William for the rest of the night."

"Was she upset by William's behavior?"

Harriet looked a trifle disconcerted. "Not really, which I found very strange. Normally she's so careful about her interactions with young men. But then she went off with one of the other teachers, and I didn't speak to her again that evening."

"Huh," Emma muttered.

It seemed a bizarre episode, and not very helpful in illuminating William's subsequent behavior toward Prudence.

"Is that everything you've heard about William?" she asked.

Harriet flapped a hand. "Oh, I forgot. There is one more thing. Mrs. Cox asked Mr. Barlowe to speak to William about his naughty behavior. She hoped the vicar could persuade William to give up his new friends and spend more time helping his father."

"Yes, I was aware of that. I wonder if—"

"Auntie Emma, I finished my book," Henry loudly announced.

Emma all but fell off the settee, since her nephew was now standing right on the other side of the tea table. Obviously, he was *quite* adept at sneaking—something she'd have to remember.

"Was it good?" she brightly asked.

"It was very good, but I'm not sure what to do next."

Emma felt a stab of guilt. The poor lad was probably bored to tears listening to all this adult gossip.

Except it wasn't really gossip. It was information gathering. Still, it was clear she'd gotten as much out of Harriet as was to be had. Emma needed to ponder her next steps, because she'd reached something of an impasse.

For now, that could wait. Henry needed some attention.

"I have an idea," she said. "Why don't we do a little exploring? Some of the storerooms and cellars have been neglected these past several years. I need to make an assessment for your Uncle George so we can decide what must be cleaned and repaired."

Harriet looked surprised. "I cannot imagine Mr. Knightley or Mr. Larkins neglecting anything. Donwell always looks perfectly maintained to me."

"The main living quarters, yes. But with only George residing here for so many years, it wasn't practical to employ the number of servants necessary to maintain those parts of the house for regular use. And, of course, he's been at Hartfield these twelve months and more, so much of the abbey has been shut up during that time."

Henry jiggled with excitement. "I love to explore! Mama never lets me do that at home. She says it's too dangerous in London."

"It's not dangerous here, so I'm sure Mama couldn't possibly object." Emma stood. "I'd like to start at the bottom of the house and work my way to the top. There are two cellars in particular that I'd like to examine. Your Uncle George says they're very interesting chambers that the monks used for storage when Donwell was still a working abbey."

"Do you think we might see a ghost? Perhaps one of the monks who was killed during the Dissolution?" Henry eagerly asked. "Some of them were hung, drawn, and quartered. Maybe we'll even spot a headless ghost!"

Emma waggled a hand. "I've never heard of ghosts in the abbey, but perhaps we might get lucky."

"That doesn't sound very lucky to me," Harriet said, trying not to laugh. "May I come along?"

Emma hesitated. "I'm not sure that's a good idea. It's bound to be too cold and damp for you."

"Cold and damp won't bother me. I'm warm all the time. Because of . . . you know." Harriet pointed to her stomach. "Besides, the abbey is such a beautiful building. I should like to see a different part of it."

When Emma eyed her askance, Harriet gave her a pleading look. "Robert's mother and sisters hardly let me do anything anymore. They want me to sit and be quiet all the time. I should love to do something different, for once."

She sometimes forgot that Harriet was still quite young and energetic. Being treated like a delicate piece of porcelain by her anxious in-laws was clearly wearing on her.

"As long as you promise to let me know the moment you get cold or uncomfortable." She glanced at Henry. "That goes for you, too."

"I promise," the two replied in tandem.

"All right, then. Henry, fetch your warmest coat and gloves while Mrs. Martin and I get on our pelisses."

It took but a few minutes to get ready, and then Emma led her little band of assistants to the kitchen.

Mrs. Hodges poked her head out from the pantry. "Is there anything you're needing, Mrs. Knightley?"

"We're going down to examine the cellars. Henry and Mrs. Martin have volunteered to assist me."

The housekeeper nodded. "I'll have a fresh pot of tea waiting for you when you're finished, but I'd advise not staying too long in that cold and damp."

Once through the door to the stable yard, Emma turned right toward the small cellar beneath the kitchen that was currently in use as cold storage. She knew that was in prime shape, so she led them farther along the back of the house toward one of the older wings.

"I see it," said Henry, running ahead to stone steps that led down to a door well below grade. From the looks of it, this cellar was more akin to an undercroft, running deep beneath the abbey.

Her nephew hurried down the steps and disappeared from view. When a loud voice bellowed out from behind them, Emma almost jumped out of her skin.

"Hold up, Mrs. Knightley! Them steps aren't safe."

She spun about to see Harry striding toward them, a frown marking his normally placid features.

"Harry, you gave me quite the fright," she exclaimed.

"Begging your pardon, ma'am. I just don't want Master Henry hurting himself. Them steps are terrible crumbly. I've been telling Mr. Larkins they need to be fixed, but I guess he's not gotten around to it yet."

Those were quite a lot of words from Harry. And it was not the usual purview of a footman to worry about things such as cellars—especially a footman like Harry.

Her nephew's head popped up at the top of the stairs. "The steps are a little crumbly, Auntie Emma, but I think it's fine."

While it was true that edges of the stone steps were worn

down and cracked, they looked solid enough. Besides, George would never have agreed to her going down to the cellars if it weren't safe.

"I agree, Henry." She glanced at their footman. "But I take your point. I'll be sure to mention the steps to Mr. Larkins."

Harriet pointed to the bottom of the stairs. "The door seems sturdy, and the lock looks quite new. I thought you said this cellar hadn't been in use."

Emma frowned. "It hasn't, as far as I know."

"Mr. Larkins had the locksmith out last summer to change all the locks on the outside buildings and entrances," said Harry.

"Why is that?"

He shrugged. "I think it might have had something to do with the poultry thief."

Highbury had suffered a rash of thefts by a poultry thief, both last summer and the one before. The thief had never been caught, much to the consternation of the good citizens of Highbury.

"I suppose that makes sense," Emma replied, "though we're hardly keeping chickens down there."

"You'll have to ask Mr. Larkins, ma'am." Harry gave her a sheepish smile. "He generally don't tell me what's going on around the place."

"I suppose we'll need a key, then. Harry, could you find Mr. Larkins and fetch it for me?"

"I think he's gone off to the village, ma'am. Not sure when he'll be back."

"Oh, bother. Then I suppose—"

"It's open," Henry said.

He'd scampered back down and was now standing in the door. Emma hadn't heard a thing. Given the age of the oak door, she could only surmise that the hardware had been cleaned and oiled, as well.

"Excellent." She snapped her fingers. "We need light. Harry, please run back to the kitchen and fetch a lantern."

The footman scrunched up his face. "Are you sure you want to go down there, missus? It's bound to be dirty as anything. You won't want to be mucking up your shoes."

"I'm wearing my half-boots," said Harriet. "I wear them around the farm all the time."

"Harry, fetch the lamp now," Emma said in a firm voice.

With a sigh, he trudged off toward the kitchen with a distinct lack of enthusiasm.

Harriet peered after him. "Harry makes for a rather odd footman. Robert says he's quite lazy."

"An opinion shared by more than one at Donwell. He does try his best, though. I think George feels sorry for him, since he's not very bright."

"Poor man. One can't blame him for that."

"Indeed."

Emma lifted her skirts and made her way down to join her nephew. "See anything interesting, Henry?"

"Just some of the floor. But the smell isn't too bad."

She took a cautious sniff and was pleasantly surprised. There was a musty odor, which wasn't surprising, but it could have been worse.

Ducking under the lintel, she followed her nephew past the cellar entrance, with Harriet in the rear.

Emma couldn't see much, since the weak afternoon light illuminated only the entrance. Still, she got the impression of a space larger than anticipated.

When Henry started forward, she clamped a hand on his shoulder. "Wait, dear. There might be holes in the floor. We need the lantern."

The boy expelled an aggrieved sigh but held fast.

Emma glanced at Harriet. "Are you warm enough?"

Her friend nodded. "It's not as chilly as I thought it would be." She glanced down. "Or as dirty. The floor around here seems rather clean."

Emma followed her gaze, and was surprised to see only some dust. "I wonder if Mr. Larkins is using this cellar for storage after all. I know the attics are full of furniture and various items, so perhaps he's using this for overflow."

"Or he might be storing cider," Henry suggested. "Uncle George said Donwell had a bumper apple crop this year, and it made an awful lot of cider."

Emma turned around at the sound of footsteps. "Ah, here's Harry."

The footman joined them, lantern in hand. "Do you want me to go ahead of you, Mrs. Knightley? That way I can see if there's anything nasty."

Consternation crossed Harriet's face. "What do you mean by nasty?"

"Big spiderwebs. Maybe even a snake."

"Oh dear," Harriet faintly replied. "Snakes?"

Emma grabbed the lantern. "There are no snakes. And even if there were, they would be hibernating at this time of year."

She held the lantern high, letting its rays play over the space in front of them.

"Goodness," she murmured.

It *was* an undercroft, and a large one. She wouldn't have been surprised if the chamber stretched almost halfway under the abbey. The floor and the walls were old but well-made brick, likely from the original construction. The brick ceiling was vaulted, held up by sturdy arches.

"This is quite something, isn't it, Henry?" Emma commented.

Henry peered at the ceiling. "It's an undercroft, not really a cellar at all."

Harriet squeaked. "I thought undercrofts were used to bury the dead."

"Aye," said Harry. "I heard tales that some of the old monks were buried down here."

"That is certainly not true," Emma crisply replied. "You may go, Harry."

"Are you sure, Mrs. Knightley?"

"Mrs. Hodges will be wondering where you are. You don't want to annoy her."

At that verbal prod, his eyes went wide. "Yes, ma'am."

When he turned and clattered hastily up the steps, Emma had to stifle a laugh.

"Mrs. Knightley, are you sure there are no monks buried here?" Harriet asked in an anxious voice.

"Quite certain. The monks' graveyard is north of the abbey. It was destroyed after the Dissolution, and it's mostly woodland now."

Harriet grimaced. "The poor monks."

"Indeed. Henry, make sure you stay in the light."

"Yes, Auntie Emma," he replied as he wandered ahead.

Emma began to walk around the perimeter of the chamber. She was pleased to see it had no visible signs of damp. Likely, it had once been used as storage space for ale and cider. Since George intended to increase production of both those commodities, this undercroft would be put to good use.

She held up the lantern. "Henry, where are you?"

He scampered back out of the gloom. "Here I am."

His pants and shoes were now covered with dust. "Hmm. Not so clean here after all, I see."

"Only toward the back." Henry pointed down to the floor. "See, it's clean here by the front."

She turned in a slow circle, casting the lantern's rays onto the floor. "That's rather odd."

"Maybe the wind comes under the door and blows the dust toward the back," Henry suggested.

"Perhaps." Emma glanced up to see Harriet standing by the doorway. "Are you all right, dear? I assure you, it's perfectly dry and safe."

"I'm sorry, Mrs. Knightley," her friend replied. "It's the smell. It's making me queasy."

Emma took an experimental sniff. "I suppose it's rather musty from being closed up for so long."

"It smells like tobacco to me. It's because I'm . . ." Harriet pointed at her stomach. "I've become very sensitive to odors. Poor Robert has to go outside to smoke his pipe because I can't stand the smell of the tobacco."

Emma didn't smell anything akin to tobacco, but she wasn't going to make her friend suffer with a queasy stomach.

"Come along, Henry," she said. "We don't want Mrs. Martin to become ill."

"I'm fine," Harriet protested. "I'll just go stand outside."

Emma took her arm and escorted her to the stairs. "Nonsense. We'll get you a nice cup of tea, and then I'll ask Harry to walk you home."

Harriet gave her a grateful smile. "There's no need for Harry to put himself out."

Henry skipped ahead of them. "I'll walk you home, Mrs. Martin. I'd like to check the pond and see if it's frozen yet for skating."

Emma closed the door to the undercroft and followed the others up the stairs. As they approached the kitchen, the door opened and Larkins came out.

"I was just coming to look for you, Mrs. Knightley. Mrs. Hodges said you were down in the old cellar."

"It's really more of an undercroft, isn't it? I had no idea there was one so big under the abbey."

"I understand it was used for storing cider and ale, as well as the cheeses the monks used to make."

"I was surprised at how clean it is."

Harriet crinkled her nose. "Except for the smell."

Larkins frowned. "What smell is that, Mrs. Martin?"

"Harriet thought it was tobacco," Emma explained, "but I couldn't smell it. I don't suppose anyone was storing tobacco down there, were they?"

"Not for a long time, if ever." Then he scowled. "Mayhap it's Harry smoking his pipe. He's been told more than once not to smoke in the house. I wouldn't be surprised if he was sneaking off there to have a smoke."

No wonder Harry tried to stop them from going in there.

"We cannot have that," Emma replied in a humorous tone.

"I'll speak to him, ma'am." Larkins looked most put out. "He won't be doing it again."

She waved a hand. "I shouldn't worry about it."

"And I might be wrong about it being tobacco," Harriet hastily put in. "I don't want to get the fellow in trouble."

Larkins snorted. "The fellow is never *out* of trouble."

It would seem that their estate steward had as little use for Harry as their housekeeper did.

"Whatever you think is best. Oh, Larkins," Emma said, after pausing for a moment. "Harry said that you installed new locks on all the outer entrances last year. May I ask why?"

"Just a precaution, ma'am. We're a big house with a small staff, and it's best to have the place as secure as possible."

She raised her eyebrows. "Harry thought it might have something to do with the poultry thief. Have there been any incidents of thieving?"

"As I said, ma'am, it was just a precaution." He scowled. "And Harry would do best to keep his opinions to himself, if you don't mind me saying. Now, if you'll excuse me, ma'am, I'd best be at my work."

He tipped his hat and strode off toward the stables.

"Is Mr. Larkins unwell?" asked Harriet. "He's generally so even-tempered."

Emma stared after the estate steward as he disappeared into the stables.

"Generally, yes, he is," she absently replied.

Larkins's unusual behavior was yet another sign that, despite appearances, life was far from normal at Donwell Abbey.

Chapter 14

Emma's father gazed morosely out the carriage window. "I cannot fathom how I allowed myself to be talked into this frightful outing. One can tolerate going to Randalls for Christmas dinner, but to travel all the way to the Coles... that is quite shocking!"

Emma exchanged a glance with Isabella, sitting next to Father on the opposite side of the carriage. Unfortunately, her sister looked almost as out of sorts with this excursion as he did.

"I know, dear, but Mrs. Cole's house is actually closer to Hartfield than Randalls," Emma apologetically said.

He sighed. "If you say so. But you know how I feel about parties, Emma, especially large parties."

"The Coles are simply hosting a lovely dinner in honor of your betrothal, not a large party at all. And Miss Bates is very excited about it."

"Well, I suppose we must hope there will be no accidents tonight, particularly fatal ones. Or that one of the guests doesn't arrive with an infectious complaint. That would be *most* distressing."

"Emma!" exclaimed Isabella. "You didn't tell me that one of the guests might have an infectious complaint. Do I need to worry about the children?"

Emma resisted the urge to thump her head against the padded side of the carriage. "No one has an infectious complaint. Mrs. Cole made it very clear to *all* the guests that they were to send their excuses if any of them had so much as a sniffle."

Isabella gave her a sheepish smile. "That was very kind of her."

Although no one in the family was particularly enthused about this party, it might still have its uses. The Coxes were on the guest list, at Miss Bates's request, which would give Emma the opportunity to observe William Cox in a more intimate setting. Perhaps it might even give her the chance to ask him about Prudence—very discreetly, of course.

The past several days had been uneventful. Despite her best efforts, Emma had been unable to unearth any additional information about William Cox and his connection to Prudence, from either the servants or anyone else. Sadly, when she'd shared her frustrations with George, he'd rather tartly replied that the lack of any such information no doubt illustrated that William had nothing to do with Prudence's death.

Emma, however, remained unconvinced that it did not. Her instincts had served her well last year in helping to bring Mrs. Elton's killer to justice, and she wasn't about to ignore those instincts now. Even if there was no proof that Prudence had been murdered, which her husband had annoyingly pointed out, it didn't mean something untoward hadn't happened. There were simply too many strange aspects to the case and too many questions that left her vastly unsatisfied.

Father sighed again. "I suppose we cannot be neglectful of Mr. and Mrs. Cole since they have gone to so much trouble. One wishes, however, that they would not host so many parties. They seem to host a great many of them, indeed." He smoothed the lap blanket over his knees. "I do hope Miss Bates will not wish to hold many parties at Hartfield. I must remember to speak with her about that."

"I'm sure she won't, Father," said Emma. "Miss Bates is always very attentive to the needs of others. She's so kind."

That finally won a smile from her father. "She is. She also has a very keen awareness of drafts. I don't think I've ever met anyone who could sense a draft more accurately than Miss Bates."

"John is also very good at detecting drafts," Isabella said. "He likes to tease me about my fear of drafts, but he's really very attentive in that regard, especially with the children."

Her father regarded her with alarm. "My dear, one must *never* tease about drafts. They can be fatal."

Emma cut into the conversation before it could deteriorate any further. "We've arrived. And how lovely the house looks! So bright and cheery, don't you think?"

"I hope it's not *too* bright," her father fretfully said. "Too much light can strain the eyes."

She was thankfully spared a reply when a footman came to the carriage door and lowered the steps.

"Good evening, Mrs. Knightley," he said as he helped her alight.

The young man was garbed in rather startling red and gold livery. It was a trifle much for Highbury, but that was the Coles' style. They were good folk with a great deal of money and an equally great desire to spread it around as lavishly as possible. After Hartfield, they owned the largest house in Highbury, and Mrs. Cole was continually undertaking improvements, determined to keep up with the latest styles from London.

"Has Mr. Knightley and his party arrived yet?" Emma asked.

George had gone on ahead to escort Miss Bates and her mother to the party in the abbey's carriage.

"They arrived a few minutes ago, ma'am."

Another elaborately garbed footman, who took their wraps, ushered them to the drawing room.

"Mr. Woodhouse, Mrs. John Knightley, and Mrs. George Knightley," he announced with a full measure of solemnity.

"One would think we're being introduced at court instead of in Mrs. Coles' drawing room," Emma whispered to her sister.

Isabella choked. "Hush, Emma."

Mrs. Cole, resplendent in a purple satin gown and matching turban topped with an enormous purple feather, sailed over to greet them. Her husband followed dutifully at her heels.

"Mr. Woodhouse," she enthused. "We are so honored to have you grace us with your presence. It is quite the occasion when Mr. Woodhouse comes to visit, and a real cause for celebration."

Mr. Cole bowed so low that his shirt points climbed almost up around his ears. "Pleased as punch that you could make it, sir, along with your lovely daughters and Mr. Knightley."

Father, ever the gentleman, replied with a sweet smile. "It was exceedingly kind of you to have us. Miss Bates was very much looking forward to it."

"And here is the blushing bride herself," Mr. Cole jovially announced as Miss Bates bustled up.

"Goodness, Mr. Cole," she exclaimed. "You are too kind, but I'm well past the age of blushing. Although I did use to blush a great deal when I was younger, much to my father's consternation. Hetty, he used to say, you're much too sensitive to the opinions of others. Seek only God's good will, and then there will be no need for your blushes."

"Er . . ." said Mr. Cole, his eyes going wide.

"Mr. Woodhouse," continued Miss Bates, "you must be perishing from the cold. Fortunately, Mrs. Cole has arranged everything beautifully by the fireplace." She touched Isabella's arm. "You, too, Mrs. Knightley. Do come get warm."

As she led them off, the Coles effusively expressed their gratitude to Emma for her family's presence—so much so that she began to feel embarrassed.

Thankfully, George broke off from his chat with a group of men and came to her rescue.

"Mr. Knightley, you must excuse me while I speak with Mrs. Cole about getting dinner on the table. I'm sure everyone's famished." Mr. Cole winked at Emma. "We have a splendid goose for dinner, come all the way from London. Only the best for Mr. Woodhouse, eh?"

He then took his wife by the arm and steered her toward the dining room.

"I do hope the goose came by chaise," Emma commented. "He would be dreadfully uncomfortable in the mail coach."

"The Coles are genuinely excited that your father is here tonight," George said in a mildly admonishing tone. "He never goes anywhere but to Randalls or Donwell, so it's quite the occasion for them."

"It's terribly sweet, but one would think the Prince Regent himself had come to sup. The footmen even have new livery."

"I seem to recall that not very long ago you wouldn't deign to cross the Coles' threshold. And yet here you are."

She wrinkled her nose. "How dreadful of you to remind me. I was a terrible snob, wasn't I?"

"My dear, I would never say that."

"Wretch. You are certainly thinking it."

He laughed. "Come and greet some of the other guests."

As was usual for the Coles, dinner was a more intimate affair held before more guests arrived later to make up the sets for dancing. The Westons were present, as was Mrs. Goddard, along with—surprisingly—Miss Nash, the head teacher at Mrs. Goddard's school. Mr. Barlowe hovered nearby the ladies, pretending to be part of the conversation but looking his usual awkward self.

Most interesting from Emma's point of view was the presence of Mr. Cox and William Cox, who were chatting with the Perrys. She had to admit that William looked perfectly respectable as he stood by his father, politely listening to Mrs. Perry.

"In case you're wondering," George murmured, "William has been conducting himself in an exemplary fashion."

Emma darted him a look. "The evening is young, dearest."

Not that she truly expected William to descend into his cups at such a small gathering. But it should be interesting to observe how he interacted with Miss Nash or some of the other young ladies later in the evening.

George refrained from making a reply as they joined Guy Plumtree and an older gentleman.

"My dear, I'm sure you remember Mr. Guy Plumtree from our party," said George. "But let me introduce you to Squire Plumtree. Sir, my wife."

Emma extended a hand. "It's a pleasure to meet you."

The squire bowed over her hand. "The pleasure is mine, Mrs. Knightley. I've known Mr. Knightley for some years—we farming fellows generally talk, you know. I was most eager to make your acquaintance. My son told me all about your splendid kick-up at Donwell Abbey."

Emma had to school her features, since that was *not* how she would have described that evening. But Squire Plumtree seemed a sincere man, if perhaps a slight rough about the edges. Neatly dressed, although not in the first style, he presented the very image of a respectable country squire.

Unlike his father, Guy looked extremely fashionable, sporting a finely tailored coat, a bright yellow vest, and an exceptionally complicated cravat. The outfit should have looked ridiculous in a place like Highbury, but the younger Plumtree carried it off with an easy confidence.

His smile was charmingly rueful as he regarded his father. "Sir, I don't believe I described that evening as a kick-up. You might also remember that a tragic event concluded the evening."

The squire grimaced. "My blasted memory again. Mrs. Knightly, you'll have to allow me to extend both my apologies and my condolences. You must have been utterly aghast by the whole, sad thing."

"Yes, it was quite awful," said Emma. "But there's no need to apologize. None of the guests were aware at the time."

"As for your memory," George smoothly interjected, "you must allow me to disagree. I've never met a man with a stronger head for detail than you. Over the years, I've greatly enjoyed our discussions about estate management."

Squire Plumtree hooked his thumbs in his collar. "If it's facts and figures you want, I'm your man. When it comes to social occasions and making decent conversation, though, Guy will tell you I'm quite hopeless."

Guy waggled a hand. "Perhaps you're a trifle consumed by business, sir, but since I am equally hopeless when it comes to estate management, I think you might call us square." He smiled at Emma. "I find the farming business to be tedious, Mrs. Knightley, much to my dear father's dismay. I'm rather a disappointment to him."

"Nonsense, my boy," his father replied in a jovial tone. "I'll make a farmer out of you yet. Especially now that I'm in residence at Plumtree Manor for the foreseeable future."

Guy's answering smile was affectionate. "And I'm very happy you are, sir."

Before they could continue their conversation, Mrs. Cole called them to the table and fluttered about as she directed them to their seats. Emma found herself between Mr. Barlowe and Guy Plumtree, and across from Mrs. Weston. She'd not yet had a chance to greet her friend, so she simply flashed her a smile. Conversation would have to wait, since a dinner this formal confined one to chatting only with those on one's immediate left and right.

Emma was glad to be seated next to Guy. Their curate was

another matter, however. Still, she would do her best to make him feel comfortable.

"How are you, Mr. Barlowe?" she asked as the footmen began the soup course. "Well, I hope?"

"Tolerable, Mrs. Knightley." There was an awkward pause. "Thank you for asking," he finally added.

Then, with a degree of concentration one would apply to a difficult puzzle, he focused on his soup, clearly determined to stymie further conversation. Emma could almost believe he'd taken a dislike to her but for the fact that he seemed awkward with most everyone.

After the footman had served her, Guy leaned in with a wry smile. "Don't mind Barlowe, Mrs. Knightley. The poor fellow is terribly shy. Can't help but wonder why he became a curate in the first place. He can barely bring himself to speak with his own parishioners."

"Did you know him before he came to Highbury?" she asked. "Perhaps you met at university?"

Guy took a spoonful of soup before answering. "I met him quite by chance shortly after he came to Highbury. Oddly, he took a shine to me, and we've been friendly ever since."

Emma cast a glance at Mr. Barlowe, grimly eating his soup and doing his best to ignore Miss Bates on his other side.

"I'm happy to hear he has made a friend," she said to Guy.

The young man flashed another wry grin. "I suspect you're probably thinking we're strange bedfellows, but there's no explaining the vagaries of friendship. And he's truly a decent and kind fellow once one gets to know him."

Emma could well understand the vagaries of friendship. No one would have ever thought she would become fast friends with Harriet, who was unaware of her own parentage until only last year and was now married to a tenant farmer.

"Not that old Barlowe and I get much chance to see each other," Guy added. "I don't get into Highbury often these days, now that my father has returned to Plumtree Manor from London. He's greatly taken up with the estate and is determined to teach me what I must know to follow in his footsteps."

She heard a slight tinge of bitterness in his voice. "He sounds like an excellent father."

"That he is. I am indeed a fortunate son."

"I imagine you're only recently down from university," Emma said. "So it must be quite a change for you, moving back to the country. We're so quiet here."

Given his social polish, Emma imagined he cut a dashing figure at Oxford or Cambridge.

"Ah, but I never attended university, ma'am. I've always lived at Plumtree Manor and received all my schooling at home. Tutors." He gave a comical shudder. "They were almost the death of me. Or I of them, more like."

A clever young man from a good family of means who hadn't gone to university? While Emma couldn't help but wonder why, it would be rude to inquire.

"Your father mentioned he is now spending more time at Plumtree Manor," she said instead. "I take it he was often away from home."

"As you might recall, he has substantial business concerns in the city. He spent much of my youth in London, looking after his wool business. It is only in the past six months that he's begun to spend most of his time at the manor."

Before Emma could ask why his father was now spending more time at home, the covers were removed and the next course served. Guy turned away to reply to a comment from Mrs. Perry, seated on his other side. Emma reminded herself that she should make another effort to speak to their young curate.

"Mr. Barlowe," she said, "Mr. Plumtree tells me that you struck up a friendship shortly after your arrival in Highbury. That is a happy occurrence."

The man froze, his cutlery suspended above his plate. Several seconds passed before he resumed cutting a slice of ham into small, identically sized pieces.

"Yes, Plumtree was most kind to take notice of me," he flatly replied.

What an odd way of expressing it.

"Have you had an opportunity to visit Plumtree Manor?" she asked. "I understand it's quite a lovely old house. In the style of Queen Anne, I believe."

"I cannot render an opinion, Mrs. Knightley, since I am not familiar with architectural styles."

Well.

Emma ate some veal, fricasseed in an excellent sauce, she was happy to note, before trying again.

"I understand from Miss Bates that Mrs. Sutcliffe has been feeling poorly," she said. "Please do let me know if I can be of any assistance. I should be happy to ask Mr. Perry to visit her, if you think that might be helpful."

"I've not yet had a chance to see her," came the blighting reply.

Emma frowned. Mrs. Sutcliffe was a widow who'd fallen on difficult times. She and George often sent baskets of foodstuff and any other necessities that might be helpful, as did Mrs. Weston. It was surprising that the village clergyman had yet to visit her.

The curate glanced at her and pulled a slight grimace, which suggested he'd read her expression.

"I intend to visit her tomorrow, though," he said. "Church matters have kept me very busy. The vestry council, you understand."

"Of course," she politely replied.

When the curate again turned to his plate with single-minded focus, Emma gave up. Glancing to her right, she briefly studied Guy Plumtree, still engaged in easy conversation with Mrs. Perry. It seemed difficult to believe that such an amiable young man would have established a friendship with a charmless, taciturn stick like Mr. Barlowe.

She was about to turn her attention to her own excellent dinner when she glanced down the table and noticed William Cox staring intently at her. When their gazes locked, Emma felt her heart skip a beat. Immediately, William flushed a bright red and turned away, holding up his wineglass as the footmen came round with a fresh bottle of wine.

And the hand that held that wineglass was trembling.

"Dear girl, you've barely heard a word I've said!" Mrs. Weston exclaimed in a humorously exasperated tone.

Guilty as charged.

"You were telling me that the chimney in your dining room was, ah, misbehaving," Emma replied.

"As I said, it was more than misbehaving. It filled the entire room with smoke," her friend dryly noted. "I also recognize that expression on your face. You're stewing about something."

Inadvertently, Emma's gaze darted to the other side of the drawing room, where William Cox sat with Miss Nash in deep conversation.

The ladies had repaired to the drawing room after dinner to allow the gentlemen to remain and enjoy their brandy, but Mr. Cole was not one to linger at the table. The other guests had arrived as well, so the party had grown lively, especially among the young people. While not honored with an invitation to dinner, the young people never seemed to mind, since there was always a great deal of music and dancing. Emma certainly didn't begrudge them a bit of fun, although it did mean having to mingle with the likes of the Cox sisters, who had arrived with their mother.

Before her marriage, Emma would have been horrified at the notion of socializing with the Coxes. In truth, she was *still* horrified by it. She hoped, however, that she'd learned not to be quite as judgmental as she'd been in the days before her marriage.

Mrs. Weston leaned in close. "Why are you staring at William Cox?"

Emma affected surprise. "Was I? I didn't even notice. Tell me, what do you think of Mrs. Cole's new chimneypiece? I must confess I'm not a fan of Mona Marble. Quite hideous, if you ask me."

Not surprisingly, her former governess was not fooled. "Emma, I hope you've given over the notion that William had anything to do with Prudence's death."

"Hush," Emma hissed by way of reply.

Fortunately, no one was standing nearby. Father, Miss Bates, and their friends were seated in front of the fireplace—the new chimneypiece really *was* quite ugly—and George was engaged with Mr. Weston, Mr. Cole, and Squire Plumtree across the room. Most of the young people were in the parlor, which opened up off the drawing room.

"You can speak freely," said Mrs. Weston. "Although I shudder to think what you *actually* might be thinking about poor William."

"*Poor* William was acting very suspiciously at dinner."

"Really? In what way?"

"I caught him staring at me intently. When our gazes met, he turned bright red and quickly looked away." Emma glanced at the young man again. "It felt as if he had something to hide."

"I suspect he's feeling embarrassed about his conduct during the party at Donwell Abbey."

"Exactly," Emma triumphantly said. "Or guilty, rather."

"My dear, he likely wants to apologize for his bad behavior and is trying to work up the nerve," Mrs. Weston replied.

Emma shook her head. "It was more than just bad behavior. He upset Prudence very badly."

And possibly did much worse than that.

"That was indeed dreadful," her friend patiently replied. "Which is why he probably wishes to apologize."

"Then why hasn't he?"

"Likely because you keep glowering at him. It's quite noticeable."

Oh dear.

"Then I suppose I'll have to be more subtle about it."

"Emma, you must—"

"Oh, look! Here comes Mrs. Cole."

Their hostess greeted them, all smiles. "Mrs. Weston, I was hoping to impose on you to play the pianoforte for us. The young people are greatly longing to dance."

"I should be happy to," Mrs. Weston replied.

"Wonderful. Perhaps you would like to look over some of the music? The Gilbert and the Otway girls have already been making some selections."

With another nod—and a quick warning glance to Emma—Mrs. Weston departed for the other room.

"What a kind woman," Mrs. Cole said. "As are you, Mrs. Knightley. I was sorry to have to place you next to Mr. Barlowe. He's terribly shy, but I knew that if anyone could pull him out of his shell, it would be you."

"I'm afraid I was rather a failure in that department," Emma ruefully admitted.

"I hope you enjoyed chatting with Mr. Plumtree, though. He's a truly amiable young man, and Squire Plumtree is a most worthy addition to the neighborhood after such a long time away in London."

"Yes, Mr. Plumtree mentioned that. What precipitated his return, if I may ask?"

Mrs. Cole sighed. "It's a very sad story, really. The poor squire—"

"Oh, Mrs. Knightley, there you are! Anne and I have been longing to speak with you."

Emma turned to find herself confronted by the Cox girls, forcing her to grit her teeth and try to manage a smile at the same time. Both Susan and Anne did appear eager to speak with her. That was more than a little strange, since normally they tried to avoid her.

"Now, Susan," admonished Mrs. Cole. "You mustn't barge into conversations. Your mother would not be pleased."

"It was Mama's idea," Anne said. "Because the music is about to start, we thought we'd better speak with Mrs. Knightley now. We won't want to speak to anyone once the dancing starts."

Susan giggled. "Except to young men like Mr. Plumtree. Anne and I could talk to him forever."

Her sister tossed a fat curl over her shoulder. "La, I barely took notice of him. You're the one who was making sheep's eyes at him."

"I was not," Susan indignantly replied.

"You were both flirting with him, from what I could see," Mrs. Cole replied with a wink. "And I don't blame you one bit. He's a very nice young man."

Since her marriage last year, Emma had given up her rather checkered career of matchmaking. Perhaps, though, she could be persuaded to make an exception for Guy. If nothing else, it would be an act of charity to introduce him to a few eligible young ladies and save him from the likes of the Cox sisters.

Perhaps the oldest Otway girl?

Susan beamed at Mrs. Cole. "And Mr. Plumtree is so stylish, too. I vow, no young man has been so stylish in Highbury since Mr. Frank Churchill."

Anne scoffed. "He's not nearly a patch on Frank Churchill—not that Frank had eyes for anyone but Jane. Although everyone *did* think he was sweet on you, Mrs. Knightley. To think he was secretly engaged to Jane the entire time that he flirted with you."

Talking to the Cox girls was just as unpleasant as stepping into a mud puddle while wearing one's best shoes.

Mrs. Cole cast a severe look on the sisters. "That's no way to speak to Mrs. Knightley. I doubt Mr. Knightley would be very pleased."

Susan had the grace to look abashed. Unfortunately, Anne wouldn't know how to look abashed if her life depended on it.

"We don't mean to offend, Mrs. Knightley," Susan apologetically said.

"It's fine," Emma said. "What did you wish to speak to me about?"

The sisters exchanged an uncomfortable glance, as if at a loss as to how to begin.

"If you'll excuse me," Mrs. Cole said with a surprising degree of tact. "I must speak to Mr. Cole."

"We're sorry again to interrupt your conversation, Mrs. Knightley," said Susan after their hostess departed. "I hope you don't think us too rude."

Anne again tossed a curl over her shoulder. "You apologize too much, Susan. I'm sure you're boring Mrs. Knightley to tears."

"A well-intentioned apology is never amiss," Emma said sternly. "Again, what did you wish to speak to me about?"

After several seconds of fraught silence, Anne elbowed her sister. "Go on, Susan."

Susan bristled. "You're the oldest, so you should say it."

"Coward," Anne muttered before looking at Emma.

Interestingly, the girl's gaze mingled a curious mixture of defiance and embarrassment, if Emma didn't miss her guess.

"Is this about your brother?" she asked.

Anne gave a reluctant nod. "Mama wanted us to apologize to you for his bad behavior at your party. She said you would be very upset about what happened to your maid, and that William's behavior just made everything worse."

Emma's heart jolted against her rib cage. "How did William's behavior make it worse?"

Susan's eyes popped wide. "Because that poor girl had such a horrible end, Mrs. Knightley. When William heard the next day, he felt dreadful because he'd been . . ."

"Flirting with her," Anne finished. "When she didn't want him to."

Emma frowned. "Your brother told your mother that he was pestering Miss Parr?"

Anne nodded. "Yes, and Papa, too. Papa rang a terrible peal over him. Poor William was miserable."

"He deserved to be miserable," Emma tartly replied.

Susan grimaced an apology. "He's ever so sorry, Mrs. Knightley, and he's dreadfully ashamed that he acted so poorly."

"Then why are you apologizing instead of him?"

"He's afraid that you or Mr. Knightley will give him a thundering scold," Anne replied, sneering a bit. "I've told him to stop being such a coward."

Emma glanced at the young man, still sitting with Miss Nash. She found him gazing at her with a woebegone expression that was more akin to a puppy that had just been kicked than a ruthless killer.

He blushed and quickly returned his attention to Miss Nash.

Emma sighed. "He certainly deserves a thundering scold. Gentlemen shouldn't be acting so poorly, especially in public."

Anne bristled. "Lots of young men drink and flirt. I don't see why William should be any different."

"He greatly embarrassed your parents. And I can assure you that a true gentleman does not act that way in public *or* private."

Anne flapped her hands like an agitated goose. "How else are you supposed to meet young men if they don't flirt with you?"

Emma wondered what she'd done to earn the ghastly task of having to school such a silly young woman in appropriate social behavior. "You do it by having a rational conversation with them about something that interests you both."

Susan looked perplexed. "But what if you don't know what interests them?"

"You ask them. Young men like nothing better than talking about themselves."

Anne scoffed. "But that's so boring."

Hopeless.

"To return to your brother," Emma said. "You said your mother wished you to apologize for him. Did William also ask you to approach me on his behalf?"

Susan nodded. "He's truly sorry, and he also apologizes for . . ." She trailed off with a grimace.

"For what?"

The sisters exchanged a glance. For the first time, they looked genuinely uncomfortable.

"After you told us to remove him from the hall," Anne reluctantly said, "we took him to one of the drawing rooms."

"The yellow one," added Susan. "It's ever so nice a room, Mrs. Knightley. And we're very sorry what happened."

"Which was what?"

"William got sick," Susan reluctantly admitted. "He, um . . ."

"Cast up his crumpets?" Emma dryly supplied.

She nodded.

"But he didn't get any on the furniture," Anne said. "And only a bit on the carpet. So it wasn't so bad, after all."

"Didn't one of the servants tell you?" Susan asked. "We felt sure that they would."

"As you recall, we were a trifle busy that evening." Emma suddenly frowned. "And you said this happened immediately after I spoke with you?"

Susan nodded.

"So, after your brother became ill, what happened next?"

"He fell asleep on one of the sofas," Anne replied. "We had a terrible time waking him up to take him home. Father had to practically carry him. It was *dreadfully* embarrassing."

"And someone was with your brother that entire time in the drawing room?"

"Yes, Mrs. Knightley," Susan earnestly said. "I stayed with him the whole time. Papa was very angry and wanted William to apologize right away, but Mama said there was no point, since he could hardly even talk."

And that was the final blow to Emma's theory about William Cox. Had he pestered Prudence earlier in the evening, upsetting the poor girl? Yes. But unless the entire Cox family was in league with him, which was a ridiculous notion, the foolish man was not guilty of anything but being a cad.

George had been right all along. Whatever the young man's faults, he wasn't a murderer.

"William truly *is* very sorry, Mrs. Knightley," said Susan.

"I believe you," Emma replied with a sigh. "But I would still like him to call on Mr. Knightley and offer a formal apology. I promise Mr. Knightley will not give him a thundering scold, but it would be appropriate for your brother to acknowledge his shortcomings."

Anne scowled. "I don't see why—"

Her sister elbowed her into silence. "I'm sure William will be happy to do that. And he's ever so much better now. He's quite smitten with Miss Nash, and Mama thinks she will be a good influence on him."

Poor Miss Nash.

"One can only hope so," Emma replied.

Anne grabbed her sister's arm. "Mr. Knightley is finished talking to Guy Plumtree. And all the other girls are in the parlor, so now's our chance to get him all to ourselves."

Susan glanced at Emma with pleading eyes. "Do you mind, Mrs. Knightley?"

"Not in the slightest."

Susan gave her a grateful smile before Anne hurried her across the room.

Emma stood quietly for a few moments, gathering her thoughts. Although it seemed she must absolve William of culpability in Prudence's death, there were still too many questions. For one thing, both Mrs. Hodges and Harry had been adamant that the young man had been the cause of the girl's extreme emotional distress. But if William wasn't, who was?

The situation defied rational explanation. Emma simply couldn't convince herself that Prudence had accidentally fallen out a narrow window, even if she *had* been inebriated—which, according to those who knew her best, was most unlikely.

George, conversing with Father and Isabella by the fire, sent her an inquiring look. Emma went to join her family.

"You were having quite an extended conversation with the Cox girls," he said.

"Yes, and I'm already doing my best to forget it."

When George raised his eyebrows, Emma smiled. "I'll explain later. You were conversing at length with young Mr. Plumtree, I noticed."

"He was asking me about Donwell Abbey."

"That's rather odd, isn't it?"

"His father encouraged him to do it. Guy strikes me as a bright young man, if a bit aimless."

"But he wants nothing to do with estate management. He was emphatic about that," Emma replied.

George shrugged. "Perhaps he was simply trying to please his father by quizzing me. Squire Plumtree apparently thinks I'm a good role model."

"He's correct, but I hope the squire doesn't expect *you* to tutor his son on estate management. You're terribly busy at it is."

"That's why I suggested he speak with Larkins. I'm hoping he will relieve me of the burden of mentoring Guy Plumtree."

Emma tried to repress a laugh. "Dearest, that is really quite dreadful of you. Poor Larkins."

"Your father apparently shares your opinion," George dryly replied.

Father huffed. "I cannot approve of Squire Plumtree, Emma. He's too loud and bluff. He reminds me of that dreadful Constable Sharpe, going about constantly annoying everyone."

She cast a hasty glance around the room.

"You needn't worry," said Isabella. "Mrs. Cole set up card tables in the dining room, and Squire Plumtree is in there with Miss Bates."

"I do hope the squire will not upset Miss Bates by speaking about that terrible incident at Donwell," Father fretfully commented.

Emma frowned. "Why would he?"

"He did so earlier in the evening," Isabella explained. "I believe Squire Plumtree thought he was commiserating with Father, but it was quite a distressing conversation."

George cocked his head. "In what way?"

Father fluttered a hand. "Because one shouldn't speak about such things in polite company."

"But what did he actually say?" Emma asked.

"He pointed out how sorry his son was about the episode," said Isabella. "Apparently, Mr. Barlowe was very upset, too. The squire made a point of saying that Guy was quite concerned for Mr. Barlowe's emotional state."

Emma frowned. "But Mr. Barlowe knew nothing about Prudence's death until the next day. Why would he be so upset?"

"I suppose any right-thinking cleric would be upset about such a tragedy," George replied.

"That cannot be right," Emma said. "Mr. Barlowe told me that he barely knew Prudence. He certainly didn't seem particularly upset by her death."

"It certainly isn't right," Father huffed. "It was poor Miss Bates who suffered the shock of discovering the body, not Mr. Plumtree or Mr. Barlowe. Emma, you must check on Miss Bates. I will not have the squire disturbing her with any more mention of those dreadful events."

"Father, do not upset yourself," Isabella exclaimed in an agitated tone. "Your nerves. What will Mr. Perry say?"

"I will see to Miss Bates," George calmly interjected. "Perhaps she's had enough cards for the evening and would like to watch the dancing."

As he went off to fetch Miss Bates, Emma set to work calming her father and sister's shared agitation.

Her mind, however, was engaged elsewhere. While William Cox was no longer in the picture, Mr. Barlowe had just entered the frame. And wasn't that an interesting development?

Chapter 15

Emma came sharply awake with the sense that someone was watching her. She blinked, blinded by the light of a candle flickering next to the bed. When her vision cleared, she saw that someone was indeed watching her.

Looking like a solemn little ghost in a robe and tasseled nightcap, Henry silently stood by the bed with a candle, waiting for her to come fully awake.

The apple didn't drop far from the Woodhouse tree in that regard. When she was a little girl, Emma had done much the same with Isabella whenever she'd had a nightmare or struggled to sleep. She would tiptoe from the nursery to Isabella's room and stand by the bed, staring at her until she woke up. The first few times, she'd scared Isabella out of her wits. Soon, though, her sister had grown used to her nocturnal visitations and simply lifted the covers to let Emma slide in next to her. Snuggled close to her big sister, Emma's young self had invariably slipped back to sleep safe in the knowledge she was no longer alone.

However, she doubted that Henry was looking for snuggles. Something was clearly afoot.

George was sprawled on his stomach in a deep sleep, apparently worn out by the sedate revelries endured at Mr. and Mrs. Cole's party. Emma took a moment to cover up his shoulders and then slipped out of bed.

"What's wrong?" she whispered to Henry as she felt around for her slippers.

"I saw something," he whispered back.

She finally got her feet into the dratted slippers and grabbed her wrapper from the foot of the bed. Belting it around her, she nodded at Henry to lead the way into the hall.

After carefully closing the door behind them, she eyed his thin, worried features.

"What did you see, dearest?" she asked.

"Lights in the back garden. And I heard something, too."

Emma frowned. "What time is it?"

"Just past three o'clock."

No one should be about at this hour, certainly not on Donwell's grounds.

"What did you hear?"

"There were scraping noises, like . . . like something being dragged over the stones. That's what woke me up. Then I looked out the window and saw lights in the garden." Henry cast a nervous glance down the darkened hallway. "Do you think it might be a . . . a ghost? *Her* ghost?"

Emma gave his shoulder a reassuring squeeze. "Absolutely not. But shall we go to your bedroom and take a look?"

They crossed the hall to his bedroom. Since he'd pulled back the curtains, the room wasn't entirely dark. Emma followed him to the window and peered out into the garden. There was no moon tonight, but the sky was clear and full of stars. The snow-covered lawn gleamed like an ice-covered pond. The bushes were misshapen blots against the white, with the trees stretching their bare limbs to the night sky. It was a forbidding landscape, one entirely empty of life.

"Are you sure you saw lights?" she asked.

He pointed to the left, toward the kitchen and service rooms. "Yes. Just over there, then they disappeared."

She thought for a moment. There was no harm in looking into what it might have been, more to reassure Henry than anything else. Perhaps one of the servants had been up late—a groom, possibly. Although what they would be doing tramping around the garden in the middle of the night was hard to fathom.

Emma took her nephew's hand. "Why don't we go down to the long gallery? We can see almost the entire garden from there."

"Should we wake Uncle George?" he asked, sounding a trifle anxious.

"I don't think so, dear. I'm sure there's nothing to worry about."

Besides, if there were something amiss, she would send Henry running back to fetch George. But she felt confident they were perfectly safe within the strong walls of Donwell Abbey.

They made their way down the shadowed staircase lit by Henry's flickering candle and crossed the great hall into the long gallery. There, the windows ran the entire length of one side of the gallery, affording a look into the garden.

They again saw under the starry canopy no evidence of life but for the tracks of a deer across the snow-crusted lawn.

"I don't see anything," Emma said.

He grabbed her arm and pointed. "Look, over there."

Was that a flicker of light near the old footpath that ran across Donwell's grounds? Yes, it was, and it seemed to be moving *away* from the abbey. Emma hurried down the gallery toward the kitchen to get a better view. At the last window, she stretched up on her toes, trying to see over the shrubbery that partially blocked her sightline.

There it was again. *Two* lights if she wasn't mistaken—lanterns most likely, and they were definitely near the old footpath.

"Do you see it now?" Henry whispered.

"I do. And I cannot imagine what they're doing on Donwell lands at this hour."

He tugged on her sleeve. "Perhaps we should get Uncle George now."

"Drat," she muttered.

Though the lights had moved out of sight, she might still be able to catch a glimpse of them again from the kitchen. Not that she had any intention of stumbling out into the snow, but if anyone had been near the house there would likely be tracks visible from the kitchen doorway.

"Auntie Emma?"

She flashed him a reassuring smile. "Everything's fine, dear. I'm sure they're quite far away by now, but I want to see if someone has come tromping around the back of the house. Then, if there's any cause for concern, we'll wake up Uncle George."

Henry gave her a dubious glance but followed her down the service stairs to the kitchen.

"You're only wearing slippers and a robe," he said. "Your feet will get wet if you go out."

"There are cloaks by the back door, and some clogs stored there as—"

"Mrs. Knightley?"

Emma practically leapt out of her slippers, and her heart *did* leap up into her throat. Slapping a hand to her chest, she spun around. Seeing their footman, she blew out an exasperated sigh.

"Harry, what *are* you doing?" she exclaimed.

Clad only in breeches, stockings, and a shirt hanging down over his thighs, Harry stood in the entrance to the pantry. He held a lamp in one hand and a plate piled high with food—including a large slice of Serle's special plum cake and a hefty piece of cheddar—in the other. He gaped at her and Henry as if he'd just seen a ghost.

"Er . . ." he finally managed to stutter.

Emma eyed the plate in his hand. "Making a late-night raid on the pantry, are we?"

In the lantern light, his expression was comically dismayed. He came out from the pantry and carefully put the plate on the big table in the center of the kitchen.

"Begging your pardon, Mrs. Knightley. I was feeling a mite peckish, so I slipped down for a bite to eat. Mrs. H generally don't mind if I have a little something, now and again."

Emma frowned at another item on his pile. "Is that one of the orange scones that Serle sent over from Hartfield?"

He scrunched up his face. "Um . . . I guess it is."

"Mrs. Hodges *will* have your head if she finds out you've been filching those. They're intended for Mr. Knightley's breakfast."

His eyes popped with alarm. "They're seven or eight left, so I was hoping Mrs. H wouldn't miss one." He grabbed up the scone. "But I'll put it back right away."

Emma finally cracked a smile. "As long as you left the rest, you might as well eat it."

Besides, Harry's hands looked slightly grubby at the moment, so best to let the matter rest.

He blew out a relieved breath. "Thank you, ma'am. And you won't tell Mrs. H, will you?"

"Only if you keep calling her Mrs. H. Harry, how long have you been up?"

He squinted at her and Henry, as if finally registering how odd it was for them to appear in the kitchen in the middle of the night.

"About twenty minutes or so, ma'am. Is something wrong?"

"Henry thought he heard something in the garden, and we both saw lights out there—or, at least, I saw them. They were near the path that leads to Langham."

He frowned. "Lights? Like lanterns?"

"Yes. I was just going to go out and see if there are footprints in the back garden."

He shook his head. "You'll catch your death, Mrs. Knightley. I'll pop out and look for you."

Harry hurried over to the door to the stable yard, slipped on a pair of wooden clogs, and then shrugged into a greatcoat that hung on a peg. When he opened the door, Emma moved her nephew away from the blast of cold air that rushed in.

"Should we go out, too?" the lad asked.

"No, Harry will tell us if he saw anything."

The footman returned a few minutes later, clattering into the mudroom and slamming the door behind him.

"There's no one out there now, Mrs. Knightley," he said, coming down into the kitchen after divesting himself of his outerwear. "I walked past the stable and took a good look toward the path, and I didn't see anything at all."

That wasn't entirely unexpected.

"Did you notice any tracks across the garden?" she asked.

Harry shook his head. "No, but I didn't go round that side of the house. Why would someone be out in the garden at this time of night?"

Emma glanced at Henry, standing quietly by her side. "You're sure you saw the lights in the garden?"

He nodded. "Yes. Farther out, between the stand of oaks and the strawberry beds."

"Mayhap it was someone taking a shortcut home from Highbury to Donwell village," Harry suggested. "Some lads who were visiting friends or at the Crown Inn."

Emma shook her head. "It's too late for the Crown. Besides,

the lights were moving in the other direction, toward Langham. If it was someone coming from the village, they would have taken the other path, straight to Donwell Road."

Harry thought about that for a few moments and then grimaced. "Could it be the poultry thief, Mrs. Knightley? I hear tell he's at it again. Got into some coops over at Plumtree Manor, not three nights ago."

Emma repressed the instinct to voice a most unladylike oath. The blasted poultry thief had been the bane of Highbury's existence these past few years. If he were back in action, her father would have a fit.

"That is decidedly unpleasant news," she said.

And if true, it could very well explain the lights. It made perfect sense that the varlet would utilize the old paths that were seldom used by anyone but the occasional local.

"Do you want me to go back out and check the coops?" Harry asked.

"I think you'd better. And while you're out there, please look for any evidence that someone might have been in the garden."

"Yes, ma'am. Do you want me to come knock on your bedroom door if that bloody—" He grimaced and then corrected himself. "If the thief got into the coops?"

There was little point in that, since the thief would be long gone.

"No," she said. "Just secure the coops, and we'll deal with it in the morning."

"Let me fetch my boots, and I'll have a proper look."

"Thank you, Harry." Emma turned to her nephew. "I think we should get you back to bed before you freeze. Your mother will have my head if you get chilblains."

The boy smiled at her. "I'm fine, Auntie Emma. But Uncle George wouldn't like it if you got cold, either."

"Indeed he wouldn't."

She nodded good night to Harry, and then escorted her nephew out of the kitchen. Now truly starting to feel the chill, she hurried him through the silent abbey and up the stairs to their bedrooms.

"There you go," she said as she tucked him into bed. "Now, with all this excitement you're to sleep as late as you want. You can have breakfast whenever you get up."

The small boy looked even smaller, and rather forlorn as he was almost swallowed up by all the pillows and blankets on the big bed. Emma studied him for a few seconds.

"Henry, is anything wrong?"

He stared at his hands, curled in a little ball over his chest, and then shrugged.

She hazarded a guess. "Do you miss your father, dearest? Do you miss London?"

"Yes," he said in a small voice. "But I like it here, too," he hastened to add. "You and Uncle George are fun."

Emma felt a twinge of guilt. The children had never been away from their father for so long—and neither had Isabella, who was no doubt also missing John very much.

"Perhaps we can write to your Papa and persuade him to make a visit to Hartfield. And don't forget we have a skating party to look forward to. Just a few more days and I think the pond will be properly good and frozen."

As they'd been preparing to leave Mrs. Cole's party this evening, their hostess had petitioned Emma for a skating party on Donwell's pond. Her daughters had recently acquired new skates and were pleading for the treat. Emma had been happy to comply, since it would be a good distraction for Isabella and a lovely outing for all the children.

"Would you like me to stay for a few minutes, until you fall asleep?" Emma asked the boy.

"Yes, please," he said with a shy smile.

She kissed him, and then plucked up a blanket from the back of a nearby chair, wrapping it around her shoulders. Wandering over to the window, she stared out at the night-shrouded garden. All was quiet, the scene a peaceful one under the glittering sky. Whoever had been there was now long gone, taking their business—and yet another mystery—with them.

Chapter 16

Having overslept, Emma hurried along to the dining room. When Henry had finally drifted off, she'd stolen back to bed. George had muttered in his sleep, and then rolled over and wrapped an arm around her waist. Eventually, with the reassuring warmth of her husband's body enveloping hers, she'd managed to quiet her restless thoughts and fall into slumber.

When she'd finally awakened, it was full daylight and George was gone from their room. She'd hoped to speak with him and explain last night's activities before Henry got to him. Her husband would likely be less than impressed with her failure to wake him and instead investigated on her own.

She almost ran into Harry as he exited from the dining room, carrying a teapot.

"Good morning, Mrs. Knightley. I was just going to fetch a fresh pot. Can I get you anything?"

"Are there any of Serle's lovely scones left?" she innocently asked.

He winced. "I believe Master Henry just ate the last one."

"Drat. I was so looking forward to one, too."

Harry's expression conveyed sheepish guilt. He might not be the best footman in England—well, it was doubtful he'd be the best footman anywhere—but his bumbling ways were rather endearing.

"Sorry, ma'am. Can I bring up some muffins? I think Mrs. Hodges just took them nice ones she makes out of the oven."

Emma smiled. "I was teasing, Harry. Is there any coffee?"

"Yes, ma'am. I just brought up a fresh pot."

"That'll do for now."

He bobbed his head and started to hurry down the hall when Emma recalled the question she should have asked him at the outset.

"Harry, what about the chicken coops?"

He half turned to look back at her. "All right and tight, Mrs. Knightley. No sign of the poultry thief or anyone else."

"So no poultry predations. Excellent. And you saw no evidence of anyone else who'd been in the garden or behind the house?"

"Nothing out of the ordinary, ma'am. Just the usual comings and goings from the kitchen to the stable, and from the outbuildings past the gardens."

"Please check again this morning. You could have missed something in the dark." She paused for a moment. "Better yet, have Larkins take a look. He should be made aware, regardless."

"Mr. Knightley already told me to do that, ma'am. As soon as Mr. Larkins comes into the house."

She winced. "So Mr. Knightley knows about last night?"

"Master Henry told him, and then he asked me about it."

Emma sighed. She hated being caught on the back foot, especially by her husband.

"That will be all, Harry. Thank you."

She adjusted her collar and tugged her cuffs into place. Then she plastered on a bright smile and sailed into the dining room.

"Good morning, everyone," she called out in a cheery voice.

Calling out was necessary, since the dining room was enormous. It was one of the largest rooms in the abbey, with circular, recessed alcoves where the sideboards were situated. Several floor-to-ceiling windows lined one wall, adorned with red velvet draperies tied back with black cords. A long, heavy-looking mahogany table in the Jacobean style with matching padded chairs held court down the length of the room. Family lore claimed the room had once served as the refractory for the monks who, one would assume, would be willing to endure the chilly atmosphere for the good of their souls. More than three or four seats away from the fireplace meant one's toes and fingers were likely to freeze at more inclement times of year.

George and Henry sensibly sat at the far end near the merrily crackling fire in the hearth.

Her husband rose and came to meet her. "Forgive us for not waiting for you. I certainly understand why you'd wish to sleep in a trifle."

Emma tried not to wince at his dry tone. "I apologize for being so late. The morning is already half-advanced."

George pushed in her chair as she took her place opposite Henry.

"Not as bad as that," he replied. "And not surprising, considering you were up half the night."

She cast him a reproachful glance over her shoulder. "It wasn't half the night, I assure you."

"No? I am glad to hear it. May I fetch you something from the sideboard?"

"Are there any coddled eggs?"

"There are, indeed. I think toast and jam might be in order, as well. You're looking rather pale this morning, my Emma."

"I'm perfectly fine, George. Please don't worry."

He crossed to the sideboard. "I do tend to worry when I hear that my wife was up in the middle of the night pursuing mysterious intruders."

Emma looked at her nephew, who crinkled his nose.

"Sorry," he whispered.

"It's fine," she whispered back.

"I wasn't exactly engaged in a hot pursuit of villains," she said as he placed a very full plate of food in front of her. "George, I cannot possibly eat all this."

He resumed his seat. "Do your best, please. I don't want you falling ill, especially in this cold weather."

"Now you sound like my father. Which reminds me," she said as she took up her knife. "Please do *not* mention anything about last night to him. Or to your mother," she added, raising her eyebrows at her nephew.

"I won't," Henry replied. "She'd want me to come back to Hartfield."

"I take it that you would prefer to stay with us for the time being?" George asked.

"Yes, please. It's more fun here than at Hartfield."

George's smile was wry. "Apparently so, since there are no potential villains skulking about Hartfield's shrubbery."

Emma sighed. "Henry has clearly alerted you to our nocturnal adventures."

"I cannot be happy you didn't wake me, Emma."

"I understand, but you needed your rest. To be fair, you were dead to the world, George."

"Emma—"

She held up a hand—or, rather, she held up her piece of toast. "I truly didn't think it was anything to worry about. I couldn't see anything from Henry's room, so I thought to pop down to the long gallery to have a look. And there *was* someone out there, George," she said. "But he was quite far from the house by that point," she hastily added when she saw the expression on his face.

"And at *that* point, you apparently decided it was wise to go outside and investigate. In the dead of night and at the opposite end of the house, where I couldn't hear you if anything went wrong."

Emma cast a jaundiced eye at her nephew. "Henry, one thing you must learn as an accomplice is when *not* to share information."

"Sorry, Auntie Emma," he said. "I'll do better next time."

She smiled at him. "I'm sure you will, dear."

"There won't be a next time," George sternly noted. "If either of you ever see anything amiss, you are to come for me immediately. Failing that, send Harry or one of the grooms to fetch Larkins."

Emma regarded him with some surprise. "George, I simply saw some lights on the path leading to Langham. And as it turns out, Harry happened to be raiding the larder, so he went out and checked for me."

Her husband scoffed. "It was by sheer happenstance that he happened to be there."

She thought about that. "Actually, I shouldn't be surprised if Harry raids the larder on a regular basis. I can't think Mrs. Hodges would approve of such behavior."

"Emma—"

"I take your point, dearest. Next time we see lights in the middle of the night, I will fetch you immediately."

"That would be wise," he said in a surprisingly serious tone.

She frowned. "George, why so—"

As the door opened and Harry entered with the tea service, Emma breathed a grateful sigh. She was never at her best when on the receiving end of one of George's scolds, although they were thankfully rare since their marriage. But an early-morning scold with only a sip of coffee was quite intolerable.

"Thank you, Harry," she said. "Have you had a chance to look about the garden, yet?"

He set the tea tray in front of her. "Yes, ma'am. Nothing out of the ordinary, as far as I could tell."

"No unusual sets of tracks?" George asked.

"Not sure what you mean by unusual tracks, sir," he replied. "Everything seemed normal to me. And nothing around the chicken coops except the regular comings and goings from the kitchen staff."

"Nothing *in* the garden?" Emma asked, just to be sure.

Harry paused to think. "I did see deer tracks up by the shrubbery. I expect Mr. Larkins won't be happy, since they trampled some of the low shrubs and made a mess of things."

Emma smiled. "It certainly wasn't deer carrying those lanterns."

"No, ma'am," he replied, completely serious.

George cleared his throat. "Thank you, Harry."

The footman was barely out the door before Henry turned an earnest gaze on his uncle. "But I *know* I saw lights in the garden, Uncle George. Auntie Emma saw them, too."

"To be fair, I only saw the lights out by the path," Emma apologetically said. "And there are apparently no suspicious tracks in the garden."

The little boy crossed his arms and lifted his chin in a stubborn tilt. In that moment, he looked remarkably like his father. "I know what I saw."

"We're not doubting you," George replied in a kind voice. "But at night, distances can be deceiving. Lights can actually be farther away than they appear. But there's no doubt you and your aunt saw something—or someone—on Donwell lands, and that concerns me."

Emma sighed. "Please don't tell me it's the poultry thief. Father will be so upset."

"I doubt it's the poultry thief, either," he rather grimly replied.

Oh dear.

"That sounds ominous, dearest."

Her husband glanced at Henry, as if suddenly realizing that

perhaps what they were about to discuss wasn't fit for younger ears.

Their nephew, however, gazed calmly back at his uncle. "You needn't worry about me, Uncle George. Papa is a barrister. He hears all sorts of horrid things."

Emma raised her eyebrows. "And how do you know about these horrid things?"

"Well... I suppose I overhear Papa sometimes when he talks to Mama about them."

"Apparently you take after your aunt in that regard," George sardonically commented.

"I have no idea what you're talking about," Emma replied in a lofty tone. "And now that it's clear Henry will *not* be shocked, perhaps you can tell us what we saw last night."

"I suspect that what you saw could have been smugglers using the old Langham path on their way to Kingston or Richmond."

Emma felt her jaw sag as she stared at her husband.

"I heard Papa talking about smugglers a few times," Henry said as he returned to his toast and jam. "He said it was much worse back in the old days."

Emma finally recovered her voice. "Smugglers, this far from the coast? We're so out of the way, why would they come here?"

"While the majority of the activity happens on the coast, a significant portion of contraband makes its way up to London by various means," replied her husband. "The goods then find their way into shops in the city, or even into the hands of private citizens who wish to import luxuries like French brandy or Belgian lace while escaping the taxes."

"And these people *know* they're trading in smuggled goods?"

Her husband seemed rather amused by her response. "Indeed. Sometimes they arrange and finance the smuggling runs in the first place."

"I realize I must sound terribly naïve about all this, but it's truly awful, George."

"It is. Still, it's also a very old business and a well-established one. There have been smugglers since the first kings of England began imposing taxation on goods centuries ago."

"That may be so, but I do *not* approve," she huffed, sounding just like her father.

George nodded. "Neither do I, especially when they might be using Donwell lands to make their runs."

Emma shook her head. "I don't understand. Why transport goods along such an old path? It's not exactly convenient."

"That's precisely why land smugglers might be using it. They tend to favor the ancient roads and paths that have fallen into disuse or disrepair. Few ordinary people travel those routes anymore, which makes them perfect for smuggling." He leaned forward, his gaze intent. "Which is why neither of you are to regard this as a trifling matter. These gangs are well organized and know their business. They are not to be taken lightly."

Emma's toast now felt like a lump in her stomach. "I understand, and I'm sure Henry does, too."

Her nephew shrugged. "Papa says you can't really blame smugglers because people hate paying so much tax. He also says lots of people buy things from smugglers—regular people and shopkeepers."

Emma tried to ignore her nephew's alarming insouciance. "George, how did you become aware of this?"

"A few days ago, Constable Sharpe was informed by the revenue agent in Leatherhead that smugglers might be using land routes in the area and possibly selling goods in Highbury and other local villages."

Emma gaped at him. "Who in Highbury would buy contraband goods?"

"You'd be surprised," he dryly replied.

She decided she'd rather *not* be surprised, so refrained from pursuing that line of questioning.

"What do you intend to do?" she asked.

"I'll ride to Leatherhead and discuss the matter with our local revenue agent. At the very least, he should be alerted to this development."

Emma cast a glance at her nephew, who continued to appear remarkably unconcerned. "Do you think there's anything to worry about here at Donwell?"

George gave her a reassuring smile. "Not at all. As a precaution, I'll instruct Larkins to have our grooms and Harry take turns keeping watch over the next few nights. Just to see if there's any more activity on the old path."

"Henry, would you feel more comfortable staying at Hartfield?" Emma asked. "I don't want you feeling unsettled by this."

"I'd rather stay here, if it's all right," the lad stoutly said. "I'm not scared of smugglers."

George's smile turned wry. "I cannot see smugglers using the path with any great regularity. I suspect they'd prefer to avoid Donwell lands, since I'm the local magistrate."

That was a comforting thought—if it was true. Still, Emma felt strangely unsettled. First there was Prudence's tragic death, and now there was a distinct possibility of smugglers in or around Highbury. She would vastly prefer the poultry thief to a potentially dangerous gang of criminals.

Emma had a notion, however, that she wouldn't be getting her wish.

After lunch, Emma and Henry set off for Hartfield. If weather permitted, Henry made a point of visiting his family every day. This time, Emma had decided to accompany him to make sure that all was well at Hartfield in her absence.

As they passed by the turning into Vicarage Lane, Mr. Barlowe stomped toward them, his gaze directed at the ground and a scowl on his face.

"Good afternoon, Mr. Barlowe," Emma said as he came abreast of them.

He jerked to a halt, almost tripping over his feet. "Er, sorry. I didn't see you there, Mrs. Knightley." He looked at Henry. "And, ah . . ."

"Henry," she supplied. "My oldest nephew."

"Of course." He touched the brim of his wide cleric's hat. "If you'll excuse me, I must be off."

"I hope all is well, sir," she replied, rather put out by his rudeness.

His glance darted past her toward the village. "Nothing is wrong, Mrs. Knightley. Goodbye."

He dashed off, giving her no chance to reply.

"Goodness," she said, more to herself than to Henry.

"Papa said Mr. Barlowe is a scrub. I don't exactly know what that means, but I think I agree with him."

Emma choked on a laugh. "A scrub is a low, mean person. It's an exaggeration in Mr. Barlowe's case, although I'll grant his manners leave something to be desired."

A few minutes later found them stepping through Hartfield's front door. Simon appeared from the back hall to take their coats and hats.

"Are my father and sister having tea?" Emma asked the footman.

"Mr. Woodhouse said he would join you after Miss Bates arrives and you go over the household accounts."

Drat. She'd completely forgotten she was to meet with Miss Bates about the accounts—likely because she was dreading the entire process.

She repressed a sigh. "And my sister?"

"Mrs. Knightley is in the drawing room. Should I bring up tea?"

"Yes, please."

John, one of Emma's other nephews, came pelting down the stairs.

"There you are," he exclaimed, bashing into Henry. "I've been waiting for you forever."

Henry gave him a brotherly shove. "I have to see Mama first. Then we can play in the garden."

"Mama's busy writing boring letters. You can say hello later."

The boys gave Emma a pleading look.

She waved them off. "Fine, go play. You can have tea with your mother later."

They chorused their thanks before barreling down the hall. Emma followed at a more reasonable pace, then entered the drawing room to find Isabella seated at their father's writing desk.

"Good afternoon," she said.

When Isabella turned round to greet her, Emma frowned. Her sister looked rather out of sorts.

"Emma, there you are. Is Henry with you?"

"He and John are having a jaunt about the garden but will be in for tea."

Isabella frowned. "I do hope they remembered to wear their gloves."

"Isabella, is everything all right?" Emma asked.

Her sister fluttered a hand. "It's nothing. All is well. Have you seen Father?"

Emma simply stared at her.

Isabella grudgingly laughed. "I could never keep anything from you, could I?"

"No, and it's best not to try. Please tell me what's wrong."

"It's nothing, truly," she replied, rising from the desk. "John is simply being . . . unhelpful."

Now it was Emma's turn to frown. "In what way?"

"I wrote asking if he wished us to return to London. He replied this morning and all but stated he didn't have an opinion on the matter."

As brusque as John could be, he adored his wife and children. "That sounds most unlike him. Did he actually write those words?"

"Well . . . not precisely."

Noting the way her sister was fiddling with her necklace, Emma drew her to a seat on the chaise. "Then what, precisely, did he say?"

"He said that if we were enjoying our stay at Hartfield we should extend it. That he was very busy at work and had very little time to be at home." Isabella blew out an exasperated breath. "John works too hard, Emma. I'm afraid he'll ruin his health if I'm not there."

"Do you want to go back to London?"

"I think so, but I don't want to disturb John if he'd rather be left alone."

"Nonsense. I'm sure he would much rather have you and the children there with him. He's simply giving you the choice because he knows how much you want to support Father and me."

Isabella grimaced. "I do, and I certainly don't wish to leave you in the lurch."

"Don't worry about that. I should probably be at Hartfield for the next little while anyway, since I need to help Miss Bates take over the accounts." She scrunched her nose. "Joy of joys."

That elicited a small smile. "Thank you, Emma. I think we will go home then—but not until after your skating party. The children are so looking forward to it."

Emma sighed. "Of course, the skating party."

"Did you forget?"

"No, I was just ignoring it."

"Emma, I suggest you start paying attention, since it's the day after tomorrow."

Before she could reply, Simon ushered Miss Bates and Mrs. Weston into the room.

"Oh, Mrs. Knightley, Mrs. Knightley," exclaimed Miss Bates. "Look who I ran into in the lane. Mrs. Weston! She was coming to call on Mr. Woodhouse and was so happy to hear that I'd arranged to meet with you. With Mrs. George Knightley, that is."

Emma rose. "Miss Bates, you truly need to start calling us by our given names, or we shall forever be in a state of confusion."

The spinster hesitated. "I can try, but it will seem so very odd."

Isabella smiled at her. "Once I return to London, you'll only have one Mrs. Knightley to worry about."

"I hope I'm not interrupting," interjected Mrs. Weston. "Miss Bates informed me that you were to go over the household accounts."

Emma was happy to forego that particular chore. "We can do it another day, if Miss Bates is amenable."

"Indeed yes," Miss Bates enthused. "It's ever so much better to chat with friends than go over dreary accounts. Not that Hartfield's accounts could ever be dreary, especially with Mrs. Knightley's superior management. Mr. Woodhouse assures me there is nothing to be nervous about, since everything is already so well organized."

"Clearly, I'm a prodigy of household management," Emma cheerfully replied. "But since we've decided to dispense with the accounts, surely we can think of something more enjoyable to speak about."

Miss Bates put up a hand, like a schoolgirl asking permission to speak.

"Yes, ma'am?" Emma said.

"I do have something I wish to discuss—the guest list for the wedding breakfast." She looked apologetic. "I realize it's very soon after that poor girl's death, but Mr. Woodhouse would like the matter settled. He's hoping the ceremony can be held next month, which will give Jane and Frank plenty of time to travel from Yorkshire."

Emma was doing her best to ignore the upcoming blessed event, as well.

Fortunately, she was spared an immediate response when Simon wheeled in the tea cart. The next few minutes were taken up with dispensing cups and filling plates.

After consuming a small meringue, Miss Bates let out a happy sigh. "These are so delicious, Mrs. Knightley. I do hope we can serve them at the wedding breakfast."

"You can have whatever you wish, ma'am. With the exception of cake, of course."

Miss Bates looked crestfallen. "Indeed, no. Mr. Woodhouse would be quite shocked to serve cake at his own wedding."

Emma smiled. "I'm jesting, ma'am. There will certainly be cake. As for the guest list, you can invite whomever you want. It's your wedding, after all."

Miss Bates gave her the sweetest smile. "Thank you, Mrs. Knightley. Sometimes I can hardly believe it. I'm going to be married!"

The rest of us can hardly believe it, either.

Isabella glanced at Emma, clearly trying to suppress a smile, before addressing Miss Bates. "What are your thoughts on the guest list?"

"Since the breakfast is to be held at Hartfield, the numbers will not be large," she replied. "Family, of course. And then just our special friends—the Coles, the Gilberts, Mrs. Goddard, and Miss Nash."

Please, not the Coxes.

"And I rather thought we should invite Squire Plumtree and his son," Miss Bates finished.

"I didn't realize you were friendly with the Plumtrees," said Emma.

Miss Bates set down her teacup. "My mother was very friendly with Squire Plumtree's mother. The entire Plumtree family would sometimes come to Highbury for Sunday services and then stay for lunch at the vicarage." A wistful expression crossed her features. "Those were such pleasant times, and Mrs. Plumtree was such a kind lady. But it was a long time ago, before..."

Before the Reverend Bates died, leaving his wife and daughter on the verge of destitution.

"What made you think to invite the Plumtrees now?" Emma tactfully asked.

Miss Bates brightened. "I hadn't really thought of it until I saw Mr. Guy Plumtree at the party at Donwell Abbey. He's such a lovely young man, don't you think? I just ran into him in the village before I met Mrs. Weston. He was with Mr. Barlowe. They were obviously going off somewhere, but Guy stopped to pay his regards. Such excellent manners."

Emma recalled the curate's odd behavior. "Did they mention where they were going?"

Miss Bates pressed a finger to her chin. "I forgot to ask. But Guy inquired about the wedding preparations and I became distracted—which is so like me, of course. He seemed genuinely interested in our plans, so I thought it only right if we invited him and his father. For old times' sake, you know."

"It would certainly be a kindness," put in Mrs. Weston. "The Plumtrees have not had an easy time of it this past year."

"Why is that?" Emma asked.

"The squire's wife died about nine months ago. While she was always frail in health, her death was unexpected," Mrs. Weston explained. "Squire Plumtree was in London at the time."

Emma grimaced. "How sad. I didn't realize."

"I'm sure it was a monstrous blow to poor Guy," said Miss Bates. "He and his mother were very close, what with Squire

Plumtree in London so much. There was great worry over Guy's health, too, though he grew out of his childhood illnesses. But Mrs. Plumtree still fretted over him."

"I understand that Guy Plumtree was not sent away to school," said Emma.

"Indeed, no. Mrs. Plumtree couldn't bear the thought of it."

"According to my husband," said Mrs. Weston, "Squire Plumtree preferred Guy to remain at home as well. He wanted his wife to have the company. I think he also worried that Guy had received such a sheltered upbringing that he might fare poorly at university. The squire was afraid he would succumb to bad influences."

Miss Bates, who'd been selecting a macaroon from the tea tray, glanced up. "I can understand the squire's concern. Guy was so delicate when he was younger."

Emma couldn't help but feel sympathy for Guy. She also knew what it was like to be smothered by the love of a well-meaning but fretful parent. "He certainly doesn't seem delicate now. What a shame that such a promising young man was denied the same opportunity given to others of his standing."

"True," said Mrs. Weston. "But his father is now determined that Guy take up his responsibilities as his heir, including learning how to manage the estate. According to Mr. Weston, that's why the squire has moved back to Plumtree Manor."

"I'm not sure young Mr. Plumtree is as eager to be a country squire as his father," Emma dryly noted.

Mrs. Weston hesitated. "Mr. Weston says he's terribly spoiled, but I wouldn't really know."

Emma laughed. "He reminds me of Frank—a trifle spoiled but very charming nonetheless. I must say that I like him."

"I think him a terribly nice young person, and his father is truly a good-hearted man," said Miss Bates. "I do think it would be a kindness to invite them to the wedding breakfast, and Guy would be happy for the chance to be social. Of course,

I will have to explain to your father that the squire is really a good man and not like Constable Sharpe at all."

"It's your wedding, ma'am," said Emma. "You should invite whomever you wish."

That led to a lengthy disquisition that mingled gratitude with ruminations on who else should be invited. With a degree of alarm, Emma began to realize she might have spoken too soon. If they weren't careful, they might end up with a guest list that once again included half the inhabitants of Highbury.

As long as no one falls out a window.

It was an ugly and foolish thought, and she put it out of her mind.

Chapter 17

The day had dawned bright and clear, with frost to nip the nose and not a trace of wind. In other words, it was the perfect winter's day.

"Drat," she muttered.

George glanced up from his breakfast. "Is something amiss, my dear?"

"No," she crossly replied. "It's a beautiful day."

"So, no reason to cancel our skating party, I take it."

She returned to the dining table and sank into the chair next to him. "No, and I'm a dreadful person for even wishing we could. But with everything that's been going on, it seems such a bother. And now smugglers, on top of it all."

"Be assured that Mr. Clarke and I have everything in hand."

George had ridden to Leatherhead yesterday to meet Mr. Algernon Clarke, the revenue agent for the Crown.

"I thought you said he wasn't terribly helpful."

"He wasn't *un*helpful, either. Mr. Clarke simply reiterated that the old Langham Path hadn't been used as a smuggling route for some time, which is not to say there hasn't been any activity in the district. He felt confident, however, that there was no cause for alarm for Donwell or the surrounding estates."

"That's reassuring, I suppose," Emma said.

"Mr. Clarke also asked me to keep him apprised of any new developments—not that I expect any."

"I hope you're right. We have enough to worry about these days without dangerous criminals larking about the village."

"Generally speaking, criminals do not lark, Emma."

When she stuck her tongue out, George grinned.

"You know very well what I mean," she said.

"I do. But you're not to fret, my Emma. The skating party will serve as a happy diversion for everyone, including you."

"Dearest, you always have an answer for everything. It's very annoying."

"I live to serve. And annoy."

She had to laugh. "You are the opposite of annoying, George. In fact, you spoil me terribly, and it's no credit to my character that I could complain about a silly skating party. Speaking of which, I should get down to the kitchen to see how the preparations are proceeding."

"I understand the Westons are coming, as well as Harriet and Robert."

"Yes. Now, if you'll excuse—"

The door flew open and Henry pelted into the room. "Mr. Larkins and I just went down to check the pond. He says it's perfect for skating, and he sharpened my skates so they're perfect, too."

Emma ruffled his hair, his boyish enthusiasm lifting her spirits. "I have little doubt you'll outskate everyone today. Now, sit with your uncle and have some breakfast. I'm going to the kitchen to check on our progress."

She spent the rest of the morning overseeing the party preparations, assisted by Larkins and Mrs. Hodges. Harry and the grooms had set up a large trestle table by the pond, and Simon arrived with two enormous baskets of baked goods and treats from Hartfield's kitchens. By the time Larkins built up a fire off to the side, the day was well advanced and the guests would soon be arriving.

Garbed in her warmest pelisse, a wool hat, and her sturdiest boots, Emma made her way to the pond at the base of the garden. It really *was* a beautiful day, with the crust of snow a gleaming white, the sky as blue as periwinkle, and the sun reflecting off the mirrored pond. The bonfire merrily blazed, and the trestle table presented a cornucopia of cakes, pastries, tarts, and pots of hot chocolate and mulled wine. Emma inspected everything with a critical eye before giving Harry, who stood at attention behind the table, an approving nod.

"Everything looks excellent, Harry," she said.

The footman grinned. "Thank you, ma'am. If you wouldn't mind saying a word to Mrs. Hodges, I'd be grateful. She was a mite peeved with me for dropping a pitcher of chocolate on the floor this morning."

Emma mentally winced. Given the cost of chocolate, she could well imagine the housekeeper's response.

Larkins turned from the fire and scowled at the hapless fellow. "Don't be bothering Mrs. Knightley with your foolishness. Go up to the stables and fetch that other bench. We'll need it for the skaters."

"Sorry, Mr. Larkins. I forgot."

"You'd forget your head if it wasn't attached to your shoulders," Larkins sternly replied.

"Happen you're right, sir," Harry said with a comical grimace.

He hurried off in the direction of the stables.

"I apologize, Mrs. Knightley," said Larkins.

"Harry means well, though I know he's something of a trial for you and Mrs. Hodges."

"Aye, but we'll manage." He breathed out a sigh. "It's Prudence we're really missing."

The flash of sorrow that passed over the man's features instantly aged him.

Emma patted his arm. "I know. She was dear to all of you."

Larkins cleared his throat, embarrassed at his display of emotion. "Thank you, ma'am. I think your guests are arriving," he added before swiftly moving to tend to the fire.

Emma went to greet the first arrivals. Harriet and Robert Martin led the way, with Mrs. Weston and Miss Bates following.

Miss Bates fluttered around the trestle table, exclaiming her delight. "Mrs. Knightley, I vow this is the prettiest scene one could imagine. Why, it's like something out of a rousing medieval tale. I can practically see the jousting knights in my head."

Since many medieval tales involved an irritating degree of mayhem, Emma could only hope their day would pass more peacefully.

"You're very kind," Emma said. "Did you come with Isabella and the children? Are they up at the house?"

"I thought to come with them. But Mr. Woodhouse was fretting a bit over the children, so I came ahead to tell you they would be late."

Mrs. Weston looked concerned. "Did you walk all the way from Hartfield? Miss Bates, you must be frozen."

The spinster flapped her gloved hands. "Nothing of the sort. I walk very quickly, you know, and I have these splendid boots that Jane sent for Christmas. I am as warm as toast."

"Still, you must come by the fire," said Emma. "And let me fetch you a cup of mulled wine."

"I'll do it, Mrs. Knightley," Harriet cheerfully offered.

"Thank you, dear. Harry should be returning soon. I cannot imagine what's taking him so long."

A sardonic snort coming from the direction of the bonfire signaled Larkins's thoughts on the matter.

Mrs. Cole and her daughters then joined them, the girls chattering excitedly while their mother profusely thanked Emma for the splendid treat. Robert Martin soon took command, helping the girls and Henry put on their skates before he shepherded them onto the ice.

"Where is Mr. Weston?" Emma asked Mrs. Weston.

"Here he is, coming with Isabella and the children."

Bella and John raced across the lawn as quickly as their little legs could carry them. Mr. Weston escorted Isabella, while George brought up the rear. Harry, several yards behind, lugged the extra bench.

After greeting the children, Emma shooed them off to Robert and Larkins. She went to hug her sister, who was charmingly attired in a hunter green pelisse and matching hat. Isabella appeared more cheerful today, with color in her cheeks and a smile for the other guests.

"Such a lovely pelisse!" Emma exclaimed. "I'm eaten up with envy."

Her sister blushed, her cheeks turning rosy. Emma wished Isabella's annoying husband were here, so he could be reminded how lucky he was to have such a sweet wife.

"I bought it in a shop in New Bond Street, just before Christmas. I do think it's rather nice."

"Ah, a London milliner," said Mrs. Weston with a twinkle. "We provincials can't possibly compete."

Miss Bates clasped her hands together. "You outshine us all—and that is truly saying something, given that Mrs. Knightley and Mrs. Weston are always dressed with such style. I could look at their lovely gowns forever."

"Nonsense," Mr. Weston heartily cut in. "You all look first-rate. Then again, I was never one for frills and furbelows. Leave the fashion to the ladies, I say." He elbowed George. "Isn't that right?"

"I would agree that all our guests are charmingly attired," George tactfully agreed.

"Mr. Knightley, you are always so kind," said Miss Bates. "But I am like a little brown sparrow amongst a flock of kingfishers."

That set off a round of good-natured denials. Emma took the opportunity to speak to her sister.

"Did Father try to talk you out of coming?" she wryly asked.

"I had to promise I would take the children inside at the first sign of a chill."

"No fear of anyone taking a chill," Mr. Weston said, overhearing them. "Not with the capital bonfire Larkins is tending." He slapped George forcefully on the back, making him slide a bit in the snow. "Well done, Knightley. Leave it to you to do everything in style."

Mrs. Weston frowned. "My dear, you will knock Mr. Knightley off his feet."

Now that Harry was back, Emma encouraged the others to avail themselves of the refreshments. The ladies gratefully accepted steaming cups of hot chocolate, while the men partook of the mulled wine, as did Emma. While she rarely imbibed this early in the afternoon, she rather felt she'd earned it.

Her sister raised her eyebrows. "You know Father's opinion on mulled wine. He thinks it much too sweet. Almost as bad as cake."

"I'm aware," she dryly replied. "I have this argument with him every Christmas. Nevertheless, I would suggest that it's a great deal more medicinal than hot chocolate."

"Far be it from me to gainsay Mr. Woodhouse," Miss Bates earnestly said. "But Mother is quite fond of mulled wine. And, of course, Mrs. Knightley—Mrs. George Knightley, that is—would never do anything inappropriate."

When George started to laugh before quickly changing it to a cough, Emma widened her eyes at him.

"Did you wish to say something, dearest?" she asked.

"I wouldn't dream of it," he replied.

After all were supplied with refreshments, the group scattered. The ladies occupied the benches and watched the children, while George and Mr. Weston stood by the fire discussing the state of the last harvest with Larkins. It was a cheerful scene—and all slightly boring.

Emma knew the fault for that lay with her. There were simply too many matters weighing on her mind, including the still-unanswered questions regarding Prudence's death.

And now this vexing issue of smugglers. George had tried to reassure her, but she knew what she saw the other night. Those mysterious lights had been moving away from the house and onto the path to Langham. Henry had also insisted that he'd seen them much closer to the house, possibly even in the garden.

Emma eyed the distance from the gardens to the old path, mentally adding it up. It was really quite near to the house, as it ran right by Donwell on the other side of the kitchen gardens—especially if one took a shortcut across the lawn to reach it. The path proper was just past the stand of oak trees that marked the perimeter of their gardens and lawns.

Perhaps if she took just a quick peek . . .

She glanced around and put her cup on the table.

"Can I get you another one, Mrs. Knightley?" asked Harry.

"I'm fine. If anyone asks, tell them I've gone for a stroll over by the trees to stretch my legs."

Harry registered a vague alarm. "It's a bit icy by that path, ma'am."

"Duly warned."

She slipped around the other side of the bonfire, thankful that the men were too deeply involved in their discussion of corn prices to notice her. Following the edge of the lawn, she made her way toward the trees. When the snow crunched under her boots, she winced and glanced over her shoulder. Fortunately, no one was watching.

Emma slowly circled the trees, looking for footprints or other signs of disturbance. The snow was pristine, glimmering with a coating that was indeed a trifle slippery, as Harry had warned. Treading carefully, she walked toward shrubbery that partially hid the Langham path from view.

Halfway there, she found what she was looking for. There were footprints in the snow, running from the kitchen garden toward the path. She bent down to inspect them, trying to ignore her accelerated heartbeat. The footprints were intermingled, making it challenging to deduce how many sets there actually were.

"Hmm," she muttered. "That one's definitely a different boot from that other set . . . and I think . . ."

Three.

There appeared to be three sets of—

"Mrs. Knightley, what are you doing?"

Emma bit back a yelp as she jerked upright. Her feet slipped, and she began to flail.

Miss Bates grasped her arm, steadying her. "Oh dear! Please forgive me. When I saw you crouching down like that, I thought something was wrong."

"No . . . no, I'm fine." Emma straightened her hat, which had tipped forward over her eyes. "Miss Bates, what are you doing here?"

The spinster peered at her with concern. "When I noticed you were gone, Harry told me that you were taking a little stroll—" She suddenly glanced down at the ground. "Is that what you were looking at?"

George would *not* be happy about this. The last thing he would want was rumors starting to spread about smugglers.

"Yes," she reluctantly replied. "I was a bit surprised to see so many footprints coming from the abbey to the path, but I'm sure it's nothing."

Miss Bates frowned. "Actually that is rather odd, especially at this time of year."

"It's likely just the grooms taking a shortcut into the village—probably to go to the Crown."

"I hate to disagree with you, Mrs. Knightley, because you are generally right about everything, but isn't the shortest way into the village along Randalls Road?"

Miss Bates was more perceptive than Emma could wish at the moment.

She pinned a smile on her face and took her future stepmother by the arm. "I'm sure there's reasonable explanation—"

Miss Bates interrupted her. "Is that a package under those bushes? Yes, it is. Someone must have dropped it."

Emma turned to look. There was indeed a package peeking out from under the shrubbery, just off the trail of footprints.

"Apparently," she said.

She picked her way to the shrubs, with Miss Bates following in her wake, and gingerly retrieved the package. About the size of a brick, it was wrapped in oilcloth and bound with string. It also gave off a distinct, familiar odor.

Cautiously, she lifted it to her nose.

Tobacco.

Emma gritted her teeth. If George had needed proof of smugglers, this would be it.

"What is it? Can you tell?" asked Miss Bates.

Emma thought for a moment. Then she placed the package back where she found it. "Miss Bates, I need you to do something for me."

"Of course, Mrs. Knightley. But why did you put that back?"

"Because I need Mr. Knightley to see exactly where I found

it. Could you please go back and fetch him? Simply tell him that I have something to show him by the Langham Path, and please do it as quietly as you can."

Miss Bates's thin features registered consternation. "Mrs. Knightley, you begin to worry me."

Emma gave her a reassuring smile. "It's nothing, I'm quite sure, but Mr. Knightley will wish to see this. Do you think you can fetch him without attracting much attention?"

"I'll try."

"Thank you."

Miss Bates picked up her skirts and hurried back toward the pond.

While Emma waited for George, she circled to the other side of the shrubbery. There was nothing else to be found there, so the only reasonable surmise was that one of the smugglers had accidentally dropped the package. It was, however, some feet away from the tracks in the snow, almost as if someone had tossed it there.

That made no sense.

And why had the smugglers travelled so close to Donwell in the first place? Were they coming from the direction of Abbey Mill Farm? That also seemed strange, since they would have had to travel across fields and wooded land. Why not just stick to the Langham Path, which would surely be easier for them than trudging across stubbled fields in the snow.

She glanced up when she heard George and Larkins coming to meet her. Unfortunately, they weren't alone, as Mr. and Mrs. Weston followed behind. Emma had complete confidence in Mrs. Weston's ability to keep a secret, but her husband was a different matter. While Mr. Weston did try his best to be discreet, it was often simply too high a hill for him to climb.

George's long strides ate up the distance between them. "I wondered where you'd gone off to. Miss Bates said you found something I needed to see."

"There's Mrs. Knightley," exclaimed Mr. Weston to his wife. "I told you there was nothing to worry about. No crisis in the offing, so no need to rush off."

Unfortunately, there *was* another crisis in the offing.

Mrs. Weston leveled an exasperated look at her husband. "I was not inclined to rush off—you were. I only followed to keep you out of Mr. Knightley's way."

He grimaced. "Dash it, my dear, I'm only trying to help. Miss Bates was in such a tizzy when she arrived back at the pond, it was hard not to imagine at least a minor calamity."

Emma sighed. "Was she truly in a tizzy?"

"Not really," George replied. "Just a trifle rattled. She said you found something."

"I suppose by now everyone knows something is wrong."

Mr. Weston waved a hand. "Never fear, Emma. The children don't realize a thing."

"It's not the children she's worried about," Mrs. Weston dryly replied.

"Dash it," he muttered.

"Emma, perhaps you can show us what you found," said George in a long-suffering voice.

"Of course."

First, she showed him the tracks in the snow. Both George and Mr. Weston crouched down to study them, but Larkins stalked back toward the house, obviously following the trail backward.

Mrs. Weston came over to stand by Emma. "What do you think it means?"

Emma hesitated for a moment. "It would appear we had smugglers crossing Donwell lands a few nights ago."

Her friend let out a small gasp. "Can you be sure of that?"

Emma pointed at the tracks. "I wasn't until I found these, but Henry and I both saw lights near the path that night. They appeared to be quite near to Donwell."

Mr. Weston straightened up from his perusal of the footprints. "Wouldn't surprise me. I've heard rumors for years about land smugglers running through these parts."

Mrs. Weston gazed at him with dismay. "Why did you never mention it, then?"

"It's not really a worry, my dear. Flaskers and owlers have been operating around here on and off forever."

"That's dreadful."

He shrugged. "Leave them alone and they'll leave you alone."

When a marked expression of disapproval gathered on Mrs. Weston's features, Emma hastily intervened to forestall a scold.

"What are flaskers and owlers?" she asked

"A flasker traffics in liquor," replied Mr. Weston. "An owler transports wool." He pointed to his wife's burgundy wool pelisse. "Shouldn't be surprised if that wool didn't come from an owler's hands. I thought at the time you snagged it for a very reasonable price."

"Are you truly suggesting that Mrs. Ford is engaging with smugglers?" Mrs. Weston demanded.

Mr. Weston put up his hands. "I'm not saying that's the case, m'dear, but it happens more often than you think."

Poor Mrs. Weston looked aghast.

"There appear to be three distinct sets of tracks," George said as he joined them.

Emma nodded. "I agree. And, clearly, they were not sticking to the path."

"No," George grimly replied. "That obviously rules out the possibility that they were local people taking the path home at night."

"Perhaps they lived in one of the cottages beyond Abbey Mill Farm and were taking a shortcut," Mrs. Weston hopefully suggested.

"Across fields when there's perfectly good road nearby?" Mr. Weston shook his head. "Unlikely."

"Miss Bates said you found something," George said to Emma.

She led them to the shrubbery. "I put it back so you could see exactly where I found it."

George retrieved the bundle.

"What is it?" Mr. Weston asked.

"Tobacco."

Emma sighed. While she'd been quite certain that's what it was, it was discouraging to get confirmation.

"Why is it wrapped in oilcloth?" Mrs. Weston asked.

"To keep it dry, should the freetraders be forced to toss their cargo overboard," explained Mr. Weston. "They return when the coast is clear and retrieve their cargo from the water. Devilish clever of them, really."

Mrs. Weston rounded on her husband. "I do *not* comprehend your attitude. You seem completely undisturbed by such criminal behavior."

Her husband looked surprised. "I wouldn't say I approve, but the taxes on imports are shocking, which is why smugglers exist in the first place. A body can hardly afford a decent tin of tea these days without paying a king's ransom."

"It's just a shame the smugglers feel the need to conduct their business on my lands," George sardonically commented.

Mr. Weston winced. "Sorry, old man. I wasn't thinking of it that way."

"Perhaps you should," Mrs. Weston tartly said. "The very notion of smugglers at Donwell makes me feel *quite* uneasy."

"I suspect this was a one-time occurrence," said George. "Freetraders are greatly inclined to avoid contact with anyone who might cause them trouble, especially the local magistrate."

"We can only hope," Mrs. Weston replied. "Does Isabella know about this?"

Emma glanced toward the pond. Her sister was now marching toward them, agitation evident in every step. "I think she does now."

Larkins was also on his way back, and he and Isabella converged on their group at the same time.

"Why didn't you tell me that Henry saw smugglers in the back garden?" Isabella exclaimed in markedly shrill tones. "What if they had seen him? You could have all been murdered in your beds!"

Emma tried to capture her sister's flailing hands. "Dearest, I assure you, there was never any danger. We couldn't even confirm they were smugglers at the time, which is why we didn't tell you."

Isabella flapped her hands even harder. "Henry says they were in the back garden! Why would anyone be that close to the house?"

George intervened. "We don't know that they were. As I explained to Henry, it can be difficult to ascertain distance at night. One might think a light is closer than it appears."

Emma suddenly frowned. "Isabella, how did you find out?"

"Miss Bates said you found something, and Henry wanted to go see what it was. When I asked him why, he told me that he'd seen smugglers."

That didn't sound like Emma's nephew. "Henry actually told you that he saw smugglers?"

Isabella hesitated. "Well . . . no. He said he saw lights that night. It was Harry who told Miss Bates it might have been smugglers."

George let out a sigh. Larkins muttered under his breath.

"And why does your footman know about smugglers and I don't?" asked Isabella, winding herself up again.

Emma's patience started to wear a trifle thin. "As I said, we didn't actually know it was smugglers."

"My dear, why don't you take Isabella and Mrs. Weston back to the pond," George said. "I'm sure the others must be wondering what we're doing."

She flashed him a grateful smile. "How rude of us to abandon our guests. I'll take everyone back to the house to warm up."

"That would be wise."

Emma cast Mrs. Weston a significant glance. Her friend gave an understanding nod and then took Isabella by the arm and led her back to the pond, speaking in reassuring tones.

"What are you going to do?" Emma asked her husband.

"I'd like to follow these tracks to see which direction they continue in."

"I'll come with you," Mr. Weston quickly volunteered.

The poor man, having finally realized he'd plunged himself into hot water with his wife, had clearly deemed it wise to avoid her for a spell.

"Emma, please do your best to quell any gossip," said George. "It would be most unhelpful at this juncture."

"I'll try," she replied. "But I fear that cat is well and truly out of the bag."

George briefly cupped her cheek with his gloved hand. "We'll sort it out, my darling. Never fear."

She dredged up a smile for him before trudging back through the snow. Another party with another disastrous outcome. Still, at least no one had died, and for that she was profoundly grateful.

As she made her way back to the others, Emma decided there would be no more parties at Donwell Abbey for *quite* some time.

Chapter 18

Emma studied her breakfast plate with a jaundiced eye. For her to lose her appetite was rare, but yesterday's events had done the trick. Mrs. Cole, upon hearing that smugglers might be operating in the vicinity, had taken her daughters and fled as if a bloodthirsty band of freetraders was hot on their heels. Isabella had reacted in equally an overdone fashion, moaning that Highbury had become infested with criminals and vowing to return to London immediately. Only when an exasperated George had pointed out that the day was too far advanced for travel had Isabella regained a measure of sense.

George walked into the dining room. He'd been up exceedingly early, busy with the repercussions of yesterday's events.

He dropped a kiss on her head. "Good morning, my Emma."

"Good morning, dearest. Have you had breakfast, or have you been too busy searching for smugglers since dawn?"

"I confess I have yet to eat."

Shaking her head at the foolishness of husbands, Emma rose and went to the sideboard. She piled ham, coddled eggs, and a cheddar scone on a plate and took it to him.

"I imagine you think I'll eat all of this," he mildly commented.

"I know that otherwise you'll spend the rest of the day running about without a thing to eat. So, yes."

"You know me too well."

"The study of Mr. Knightley has been a favorite subject of mine since I was a little girl."

He scoffed before taking up his fork.

Emma let him eat for several minutes as she drank her coffee and pretended that everything was just fine. After a few minutes, he shot her a wry glance.

"You *can* speak to me, my dear. I'm capable of doing two things at once."

"Of course, but I didn't wish to disturb you."

"You never could, anyway. To your earlier point, I have been walking the grounds with Larkins. As he noted yesterday, there are suspicious tracks that cut across the back gardens. It's hard to ascertain where they originate, unfortunately, because others cross through the gardens on a regular basis, as you know, including the staff and people coming up from Abbey Mill Farm."

"Has Larkins noticed any unusual activity? He's best placed to do so, given that he's all over the estate on a daily basis."

George shook his head. "No, and he wouldn't see anything after he retreats to his cottage at night. He has no view of the gardens from there and can see the Langham Path only where it intersects Donwell Road."

Emma grimaced. "What do you intend to do?"

"I've already dispatched a message to the revenue agent in Leatherhead to apprise him of yesterday's events. I have no doubt Mr. Clarke will wish to investigate."

"Splendid," she sardonically replied. "Now we'll have a revenue agent skulking about the village. I'm sure everyone will be thrilled."

"Mr. Clarke will simply conduct his investigation and present the results to me and to his superiors. No one in Highbury has anything to fear."

"Nevertheless, Father will be in a complete flap about this. I hope you realize that once Isabella leaves for London, I'll need to return to Hartfield."

"I know. But given the circumstances, I'll have to remain at Donwell for the time being."

Since their marriage, they'd not spent even a single night apart. Still, there was no point in making a fuss over it. "Gracious me, it would seem Highbury *is* turning into a hotbed of criminality, first with murders and now with smuggling."

"Murders?" George looked puzzled for a moment but then sighed. "Surely you're not suggesting that smugglers had anything to do with Prudence's death?"

Emma wavered but then decided to voice her concerns, no matter how improbable. "I know it's an odd connection to make, yet the explanation surrounding her death has always struck me as improbable. What if Prudence *had* discovered something bad but didn't know what to do about it?"

"Is there any indication of that? From one of the other servants, perhaps?"

"Well . . . no."

"Then it serves little purpose to try to connect what are very likely separate events when one lacks evidence."

She was debating whether to argue the point when Henry burst into the room. His coat was open and his hat askew.

"Henry, what's wrong?" she exclaimed, taking in his panicked expression.

George rose and went to the boy. "Sit, Henry. Catch your breath."

"No . . . no time," Henry stuttered. "You have to come right now, Uncle George!"

"Come where?"

"To Mr. Larkins's cottage. Constable Sharpe is trying to arrest him!"

"I walked over from Hartfield to say goodbye to Mr. Larkins," Henry explained as the three of them hurried down the drive to the estate steward's cottage. "He's been ever so nice, and I wanted to thank him."

"Was Constable Sharpe already at the cottage when you arrived?" asked Emma.

"No. Mr. Larkins was making me a cup of tea when the constable banged on the door. He yelled at Mr. Larkins and told him to surrender himself to the law."

"The nerve of the man," Emma huffed. "With you right in the room, too?"

"Mr. Larkins went outside, but I still heard everything. Constable Sharpe said he'd come to search the cottage, and then they got in a big fight. So I slipped by them and ran for you."

George dropped a comforting hand on the boy's shoulder. "That was very quick thinking, Henry."

"I didn't know what else to d-do."

Emma's heart twisted at the quaver in the boy's voice. She'd like nothing better than to box Sharpe's ears for his outrageous behavior. And she just might, yet.

"George, how could Sharpe not tell you of this?" she asked.

Her husband looked grim. "Believe me, I will have more than a few things to say to the constable."

They rounded the curve in the drive to the distressing sight of Larkins standing athwart his doorway, fists raised as if ready to pummel Sharpe. In a pugnacious stance, Sharpe barked back, ordering Larkins to step aside.

Just as dismaying, the scene had attracted an audience. Mr. Gilbert and Mr. Otway were avidly watching from a short distance, taking in every nasty detail.

"This is very bad," Emma said as they hastened forward. "Mr. Otway and Mr. Gilbert will tell *everyone* in Highbury about this."

"Perhaps you can send them on their way," said George, "while I try to calm down the combatants. Take Henry with you."

"But I want to help Mr. Larkins," Henry protested.

"The best way to help is to help send those gentlemen over there on their way."

George lengthened his stride and headed for the brangling men. Emma hastened to intercept the onlookers, who were now creeping forward, obviously the better to hear what Mr. Knightley had to say.

She blocked their path. "Mr. Otway and Mr. Gilbert, I see. How are you?"

"Er..." replied Mr. Gilbert, clearly thrown by her bland comment.

"Have you met my nephew?" She tugged Henry forward. "He's my sister's eldest son, Henry. Dear, please make your bow to Mr. Gilbert and Mr. Otway."

Smart lad that he was, Henry realized she wished to create a distraction from the ugly scene going on behind them.

He gave the two men a courteous bow. "Good morning, Mr. Otway, Mr. Gilbert. It's a pleasure to meet you."

The men exchanged puzzled glances. Mr. Otway managed to pull himself together first.

"It's a pleasure to meet you, Master Henry," he replied. "I hope you've been enjoying your stay in Highbury."

Then he winced, as if realizing how silly that might sound. Henry, however, responded with remarkable aplomb.

"Thank you, sir. I have. We had a splendid skating party on the pond yesterday. I very much enjoyed it."

Oh dear.

Mr. Gilbert leapt into that unfortunate breach. "Speaking

of yesterday, Mrs. Knightley, I understand that you discovered smuggled goods on Donwell's grounds. Most shocking, I must say!"

Emma gave him a regretful smile. "I'm afraid that report is *quite* exaggerated, sir. Nothing was actually found at Donwell, although a packet of tobacco was dropped near the Langham Path. There's no telling who mislaid it."

Mr. Otway frowned. "That's not what Mr. Weston told Mr. Cole. He said it was clear it was smuggled goods."

It was time for Emma to have a little chat with Mr. Weston about his fatal inability to keep his counsel.

"There's no certainty about anything," she calmly replied. "But rest assured that Mr. Knightley is taking all proper steps."

Unfortunately, said Mr. Knightley was currently raising his voice to unaccustomed levels.

"I hate to contradict a lady," Mr. Gilbert said, "but Mr. Larkins and Constable Sharpe had been a hair's breadth from a walloping bout before you and Mr. Knightley arrived on the scene. Constable Sharpe was yelling about smuggling and demanding to search Mr. Larkins's cottage."

Drat, drat, drat.

Henry adopted an expression of angelic innocence. "What's a walloping bout, Auntie Emma?"

"It's best not discussed in polite company, dear," she replied, directing a severe gaze at Mr. Gilbert.

He had the grace to blush.

"Now," she added, "I know this situation seems most interesting, but I assure you it's a private matter between Mr. Knightley and Mr. Larkins."

Mr. Otway frowned. "Then what's Constable Sharpe doing here?"

Emma adopted her best *lady of the manor* stance.

"Since I'm not privy to the workings of Constable Sharpe's

mind, I have no idea," she frostily replied. "But as magistrate, Mr. Knightley will be responding to any concerns Mr. Sharpe may have. *And* as magistrate, he's directed me to ask you to proceed about your daily business. Engaging in idle speculation and gossip will only lead to confusion and misunderstandings. I think we can all agree that would be *most* unfortunate." She gave them a curt nod. "Good day, gentlemen."

Under such direct fire, the two men had no choice but to tip their hats and reluctantly continue on their way to Highbury.

Henry cast her an admiring glance. "Thunderbolts, Auntie Emma! I wish I could do that to people."

"I'm sure you will one day. Unfortunately, this time I suspect it was too little, too late."

By now, the argument seemed to have subsided to a dull roar. Emma and Henry hurried over to the cottage.

Mr. Larkins grimaced with embarrassment. "I'm sorry you had to be exposed to this, ma'am. My apologies."

"There's no need to apologize, dear sir." She glanced at Constable Sharpe and sniffed. "I'm *quite* sure someone else was responsible for this unfortunate scene."

George let out a quiet sigh. Constable Sharpe just glared at her.

"If some people would stop obstructing justice," Sharpe finally snapped, "there wouldn't be no need for a scene."

"I find there is never a need for a scene, Constable," she loftily replied. "And I hope the problem will be sorted before any more locals wander by to witness so unfortunate a performance."

He pointed at Larkins. "That's up to him."

"Constable Sharpe has apparently received information that Larkins is in receipt of smuggled goods," George explained. "He's insisting on searching the cottage."

"That's the most ridiculous thing I've ever heard," she exclaimed. "Larkins would never purchase smuggled goods."

The steward looked grim as death. "That's what I said. But Sharpe, here, he's insisting to nose around in my things."

Emma tsked. "How very rude."

"It makes no difference if it's rude," the constable retorted. "I've got a duty to follow up on the information, especially in light of yesterday's discovery."

"This supposed information sounds very fishy to me," she shot back.

Constable Sharpe bristled like a terrier ready to go down a rat hole, but George held up a restraining hand.

"We have set that matter aside for the moment," he said. "As we know Larkins has nothing to hide, I have convinced him to let you search the cottage—under my supervision."

"Just as you say, Mr. Knightley," Constable Sharpe stiffly replied.

"That's very accommodating of Mr. Larkins," Emma said. "I will keep him company while you conduct the search *under* Mr. Knightley's supervision."

The constable scowled. "There's no need for you to be present, ma'am."

"Nonetheless, I will remain."

"Well, then, I certainly won't have a child at my crime scene," he blustered.

"This is *not* a crime scene," George austerely replied. "I agree, however, that Henry should return to Hartfield."

"But Mr. Larkins is my friend," their nephew protested.

Emma stroked his hair. "Your mother will be wondering where you are, dearest. I promise to come straight to Hartfield once we're finished here."

The lad reluctantly nodded. "All right. Goodbye, Mr. Larkins. Thank you for everything."

Larkins crouched down to meet Henry at eye level. "It's I who should be thanking you, Master Henry. Give my best to your mother, and here's wishing you safe travels back to London."

"Off with you," Emma said, giving her nephew a gentle nudge. He sighed and trudged off toward Highbury.

"Are you finished now, Mrs. Knightley?" the constable asked in a sardonic tone.

Not deigning to respond to his rudeness, Emma swept past him and into the cottage. The warmth inside made her sigh with relief. It was a dreary, cold day, and although engaging in a fractious debate with someone as stupid as the constable may boil one's brain, it did little to heat the limbs.

The estate steward's domicile was an old stone cottage with thatched roof. Although not large, it had been lovingly maintained over the decades, and its current resident had made a number of improvements. The walls were painted a cheery yellow, while comfortable furniture adorned the main room, with the living area set off from a small pantry and basic kitchen. A door to the side of the fireplace led to a nicely sized bedroom, and a steep set of stairs in one corner climbed up to a tidy garret. All in all, the cottage was just right for a bachelor—perfectly cozy and comfortable, and near enough to Donwell to attend to work yet far enough away to provide a spot of privacy.

Emma moved to the cheerfully blazing fire to warm her hands. A kettle hung off to the side, ready to be heated. A plate of scones, along with tea-making necessities, were at the ready on a small kitchen table.

"Can I get you a cup of tea while you wait, ma'am?" Larkins asked.

The poor man looked exhausted. His color was high, likely from arguing with their idiotic constable. Lines scored his face, and his eyes were red-rimmed and shadowed. His gaze seemed haunted, as if something unbearably heavy was dragging on his spirit.

Prudence.

"I'm fine," she said, "but it looks like we interrupted your breakfast. Please do have your tea, Mr. Larkins." She leaned in a bit. "You look like you could use a cup."

He dredged up an answering smile, and Emma could feel the effort he made in doing so.

Larkins jerked his head toward the constable making a show of searching the cottage, even crouching down to look under the small sofa. "I'll have a bit once his worship is done and gone," he said.

Predictably, the constable glared at him. "You won't be getting rid of me that easily, laddie boy."

George narrowed his gaze to irritated slits. "His name is Mr. Larkins, Constable."

Sharpe's only response was to mutter something about *bloody Irishmen* under his breath.

That was *not* good.

When she cast a significant gaze at George, he gave her an unhappy little nod. Larkins had encountered his fair share of bigotry when he'd first been hired, but that had mostly evaporated over the years. Unfortunately, it seemed that the old hatred against the Irish still lurked beneath the surface, at least for Sharpe—who happened to be in a position of authority.

They stood in tense silence while the constable continued to conduct a thorough search. He even thumped down his booted foot on sections of the floor, and once he got on his hands and knees to inspect the floorboards. When he dug through the firebox, looking for heaven knew what, Emma could no longer keep silent.

"Good heavens," she exclaimed. "You can actually see what's in there, sir—just kindling."

"I know my business, Mrs. Knightley," the constable snapped, apparently finished digging. "I'll thank you to let me get on with it."

"And may I point out that you did *not* find anything in the firebox, which is no surprise."

"Emma," her husband warned.

"Really, George, it's all quite absurd. And why is he inspecting the floor like that? One would think Constable Sharpe might be about to effect repairs on a loose board or two."

The constable failed to bristle up, instead giving her an odd little smile, and it sent a chill slithering down her spine.

"An interesting comment about the floorboards, Mrs. Knightley," he said.

"There's nothing interesting about floorboards," she replied.

"We'll see about that."

"Constable, are you finished in this room?" George asked in a long-suffering tone.

"I am, sir. For now."

"Then I suggest you move into the bedroom so we can put this matter behind us as quickly as possible."

The constable stalked off to the bedroom. George followed.

Emma glanced at Larkins, who'd moved to stand by the fireplace. His arms were crossed over his chest as he gazed absently into the flames.

"I'm sure there's nothing to worry about," she said. "This is just a silly misunderstanding."

"I know, ma'am," he calmly replied. "I was that upset that Sharpe made such a fuss and bother in front of Master Henry. That's what set me off more than anything."

"I don't blame you." She lowered her voice. "The constable can be quite annoying. I've had more than one run-in with him, I'm sorry to say."

Larkins seemed about to reply when a triumphant exclamation sounded from the bedroom.

"What in the world?" Emma said.

She hurried over to the door to see Sharpe once more on the

floor. He'd somehow removed a floorboard—it must have been loose—revealing an open space.

"I told you, Mr. Knightley," the constable crowed.

Larkins slid past Emma into the room. "What are you about, man? Why are you taking up my floor?"

Sharpe reached down and extracted a small package, holding it up and waggling it. Emma's heart plunged down to the pit of her stomach.

"A tidy stash you have here, *Mr.* Larkins," the constable said. "Smuggled tobacco it is, hidden under a loose board. That is exactly the information I received."

He reached down and extracted a second package. Both were identical to the one Emma had found in the bushes off the old footpath.

When she glanced at Larkins, his entire expression suggested extreme surprise and shock. In that moment, Emma would swear on the Good Book that Larkins was as stunned as she was. He'd obviously had no idea what had been hidden under the bedroom floor like a hideous secret.

"Larkins, what can you tell me about this?" George asked in a troubled voice.

The steward rubbed an agitated hand over his head. "I don't know what to say, sir. I've never seen those packages in my life."

"So, you're saying that someone snuck into your cottage and stowed them there?" the constable sarcastically asked.

"Well, I damn well didn't put them there," Larkins retorted. Then he grimaced. "Begging your pardon, Mrs. Knightley, but I swear I don't know how they got there."

"I believe you, Mr. Larkins," Emma replied.

"And that board has never been loose, at least not recently," he added. "I would have noticed if it was."

"I'm sure you would have," she soothingly replied. "George, there must be a reasonable explanation for this."

"Larkins, do you lock your door when you leave your cottage?" George asked.

He nodded. "Always, sir. I have some good pieces of silver I inherited from my ma. I'd be that upset if they were stolen."

Emma mentally winced. Clearly, the poor man had no idea that his reply was a problem. His brogue was also starting to manifest itself, a sure sign he was perturbed.

"An enterprising thief could certainly pick the lock to your door," she said.

"Mrs. Knightley, thieves don't pick doors to come in and stash stolen goods," said Constable Sharpe. "They pick locks to come in and *steal* things, not stow them."

Sadly, his logic was sound.

"Constable, the information you received specifically stated you would find smuggled goods under the floorboards?" said George.

"It did, sir."

Emma scrambled to think. "That makes no sense. How would that person even know about the loose floorboard unless he'd broken in and planted those packages himself, to deliberately cast suspicion on Mr. Larkins."

The constable scoffed. "That's a leap if I ever heard one. People don't go around framing people for smuggling and such like."

She stared at him, incredulous. "People *do* frame innocent people, you might recall, even for murder. And, again, how would someone know about a loose floorboard in the bedroom, so as to alert you to its presence?"

"Who said it was in the bedroom?" the constable retorted. "And I don't need to be explaining myself to you, Mrs. Knightley."

"No, but you will explain yourself to me," said George in a stern voice. "My wife has asked a very reasonable question, one I would like answered."

When Sharpe began to protest, George cut him off. "Immediately, Constable Sharpe."

The annoying man grumbled but finally replied. "I received an anonymous note this morning."

"When?"

"Early, it was slipped under my door."

Larkins snorted, his disdain clear.

"May I see this note?" George asked.

Sharpe squirmed a bit. "I left it back at my house."

Emma huffed with growing outrage. "This is utterly ridiculous. The very fact that it's an anonymous note proves my point. Someone is clearly trying to cast suspicion on Larkins, although why they would wish to do so I cannot imagine. It's not as if there's any evidence of smugglers actually *in* Highbury."

"Of course there is," said Sharpe. "He's standing right in front of us."

"I'm no smuggler," Larkins gritted out.

"Constable Sharpe," said George, "I wish to see that note as soon as possible. In the meantime—"

"In the meantime I'll be arresting Larkins for smuggling," Sharpe cut in. "Especially in light of the information you gave me the other day, sir."

Emma could practically feel Larkins vibrating with repressed fury.

"George, surely that's not necessary," she hastily said. "All this shows is that Mr. Larkins's home contained smuggled goods. And although that would certainly be regrettable, possession is hardly a capital crime. As Mr. Weston said the other day, it's a fairly frequent occurrence."

Her husband nodded. "I agree."

"Sir, I swear I don't know where those packages came from," Larkins protested.

"And I believe you," George calmly replied. "We are simply

making the point that simple possession of these items does not justify an arrest."

Larkins grimaced. "But people will already be talking about it. It's my good name that's on the line, and if folks around here think I've been taking in smuggled goods, well, that reflects badly on you too, Mr. Knightley."

"You're not to worry about that now, Larkins."

Emma patted Larkins's arm. "The most important thing is that Mr. Knightley and I believe you. You've not done anything wrong, and there's no reason to arrest you."

"I wouldn't be so sure of that," Constable Sharpe said in a queer sort of voice.

He was still on his knees on the floor. He'd been silent for a few minutes, as he continued to search under the boards.

Carefully, he extracted what looked like a scrap of fabric from the hole. Was that a . . . pink ribbon in his hand?

"What is that?" asked George.

Holding the items with great care, the constable rose to his feet. Then he held them up to the light coming in from the window over the bed.

Emma found a sense of dread creeping over her.

"It's a mobcap, like the kind a maid would wear," the constable said. "And a hair ribbon."

George swiftly took the mobcap from the constable. The plain white cap was indeed the sort of thing a maid would wear as she went about her day. It would fully cover her hair, with minimal trimming.

George turned it over, exposing the other side, and Emma's stomach lurched sideways. She had to struggle to force out the words.

"Is that . . . ?" she whispered.

"Blood," George tersely replied.

Larkins breathed out a groan. Every ounce of color had

drained from his ruddy complexion, leaving him as pale as a corpse.

Constable Sharpe aggressively elbowed George out of the way. "William Larkins, I'm arresting you for smuggling *and* for the murder of Prudence Parr."

Chapter 19

Emma marched into her husband's study. "George, was it truly necessary to ship poor Larkins off to the Guildford gaol? Why could he not be confined here at Donwell until further investigations were made?"

He rose from his desk to meet her. "My Emma, come sit by the fire. You must be chilled to the bone from the walk back from Hartfield."

"My fury with Constable Sharpe has kept me warm enough, I assure you."

George led her to the sofa in front of the fireplace, and Emma gratefully sank down onto the cushions. She *was* feeling a trifle worn out—it had been a very trying day.

When Sharpe made his dramatic pronouncement, Emma had kicked up a tremendous fuss. Surely any self-respecting murderer wouldn't keep a damning clue like a bloodstained mobcap in his house. It seemed obvious to her that the anonymous note-writer had placed them there in an attempt to frame Larkins.

Unfortunately, her arguments had been hampered by the

fact that Larkins had fallen into a strange sort of paralysis, looking as white and lifeless as a marble statue. It was the shock, she supposed, but it didn't help the situation. And although George was inclined to believe Larkins was innocent, he was still the magistrate, so he'd been forced to concede that the items found under the floor were enough to place Larkins under arrest, at least temporarily.

While Sharpe was taking custody of their poor estate steward, George had asked Emma to hurry to Hartfield in order to get ahead of whatever garbled tale was no doubt spreading through the household—and soon farther afield. Of course, the truth was now much worse than what it had initially seemed, but she'd seen George's point.

And a good thing she'd gone, since Henry had returned to Hartfield most upset. That had predictably resulted in Isabella and Father giving free rein to their emotions and kicking up a fuss. It had taken Emma a good two hours to calm everyone down and convince Isabella to delay her departure for London until the morning.

She'd then trudged back home through the cold of a dreary winter afternoon, only to be met with the news that the dratted constable had carted Larkins off to prison.

George added another log to the grate. Once he had the flames crackling to his satisfaction, he straightened up and studied her with concern.

"Can I get you something to drink, love?"

She blew out a frustrated breath. "A sherry wouldn't go amiss, but then I would like some answers."

"Of course."

He fetched drinks for both of them and then joined her on the sofa.

"I know this has been a very distressing turn of events," he somberly said. "But I truly didn't have a choice."

Emma grimaced, desperately sorry for him. While George

had known Larkins for years and greatly depended on the man's support, he also considered his estate manager to be a good friend. Whatever anger and worry she was struggling with, George was bound to be feeling all of it and doubly so.

She pressed a hand to his knee. "I apologize. I let my anger get the best of me. Now, what transpired while I was gone that necessitated such drastic measures as sending Larkins to Guildford? I thought you were going to confine him here at the abbey for the time being?"

"Initially, we held him in the old butler's pantry, with one of the grooms to stand guard." He shook his head. "You can imagine how well that was received by the staff."

"Not well at all, I imagine."

"Mrs. Hodges was exceedingly upset and made no bones about expressing her opinion to Constable Sharpe. He was not well pleased."

Emma briefly smiled. "Huzzah for Mrs. Hodges. Then what happened?"

"We showed her the mobcap." He grimaced. "Frankly, I was afraid the poor woman would faint on the spot."

Emma's fleeting sense of amusement died a quick death. "Of course she identified the mobcap as belonging to Prudence."

"Indeed, and the pink ribbon as well."

That unwelcome revelation prompted Emma to take a fortifying sip of sherry before responding. "She didn't have any doubts?"

"Certainly not about the mobcap. Harry also confirmed the ribbon belonged to Prudence. It was a present from her father at Christmas. Harry said she was very proud of it and showed it to him when she returned to Donwell."

She shook her head. "That's very bad."

"If it's any consolation, both Mrs. Hodges and Harry were adamant that Larkins would never harm Prudence. They were both vociferous in their defense of him, as was our head groom."

"Sharpe was no doubt unimpressed by any of that," she dryly replied.

George extended his booted legs toward the fire, staring moodily into the flames. "Unfortunately, what other conclusion could one arrive at, based on the existing evidence?"

"I can think of one easily—that Larkins was framed by this anonymous person."

"I agree, but the constable was unmoved by that argument, given no evidence in that regard. Nor could I deny compelling prima facie evidence of Larkins's guilt. As such, I had no grounds to prevent Sharpe from carrying out his lawful duties."

"I hope the constable intends to show you the note."

"I made it very clear that he was to do so as soon as he returned from Guildford, as well as report to me anything that Larkins might communicate."

"I take it that Larkins was still declining to defend himself? I simply don't understand why. His reaction seems so very odd."

"I think he's in a state of shock, as well as feeling a measure of guilt."

She frowned. "What can he possibly have to feel guilty about?"

"I believe it stems from feeling that he failed to prevent Prudence's death in the first place. He's always taken on a great sense of responsibility toward all who reside at Donwell. And in Prudence's case . . ."

Emma finished his thought. "He was in love with her."

"Correct, which unfortunately does not help his case. It's clear to me that Constable Sharpe is already casting Larkins as the spurned lover, whose anger and disappointment took a violent turn."

"Anyone who knows Larkins can see that's a ridiculous conclusion. And according to Mrs. Hodges, Prudence didn't even know about his feelings for her." She let out a snort of disgust.

"Constable Sharpe is a menace. First, he insists that Prudence jumped out the window, and now he's trying to cast Larkins in the role of the spurned lover. He changes theories as easily as one changes a waistcoat."

"Unfortunately, the bloodstained mobcap does indeed suggest violence was committed against her. And then there is the presence of the ribbon. One might conclude that the murderer kept it as a keepsake."

Emma couldn't help feeling queasy. Yes, she'd had early suspicions that foul play might have been involved in the poor girl's death, but nothing so close to home or as dramatic as this.

A thought struck her. "How did the constable come to know about his feelings for Prudence? It wasn't common knowledge."

"Mrs. Hodges and Harry were a bit too vociferous in their claims, perhaps, that Larkins would never hurt Prudence."

She winced. "Oh dear."

Sharpe would react to that bit of information like a hound bolting after a fox.

"Did Larkins say anything at all before he was taken away?" she asked.

"He did tell Mrs. Hodges that he didn't do it. Not that Sharpe gave him more than a moment to put on his coat and hat before hustling him into the carriage."

"The poor man. I assume you're going to visit him tomorrow?"

"Yes. I've already asked Mrs. Hodges to pack some essentials, as well as food."

Prisoners—or their families—had to provide for their own needs. Thankfully, she and George could take care of making Larkins's stay in prison at least marginally comfortable.

They both fell silent, staring into the fire and lost in their own dark thoughts. Absently, Emma picked up her glass only to discover it was empty.

George cocked an eyebrow at her. "Would you like another?"

"Best not until I've had something to eat. I should bestir myself and see what's afoot in the kitchen, but I can't bring myself to face Mrs. Hodges yet."

George took her hand and cupped it on top of his thigh. "There's no rush. We all need time to absorb the events of the day."

"I keep trying to make sense of it, and I simply cannot." She held up her other hand. "Just for the sake of argument—and I hate to even think it, much less voice it—let's say that Larkins *did* kill Prudence. Why would he keep those incriminating items? Such an intelligent man would get rid of them immediately, and certainly never take them back to his home."

"I agree. Larkins is the sanest, most even-tempered fellow I've ever met. And when he does express irritation, it's invariably something to do with Donwell rather than a personal matter."

Emma hesitated for a few seconds. "Until Prudence came along. He's changed because of her, especially since her death. I've never seen him so . . . unlike himself."

He frowned. "Emma, are you suggesting that he might be guilty after all?"

She dodged the question. "Has it been determined exactly where Larkins was at the time of Prudence's death? All the other servants have been accounted for, and we know now that William Cox had nothing to do with it."

"I never thought Cox had anything to do with it," he replied. "But to answer your question, not really. Larkins stopped at the Crown for his supper, then walked back to his cottage to await the end of the party. Unfortunately, there's no way to corroborate his claims that he was actually at his cottage the entire time."

"That's not good, George."

"I'm aware."

She hesitated. "Again, just for the sake of argument, what if Larkins *did* declare his feelings to Prudence that night? And suppose Prudence rejected him, and . . . and then they fell into an argument. People can grow heated or even overwrought when it comes to matters of the heart, and it can prompt them to act in ways totally out of character."

"No matter the provocation, I find it impossible to believe that Larkins would deliberately commit violence against Prudence," George firmly said.

"I agree. Something happened in that room, though. Prudence didn't just fall out the window. I can't seem to bring the sequence of events into focus, which is immensely frustrating."

"Perhaps because you're imagining the wrong person in the role of the villain," George calmly replied. "The bloodstained mobcap does make clear that some sort of violence took place. But even if there had been an argument and a dreadful accident—or worse—occurred, Larkins would never try to cover it up. He would take responsibility, no matter the consequences."

She eyed him with a degree of skepticism. "Even if it meant going to the gallows?"

"Even then. I would stake my reputation on it."

Emma felt some of the tension bleed from her shoulders. Of course George was right about Larkins. He would never hurt anyone, much less someone he loved.

"Besides," George added, "I find it highly unlikely that Larkins would declare himself to Prudence under any circumstances. From what you've told me, he knew the girl didn't love him, and he would never put her in so uncomfortable a position."

Emma nodded. "Mrs. Hodges would certainly swear to that."

"She may have to do so at the inquest."

Ugh.

"I forgot about that," she said. "I suppose Dr. Hughes will now call a coroner's inquest."

"Without a doubt. Given the evidence, he has no choice but to empanel a jury to make a determination as to whether Prudence's death was an accident or murder."

That was a gruesome prospect. The inquest into Mrs. Elton's death had turned Highbury into a veritable circus, as people from the surrounding parishes had streamed into the village to watch the proceedings. The thought of going through another such event was appalling.

"If one can't be avoided," she said, "then we must do everything we can there to prove Larkins's innocence."

"Remember, the coroner's jury only determines if murder has been committed. The murder trial itself will take place at the Assizes. That's where Larkins will have the chance to plead his innocence."

Emma suddenly froze. Of course Larkins was innocent, and of course someone was trying to frame him. But thus far their focus had been on Larkins and his dilemma, not on the person who was doing this to him. And certainly not on the person who'd . . .

George tapped her nose. "What are you thinking?"

"That I'm a great fool. We've been so focused on proving to ourselves and that stupid constable that Larkins is innocent that we've barely touched on an even more pressing concern."

His expression was somber. "You mean that the real killer is still out there."

"Yes, the person trying to frame Larkins."

"One would assume it's the same person."

She gently thumped a fist against her forehead. "I am such a henwit. Even Isabella figured it out."

"What do you mean by that?"

"When I arrived at Hartfield, Henry had already told Isabella and my father that Constable Sharpe had tried to arrest Larkins for smuggling. Naturally, Isabella was very upset that Henry had witnessed such a distressing scene." She gave her husband a speaking look. "*Very* upset."

"I'm sorry you had to manage such an unpleasant interlude, although I cannot blame Isabella for her reaction. Constable Sharpe was most remiss in behaving as he did in front of a child—a point I intend to pursue with him."

"I'm inclined to give him a piece of mind as well, but I will defer to your position."

"My dear, you already gave him a piece of your mind," he sardonically replied.

"And I should be happy to do so again."

"It might be best if you held off for now. But, returning to Hartfield, what makes you say that Isabella had the right of it?"

"Because when I told her that Larkins was being accused of murder as well as smuggling, she instantly fell into a fit of the vapors."

George's eyes narrowed. "I don't follow."

"She immediately deduced that the real killer was still on the loose. In the back of my mind, I understood that to be the case as well, yet I was too busy managing the situation to fully grasp it. Isabella, however, was convinced that murderous smugglers were about to descend on Highbury en masse. She was ready to run to the stables and prepare the carriage for departure, on the spot."

"Ah, yes, the smugglers. Isabella's assumption makes a great deal of sense, given that the smuggled tobacco and the mobcap were so conveniently found together."

"First, I find a package of smuggled tobacco on the path. Then Sharpe receives an anonymous tip and goes to find two similar packages in Larkins's cottage along with the bloodstained mobcap. It's all very neat, isn't it?"

"Too neat. It also clearly suggests that this person was close enough at hand to know *when* to plant the items in Larkins's cottage."

She stared at him in abject dismay. "And knew enough about Donwell and Highbury to frame a credible suspect. George, this is *dreadful*."

So dreadful that she found herself longing for another glass of sherry—one considerably more generous than the last one.

"What are we going to do?" she asked him.

"I'll contact the revenue agent again and insist that he make a more detailed investigation of smuggling activity in and around Highbury. I was doing exactly that when you returned home."

"That makes perfect sense, but what about poor Larkins?"

"I'll hire a solicitor for him, though I fear there's little we can do until we can discover who's behind this smuggling scheme. I suspect that will then lead us to the real killer."

"And you're truly convinced of that connection?"

He shrugged. "Nothing else makes sense."

She pressed a hand to her chest, as if to hold back the growing sense of dread. "Do you know what this means? At least one smuggler was here the night of Prudence's death. Do you think anyone connected to Donwell could be part of all this?"

"Do I think any on our staff are involved? Emphatically no. As to our tenants, it's unlikely, although I will follow up on that. But please remember that the house was bursting with people that night. It would have been entirely possible for someone to slip in unobserved."

"Or, perhaps, it could have been a guest at the party. After all, Mr. Weston told me that even wealthy and supposedly respectable people sometimes participate in smuggling."

"Unfortunately true."

Another ghastly thought struck her. "Prudence . . . she was the one involved with the smugglers, wasn't she?"

George now looked as grim as a hanging judge. "So it would seem, but in what way we don't yet know."

Emma rubbed her forehead. "This is so awfully complicated. How will we ever figure it out?"

"As we did last time. One step at a time."

"Last time also involved a great deal of luck, as you recall," she ruefully commented.

"You sell yourself short, my dear. In the meantime, how did you leave things with Isabella and your father?"

"After Isabella regained some composure, I convinced her to postpone her departure until the morning." She crinkled her nose in apology. "I'll have to move back to Hartfield, first thing. I cannot leave Father alone."

He briefly cupped her cheek. "I would expect nothing less."

"Father also wants you to move back to Hartfield with me. He fears that Donwell Abbey has become a den of killers and smugglers. It took some work on my part to disabuse him of that notion."

George cracked a half-smile. "I think it's wise for me to remain at Donwell for at least the next few days. Once the revenue agent arrives, I will reassess the situation."

"I know you will do whatever is appropriate, dearest. You are not to worry about us at Hartfield."

"Perhaps you can enlist Miss Bates to help you. She all but lives at Hartfield as it is."

"Good heavens, I'd completely forgotten about Miss Bates. Father will have told her everything by now, and I'm sure the two of them have perfectly wound themselves up. You remember that the last time we had a killer running about Highbury, I had to keep my smelling salts at the ready for the both of them."

George tipped up her chin and gave her a brief kiss. "I have no doubt you will manage everything with your usual aplomb."

Emma eyed the drinks trolley as she contemplated life for the foreseeable future. "I think I'll take that second sherry now, George."

And make it a generous one, at that.

Chapter 20

Emma's father turned a severe gaze on their surroundings. The ballroom of the Crown Inn had once more been transformed into a courtroom for the coroner's inquest.

"I object to participating in yet another one of these unpleasant exercises," he groused. "For one thing, it is a breeding ground for contagion. Dr. Hughes has much to answer for in that regard."

"Because Mr. Larkins was arrested for murder, a coroner's inquest was required by law," Emma replied. "I'm afraid there's no avoiding it."

Father then turned his ire on another favorite object of scorn. "That Sharpe person seems to think he can go about arresting people, regardless of how the rest of us think. I do *not* approve."

Emma glanced toward the coroner's table, only a few feet away from where they sat in the front row. The constable stood behind it, scowling ferociously at them.

"Mr. Sharpe is right there," she whispered. "He can hear you."

Undeterred, her father continued. "*You* would make a better constable, my dear. Certainly you would never go about arresting innocent people at the drop of a hat."

Miss Bates, sitting on his other side, leaned forward. "Indeed, Mrs. Knightley. You possess such keen intelligence. You would make a splendid constable."

Emma had to smile. "I doubt Mr. Knightley would approve. Nor can I see myself lurking about the village in the dead of night, lantern and staff at the ready to apprehend villains."

Her father gasped. "Emma, recall the danger you faced last summer when Mrs. Elton was murdered. You must promise never to put yourself in danger again!"

"Father, I was simply making a little joke."

"You mustn't joke about murder, my dear. People might misinterpret your meaning."

She sighed. "Yes, Father."

Fortunately, Miss Bates diverted his attention by speaking of her latest letter from Jane Churchill.

Three days had passed since Larkins's arrest. Dr. Hughes, assisted by George, had quickly assembled a jury and convened the inquest. At the moment, the jury was on a break after a long morning of witness testimony. While the jury had retired to another room, most everyone else—a large turnout of locals—had remained and were stretching their legs or consuming their lunches, all while avidly gossiping about the proceedings.

Sadly, the inquest was generally viewed as a form of entertainment by some, who then acted accordingly—sometimes even loudly offering opinions, much to the annoyance of Dr. Hughes. To think Emma had once considered Frank Churchill's secret betrothal to Jane Fairfax the height of drama. Now, Highbury had been the scene of not one but *two* murders, and might be a hotbed of smuggling as well.

Mrs. Weston tapped her shoulder from behind.

"Emma, are you well?" she asked in a low voice.

Forcing a smile, Emma turned in her seat. "I'm fine. Just impatient with the delay."

"This break does seem rather long," Mrs. Weston replied. "Most of the witnesses gave their testimony this morning."

Emma and George had both testified, as had Father and Miss Bates. It had taken a great deal of persuasion on George's part to convince Father that he was required to appear as a witness. Father had seen it as a great affront to his dignity and had made a point of expressing that opinion on the stand, much to the amusement of the locals. At least his testimony had been to the point, unlike that of Miss Bates. The poor woman had tried her best to be helpful, but she'd buried the coroner under her usual avalanche of words.

The one person who would not be called as a witness was William Larkins. Since he'd already been remanded for murder, his testimony was deemed unreliable. Emma and George had done their best to discount the evidence against their steward, but even she had to admit it was incriminating.

Even worse were the testimonies given by Mrs. Hodges and Harry. Both were clearly reluctant witnesses, and their statements had been damning. Mrs. Hodges had been forced to confirm the bloodstained mobcap as belonging to Prudence, and Harry—in his usual awkward fashion—had alleged that Larkins cherished tender feelings for the girl. Dr. Hughes had then asked if Prudence returned those feelings. Harry had squirmed a bit before admitting that he believed such was not the case.

Those observations by the staff had elicited a great deal of murmuring from the crowd. Clearly, many were drawing the disastrous conclusion that Prudence's death had been at the hands of a spurned lover. Knowing Larkins as they did, most of the villagers should have rejected such a ridiculous conclusion but, unfortunately, that now seemed a faint hope.

Hearing a stir at the back of the room, Emma turned to see

three men enter, their coats dusted with snow. Two were so alike they could only be brothers. The other man, although of a strong and upright bearing, was much older. His hair was liberally sprinkled with gray and his complexion was weather-beaten and worn.

"Prudence's father and brothers, I believe," Emma said to Mrs. Weston. "That's who we've been waiting for. They had to travel from Leatherhead."

"The poor men," Mrs. Weston replied in a sympathetic tone. "And in this dreadful weather, too."

George, who'd been at the front of the room with Dr. Hughes, strode down the aisle to meet the Parrs. Naturally, all heads turned to look at the victim's family, some even standing up to do so. Murmurs rippled through the room, following Mr. Parr and his sons as they moved up front.

The group paused by Emma's chair.

"My dear," said George. "Allow me to introduce Mr. Parr and his sons, David and Marcus."

She rose and extended her hand. "Sirs, please accept my condolences on your great loss. We are so grieved for you."

Mr. Parr's hand, rough from his smithing work, engulfed hers. "That's kind of you, ma'am. We're ever so grateful to you and Mr. Knightley for taking care of our girl. She loved working at Donwell, and—"

He broke off, his features distorting with grief.

David placed a hand on his father's shoulder. "It's all right, Pa. You don't need to say anything else."

Mr. Parr cleared his throat as he released Emma's hand. "Apologies, Mrs. Knightley. I can hardly believe my Prudence is gone. It's not right. She should be here with us."

"There is certainly no need to apologize," Emma said. "What happened to your daughter is an utter tragedy."

His grief-stricken expression suddenly turned hard. "It is at that, and I intend that my girl gets justice."

A loud throat-clearing from the dais drew their attention to Dr. Hughes, his usual pompous self. "I believe we are now ready to reconvene. If the witnesses will take their seats, the jury can be recalled."

In quick order, the Parrs were seated at the end of the first row as the jury filed in.

"I now call Mr. Parr, father of Miss Prudence Parr, to the stand," announced Dr. Hughes.

Murmurs of sympathy rose as Mr. Parr took a seat next to the coroner's desk.

Dr. Hughes stood before him. "Sir, if you will please state your full name and your relationship to the victim for the records."

The first few minutes of Mr. Parr's testimony were mostly comprised of mundane details, as well as a brief history as to how Prudence came to work at Donwell. Mr. Parr was also asked to give a description of Prudence's character and temperament. As one would expect, it was glowing. It was also, as far as Emma knew, accurate. That everyone at Donwell thought highly of Prudence was a fact already established.

"When was the last time you saw your daughter?" asked Dr. Hughes.

"It was about three weeks before—" The man clamped his lips shut, as if emotion threatened to overwhelm him.

"Take your time, sir," the coroner said with more kindness than his usual wont.

Mr. Parr struggled for control. "It was about three weeks before her death. Prudence always came home once a month on her day off." He managed a wobbly smile. "She was a good girl that way. Never forgot her family."

More sympathetic murmurings swelled like a gentle chorus. Emma mentally grimaced. Although she felt tremendous compassion for the Parrs, the father's emotional testimony boded ill for Larkins. The portrait being drawn of Prudence was that of a sweet, kind girl who was an innocent victim of a heinous crime. The people would want justice—or vengeance, and Larkins would make a convenient target.

"On her last visit, how did Miss Parr seem?" the coroner asked. "Was she concerned about anything? Did she refer to anything that might be troubling her?"

"I could tell something was bothering her. Not like herself, she was. Prudence was very quiet-like that visit. My boys noticed it, too."

Emma glanced down the row to see the Parr brothers grimly nodding agreement.

Dr. Hughes looked grave. "Did you ask your daughter what troubled her?"

"I did, sir. At first, she tried to brush off my questions. When I wouldn't let it go, she finally said that she was a bit worried about something but was sure it would sort itself out."

"So, she didn't say specifically what the worry was about?"

Mr. Parr shook his head. "No. I asked her if anyone at the abbey was bothering her and she said no, and that it weren't nothing to speak of. When I told her to go to Mr. Knightley about it anyway, she got all bothered and said she wouldn't dream of worrying the master. Then she told me again that it would sort itself out in a few weeks."

Now seated next to her, George exhaled a quiet sigh. Emma placed a hand on his knee, knowing that he still felt that he'd failed the girl.

Dr. Hughes stooped to retrieve an item from a large basket under the table, and then he showed it to Mr. Parr.

"Sir," he asked, "do you know if this lace ribbon belonged to your daughter?"

The blacksmith's face crumpled. "My Davey gave it to her last Christmas. Prudence loved pink."

Emma glanced down the row to see David Parr cover his eyes as his brother placed a consoling arm around his shoulders. A few sniffles could be heard from the women in the crowd, and who could blame them? It was utterly heart-wrenching.

Holding up the ribbon, Dr. Hughes brought it over to the jury box.

"Gentlemen," he said. "This is the ribbon that was found under the floorboards of Mr. Larkins's cottage, and which Mr. Parr has now confirmed belonged to his daughter."

Dark murmurings arose.

"Hang the bastard," someone growled. "He clearly did it."

"Hanging's too good for the likes of him," exclaimed another. "Chop off his bleeding head."

Emma spun in her chair to glare across the room, trying to identify the culprits. Unfortunately, most of the people glared back at her or refused to meet her eye.

"Quiet in the courtroom," barked Constable Sharpe.

"Emma, turn around," whispered George.

She gave one last glower for good measure before facing forward again.

George took her hand. "It does no good to be angry with them. The evidence against Larkins is hard to deny, based on what they've heard."

"But they *know* him, and they know him to be a good man."

"Order in the courtroom," intoned Dr. Hughes.

Since he was obviously directing his statement at her, Emma mustered an apologetic smile. The coroner simply nodded and—surprisingly—moved on. He'd never been a fan of hers, but she had to admit he was conducting the inquest in a fair if rather long-winded fashion.

"Mr. Parr," said Dr. Hughes, "according to the testimony of those at Donwell Abbey, your daughter was not given to strong drink. And yet on the night of her death, there was evidence that she had been drinking spirits, possibly to excess."

Mr. Parr's cheeks flushed a deep red. "That's a blasted lie, or my name's not Parr. Prudence never touched strong drink. Hated the way it tasted. Nor would she risk her job, either by filching a bottle from Mr. Knightley or by getting fuddled."

Dr. Hughes held up his hands. "It is not my intention to besmirch your daughter's reputation, sir."

"You'd best not, you nor anyone else," barked David Parr from the front row.

With a fair degree of tact, the coroner decided to ignore him.

"Only one more question, Mr. Parr," he said. "Do you know if your daughter had a suitor, or was romantically involved with anyone?"

Mr. Parr sucked in a deep breath, as if trying to temper his emotions. "I don't know, sir. I thought she might have a beau, but she was very closemouthed about such things. Which was unlike Prudence, I'll add."

Then the bereaved father's anger slipped the traces again, his voice rising in agitation. "I'll tell you one thing for sure. If she were involved, it weren't with that Larkins." He glared at the crowd. "She'd never involve herself with the likes of him."

The coroner frowned. "What do you mean?"

"A bloody Irishman! I wouldn't stand for it, and neither would her brothers. Everyone knows you can't trust the Irish. They should have stayed in that godforsaken country where they belong." He jabbed a finger at the jury. "Take my word for it—Larkins is guilty of murdering my poor girl, and he'd better hang for it."

As if someone had stuck a pin in her backside, outrage shot Emma to her feet. "I'm very grieved for your loss, sir, but that is most unfair. Mr. Larkins is a good, kind man, and he would never hurt anyone."

Dr. Hughes glowered at her over his too-small spectacles. "Mrs. Knightley, you must not interrupt the witness. Please take your seat."

Emma ignored him and spun to face the jury. "You know

what I'm saying is true. Mr. Larkins has never been anything but good and helpful to everyone here in Highbury. He's been your neighbor for years!"

A tall man in a shabby greatcoat, seated near the back, jumped to his feet. "Parr has it right. You can't trust them Irish. Papists and criminals, the lot of them, and Larkins ain't no different. It's clear as day he killed the poor girl."

For a moment, the room froze in a shocked tableau. Then it exploded into a maelstrom of voices, with the remaining friends of Larkins jumping to their feet to admonish the man in the greatcoat. Others did the opposite, proclaiming their agreement that the Irish could never be trusted. Even the dreadful Anne Cox added to the din, loudly stating to the room at large that everyone knew Mr. Larkins was a *dodgy one.*

Fortunately, Mrs. Cox promptly employed her velvet muff and whacked her daughter into silence.

"Order, order," shouted Dr. Hughes, "or I'll be forced to have Constable Sharpe read the Riot Act!"

He might as well have been yelling into the void.

Emma's father tugged on her sleeve. "My dear, you must sit down! These dreadful people might hurt you!"

By now, George was on his feet. He held up an imperious hand, looking every inch the stern magistrate.

"Ladies and gentlemen," he called out in a commanding tone. "You will cease this commotion immediately. If not, Constable Sharpe *will* read the Riot Act. We will then remove people from the room and apply the full force of the law under the Act."

"Just say the word, Mr. Knightley," barked the constable, "and I'll be happy to oblige."

The combined threats did the trick, and the room was restored to order with astonishing speed. Emma couldn't help notice, though, that the man in the shabby greatcoat took the opportunity to slip out of the room.

Not from around here.

"Good riddance," she muttered.

Her husband grasped her wrist and pulled her back down into her seat. "Emma, I would prefer you not be arrested, either."

She grimaced, now rather appalled by her loss of temper. "I apologize, but I couldn't let Larkins be so besmirched."

"I understand. Nevertheless, you must make allowances for Mr. Parr's grief. I'm sure he doesn't realize what he's saying."

Emma glanced at the man, who was still glaring at the jury. Grief might have driven him to say what he did, but she also felt sure he didn't regret a word. And even if he did, the damage was done.

Now that calm had been restored, Dr. Hughes dismissed the witness. Emma was struck by the fact that the coroner declined to ask the jury if they had any questions for Mr. Parr, which was their right. Most likely he was afraid of another outburst, either from Mr. Parr, the spectators, or . . .

Me.

The next witness was Constable Sharpe, who unfortunately made it clear that he believed Larkins had murdered Prudence. After very briefly discussing the anonymous note that had tipped him off, he described the discovery of the smuggled tobacco packets, the mobcap, and the pink ribbon with what she considered distasteful relish.

"George," she whispered to her husband when the coroner moved on. "This is dreadful. Sharpe has quite glossed over that business with the anonymous note."

"Patience, love," he whispered back.

After the constable finished, Dr. Hughes asked the jury if they had any questions. Mr. Weston, the jury foreman, raised his hand. "Does Constable Sharpe know the identity of the person who wrote the note regarding Mr. Larkins's alleged culpability?"

Emma had to swallow a smile. Clearly, her husband and Mr. Weston had chatted at some point.

Constable Sharpe's pinch-face grew surly. "As I said in my testimony, the note was *anonymous*. So obviously I don't know who wrote it."

"How would the person who wrote even know that Mr. Larkins was in possession of these items, or where they were hidden?" Mr. Weston asked. "Is it not possible that this anonymous person also planted the items under the floorboards so as to divert suspicion from someone else onto Mr. Larkins?"

"A good point, sir," called Mrs. Wallis, the baker's wife. "Seems mighty strange, all this anonymous business."

Some in the crowd rumbled in agreement.

"Remind me to place a *very* large order with Mrs. Wallis next week," Emma whispered to George.

He snorted under his breath.

"Order," rapped Dr. Hughes. Then he turned to the constable. "Please answer the question."

Constable Sharpe left off glaring at Mr. Weston to reply. "The investigation is ongoing, but it could be that the person who wrote it was a smuggler like Larkins, and would therefore know where the evidence was stashed."

"If so, that person is a criminal and hardly a reliable source of information," said Mr. Weston in a disapproving tone. "Therefore, it seems premature to accuse Mr. Larkins of murder, when he may have been set up by this anonymous person for reasons unknown."

The constable looked ready to argue, but Dr. Hughes forestalled him.

"Your questions have merit, Mr. Weston," the coroner said. "And I will enter them into the record. However, we must remember that the only business of this jury is to decide *if* murder has been committed, not *who* did it. That will be decided by a trial at a later date. I will also ask you to defer any additional questions about smuggling until we hear from our next witness."

Mr. Weston nodded his compliance and resumed his seat.

"Constable Sharpe, you are released," intoned Dr. Hughes. "I now call the last witness, Officer Algernon Clarke."

Emma frowned. "Is that . . . ?"

"Yes, the prevention officer from Leatherhead," said George. "He's been watching the proceedings from the back of the room. Observing potential suspects, I would imagine."

Emma swiveled to watch the man walk up the middle aisle. A certain degree of scowling and disgruntled muttering followed in his wake. Clearly, there were those in Highbury who had more sympathy for the smugglers than they did for the officers tasked with preventing their criminal deeds.

Mr. Clarke, who appeared to be of an age with George, was a man of middling height and attractive appearance, neatly and soberly garbed. His features were regular, his expression calm, and he bore himself well. He didn't seem puffed up or particularly foolish, something that could certainly not be said of Highbury's law officers.

"He appears to be a respectable person," Emma's father commented in a lamentably loud stage whisper. "Unlike Constable Sharpe. I was dreadfully shocked by the constable's rude treatment of Mr. Weston."

When ripples of laughter sounded behind them, Emma didn't dare look at the constable, who was probably shooting death daggers at her father.

Mr. Clarke gave George an amiable nod as he took his seat in the witness chair.

"He does seem like a decent sort of fellow," Emma whispered to her husband.

"He's certainly no fool."

Mr. Clarke noted for the record that he'd been a prevention

officer in Leatherhead for almost a year, tasked with investigating smuggling operations and enforcing the law against them.

"It is my understanding," said Dr. Hughes, "that you met some days ago with Mr. Knightley, our local magistrate, regarding suspicious activity on his estate."

"I did. I also confirmed that I was investigating a gang that might be operating in the countryside and villages in this region of Surrey. Early evidence suggests that the gang has been at work for at least two years."

"Alarming news, indeed," stated the coroner. "And do you also believe these smugglers may be operating in Donwell parish, and possibly in Highbury itself?"

"It's certainly possible. It seems they used the old Langham Path on at least one occasion. As for activity in Highbury, it wouldn't be out of the question that some in the village have been in receipt of contraband goods."

Mr. Clarke punctuated his statement by sweeping the room with a stern gaze. Mrs. Stokes, the proprietor of the Crown Inn, suddenly picked up a tray of glasses from a sideboard and hastened from the room. Emma could also hear rustling and uneasy murmurs from the rows behind her.

After Dr. Hughes returned to questioning the witness, Emma leaned into George's side.

"What's going on?" she whispered.

"Mr. Clarke's testimony has obviously discomforted some of our locals," he murmured. "Mrs. Ford just made a hasty exit, as did Mr. Barlowe."

Emma all but gaped at him. "The vicar? Why would—"

"Hush, my dear. You'll interrupt the proceedings."

She did her best to refocus, although her mind boggled at the notion that Mr. Barlowe—not to mention dependable Mrs. Ford—could somehow be involved in smuggling.

"As you know, Mr. Clarke," said Dr. Hughes, "it is not within the purview of these proceedings to involve itself in matters of smuggling per se. There is, however, the potential that the tragic death of Miss Parr might have intersected with criminal proceedings of the type you are wont to investigate."

Mr. Clarke frowned. "Is that a question?"

Emma had to bite her lip to keep an inappropriate chuckle from escaping.

"I'm just getting to that, sir," the coroner huffed.

He ponderously bent to reach into the basket on the floor, his stays creaking as he did so. Retrieving a package, he placed it on the table next to Mr. Clarke.

"Do you recognize that item?" asked Dr. Hughes.

The agent inspected it. "I believe it's from the same shipment that was abandoned a few weeks ago, just outside Dorking. Along with a unit of dragoons, I was in pursuit of the aforementioned gang. The smugglers dropped their goods as they made their escape, and we were able to retrieve some of the packages."

"Only some?" the coroner queried.

"As it was a moonless night, it was difficult to ascertain whether the entire load was dumped."

"But you're sure *this* particular packet is from that load."

"Yes, because it's wrapped and tied in an identical fashion." He sniffed the packet. "Same tobacco too, unless my nose fails me."

Dr. Hughes walked over to the jury with the packet. "This is one of two packages found under the floor of Mr. Larkins's cottage, along with the items belonging to Miss Parr."

There was a commotion at the end of the front row. Emma leaned out to see Mr. Parr drop his head into his hands. His sons, looking anguished, tried to console him.

Dr. Hughes cast the family a sympathetic glance before returning to the front of the room.

"Mr. Clarke," he said. "Given this evidence, would it be reasonable to assume that Mr. Larkins is part of the smuggling gang you've been pursuing?"

Emma had to tamp down a flare of outrage on Larkins's behalf. Her father, however, felt no such compunction.

"That is a dreadful assumption to make about poor Larkins," he announced to Miss Bates. "I do not approve of Dr. Hughes asking such a leading question."

The coroner shot a baleful glare their way. Father, as usual, was oblivious.

Mr. Clarke regarded the coroner with unimpeded calm. "Without further evidence, I cannot speak to your question about involvement in the gang. All I can say is that he was in receipt of contraband goods. While that of course is illegal, it's not an unusual state of affairs anywhere in England."

Dr. Hughes looked nonplussed by that reply. "Er, yes, just as you say. Does the jury have any questions for Mr. Clarke?"

Mr. Weston glanced at the other members of the jury, who all shook their heads. "We do not, Dr. Hughes."

"Very well. Mr. Clarke, you are excused."

The imperturbable agent rose from his chair and made his way to the back of the room, ignoring the blatant curiosity of the crowd.

Dr. Hughes then noted that the only thing left at this point was the coroner's summation to the jury. With his usual pomposity, he proceeded to review the evidence in excruciating detail. Then he postulated two theories as to why Prudence had been murdered, both of which cast Larkins in a very bad light. Emma considered it most unseemly that the coroner would choose to speculate as to the motive behind a possible murder, rather than sticking to the evidence at hand.

First, the dratted man speculated that Prudence had been murdered for spurning a lovelorn suitor. Even though Emma had suspected that could have been the case with William Cox, hearing Dr. Hughes outline the particulars of that theory made her realize how thin it was. She'd seen Prudence's room herself. Aside from the open window, there'd been little sign of disturbance and not one that suggested a desperate struggle.

The coroner's second theory was directly tied to smuggling, suggesting that the killer was indeed part of a smuggling gang. Dr. Hughes postulated that Prudence had somehow discovered that her murderer was involved in this criminal endeavor, and for some reason had confronted him. In so doing, she'd sealed her own fate.

Emma reluctantly admitted that the second theory was a great deal more plausible than the first. Prudence had obviously been murdered, and smuggling was indeed taking place in the environs of Donwell. But how, exactly, had the girl's life intersected with the activities of the shadowy gang? It was a question begging to be answered, not left to vague speculations.

Once Dr. Hughes finished his summation, he sent the jury off to begin deliberations. Most people in the room quickly came to their feet, thankful for the opportunity to move about. Emma did the same, and contemplated going for a short walk down the high street. The room had grown almost unbearably stuffy and, this late in the day, odiferous as well.

Emma's father touched her arm. "I'm going to escort Miss Bates back to Hartfield. She is most distressed by the dreadful accusations made against poor Mr. Larkins."

"You mustn't worry about me, sir," Miss Bates earnestly exclaimed. "Although I am indeed terribly shocked by what has been said about Mr. Larkins. I've never met a gentler person than Mr. Larkins—excepting you, Mr. Knightley, and of course my dear Mr. Woodhouse. Oh, and dear Mr. Weston, who has always been so generous to Mother and me. But I grow quite faint at the very notion of Mr. Larkins locked away in that hideous gaol. However will he survive?"

Emma was a great deal more concerned about Larkins escaping the gallows than surviving the gaol.

"There's no need for either of you to stay," she said to her father. "I'll return home as soon as the verdict is rendered."

"Very well, my dear. But do not linger. I heard someone cough only a few minutes ago."

Naturally, their exit took several minutes since Miss Bates wished to make her goodbyes to half the room. Father finally took his betrothed by the elbow and marched her out.

"George, I am constantly amazed by the changes in my father since his romantic involvement with Miss Bates," Emma commented. "He has certainly developed a more forceful personality."

"I suspect it has more to do with his fear of contracting a contagion," he dryly replied.

Mrs. Weston tapped George on the shoulder. "How long do you think it will take the jury to arrive at a verdict?"

George checked his pocket watch. "Not long, I would imagine. The physical evidence was compelling."

"I have to echo Father's complaint about Dr. Hughes's concluding statement," Emma said with disapproval. "There was an astounding degree of speculation."

He grimaced. "I was also not well pleased. Remember, though, that the coroner's inquest doesn't determine guilt."

The three of them then chatted in a desultory manner for ten minutes or so, waiting for the jury to return.

"Ah, here they are," said George, glancing across the room.

Emma sighed. "I suppose it's no wonder that they came to such a speedy conclusion."

They resumed their seats as the men filed in.

"Gentlemen of the jury," said Dr. Hughes once they were seated. "Have you reached a verdict?"

Mr. Weston stood. "Yes, Dr. Hughes. We have determined that murder has been committed."

Excited murmurings rippled throughout the room, even though the verdict was no surprise.

"Order, please," called Dr. Hughes. "This matter shall now be turned over to Constable Sharpe for investigation. Mr. Knightley as magistrate is to be kept informed of all developments, and I will expect to receive regular reports as well."

Mr. Parr, red in the face, jumped to his feet and jabbed a finger at the constable. "And *I* expect to see justice done, with that bloody Irishman swinging from a gibbet."

Emma heard George's exasperated sigh as the room once more descended into a ruckus.

Chapter 21

Emma picked up the teapot. "Miss Bates, would you care for another cup?"

Her future stepmother waved a fluttering hand. "I don't think I could squeeze in another drop. Dinner was excellent, as it always is at Hartfield. Mother and I are forever talking about Serle and how well she does everything. We're quite convinced she's the best cook in Surrey. Of course, Mrs. Weston's cook is also excellent, and the Coles certainly set a fine table. But no one can compare with Serle, of that I feel sure."

Emma's father, sitting next to his betrothed on the sofa, graced her with an approving smile. "It gives me a great deal of pleasure to know you think so highly of our good Serle. After all, once you move to Hartfield, you will be drawing up the daily menus and giving her direction."

Miss Bates looked more than slightly alarmed at the notion, and Emma couldn't blame her. Giving Serle direction on anything was always daunting. Aside from sketching out basics for the daily menus, Emma generally left all their meal planning up to their formidable cook, and that was exactly how Serle preferred it.

Fortunately, the pedestal clock chimed out the hour, sparing Miss Bates a reply.

"Goodness, I had no idea it was so late," she said. "I must be getting home to Mother. She'll want to hear everything about that dreadful inquest today." She sighed. "Poor Mr. Larkins. I feel wretched thinking about him sitting in that dreadful prison."

Emma's father shuddered. "They are breeding grounds for every sort of nasty contagion. As much as we are all concerned for Larkins, George, you must promise me that you'll not visit him. You might catch something and bring it home to Emma."

"There's nothing to worry about, I assure you," George replied in a soothing tone.

Naturally, he failed to mention that he'd already made one visit to the gaol since Larkins's arrest three days ago. The poor man was in very low spirits, protesting his innocence but convinced that no one would believe him.

"Miss Bates, will you allow me to escort you home?" George asked as he stood.

"Dear sir, I would never dream of taking you out of your way. It is only a short walk to the village. I will be perfectly fine."

"It's no trouble, ma'am. I'm returning to Donwell regardless, so I can easily escort you."

"You must call the carriage," Father protested. "It is too long a walk, and Miss Bates should not be out in such weather."

"There is no need for that, sir," George replied. "The night is quite mild, and there is no wind."

When Father looked ready to argue, the distant sound of a knock on the front door forestalled his objections.

Emma frowned. "Who would be calling at this time of night?"

"It might be Mr. Weston," said George. "He wished to speak to me after the inquest, but we never found the opportunity."

The drawing room door opened to admit Simon. "Mr. Knightley, it's Mr. Clarke. He'd like to speak to you."

"That's odd," said Emma.

"There's only one way to find out," said George. "Simon, have him—"

"Show Mr. Clarke into the drawing room, please," she hastily intervened.

When George raised his eyebrows, Emma shrugged. "You'll have to tell me anyway, so you might as well let me hear it firsthand."

He made a scoffing noise, but nodded at Simon to follow her instruction.

Emma beamed at her husband. "Thank you, dearest, that's very considerate of you."

"As if I had a choice," he dryly replied.

"Oh dear!" exclaimed Miss Bates, all in a flutter. "Should I leave? Mr. Clarke won't wish to discuss his business in front of strangers."

"You cannot leave without George to escort you," Father fretfully said. "Emma, tell Miss Bates to stay."

When Mr. Clarke appeared, he looked slightly taken aback at the presence of a small audience but recovered quickly. He greeted them with quiet decorum, and offered a perfectly respectable bow to Emma and Miss Bates.

"I beg your pardon for disturbing your evening, Mr. Knightley," he said.

"I hope there's nothing urgent that brings you to Hartfield this evening," George replied.

Mr. Clarke shook his head. "I'm off to Guildford tomorrow, and then I'll be returning to Leatherhead for a few days to follow up on my investigations. I thought it best to apprise you of my actions beforehand."

George gave him an affable nod. "I appreciate the courtesy."

By which comment Emma deduced that prevention officers weren't obligated to report to local magistrates.

"I take it you're going to visit Mr. Larkins tomorrow," she said. "May I ask why?"

Mr. Clarke cast her an odd look, as if wondering why the lady of the house would ask such a question. Emma was used to that reaction. Women in general—and ladies in particular—did not involve themselves in criminal investigations. Experience had taught her, however, that the so-called weaker sex was just as likely to arrive at the proper conclusions as a man. Call it what you like, but Emma trusted her instincts, and certainly more than she trusted either the instincts or capacities of Constable Sharpe or Dr. Hughes.

"Yes, ma'am. I intend to question Mr. Larkins about his possible role in the smuggling gang that's at large in your district," the officer replied.

Miss Bates let out a little shriek. "Gracious! One cannot possibly imagine Mr. Larkins as a smuggler. He's the most honest person one could hope to meet. Why, he's been nothing but helpful to Mother and me. Just last month he brought us a lovely ham from Donwell Abbey. Of course, we owe so much to the generosity of our dear Mr. Knightley, but I know for a *fact* that Mr. Larkins always makes sure we get the best of everything."

"Very true," Father concurred. "Larkins is an excellent fellow. I do not approve of people besmirching his name in so hasty a manner. One should resist the temptation to jump to conclusions, like that dreadful Sharpe person did at the inquest."

Mr. Clarke eyed the pair on the sofa with a slight air of consternation, not that Emma could blame him. If one had never encountered the eccentricities of her father or Miss Bates, one couldn't help but feel a degree of bewilderment.

"I'm sure Mr. Clarke will avoid any temptation to make hasty conclusions," George tactfully intervened. "He's simply performing the required duties of his office."

The prevention officer nodded. "My only interest is in discovering the truth and bringing the guilty to justice."

"Then the only thing you'll discover with Larkins is his innocence," said Emma. "He should never have been detained in the first place."

Mr. Clarke shrugged. "Perhaps. However, given the evidence, I can understand why Sharpe and Dr. Hughes reached the conclusions they did."

Emma frowned. "Sir, only this afternoon you stated that you did *not* believe there was sufficient evidence to convict Mr. Larkins of anything more than possession of contraband tobacco. Are you now suggesting he is part of the smuggling ring? Or even guilty of murder?"

"I haven't changed my thinking, ma'am. I have yet to see conclusive evidence that Mr. Larkins *is* part of a gang. Nor is it my business to speak to the murder charge, unless that becomes directly relevant to the smuggling charges. Therefore, I wasn't prepared to make speculative statements for the record. Still, I have no choice but to proceed with a full investigation, and that includes interviewing Mr. Larkins as both a principal witness and a potential suspect."

Emma leaned forward, holding his gaze. "Sir, I know what the evidence might suggest . . . does suggest. But Larkins *is* innocent, of both murder and smuggling."

"Exactly so, Mrs. Knightley," said Miss Bates. "Mr. Clarke, let me assure you that Mrs. Knightley is always right in these matters. Why, only last summer, she saved us from a terrible fate. I still shudder to think about it!"

Mr. Clarke frowned. "What happened last summer?"

George hastily intervened before the discussion could go down *that* rabbit hole. "Nothing that's germane to this case. I will say, however, that I concur with my wife's opinion. Despite the evidence, I firmly believe Larkins is innocent, and that there are other forces at work here."

"Evil forces," Father proclaimed in dramatic tones.

"Heavens above!" exclaimed Miss Bates, falling back upon the sofa cushions.

Mr. Clarke cast a longing glance toward the door, clearly

wishing for an escape. Emma had to choke down the impulse to laugh.

The prevention officer, however, gathered himself. "I realize that Mr. Larkins is a trusted member of the Knightley household. Nevertheless, I've known respectable merchants to be heavily involved in these sorts of activities, and so have gentry. I've even known of cases where clergymen were directly involved with the gangs."

Miss Bates looked speechless with horror. Well, almost speechless. "The clergy! Every notion of good conduct revolts at the very idea."

"Very true, ma'am, but the fact remains that some clergymen have played roles in the trade, from direct involvement to simply turning a blind eye to what goes on under their noses."

Now that you mention it . . .

Emma found it all too plausible to imagine that their curate, Mr. Barlowe, was involved in a smuggling scheme. Not as a smuggler himself, of course. The man was scared of his own shadow. But she could, perhaps, see him quietly turning a blind eye so as to be compensated with contraband goods. That might be one explanation for both his excellent tea and his collection of expensive spirits. Most important, it would address his odd behavior these past few weeks whenever the subject of smuggling or Prudence came up.

"I refuse to believe that *our* Mr. Barlowe would be involved in anything so nefarious," Miss Bates stoutly replied.

"I defer to your superior local knowledge, ma'am," said Mr. Clarke. "Still, I wouldn't be surprised to hear of people in Highbury who are knowingly in receipt of contraband goods at this very moment."

"Emma," Father exclaimed, growing agitated. "Tell Mr. Clarke that such a thing cannot possibly be true."

Instead, Emma and George exchanged a quick glance before her husband rose to his feet.

"Mr. Clarke, thank you for keeping me apprised of your plans. I'll do everything in my power to assist you."

"Thank you, sir. It's always welcome to have the support of the local magistrate and law officers."

He gave Emma and Miss Bates a courtly bow before quietly departing the room.

Miss Bates fanned herself with her handkerchief. "I hardly know what to think, Mr. Woodhouse. Can there truly be such goings-on in our beloved Highbury? It's too dreadful to contemplate!"

"Then we shall not do so," responded Father as he patted her hand. "Although Mr. Clarke seems a respectable man, he *is* from London. Since the city teems with criminals, he must be in the habit of seeing villains lurking behind every bush."

Emma refrained from pointing out that villains were, in fact, doing some lurking about Highbury.

"Mrs. Otway told me after the inquest that she suspected Mrs. Ford of receiving smuggled wool," Miss Bates morosely said. "I refuted the very notion at the time, but now I must wonder if she might be correct."

Father huffed. "Nonsense. Mrs. Ford found me the most excellent pair of fur-lined gloves, just last week. She knows all about the danger of chilled hands. So sensible a woman would never engage in criminal activities."

Perceiving that her father and Miss Bates could go on in this vein all evening, Emma made a concerted effort to soothe their anxieties. She replenished their teacups and suggested they reread the contents of Isabella's latest letter. Once the pair was properly diverted, she joined her husband on the settee by the French doors.

"What a gruesome day," she said.

"One in a long line of gruesome days, I'm afraid. I've written to John about securing legal representation for Larkins. At some point, I'll have to go up to London to meet with whomever he chooses."

"Poor George. As if you don't have enough to do already—and now without Larkins."

"I'll manage." He cast a look at her father. "Besides, you have challenges aplenty at Hartfield."

She ruefully echoed him. "Yes, I'll manage, though I hate that we cannot be together. I'm afraid I'll have to spend most of my time at Hartfield. Father will fret too much without me."

"I'll come to Hartfield for dinner every evening. And we must hope that these matters resolve themselves sooner than later, so life can return to normal."

"But how? It's such a tangle, George. Smuggling, murder . . . how is it ever to be sorted?"

"Mr. Clarke will get to the bottom of it," he calmly replied. "In any event, we have no choice but to allow the investigation to play out."

Emma found herself contemplating the notion of choices. Was their only choice, in fact, to rely on the work of others?

Perhaps her hands were tied when it came to the murder investigation. But when it came to the issue of smuggling, especially as it affected Highbury, she believed there were, at least, a few avenues to pursue on the way to the truth. Nothing dramatic, mind you—just a conversation here and there with people who would be reluctant to speak to Mr. Clarke.

They wouldn't be reluctant to chat with her. Of that, Emma felt quite sure.

Chapter 22

"Mrs. Knightley, do hold up!" cried a familiar voice.

With a sigh, Emma turned to wait for Miss Bates, who was hurrying through the village square to join her. Avoiding uncomfortable questions was why she'd snuck out of Hartfield so early this morning. She'd not counted on Miss Bates's preternatural ability to be precisely where Emma did not wish her to be.

The spinster fluttered up to her like a little wren darting among the hedgerows—albeit a wren sporting a luxurious velvet muff that dangled from one wrist. Garbed as she was in her sensible brown pelisse and plain bonnet, the enormous and undoubtedly expensive muff presented quite the contrast.

"Good morning, Miss Bates," Emma said. "You're out early."

"Yes, I popped down to the bakery to place an order for an apple tart and tea cakes from Mrs. Wallis. Mrs. Goddard and Mrs. Martin are coming by this afternoon, and I wished to have something special."

"They will be happy for the treat," Emma replied. "But you must be busy, so don't let me keep you."

"Always so kind, Mrs. Knightley, but Patty will take care of everything. She's so capable, as you know."

Patty, the Bateses' maid, was indeed efficient, and Emma was running out of excuses.

Miss Bates cast her an inquiring look. "When I saw you pass by the bakery, I couldn't help but wonder why *you* were up so early. Are you off to Donwell Abbey?"

Drat.

"Actually, I'm on my way to Ford's," she reluctantly replied. "I thought to stop in first thing, before Mrs. Ford got busy."

"I suppose Mr. Woodhouse is needing new gloves? But, that cannot be right. You got him new gloves just last week."

"No, but I think he might—"

Miss Bates waved her arms. "I know! You're going to speak to her about what Mr. Clarke said last night, aren't you?"

Emma hastily stepped back to avoid being clocked in the chin by the enormous muff.

"Do forgive me," Miss Bates said, wrestling the muff under control. "I quite forget I have this around my wrist."

"It's, er, rather large," Emma replied.

Miss Bates flashed her a shy smile. "Your father gave it to me for Christmas. It's much too extravagant for me, but he insists I use it on cold days. Since I'm going to Hartfield after my errands, I thought to wear it."

"I . . . I didn't know Father gave you such a lovely gift," Emma said, trying to stifle a laugh.

The muff was indeed quite lovely, though much too large for a petite woman like Miss Bates.

The spinster leaned in, as if confiding a secret. "I've never worn muffs, since I always forget about them or misplace them. But now I don't wish to disappoint Mr. Woodhouse."

"It's splendid, and you should absolutely wear it. Now, if you'll excuse me—"

"Mrs. Knightley, I think I should go with you," Miss Bates said with uncommon determination. "Mrs. Ford might feel a *trifle* nervous regarding this subject. Why, I lay awake half the night just thinking about it! Since she and I are such particular friends, she might feel more comfortable answering questions if I'm there."

Emma had to admit that Miss Bates had been surprisingly helpful these last few weeks. She possessed such a kind presence and everyone loved her. Certainly, no one could feel threatened by her.

"Very well, but we must be careful and discreet. This is a very delicate situation."

When Miss Bates clasped her hands, the muff banged against her torso. "How exciting! I feel as if I'm living in the pages of a thrilling novel."

"Not a very good one," Emma dryly commented.

"Oh dear, I suppose that's true. I promise I will be as quiet as the proverbial church mouse while you interrogate Mrs. Ford. And no one will be able to compel me to give up *any* information we might learn, no matter how great the pressure."

Emma eyed the woman's earnest expression, rather wondering if Miss Bates had a secret predilection for sensational novels.

Highbury was starting to bustle. It promised to be a fine day with clear skies and a refreshing nip to the air. They exchanged hellos with a few of the townsfolk and nodded to Mr. Gilbert as he doffed his hat and rode by on his mare.

A glance into the wide bay window at Ford's, gaily festooned with a display of winter hats, assured Emma that no other customers were present. Those bonnets, however, gave her pause. The high feathers and trim they sported were rather too extravagant for a milliner in a place like Highbury. For the first time, she wondered how Mrs. Ford managed to so often stock her establishment with merchandise of higher quality than one would normally see in a village this size, and at reasonable prices at that.

Only one way to find out.

The little bell over the door jingled them in. Mrs. Ford was behind a long counter. Her attention was focused on a ledger, but she quickly glanced up and hurried over to greet them.

"Mrs. Knightley, Miss Bates, good morning. What brings you out so early?"

Highbury's milliner was a woman of both sensible demeanor and dress. Her gowns were well tailored but never showy, as if she preferred the focus to remain on her merchandise rather than herself. A widow of some years, her entire life revolved around the shop and her loyalty to her customers. Ford's was an institution in their village, and its proprietor had always been considered above reproach.

Until now.

"Miss Bates and I wished to speak to you before you got busy," Emma said.

"Oh? How can I be of assistance?"

"I have a question—just a little one, really. It's about something Mr. Clarke mentioned at the inquest."

Mrs. Ford sucked in a startled breath.

Emma hesitated, but then decided there was nothing for it. "As you might recall, he raised concerns about smugglers having some influence in Highbury. Naturally, one doesn't wish to believe anyone in our village would be involved in such things. I was wondering, perhaps, if you could shed some light on Mr. Clarke's observations."

"I don't see how I possibly could," Mrs. Ford stiffly replied. "I know nothing about how smugglers operate, here or anywhere else."

"Of course not," Emma said in a soothing tone. "And why would you? But we were just wondering—"

"If you've ever been in receipt of smuggled goods," Miss Bates bluntly interjected.

Mrs. Ford turned as white as the cravats displayed in her shop.

So much for making the poor woman comfortable.

Miss Bates reached over and took the shopkeeper's hand. "Dear Mrs. Ford, please don't be angry with me. No one believes you could be in league with those horrible smugglers. I almost fainted dead on the spot when Mr. Clarke suggested it!"

The poor woman began to look ill. "Mr. Clarke thinks I'm smuggling contraband goods?"

Emma put up her hands. "He simply suggested that the occasional shipment of smuggled goods *might* have found their way into some of the local shops. He has no intention of accusing anyone."

"That we know of," Miss Bates added with lamentable candor.

"What?"

Emma winced. Mrs. Ford had *quite* a loud screech.

"Ma'am, there's no need to panic," she said. "Mr. Clarke's attention is focused on the smuggling gang, not on Highbury's merchants. I promise you that."

Mrs. Ford made an effort at composing herself. "Mrs. Knightley, what do you want me to say?"

"Only the truth. As you know, Mr. Larkins has been accused of murder *and* smuggling. My husband and I are convinced that both charges are false. Naturally, the murder investigation is out of my . . . our hands, but I do think we can assist Mr. Clarke in ascertaining if there is evidence of smuggling in Highbury." She gave Mrs. Ford an encouraging smile. "And who better to ask than you, who knows everyone in our village?"

Mrs. Ford's chin tilted up, and she began to look unfortunately stubborn. "I'm still at a loss as to what you think I might know, Mrs. Knightley."

Emma could be stubborn, too. "You deal with any number of merchants and suppliers, many of them in London. Have you ever seen any indication that they might be passing on smuggled goods to Highbury's shopkeepers?"

Mrs. Ford stared back, obstreperously silent.

Miss Bates again touched her arm. "It's for Mr. Larkins. You know he's a fine man, and think of all the good he's done for Donwell's tenants. If we cannot help him, who knows what will happen?"

"He'll end up on the gallows," Emma grimly said.

"I know," Mrs. Ford finally said. "And I do wish to help the poor man. All I can say is that if Mr. Larkins is involved in smuggling, I've heard no tale of it from the other shopkeepers in the village."

"Nothing against him, not even rumors?" Emma asked, wanting to be sure.

"Not a word."

"Thank you," Emma replied. "Now, please don't think I'm judging you, but is it possible that you may sometimes be in receipt of contraband goods from some of your suppliers? The quality of your merchandise is comparable to that found in many expensive London shops. How do you manage it?"

The woman grimaced. "Mrs. Knightley, you're married to the local magistrate. I don't know how to answer such a question."

"My husband's *only* interest is in discovering who murdered Miss Parr and clearing Mr. Larkins's name. I promise you, anything you tell me will go no further than Mr. Knightley."

Of course, George probably wouldn't approve of her making such promises, but Emma was convinced there was no other way.

"My lips will also remain forever sealed," Miss Bates stoutly added.

Mrs. Ford cast her a dubious glance. Miss Bates had the least discretion of anyone in Highbury, with the possible exception of Mr. Weston.

The spinster held up a hand. "I vow on my father's grave."

The milliner blew out an exasperated breath. "Very well. I

do wonder if one of my suppliers receives contraband goods, especially the Belgian lace and a few other items." She pointed to the hats in the window. "The feathers, for one. You might have noticed the quality."

Emma nodded. "I have. Is this a London supplier?"

"No, a peddler. He visits about four or five times a year, around the biggest market days. He sells to me and also sets up a stall in the square."

Emma slowly nodded. "I think I know him."

In fact, she'd bought lace and ribbons from the man on a few occasions. Mrs. Ford was correct—the quality of his goods was excellent.

"Does he ever mention where he sources his wares?" she asked.

"No," Mrs. Ford reluctantly replied. "I suppose I should have pressed him more about that."

"I could say the same about myself," Emma candidly replied. "I've bought his goods without giving it a second thought."

The milliner gave her a grateful smile.

"Is there anyone else you can think of who might know something about smuggling in Highbury?" Emma asked.

Mrs. Ford's smile changed to a grimace. "I don't like to tattle, Mrs. Knightley."

"Again, I assure you of our discretion."

"Indeed," said an earnest Miss Bates. "I won't say a word to anyone."

Mrs. Ford finally gave a reluctant nod. "You might try Mr. Cox, ma'am. He might be able to tell you a thing or two about smuggled goods in Highbury."

Emma frowned. Mr. Cox was Highbury's solicitor. It was difficult to imagine that he was involved with smugglers.

"Do you mean Mr. Cox?" she cautiously asked. "Or William Cox?"

Miss Bates let out a little squeak, obviously realizing the import of her question.

"I don't really know," replied Mrs. Ford. "But there's been a bit of gossip about the Coxes and their fine living these past several months—living beyond their means. Mr. Cox is very proud of his snuff, at least according to Mrs. Cox. She was boasting about the quality of his Martinique just the other day. And then there's the French brandy. I heard William Cox waxing on about it when he came to pick up gloves a month or so ago. He bragged to his sister that not even Mr. Knightley or Mr. Weston could drink anything finer."

Well, well, well.

It would seem William Cox was back in the picture, after all.

"Thank you, Mrs. Ford," said Emma. "You've been very helpful, indeed."

"More tea, Mrs. Knightley?"

Emma heard the perplexed tone in Mrs. Cox's question. The poor woman had no idea why she and Miss Bates had dropped in unannounced, especially since Emma had never once visited them, nor had the Coxes to Hartfield.

It was also much too early in the day to make social calls. The Cox girls had apparently not even finished dressing. Still, Mrs. Cox had sent the housemaid up to fetch Anne and Susan, who had just appeared. Emma found that most unfortunate, since the less time spent with those two, the better.

The object of her prey, William Cox, had stepped out on an errand but was expected back shortly. Miss Bates had easily solicited that information. Since the spinster actually *was* a friend of the Coxes, her polite question hadn't seemed out of place.

Emma smiled at their hostess, who clutched a large floral teapot to her chest like a shield against unwanted intruders.

"Thank you, Mrs. Cox," she replied. "It's delicious tea. Souchong, I believe?"

The woman tentatively smiled. "Yes, that's right."

"I don't know when I've had a finer cup of tea," enthused Miss Bates. "One could imagine this tea served in the best households in England, including Hartfield, of course. The tea at Hartfield is always superior."

Anne tossed a ringlet over her shoulder. "I'm sure *our* tea is as good as anything served at Hartfield. William gets it for us, whenever he goes on one of his little jaunts to London with his friends. He always brings back the nicest things."

Mrs. Cox frowned. "Mind your manners, Anne. There's no need to make comparisons."

"It wasn't me making comparisons," the girl protested. "It was Miss Bates."

That naturally led to an extended and garbled apology from Miss Bates. Normally, Emma would have intervened, but she was too caught by the information the girl had inadvertently revealed. While the family certainly lived in decent style thanks to Mr. Cox's profession, they weren't wealthy. Nor had William yet taken up his father's profession. So how could a young man with limited resources find the means to buy such high-quality goods?

Emma had a growing conviction that William's new friends had something to do with it.

Once Miss Bates finished her garbled apology, an awkward silence fell over the room.

It wasn't the first, Emma was sorry to note.

After leaving the milliner's shop, she and Miss Bates had determined to immediately follow up on the promising lead provided by Mrs. Ford. Although the decision might have seemed a bit hasty, Emma knew there was no time to waste. There was simply too much at stake, for one thing. For another, once George found out she was making inquiries, he would be none too pleased. Better to proceed with useful information in hand rather than seek approval first.

And, yes, he would be annoyed with her, but he *would* listen. While George might not approve of her methods, he always listened to her. It was a splendid quality in a husband.

Anne finally broke the silence. "Mrs. Knightley, I found that

Mr. Clarke ever so interesting. You know, at the inquest yesterday. I was wondering what you know about him."

Mrs. Cox winced with embarrassment. "Anne, that is hardly an appropriate question."

"No one else has anything to say, so I thought I might as well ask," she pertly replied. "The inquest was so dreadfully boring, except for Mr. Clarke."

"There's nothing boring about murder, Miss Cox," Emma replied in a clipped tone.

Miss Bates looked shocked. "Indeed, no. That poor girl, and poor Mr. Larkins. One feels for his predicament."

"But isn't he guilty?" asked Susan. "Everyone seems to think he's guilty, so surely he must be."

"Mr. Larkins's guilt is very much in doubt," Emma replied. "My husband and I certainly do not believe him to be guilty."

"Nor do I," Miss Bates added. "Such a kind, good man."

Anne waved an impatient hand. "But no one really knows, do they? Besides, that's not what I was asking Mrs. Knightley about, anyway. I wish to know about Mr. Clarke. Do you know if he's married?"

"Oh, Anne," her mother sighed.

Susan stepped into her sister's unfortunate breach. "Mr. Clarke is quite handsome, even if he is a revenue officer."

Miss Bates looked confused. "How does Mr. Clarke's profession affect his looks?"

"Because most people hate prevention officers," Anne replied with a stunning lack of logic. "But who cares if he arrests smugglers? He was dressed quite smart, too, which means he must have some money."

Mrs. Cox looked ready to die a thousand social deaths. Emma could well sympathize. Having a daughter like Anne would make one wish for a swift and merciful end.

"To answer your question, Miss Cox," Emma dryly replied, "I have no idea of his marital status. Nor am I inclined to find out."

"Of course not," Mrs. Cox hastily said.

Anne ignored her mother. "I tried to get his attention after the inquest, but he was too busy talking to that silly Constable Sharpe."

"Maybe he'll return to Highbury," Susan said in a hopeful voice. "If there are smugglers running about, I expect he'll be investigating."

Anne clapped her hands. "That would be splendid."

Be careful what you wish for.

As if summoned by her thoughts, Emma heard someone come in through the front door.

"That must be William," Mrs. Cox said with relief. "Anne, why don't you fetch him? I'm sure he'd like to say hello to Mrs. Knightley and Miss Bates."

Anne scoffed. "No, he wouldn't. Not after he embarrassed himself at Donwell Abbey."

"Fetch him anyway."

"Why can't Susan do it?"

"Because I asked *you*," her mother sharply replied.

Anne got to her feet and flounced out of the room.

Mrs. Cox gave Emma an apologetic smile. "I beg your pardon, ma'am. I'm sure William will be happy to see you, especially after you so kindly forgave him for his unfortunate behavior."

He won't be happy for long.

William and Anne entered the room a few moments later. When he caught sight of Emma, he pulled up short, causing his sister to barrel into him.

Anne gave him a shove. "La, Will, don't be such a clumsy oaf. What will Mrs. Knightley think of you?"

Mrs. Knightley was thinking that William Cox was completely unnerved, even frightened. It seemed an extreme reaction when she had yet to even ask him a question.

"William, make a proper bow to Mrs. Knightley and Miss Bates and then come sit down," ordered Mrs. Cox.

The young man somewhat recovered, making a bow and then taking a seat as far from Emma as possible. He gave every appearance of preparing to bolt from the room at the first sign of trouble.

She made no immediate attempt to break the silence, instead perusing the young man with a calm gaze. He began to fidget, taking up a napkin from the table and beginning to pleat it. A steady silence could be unnerving, a trick she'd learned from observing George over the years.

William Cox was decidedly unnerved.

Mrs. Cox glanced between Emma and her son, looking puzzled. "Mrs. Knightley, I do not wish to be rude, but do you have something you wish to discuss with William?"

Emma kept her gaze on the young man. "Mr. Cox, you seemed taken aback when you first saw me. Why is that?"

He crumpled the napkin in his fist. "Did I? Gosh, I . . . I suppose it's because you've never called on us before. Yes, that's it. I was quite surprised to see you here."

"That's very true," said Anne with a dismissive sniff. "I don't know why Mrs. Knightley never thought to do so before. It's not as if we're farmers or that low sort of people."

Emma had to refrain from scoffing, since Anne had been in hot pursuit of Robert Martin, a farmer, before Harriet married him.

Mrs. Cox glared at her daughter. "Anne, hold your tongue." Then she looked at Emma. "Ma'am, is there some reason *why* my son should be discomposed to see you, other than your presence in our parlor?"

Emma pulled the trigger. "Yes, there is. I believe William is now or at least has been involved with the smuggling gang operating in the vicinity of Highbury. I'm guessing your son's reaction has something to do with that."

Mrs. Cox gaped at her, stunned into silence. Sadly, her daughters were not.

"Mrs. Knightley, how could you say such an awful thing?" Anne hotly declared. "He would never do anything so stupid and vulgar."

Susan nodded so vigorously her curls danced. "Anne's right. William would never do anything so dreadful."

"I'll bet that Harriet Martin is the cause of all this," Anne said with a sneer. "She's always been jealous of me, so she decided to get back at me by telling fibs about William."

Really, Anne was *the* most annoying girl. "It may be difficult for you to believe, Miss Cox, but this isn't about you. Not unless you've been helping your brother with his smuggling activities."

Anne's only response was to bluster, while Susan simply burst into tears.

"Oh dear," said Miss Bates. She extracted a handkerchief from her reticule and handed it to Susan.

Mrs. Cox regained her voice. "Mrs. Knightley, I'm incredulous that you would make such an accusation against my son. Please remember that my husband is a solicitor and an officer of the court."

"I mean no disrespect to you or your husband, ma'am," Emma replied. "Believe me, I wouldn't level such a charge if I didn't think it absolutely necessary."

"I'm certain my son has nothing to do with smuggling. I cannot imagine where you would get such a notion."

Emma nodded at William who, at the moment, looked like a rabbit cornered by a fox, paralyzed with fear. "Look at your son, ma'am. And please remember that you *have* been concerned for him as of late."

Mrs. Cox gazed at her son. His only response was to duck his head to avoid her searching eye.

"But William's been ever so much better since he started courting Miss Nash," Susan pleaded. "He would never do anything to displease her."

At the mention of his sweetheart, William turned a stricken gaze on Emma. "Please don't tell Miss Nash what I've done, or my father. He'll disown me if he finds out."

"Finds out that you've been involved with the smuggling ring?" Emma gently asked.

He squeezed his eyes shut.

Mrs. Cox rose from her seat and crossed to him. "William, tell me the truth. Is what Mrs. Knightley saying true?"

He opened his eyes and gazed miserably up at his mother. "Yes, but I stopped doing it months ago. And I didn't go on many runs in the first place, I swear. It was all just a lark, Mama. Really!"

Mrs. Cox fixed him with an astounded stare for several excruciating moments. Then her arm flashed up and she boxed her son's ears.

"Ouch!" yelped William. "Mama, why did you hit me?"

"Because you've disgraced this family, you foolish boy! Whatever will your father say—you've ruined him!"

At that, Susan descended into full-blown hysterics and even Anne started to cry. Ignoring her daughters, Mrs. Cox continued to berate her son. He began to defend himself while also pleading with her not to tell his father.

The din was considerable.

Miss Bates grabbed Emma's arm. "Mrs. Knightley, what should we do?"

"Use your smelling salts on Susan and try to calm her down."

Emma rose and reached for Anne's shoulder, giving her a shake. "Miss Cox, try to control yourself before the servants hear you."

Anne's dramatic sob ended on a prosaic hiccup, and her tragic expression transformed into a glare. "This is all your fault, Mrs. Knightley. We shall all be ruined."

"You will be if you don't cease acting like a henwit," Emma ruthlessly replied.

Then she inserted herself between the brangling mother and son. Never had she thought to be in the position of protecting an impudent pup like William Cox from his own mother, but it *had* been a very strange day.

And it wasn't even noon yet.

"Mrs. Cox, you must let me speak with William," Emma firmly said. "It will do no good to continue berating him."

"He deserves a good scolding, and then a trip to the woodshed!"

"I'm a grown man, not a boy," her son protested.

"What you are is a criminal, and I never thought to see such a day," Mrs. Cox replied in a quavering voice.

Emma gently guided the poor woman back to her chair. "I'm sure William did think it was just a merry lark to begin with. Young men can frequently be foolish."

Not that she'd had much experience in that regard, but William seemed typical of the breed.

"Mrs. Knightley, what are we to do?" Mrs. Cox dolefully asked.

Emma directed her attention to William. "First we will need the truth from you—all of it."

The young man spread his arms wide. "I didn't mean anything by it. You must believe me, Mrs. Knightley."

"I shall if you tell me the truth. Do not forget, a man's life is at stake."

He blinked. "You mean Mr. Larkins."

"Yes."

"But everyone knows Larkins was involved with the smuggling," Anne exclaimed. "And killed that maid, too."

Emma narrowed her eyes on the girl. "Miss Cox, do you think that for one blessed moment you might behave like a rational person?"

Anne subsided with a sullen glare.

"Thank you. Now, William, do you know if Mr. Larkins was involved with the smugglers in any way?"

He shook his head. "I never saw him or heard tell of him. I never heard anyone else mention his name, either."

Emma expelled a relieved breath. "You're certain of that?"

"Yes, ma'am. I never heard anyone mention him or Donwell Abbey."

Thank God.

"Are any of the smugglers from Highbury?"

"No. I never saw them before I . . ." He grimaced. "You know."

"Began smuggling."

"It really wasn't for that long," he miserably said. "And like I said, I didn't go on that many runs. It started off as a lark, just as you said, but then it began to feel dangerous. I didn't want anything more to do with it after that."

"How did you get involved in the first place?" asked Emma. "Where did you meet those men?"

"In a tavern in Kingston-on-Thames. I used to meet a few friends from London there, now and again."

"I told your father those London friends of yours were a bad influence," his mother bitterly said. "Your friends in Highbury weren't good enough, I suppose."

William grimaced. "Mama, you're embarrassing me."

"I think we're well beyond that," Emma noted. "You met those men in a tavern. And they convinced you to join their smuggling ring."

"Not the first time I saw them. They just seemed like bang-up fellows, and we fell to talking. So I met them again a few times after that."

"What are their names?"

"Dick and Bill Smith. They're brothers." Then he frowned. "Although they didn't look like brothers at all, come to think of it."

Emma resisted the impulse to whack him with her reticule. Was it really possible for someone to be so stupid?

"I doubt those were their real names. I presume you can identify the tavern, though."

He gave her a hesitant smile. "Oh, yes. I can do that, at least."

Emma waited. "And?"

"Oh, um, it's the Eagle and the Hare."

"Thank you. Now, how did they convince you to participate in these activities?"

"Because I was stupid," he said with a sigh. "They made it sound like it was such a jolly. Like everyone did it, and there was nothing dangerous about it. And also a bang-up way to make extra blunt."

Miss Bates tilted her head like an inquisitive wren. "What's blunt?"

"Money," Emma said. "Did they also pay you in goods?"

"Yes. Tea, mostly, and a bottle of brandy every now and again."

"But you told us you got those nice things from your friends in . . . in London," hiccupped Susan.

He grimaced, while his mother simply sighed. Clearly, the Cox family hadn't bothered to question too closely why their son was able to bring home such largesse.

"All right," Emma said. "Tell me exactly what you did and how it worked."

In a halting tone, William explained that he occasionally went on the runs for about six months. Mostly, he helped transport small casks of spirits along the abandoned roads or deserted trails that intersected this part of Surrey, trails that ran up from the coast on their way to London. The contraband goods were usually hidden in abandoned sheds or occasionally in barns—sometimes with the cooperation of the farmers, sometimes not.

"That's when I became worried," he confessed. "Most of the farmers turned a blind eye, but there were a few who didn't and, well, the smugglers threatened them."

"How, exactly?" Emma asked.

"They told one fellow they'd burn down his barn. And . . . and worse."

She had no desire to inquire into the specifics of *worse*.

"William, were you able to ascertain if those men were part of a larger operation?"

He nodded and went on to explain that the runs were well organized and apparently happened at least twice a month.

"They knew what they were about," he finished. "I thought it was just a few fellows, at first—like I said, more of a jolly than anything else." He grimaced. "Pretty stupid of me, I guess."

Anne scoffed. "How could you be such a dimwit? I wouldn't have fallen into their trap."

"They don't ask girls," he retorted. "So you'd never have the chance to show them how smart you are."

Mrs. Cox looked pained. "Children, please do not make things worse with your idiotic bickering."

"William, how did they contact you?" Emma asked, trying to reclaim the conversation.

"I met them once a month at the Eagle and the Hare," he replied.

"They never communicated in writing?"

He shook his head.

"Could you identify the farms where the goods were stored?"

He grimaced. "The runs only happened on moonless or overcast nights, so it was very dark. I . . . I don't think I could tell you specifically which farms. Only the route."

"When we're finished here," she said. "I want you to write down everything you can remember."

Mrs. Cox anxiously peered at her. "I know what William did was very bad, but if this becomes common knowledge, I cannot imagine what will happen to him or to my husband. If my boy is arrested . . ." Her mouth trembled.

"Miss Nash won't have anything to do with William if she finds out about this," Susan dolefully added.

William's face crumpled. For a horrible moment, Emma

feared he might burst into tears. George should really make the final decision on what course to take, but taking in the woeful faces of Mrs. Cox and her children—even Anne—Emma knew she couldn't subject them to scandal and even financial ruin. While William had been a reckless idiot, he'd managed to extract himself from a bad situation and was apparently trying to mend his ways.

Emma gave Mrs. Cox a reassuring smile. "I am going to share this information with Mr. Knightley, of course, and I will impress upon him the need to maintain your privacy. I see no reason to share William's name with either Mr. Clarke or Constable Sharpe. The information itself is what matters, not the source in this particular case."

She was going out on a limb with that promise, and could only pray it wouldn't crack under her weight.

William all but collapsed into his chair with relief, while Mrs. Cox clasped her hands to her breast. "I shall be eternally grateful to you, Mrs. Knightley. Thank you."

"Well, I should think Mrs. Knightley would help us," Anne said, reverting to type. "We are her neighbors, after all, and neighbors don't tattle on neighbors or lord it over them."

Miss Bates, clearly appalled by the girl's comments, shook a finger at her. "And you, Miss Cox, should learn to be grateful when one of your neighbors does you a great service. You should be thanking Mrs. Knightley, not making pert remarks."

The unexpected reprimand reduced the room to astonished silence.

In all her years, Emma had never once heard Miss Bates render even the mildest criticism against anyone. Father clearly wasn't the only person who'd undergone a remarkable change in the last year.

"Er, quite," said Emma. "William what happened when you told the smugglers you wished to stop?"

He winced. "I . . . I just stopped going to meet them, actually. I saw how they dealt with people who didn't do what they asked, and I wanted no part of it."

Perhaps not the best course of action, but she couldn't blame him. "I take it they know your real name and where you live."

"Didn't see any reason not to tell them. They seemed like regular fellows, to me."

"William," exclaimed his mother, "you have put us all in danger. Those ruthless men could come to our house and kill us in our beds!"

Susan again burst into tears, and even Anne looked frightened.

"I'm sorry, Mama," he wretchedly replied.

As she waved smelling salts in Susan's general direction, Miss Bates cast Emma a concerned glance. "Mrs. Knightley, what are we to do? Is there real danger?"

"William, when was the last time you met those men?" Emma asked.

"November. Haven't gone near Kingston-on-Thames since then."

"And no one has made any attempt to contact you?"

"Not a word. Nothing."

Emma nodded. "Then I'm sure it's fine. I wouldn't worry."

I hope.

Mrs. Cox, who'd taken refuge behind her handkerchief, resurfaced to cast Emma a hopeful glance. "Do you really think so?"

"I expect they don't want to draw attention to themselves. And if they thought William was worth the effort, they would have already tried to contact him."

The young man looked mortified by her assessment, but Emma couldn't find it in herself to be sorry. He was getting off lightly.

Mrs. Cox blinked a few times. "So . . . so this is the end of it?"

"I should think so." Emma rose to her feet. "Mrs. Cox, I'm very sorry for the distress this has caused you. I would not have brought this to your doorstep if I didn't think it absolutely necessary."

Mrs. Cox all but leaped to her feet and grasped her hand. "Mrs. Knightley, you have done us a great kindness. We can never thank you enough."

The others also rose, the Cox siblings radiating various levels of mortification.

"William, I expect you to come to me or to Mr. Knightley if you think of anything else that could be relevant," Emma said. "Or if you hear of anything else, especially if it pertains to Donwell Abbey or Mr. Larkins."

"I will, ma'am. I promise."

She and Miss Bates were halfway to the door before she realized she'd forgotten to ask a rather important question. "William, you said that as far as you know there was no connection between Donwell Abbey and this gang."

He nodded. "Yes, ma'am."

"That includes any staff who might have previously worked there, correct?"

William frowned. "Why would any of your servants be involved with those men?"

It was on the tip of her tongue to mention Prudence, but she thought better of it. It seemed clear he'd told her everything he knew.

"Thank you," she replied. "Don't forget to write down everything and send it to me."

"You may be sure he will do so immediately," said Mrs. Cox. "Please, let me show you and Miss Bates to the door."

Moments later, they found themselves on the street.

"Mrs. Cox was certainly eager to be shot of us," Emma dryly noted as they headed up the street. "I believe she almost closed the door on the skirt of my pelisse."

"I thought you were brilliant, Mrs. Knightley," Miss Bates earnestly said. "I was so horrified by William's dreadful tale that I could barely utter a word."

"Nonsense, you were most helpful." She smiled. "I especially enjoyed your reprimand of Anne."

"I was rather shocked at myself, but I truly felt for poor Mrs. Cox."

"Please feel free to deliver set-downs to Anne on a regular basis. It might even improve her manners."

Miss Bates barely seemed to hear her. "It's all such a muddle, Mrs. Knightley. What are we to do now?"

"I must speak to my husband. He'll devise an appropriate response."

Once, that is, George got through scolding her for haring off on her own yet again.

Chapter 23

Emma found herself awake as dawn slipped past the draperies. As she lay in bed, she reflected on how quickly one could become accustomed to a bedmate after a lifetime of sleeping alone, especially when that person was the beloved of one's heart.

Waking without George was a particularly dreary way to start the day.

Yesterday, after hearing her report about William Cox, her husband had decided to leave for London that very afternoon. Matters in Highbury were coming to a head, and he wished to discuss these latest developments with John, along with the possibility of hiring a Bow Street Runner to help investigate the case and clear Larkins's good name.

He would also transmit the new information to Mr. Clarke. Thankfully, George had agreed to keep William's name out of it, but he acknowledged that the revenue agent's primary focus was on catching smugglers, not murderers. Although identifying the smugglers could only help Larkins's cause, there was still the matter of Prudence's bloody mobcap and other incriminating evidence. If Mr. Clarke failed to run the smugglers to ground before the murder trial, Larkins would almost certainly go to the gallows.

Time was racing away from them.

During their discussion, George had delivered an expected and rather pithy lecture on the perils of amateurs investigating murder. Though she'd pointed out that, strictly speaking, she'd been investigating smuggling not murder, George had been unimpressed by her logic and had said so in equally pithy terms. Still, he'd taken the information to heart—as she'd known he would—and had acted upon it by planning his departure for London.

Of course, his excellent decision-making abilities meant that Emma found herself standing morosely under Hartfield's portico a short time later as she watched her husband's carriage roll down the drive. Thankfully, they'd parted on mostly excellent terms. George had pulled her into his arms for a lingering kiss and embrace, but had rather ruined the moment by admonishing her to stay out of trouble until his return. Emma had considered pointing out that trouble seemed to find *her* rather than the other way around, but had refrained in the interests of domestic harmony.

After staring up at the canopy of her bed for twenty minutes, Emma was still debating whether to climb out from under her warm blankets when the maid entered the room to light the fire. She rose and then washed, shivering slightly in the morning chill, and donned her warmest kerseymere gown. Father wouldn't be down for at least another hour, so she would have time to think about what to do while she waited for news from George. For one thing, she should probably visit Donwell this afternoon to check on the servants. With George now gone for at least three days, Mrs. Hodges and company were more in need of support and guidance than ever.

After coming downstairs, she encountered Simon on her way to the breakfast parlor.

"Good morning, ma'am," he said. "Would you prefer coffee this morning? I just brought tea in for Mr. Woodhouse."

Emma couldn't hide her surprise. "My father is up already?"

"Yes, he rang for me almost an hour ago," replied Simon in a resigned tone.

As one of Hartfield's longest-serving staff and Father's de facto valet, Simon knew the old dear almost as well as she did.

She sighed. "He's fretting about the smuggling, isn't he?"

"A bit, ma'am."

"I'll have coffee, then." Emma had a feeling that tea wouldn't be a strong enough brace for the day ahead.

"Right away, Mrs. Knightley."

She pinned a bright smile on her face as she entered the breakfast parlor. "Good morning, dearest. You're up very early."

Her father, who'd been gloomily perusing a letter, glanced up. "I feel very discomposed, my dear. I cannot stop thinking both about those dreadful smugglers and poor Larkins sitting in that damp prison. He's bound to come down with a dreadful chill, and you know how dangerous they can be if left untreated."

"Larkins is very robust, and we've made sure he has everything he needs to stay healthy. Don't forget that George has gone to London especially to procure help for Larkins. He and John will manage it, I promise."

He looked even more ruffled. "But, Emma, London is very damp at this time of year, and George is not used to London weather. I do hope he remembered to pack his flannel scarf and waistcoat."

George had never worn a flannel waistcoat in his life, and Emma suspected he never would.

"Is that a letter from Isabella?" she asked in an attempt to divert his fretting thoughts. "What does she have to say?"

"She never complains, as you know, but I surmise that she finds London quite dreary at the moment, especially with John working so much." He sighed. "I cannot help thinking that she and the children would be better off staying with us right now. City air is so injurious to one's health in the winter."

Emma studied his doleful expression. "Father, would you like to write to Isabella and ask her to come back to Hartfield with the children? I should certainly be glad for their company."

He perked up. "Do you think she would do that?" Then he hesitated. "But what of the smugglers? Is it safe? We cannot put them in danger, Emma, especially not the children."

She weighed the question. True, the smugglers had cut across Donwell's gardens, but Mr. Clarke was of the opinion that it had been a singular occurrence. There was also the fact that William Cox had precipitously quit the gang almost three months ago and had remained entirely unmolested by them. And George had spent the past several nights at Donwell, where all had been as peaceful as one could hope. It seemed clear that whoever killed Prudence was not from Highbury any more than the smugglers were.

While someone had obviously framed Larkins and that was deeply concerning, Emma had no doubt that the village, Hartfield, and Donwell were all safe from harm.

Besides, if Isabella returned to Hartfield it would allow Emma to move back to Donwell. There was much work yet to be done to bring the old pile up to snuff before she and George made their permanent move. If George wished her to stay out of trouble, the best way to do that was for her to focus on preparing for their new life as master and mistress of Donwell Abbey.

Before Emma could reply, Simon entered with the coffee service. A moment later, a knock echoed down the hall from the front of the house.

Emma frowned. "Goodness, who could be calling so early?"

"Perhaps it's Perry," her father said. "Simon, please show him in here. I'm sure he'll be happy for a cup of tea."

"Very good, sir."

"I'm surprised Mr. Perry would call so early," said Emma. "He doesn't usually do so."

"True, but he knows that I've been most—"

The door opened and Miss Bates hurried in, looking flustered.

"My dear Miss Bates, is something wrong?" Father exclaimed. "Is Mrs. Bates unwell?"

Miss Bates flashed an apologetic smile. "Dear me, no. We are both perfectly well. Forgive me for giving you a fright. I heard the most disturbing news just now, and I knew Mrs. Knightley would wish to know about it immediately."

Emma went to her. "Of course, but first you must take off your bonnet and pelisse and have a cup of tea."

Though Miss Bates protested that she was fine, Emma handed her outerwear to Simon, got her seated, and poured her a cup.

"Now," Emma said, resuming her own place. "What is this dreadful thing that sent you racing to us so early?"

"I hope this has nothing to do with those wretched smugglers," Father said. "I do not approve of all this smuggling, Emma. These villains are worse than the poultry thief."

Emma and Miss Bates exchanged a concerned look. In Father's world, there was little worse than the dreaded poultry thief.

"I don't imagine anyone approves of them, Father," Emma replied.

"I do hate to be the bearer . . . oh, are those Serle's vanilla scones?" asked Miss Bates as Simon brought the platter to the table. "Yes, I'd love a scone, Simon. And strawberry jam—such a treat! I vow, Serle makes the best strawberry jam in all of Highbury."

Emma resisted the urge to grind her molars. "Miss Bates, what is this news you so urgently needed to share?"

"Dear me, I beg your pardon." She put down her knife. "Poor Mr. Clarke was found unconscious in the churchyard this morning, lying behind one of the gravestones. Mr. Barlowe found him there. He'd been severely beaten. Mr. Clarke, that is, not Mr. Barlowe. Apparently, he'd been attacked some time in the night and left for dead. If Mr. Barlowe hadn't had business in the church first thing, poor Mr. Clarke might have frozen to death."

Emma stared at her, aghast at the news. So much for Highbury being perfectly safe.

Father threw down his napkin. "Emma, this is unacceptable! I do not say I approve of Mr. Clarke, but one should be able to visit the churchyard without being set upon by villains. You must write George immediately and tell him to come home."

"Yes, dear," she replied, her attention still on Miss Bates. "Where is Mr. Clarke now? Is he conscious?"

"Yes, he was taken to the Crown Inn. Dr. Hughes was called immediately and is still there with him."

"How did you hear of this?"

"Patty got up early to go to the bakery and she ran into one of the grooms from the Crown. He told her everything."

"Do you know anything about the extent of his injuries?"

"Only what I've told you. Dr. Hughes and Mr. Barlowe are still with him. Oh, and Constable Sharpe was there at the Crown, too."

Father let out a dismissive huff. "Mr. Clarke would be better served if Perry were to see to him. Emma, you must send a note to Perry and ask him to attend to Mr. Clarke."

"Yes, dear," Emma automatically replied. "Did the smugglers attack him?"

Miss Bates shook her head. "Constable Sharpe apparently told Mrs. Stokes that it was a robbery. Mr. Clarke's clothing was . . . was discomposed, and his watch and fob were taken."

"Thieves *and* smugglers," Father moaned. "What is to become of us? We shall all be killed in our beds!"

"We're perfectly safe here at Hartfield, Father," Emma said

in soothing tones. "And I strongly suspect that this supposed thief was actually one of the smugglers."

Most likely he made the attack on Mr. Clarke appear to be a robbery. It strained credulity to think otherwise. It also suggested that the prevention officer had been making progress—and that Mr. Clarke's apparent headway had caused someone to become very nervous.

"I wondered if that was the case," confessed Miss Bates. "To have both robbers *and* smugglers in Highbury would be too dreadful."

"And extremely coincidental," Emma replied. "I can only wonder what Mr. Clarke was doing in the churchyard in the middle of the night?"

Miss Bates held up a hand. "I think I know. He was probably investigating the strange lights."

Emma frowned. "What strange lights?"

"In the bell tower, after midnight. There was a report of strange lights up there." Miss Bates twirled a hand. "Mr. Clarke has been staying at the Crown Inn when in Highbury, according to the groom. The poor man must have seen them and gone out to investigate."

"I didn't know he was back in Highbury," Emma replied, musing on the information.

As she now knew, churches were often used as depots for contraband goods. And one certainly had to note that Mr. Barlowe had been acting rather oddly ever since Prudence's murder. Did he know something about the smuggling gang, after all, and had been frightened into silence?

"Did anyone else see those lights?" Emma asked.

Miss Bates nodded. "Apparently Mr. Perry did."

Father flapped his napkin. "Perry should not be out so late, especially with such dangerous villains roaming about."

"Miss Bates, how do you know Mr. Perry saw the lights?" asked Emma.

"After Patty ran back and told us what had happened, I set

off immediately for Hartfield. On the way, I ran into Mrs. Cole." She pulled a sympathetic grimace. "Mr. Cole was feeling poorly last night, so they were forced to call for Mr. Perry. Dyspepsia, you know. Mrs. Cole says that Mr. Cole's business gives him a nervous stomach."

Father huffed. "Nonsense. Mr. Cole eats too much cake and too many rich foods. I've told Perry as such, and he agrees with me."

Emma tried to stay on point. "So Mr. Perry saw those lights on the way to see Mr. Cole?"

Miss Bates nodded. "He mentioned it specifically to Mrs. Cole when he arrived, but was then taken up with treating Mr. Cole. And Mrs. Cole forgot all about it until this morning. But she told me that she was going to speak to Constable Sharpe as soon as she saw Mrs. Ford about procuring flannel waistcoats for her husband—to help with his dyspepsia."

"Flannel waistcoats will do nothing to help dyspepsia unless Mr. Cole leaves off eating cake," Father severely noted.

Emma ignored her father as she focused on what to do. Speaking to Constable Sharpe or Dr. Hughes was clearly out the question. They would simply dismiss her. But something was clearly going on at the church, something that likely led to the beating of Mr. Clarke. Who better a person to speak to, then, than Mr. Barlowe?

First, she needed to get into that bell tower.

She stood. "Father, it might be best if I go into Highbury and check on poor Mr. Clarke. Mrs. Stokes is always so busy, and who knows if she has the proper medicinal potions on hand at the inn. She might need help."

Her father's eyes popped wide with alarm. "Emma, you must not leave the house! Not with villains running about the village."

"I'm sure there's no danger. After all, Mrs. Cole was out and about, and Miss Bates safely came to Hartfield."

"Miss Bates should also remain here," he stubbornly replied.

The spinster pressed a feeling hand to her chest. "Dear Mr. Woodhouse, always so concerned for everyone's care. But I believe Mrs. Knightley is correct. There were quite a few people on the street, and all the shops were opening up. I even saw Mrs. Goddard and some of her pupils out for a brisk morning walk. You know she would never put her girls at risk."

"And you did say we should have Mr. Perry visit poor Mr. Clarke," Emma swiftly added. "I can stop by and ask him to do that."

Father wavered. "Perhaps if you take one of the footmen with you?"

"What a good suggestion," Emma enthused.

And a suggestion it would remain, since she had no intention of having a footman trailing along while she snuck into the church.

Miss Bates also came to her feet. "I'll walk back with you, Mrs. Knightley. I should like to see how Mr. Clarke is, too."

Drat.

She didn't need Miss Bates as a witness, either. It seemed, however, that she might have little choice.

As Hartfield's front door closed behind them, Miss Bates touched Emma's arm.

"You're not really going to call on Mr. Perry, are you? You're going to the church to investigate what happened to Mr. Clarke."

Startled, Emma could only stare at her. "How did you guess?"

"So, you *are* going to investigate."

Miss Bates looked so pleased with herself that Emma didn't have the heart to contradict her.

"You mustn't tell Father," she warned. "He'd have a conniption."

"I wouldn't dream of it. The dear man's peace is already cut up as it is. The less he thinks about these dreadful smugglers, the better. I only wonder what we can do about it."

Emma slowed as they approached the turning into Vicarage Lane. "We could try to get to the bottom of it."

Miss Bates matched her pace. "I'm not sure what you mean, Mrs. Knightley. Why else would Mr. Clarke be in the churchyard at night but for smugglers? They must have been the source of those strange lights—unless it was the ghost. Although it doesn't seem likely, I suppose one must take the ghost into consideration."

"What ghost? I've not heard any reports of ghosts in the church."

Generally speaking, Emma didn't believe in ghosts. Highbury had always been dreadfully dull in that respect, thank goodness, with nary a whisper of some idiotic spirit making a nuisance of itself.

Miss Bates fluttered a hand. "Some in the village still think Mrs. Elton's ghost is haunting the church. Although why her ghost would be up in the bell tower is beyond me. I'm quite sure she never set foot up there."

Emma sighed. "I'd forgotten about that."

After Mrs. Elton's murder, some locals were indeed convinced that her spirit was haunting Highbury's church. Emma had been forced to deliver stern admonitions to a number of young people regarding the foolishness of such irrational and irreligious beliefs.

"Mrs. Cole said Mr. Gilbert also saw the lights one night, some weeks ago," added Miss Bates. "She thought nothing of it at the time, but after last night . . ."

Emma scoffed. "Did Mrs. Cole think that Mrs. Elton's spirit attacked Mr. Clarke?"

Miss Bates waved to a few children as they ran past on their way to the village school. "Such dear little children. What did you say, Mrs. Knightley? Oh, the ghost. I asked Mrs. Cole why she thought it might be Mrs. Elton's ghost. She said that perhaps Mrs. Elton had a general opposition to paying customs fees and would therefore object to having a prevention officer on church grounds."

Emma came to a dead halt. "Did she truly say that?"

Miss Bates, who'd walked on a few steps, turned back to address her. "I'm afraid so." Then she sighed. "Poor Mrs. Elton. I'm very sure she would be happy to pay her customs fees now, if she were only alive."

Emma had to bite her lip to hold back a laugh. "Indeed. Miss Bates, you missed the turn into Highbury. Won't your mother be waiting for you?"

The spinster gave her a placid smile. "Mother is probably taking a little nap by the fire right now. Patty will see to her."

"You intended to go to the church with me all along," Emma dryly commented.

"It wouldn't do for you to go alone, Mrs. Knightley. Not with such dangerous men lurking about the village. Whatever would Mr. Knightley say if I abandoned you in such circumstances?"

Emma couldn't visualize Miss Bates in an encounter with hardened smugglers. "I think Mr. Knightley would object to either of us confronting dangerous men—which I'm sure won't happen in any event."

"I'm sure you're correct. Still, who knows what you might find up in the bell tower." She shook her head. "No, I have a responsibility to Mr. Woodhouse *and* Mr. Knightley to be present should you need me."

In a surprising development, it would seem that Miss Bates was taking her duties as future stepmother very seriously—something quite sweet but also quite dreadful.

"I suppose two sets of eyes are better than one, but you mustn't say a word to my father. And I'll tell Mr. Knightley if we find anything, agreed?"

Her companion beamed at her. "I promise I won't let you down. Oh, should I take notes? I have a pencil and a scrap of paper in my reticule. I should be happy to write down any observations we might make."

"I'm sure that won't be necessary," Emma firmly replied.

She marched Miss Bates up the path to the south porch of the church, doing her best to avoid thinking about the future with Miss Bates as her stepmother and, apparently, her partner in pursuing justice.

Miss Bates tried the door. "It's locked. Do you want me to fetch Mr. Barlowe?"

Emma bent down to try to wriggle out a brick that was part of the door trim. "I hardly think Mr. Barlowe would wish us snooping around his church."

"You make it sound so exciting, Mrs. Knightley! I cannot imagine what Mr. Woodhouse would think if he saw us now."

Nothing good, of that Emma was sure.

"Come loose, you silly thing," she muttered as she wrestled with the brick.

"Mrs. Knightley, what are you—"

"Ah, finally," Emma triumphantly exclaimed.

After pulling the brick fully out, she reached into the hole and extracted a key.

Miss Bates regarded her with wide eyes. "How did you know that was there?"

"It's where the caretaker stows an extra key. I saw him put it there one day when I brought flowers to the church."

Emma opened the door and quickly ushered in her companion. It wouldn't do to linger where they might be seen.

On an overcast winter's morning, the old church was shrouded in silence and shadows. Even the stained glass windows held barely a hint of color, the figures a muted reflection of their usual glory. The stone monuments mounted between the windows seemed to blend into the walls, and the lack of light made everything appear flat and lifeless. It seemed as if the old church was hibernating as it waited for the warmth and color of spring.

It was also so cold that Emma couldn't repress a shiver.

"It is quite drafty, isn't it?" said Miss Bates in a worried tone. "Perhaps we should leave. It wouldn't do for you to catch a chill."

"I'm fine. Anyway, we won't be long."

Emma led the way to a staircase in the back corner. Lifting their skirts, they climbed the narrow, twisting stairs, ducking their heads under the low doorframe when they reached the belfry.

The top of the tower was a tall, narrow space, with the center taken up by the frame that supported the bell and wheel. The noble old bell was not particularly large, so its timber frame left the perimeter of the room clear for storage. Emma hadn't been up in the tower since she was a girl, but remembered it had been used for storage of broken furniture and other detritus collected by vicars over the years.

Now, though, the tower was empty and surprisingly free of dust. The floor looked like it might have been recently swept.

"My word, it's very clean, isn't it?" said Miss Bates. "When my father was vicar, he used to store all manner of things up here."

"Hmm," Emma muttered as she began to make her way around the room.

She was trying to make out what seemed to be odd-looking marks on the floor when a ray of winter sunlight streamed in through the high windows.

"Ah, that's better." She crouched down, running a hand across a mark scored into the floor.

Miss Bates joined her. "What is it?"

Emma pointed. "Does this not look like something was dragged across the boards?" She glanced toward the door and pointed. "But not over there."

"How odd. What do you make of it?"

Emma straightened up. "It would appear that some object or objects were dragged away from the wall."

Miss Bates peered down at the floor. "But only partway."

"Yes. I would guess it was then picked up and carried."

"But what could it have been?"

Emma thought for a few moments. "A small cask or casks, perhaps?"

"You mean spirits?" Miss Bates replied, aghast.

"Or tea, possibly."

"Mrs. Knightley, how dreadful! To think my father's dear little church could be used in such a sinful manner." Then she blinked. "And what of Mr. Barlowe? He couldn't possibly know about this, could he?"

"That is the question," Emma replied.

Further perusal verified there was nothing more to see, so she ushered Miss Bates down the winding staircase. They'd almost reached the bottom when they heard quick footsteps coming from the back of the church. Miss Bates froze, as did Emma. She mentally crossed her fingers hoping that whoever it was hadn't heard them.

But the door at the bottom of the staircase suddenly flew open to reveal the curate. Mr. Barlowe gaped at them for a moment before his expression transformed into a scowl.

Of all the bad luck....

"Mr. Barlowe," Emma exclaimed in a dementedly bright voice. "What a surprise."

"I might say the same, ma'am," he blustered. "What could you be doing up in the bell tower?"

She scrambled to come up with a plausible excuse, but was forestalled by Miss Bates.

"My dear sir, we heard about the terrible events of last night. So shocking! We were on our way to call on Mr. Perry, to ask him to check on poor Mr. Clarke. Our dear Perry could no doubt be of great service to Mr. Clarke in his time of trial."

"I can assure you that Mr. Perry is not up in the bell tower," Barlowe frostily replied.

Emma sighed, resigned to telling the unfortunate truth. "We

heard reports of lights in the tower last night at about the time Mr. Clarke was attacked. I thought it might be useful to have a look around so I could report back to my husband when he returns from London."

Mr. Barlowe went still as death. His complexion suddenly mimicked a rather good imitation of a corpse, too.

"Is something wrong, sir?" Emma asked.

He made an effort to recover himself. "It certainly is. You are snooping about my church, where you have no business."

"Sir, I don't mean to criticize," Miss Bates apologetically said, "but my father was in the habit of leaving the church open as much as possible when he was vicar. He encouraged people to spend time in here, and the children quite enjoyed climbing up to the bell tower, back in his day."

"That may be so, but *I* do not leave the church open."

"Someone must have," Emma said, crossing her fingers behind her back. "How else would we have gotten in?"

Miss Bates made a slight choking noise but held her peace.

"Be that as it may, I would ask you to leave now," the curate impatiently replied.

He then shooed them out of the building as if they were a pair of obstreperous geese, and made a point of locking the door before turning back to them.

"I hope your curiosity was satisfied, Mrs. Knightley," he said. "Now, if you'll excuse me—"

Emma shot up a hand. "Just a quick question, Mr. Barlowe. We noticed some odd scrape marks in the belfry that looked recent. I have to wonder what could have left such marks."

His lips pressed into a thin, reluctant line. Emma simply smiled and waited him out.

"Pews," he tersely replied.

"I beg your pardon?"

"Old pews, Mrs. Knightley. They were stored in the loft. I had them taken away by a scrap dealer, which is why the floor is marked up."

"I see. And when was this?"

"Last week. I do not remember the day."

"Do you remember the name of this scrap dealer?"

He scowled. "Of course not. He was an itinerant peddler."

"Ah." That was a convenient answer.

"Did you see any lights or sign of activity in the bell tower last night?" she went on to ask.

"Of course not."

"But surely you heard something," put in Miss Bates. "Poor Mr. Clarke was attacked, and apparently quite viciously. Did you not hear sounds of a struggle or a call for help?"

"No," he huffily replied. "If I had, you may be sure I would have done something."

Emma decided to press him. "Mr. Barlowe, do you think it's possible that smugglers were using the bell loft to store their contraband goods?"

He stumbled backward, slightly banging his elbow into the church door. Muttering, he rubbed it while continuing to glare at her. "With all due respect, that is a ridiculous notion. I would certainly be aware if smugglers were using my church. Besides, Constable Sharpe has already determined that Mr. Clarke was the unfortunate victim of a robbery."

Emma made a skeptical noise. "In the churchyard, in the middle of the night? That seems very odd, especially for Highbury."

"You may ask the constable yourself, or even Mr. Clarke."

"And how is he?" asked Miss Bates.

"Very poorly, I'm afraid. The villains were harsh with him."

Emma raised her eyebrows. "So there was more than one villain?"

The curate seemed to mentally freeze for a moment before recovering himself. "Apparently, although Mr. Clarke was hazy on the details. He took a blow to the head, so his memory is impaired."

"But he remembered there was more than one attacker?" Emma clarified.

"I... yes, I believe so."

"And what led Constable Sharpe to conclude it was a robbery and not smugglers? After all, Mr. Clarke is a prevention agent. Why else would he be in the churchyard in the middle of the night?"

Miss Bates gave a vigorous nod. "Very true, Mrs. Knightley. It's most wicked, of course, but storing contraband in churches does happen, as you know. My father told us once of a church in Chiddingfold where smugglers stored their goods. In the attic, you understand, without the vicar's knowledge. The poor man was giving his Sunday sermon when one of the casks—quite a large one, apparently—fell through the ceiling and smashed into the middle of the aisle. Thankfully, no one was injured, but it took weeks to get rid of the odor of brandy."

"Oh dear," Emma said, stifling an impulse to laugh.

"And when you were snooping, did you find any brandy in the loft?" the curate angrily demanded.

Emma's fleeting amusement vanished. "There's no need to be rude, sir. We're simply asking reasonable questions."

"Then I suggest you address them to Constable Sharpe," he retorted. "As I said, he feels certain the villains were thieves. After all, Mr. Clarke's billfold and watch were missing."

Emma shrugged. "That could simply mean they were both thieves *and* smugglers."

"Mrs. Knightley, I would again ask you—"

"Ho, Barlowe," called a friendly voice. "At last I find you."

They all turned to see Guy Plumtree strolling up the church walk, an easy smile gracing his handsome features. He cast a curious glance at Emma before giving her and Miss Bates a courtly bow.

"Ladies, it's a pleasure to see you both," he said. "I hope I find you well."

Miss Bates dropped a slight curtsy. "Very well, Mr. Plumtree, thank you."

He glanced at the curate. "I've been looking all over for you, Barlowe. Did you forget we had an appointment this morning?"

"Of course I didn't forget. Now you've found me, so I fail to see the problem."

Guy's eyebrows ticked upward at the ungracious reply. "No need to snap, dear fellow. All is well."

Emma, however, was beginning to think the curate's snappishness had less to do with rudeness and more with being rattled by her questions.

Mr. Barlowe finally unbent a bit. "I was at the Crown Inn with Mr. Algernon Clarke. He was badly injured last night."

"Set upon by villains in the churchyard," Miss Bates helpfully supplied.

Guy's expression registered astonishment. "In Highbury? How appalling. Does anyone know why?"

"Thieves." Mr. Barlowe cast a sour glance at Emma. "Although Mrs. Knightley seems to think it had something to do with smuggling. Which is ridiculous, of course."

"There's no need to be snappish, dear fellow," Guy gently admonished. "Mrs. Knightley would certainly have grounds to think such a thing. After all, Donwell's estate manager has been accused of that very crime."

Now it was Emma's turn to bristle. "Unjustly, I might add."

Guy flashed her a quick, apologetic smile. "Forgive me, ma'am. I had no intention of giving offense. I've met Larkins on occasion, when my father had dealings with him. He always struck me as a sensible and decent fellow. I was sorry to hear of his predicament, and of course I extend my sympathies to both you and Mr. Knightley."

Mollified, Emma gave him a nod. "Yes, it's dreadful, but I'm certain we'll clear his name."

"I hope so," Guy replied. "And of the murder charge, as well."

"Heavens," exclaimed Miss Bates. "I refuse to believe that our dear Mr. Larkins could be guilty of such a crime. Indeed, I still struggle to believe *anyone* in our village could have *anything* to do with murder or those dreadful smugglers."

"It is shocking," Guy said with great sympathy. "Unfortunately, it's more common than one would think. Poor rural folk do it to earn extra money, and one can hardly blame them. I'm afraid many of the gentry see nothing wrong in trafficking with freetraders, either." His smile was rueful. "Or the gentlemen, as my father likes to call them. He himself has always been quite comfortable with the whole business, as is quite common in his generation. Naturally, I have discouraged him, and to good effect, I think."

"Gracious," exclaimed Miss Bates. "I would never have thought such a thing of your father."

Guy shrugged. "He's very old-fashioned, ma'am. However, I believe I've reformed him—at least I hope so."

After that further admission, an awkward silence descended on their group.

Then Guy clapped his gloved hands together. "But here we are keeping you ladies standing about in the cold. Barlowe, where are your manners? Have you not invited the ladies in for tea?"

The curate bristled. "I've hardly had the chance. Besides, we *do* have an appointment, as you recall."

"I do." Guy smiled at Emma. "Can we escort you ladies anywhere first?"

"Thank you, but no. We're just walking up the street to call on Mr. Perry."

"Then we shall make our goodbyes. Have a pleasant day, Mrs. Knightley. Miss Bates."

Guy doffed his hat and took Mr. Barlowe by the arm to lead him off in the direction of the vicarage.

"What a strange conversation," commented Miss Bates. "I'm quite shocked to hear about Squire Plumtree. I never would have thought of it."

Emma also found it hard to believe that so respectable a man could be involved with smugglers. But was he actually *involved*? Might he even know the names of the men who made up the gang, or was it just the usual arrangement—a few casks of spirits left on the doorstep in exchange for turning a blind eye to runs across his estate?

They were questions that begged for answers.

Chapter 24

When Harriet entered Hartfield's drawing room, Emma gratefully put aside her needlework and stood. "How are you, dear? I vow, it's been an age since we spoke."

Harriet gingerly returned Emma's embrace around her expanding girth.

"I apologize, Mrs. Knightley. Robert hates for me to go out when there's ice on the road. I keep telling him there *is* no ice on the road, but he's convinced I'll take a tumble."

"He's just being protective. That's his job."

"The midwife says I have almost three months to go before my lying-in, and I swear Robert would lock me away for the whole time if I let him."

Emma laughed. "How did you manage to escape today?"

"My mother-in-law gave Robert a scold. She said she worked right up to the day she gave birth to him, and that a little exercise and fresh air would be good for me."

"She's right about that, though I expect no one in the Martin household expects *you* to work right up to your lying-in."

Harriet crinkled her nose. "They all spoil me terribly."

Emma drew her to sit on the sofa. "No one deserves a little pampering more than you. Did you walk to Hartfield?"

"Yes, with my sisters-in-law. They had to do some shopping in Highbury. Robert asked, please, if one of your footmen could escort me home." She huffed. "It's so silly. I feel perfectly fine."

"I'll take you myself," Emma said. "I've been cooped up all day and would be happy to walk off the fidgets."

"Robert says Mr. Knightley has been away for a few days. When does he return home?"

"I hope to see him this afternoon. He and John are working on a defense for poor Larkins. They're also looking into hiring a Bow Street Runner to investigate the smuggling. That's doubly necessary now with Mr. Clarke out of commission."

Harriet clucked her tongue in sympathy. "Poor Mr. Clarke. But I heard Constable Sharpe deemed it a robbery that had nothing to do with the smugglers?"

"You know what a dimwit he is. Why else would Mr. Clarke be in the churchyard after midnight? He was obviously onto something. He must have been set upon by the smugglers because he was getting too close."

Harriet glanced over her shoulder before leaning in. "It's actually about the smugglers that I wanted to speak with you."

Emma smiled. "You needn't whisper, dear. I promise there are no smugglers in our household."

Harriet looked solemn. "You never know who could be listening."

"That's an alarming remark. Whatever can you mean?"

"It's rather hard to explain, because I promised someone that I wouldn't reveal their identity. Or what she . . . I mean, they, specifically told me about what was taking place . . . in the place where things were taking place."

Emma frowned. "Harriet, you're beginning to sound like Miss Bates."

"I know. But it's most important that I keep my promise, because my friend . . . this person is very frightened."

Ah. That was interesting—and disturbing.

She took a guess. "I take it your friend—clearly a woman—has been threatened by smugglers?"

"Not specifically, but . . ." Harriet hesitated, clearly torn between her promise and the need to relay important information.

Emma laid a hand on her arm. "If you wish to withhold this person's name, I completely understand. Still, the more information you can give me, the more we can do to stop these terrible men before they hurt anyone else."

Harriet wavered a bit, then nodded. "Well, my friend came to visit me this morning. Her husband is a farmer in the parish next to Donwell. The smugglers have taken over the use of his barn to store contraband on its way to London. In the beginning he tried to say no, but they beat the poor man quite terribly. After that, he was too afraid to refuse their demands."

Anger and frustration mingled in equal portions in Emma's breast. How could these awful people keep getting away with their reign of terror?

"I'm so sorry, Harriet. How long has this been going on?"

"For a year."

"And I take it your friend's husband hasn't reported this to anyone?"

Harriet shook her head. "He's too frightened. And he's afraid the revenue agents might blame him, because the smugglers insisted on paying him. He thinks it makes him look guilty."

It *would* make him look guilty, which was no doubt the gang's intent. Beat the man into compliance and then make it appear as if he were a willing participant.

"Why did your friend come to you now?" Emma asked.

"Because things are getting worse. The smugglers are demanding that her husband start storing even more goods they bring from their runs, and more frequently. She thinks something's gone wrong." Harriet twirled a hand. "With the smugglers, I mean. That something happened to their normal route, and now they have to use my friend's farm to store even more contraband."

Emma thought for a moment. "Perhaps the smugglers lost access to one of their other storage depots."

Like the bell tower of a church.

"Or," she thoughtfully added, "they had to shift their normal route because someone like Mr. Clarke was getting too close."

"All she knows is that something has changed."

Emma studied her friend. "Harriet, why did she come to you, specifically?"

"She knows you are my friend, Mrs. Knightley. She . . . she thought you could do something."

"Because I'm married to the local magistrate?"

Harriet gave her a sheepish smile.

"I understand," said Emma, "but it's not much to go on."

"I'm sorry, but I did promise her," Harriet unhappily replied. "I can't break my promise."

"I know, dear. I'll think of something."

Her friend looked dubious.

Emma tapped her knee, pondering the situation. As it was, going to George with this information wouldn't be terribly useful. There were a great many farms and tenant farmers within the surrounding parishes. Trying to identify the correct one, while not quite a needle in a haystack would still be a monumental task, especially if the farmer was too frightened to talk.

Then a piece of the puzzle suddenly clicked into place.

"I have it," she exclaimed. "We need to speak to a farmer."

Harriet blinked. "Why?"

"Given the predilection of smugglers to use farms as storage depots, it's reasonable to assume that other farmers in the area have also been coerced into working with the gang. Or, at least, have been approached by them."

"Are you saying we should try to find farmers who might be working with the smugglers?" Harriet asked in a skeptical tone. "I don't think Robert would like that. He takes a very dim view of smugglers and won't have anything to do with them."

"I'm not suggesting we do anything dangerous. I *am* suggesting that we speak to the one person who knows more about what goes on in our local farming community than anyone else. Even more than my husband."

Energized, Emma jumped to her feet. "Come along, Harriet. I'll walk you home. That person lives on the way."

A quick walk to Riverwatch Farm took them just down a tidy lane off the village high street. No one in Highbury knew the local farming community better than Farmer Mitchell. He was also an intelligent, thoughtful man whose opinion was very much worth considering. If anyone could elucidate the mystery of smugglers preying on local farmers, it would be he.

As they turned into the drive, Mr. Mitchell must have spotted them, because he came hurrying down from the farmhouse to meet them.

"Mrs. Knightley, Mrs. Martin," he exclaimed. "It's a cold day to be walking about the village. Come inside to the parlor before you catch yourself a chill."

"You sound just like my father," Emma teased.

Farmer Mitchell cast her a shrewd glance. "I'll wager Mr. Woodhouse doesn't know you're out strolling country lanes with Mrs. Martin."

She tapped the side of her nose. "Then let's keep it our little secret, shall we?"

He returned her smile as he ushered them through the front door.

Riverwatch Farm was a tidy, prosperous establishment with an excellent dairy that produced cheeses much in demand throughout the district. The Mitchells had resided in Highbury for several generations, and the farmhouse reflected its age in a hodgepodge of shapes and styles. But it was in excellent repair, and the furnishings, though not particularly stylish, were of good quality and just what one would expect of a respectable farming family.

"My missus is away for the afternoon," said Mr. Mitchell, "but if you ladies will take a seat in the parlor, I'm sure I can rustle up a decent sort of tea."

"Thank you, but no," said Emma. "Unless Harriet would like some tea."

Her friend smiled. "I'm fine. I'll have tea when I return home."

Emma took one of the low armchairs by the fireplace, and was immediately grateful for the crackling blaze. With a sigh, Harriet eased down onto the well-cushioned sofa opposite.

Farmer Mitchell planted his burly form between them, a slight expression of puzzlement marking his genial features. "Then how can I be of service this day?"

Emma hesitated. "It's rather a delicate subject, so I'm not sure—"

"It's about the smugglers," Harriet blurted out. "And how they've been threatening people."

So much for delicacy.

Then again, that was Harriet. Tact was not one of the dear girl's strong points, even when caution was the order of the day.

If Farmer Mitchell was surprised, he didn't show it. Instead, he calmly took a seat in an old leather armchair next to Emma. "Can I ask why you're talking to me instead of Mr. Knightley or Constable Sharpe?"

Emma gave him a look. "I rather think you can guess why we're not going to Constable Sharpe."

Mr. Mitchell snorted. Due to some of the events surrounding last year's investigation into the murder of Mrs. Elton, he had as low an opinion of the constable as she did.

"My husband is currently in London," Emma added. "Besides, the person who is being threatened is a farmer."

"So you thought to talk to a farmer about it, I reckon."

Emma opened her hands. "You know every farmer in the area, Mr. Mitchell, and I'm quite certain you're not involved in any smuggling operations."

His lips twitched. "Sure of that, are you?"

"I most certainly am."

"Then you'd best tell me what it's about, and I'll see if I can help."

Emma glanced at Harriet, who related the tale she'd told earlier. Mr. Mitchell asked a few questions but mostly held his peace, listening with a thoughtful frown.

"I'm sorry to hear of such goings-on right here in Highbury," he said when Harriet had finished. "But smugglers have been running up from the coast for as long as anyone in these parts can remember, often using the abandoned Roman roads. I remember flaskers and freetraders doing their runs right past Highbury when I was a boy."

Harriet tilted her head. "What's a flasker?"

"A freetrader who runs liquor."

"It appears you're not surprised to hear that smugglers are operating near or in Highbury," Emma said.

He thoughtfully rubbed his chin. "Maybe I am a bit. There's not been much activity this close to the village in years—not till that dustup with poor Mr. Larkins. If the freetraders have been operating in our vicinity, they've kept it mighty close to the vest."

Emma leaned forward. "So, you don't believe Larkins is a smuggler, either."

He scoffed. "I've never met a man more God-fearing and upright in my life. It was a barmy notion to think he'd take such a risk, much less betray Mr. Knightley. If you'll remember, ma'am, I was on the coroner's jury. It seemed pretty clear to me that your take on the matter was the right one. Mr. Larkins was set up for a fall. But as that pompous blowhard—I mean, Dr. Hughes—pointed out, our job was to decide if murder had been done, not who did it."

"So until this incident with Larkins, you'd heard nothing of any recent import about smuggling nearby?" Emma asked, to be sure.

"Mayhap one or two things, but nothing I paid much attention to. I've certainly heard no tale of farms being used for depots, or farmers being threatened."

Emma sighed. "We were hoping you'd heard something."

"I haven't, but I know someone who might be able to help."

She perked up. "Yes?"

He lumbered up from his chair. "I'll fetch him now. Won't take more than a few minutes."

As he exited the room, Emma and Harriet exchanged a surprised glance.

"I wonder who it is?" said Harriet.

They didn't have long to wait for Mr. Mitchell's return. Only a few minutes later, they heard the rumble of masculine voices. Mr. Mitchell reentered the room, followed by another man dressed in rough working clothes.

"Mr. Curtis," exclaimed Emma. "How nice to see you again."

The weather-beaten, middle-aged man flashed a broad grin. "And you, Mrs. Knightley. But it's just Dick, ma'am. There be no need to be fancy with the likes of me."

Dick Curtis was a local laborer who'd fallen on hard times

after injuring his hand in a farming accident. Thankfully, the Mitchells had taken him under their wing, giving him as much work as he could perform. Emma and George had also had occasion to help him in the past, earning Dick's undying loyalty.

"Mrs. Martin, you're lookin' well," he said with a genial nod. "And I'm happy to be helpin' you in any way I can, Mrs. Knightley. Mr. Mitchell's explained to me about them bastards—" He grimaced. "Beggin' your pardon, ladies. What them varlets are doing to your friends."

"Have you heard reports of anything like that?" Emma asked.

"Not exactly, but I'm fair certain I had a run-in with them same smugglers just a few months ago."

Emma's heart skipped a beat. "Truly? Do you have any idea who they are?"

"Sorry, Mrs. Knightley. It was night, and they were all but disguised. That don't mean I didn't take note of some things, though."

Mr. Mitchell tapped him on the shoulder. "Don't keep the ladies waiting, man. Tell her what you told me back then."

Dick scoffed. "I'm gettin' there, never fear. Anyway, it was like this, Mrs. Knightley. I was walkin' home from the Crown one night in November. I was almost there when two blokes came out of the bushes at the end of the lane. Surprised me something fierce, they did. Had no idea they were there, and by the looks of them, they were up to no good."

"How did they look?" asked Emma.

"Well, they had scarves wound up round their faces and their hats pulled down round their ears. It weren't that cold a night, so there was no reason to swaddle themselves up like that."

"They didn't want to be recognized," Emma replied.

"You got it, missus."

"So, you had a run-in with them. What did they want?"

"For me to work for them on some runs. Help them transport goods through Surrey to London."

Harriet stared at him. "They just came up to you like that and asked you to work for them?"

"It's not that unusual," interjected Farmer Mitchell. "Smugglers sometimes approach farm laborers in the winter months, when work is scarce."

"And you only spoke to them outside in the lane?" Emma asked Dick.

"Aye. I sure wasn't gonna let the likes of them into my cottage."

"Hmm."

Harriet tilted her head. "What are you thinking, Mrs. Knightley?"

She remembered that when the smugglers approached William Cox, they did so quite openly in a tavern. These men, however, had been a great deal more circumspect, and she couldn't help wondering about the difference.

"It's not important at the moment," she replied. "What did you tell them, Dick?"

He looked sheepish. "Something that ain't proper to say in front of ladies."

Emma had to laugh. "The gist of it was no."

"It definitely was, ma'am."

"Good for you. Now, what else can you tell me about them? From their voices, for instance, might they have been locals or strangers?"

Dick crossed his arms over his burly chest. "I could have sworn I recognized one voice, but now I'm not so sure."

Emma pounced on that. "Someone local?"

"Aye, but I'm sure it weren't no Mr. Larkins, I can tell you that."

"You're certain."

"Aye."

"What about the other one?"

Dick held up his good hand. "Now, he was interesting. Better dressed than the other fellow, and I was thinkin' he wasn't a workin' bloke or a farmer type. He tried to disguise his voice by talking low, but I could tell he weren't no country folk."

Emma's brain spun for a moment over that tidbit. "That's interesting. Could you tell anything else about him? Tall, broad-shouldered, short—anything like that?"

Dick frowned. "Not a brawny fellow, I can tell you. Average, I guess. He was wearing a greatcoat, so it was a bit hard to tell."

Emma pondered how to phrase the next admittedly sensitive question, but then decided to take a page from Harriet's book.

"Dick, this may seem like a strange question," she said, "but do you think either of these men could have been Mr. Barlowe?"

Harriet squeaked and Mr. Mitchell's jaw sagged, but Dick simply frowned.

"Who's Mr. Barlowe?" he asked.

Drat.

"He's Highbury's curate."

"Sorry, Mrs. Knightley," Dick apologetically said. "Don't know him. I'm not much for churchgoin' these days."

"Or at all," Mr. Mitchell tartly commented.

"Happens you're right," Dick replied with unimpaired calm. "I haven't been much for church ever since old Mr. Bates was vicar. And then when my dad passed on . . . I used to take him, you see."

"I understand," Emma said with a sigh. "I was just taking a bit of a wild guess."

Mr. Mitchell cast her a shrewd glance. "You're thinking of

what happened to that prevention officer, and the lights in the bell tower."

"You heard about the lights?"

"I expect everyone in the village has by now." Mr. Mitchell tapped his chin. "I'll say this, though. If Barlowe does have his nose in this, he wouldn't be the first clerical gent to get involved with freetraders."

Harriet squeaked again, obviously appalled by that observation.

"Dick, can you think of anything else that might be of note?" asked Emma.

He shook his head. "Sorry, missus. I wish I could."

She rose. "Don't be sorry. You've been incredibly helpful. Would you mind if I relayed this information to my husband?"

Dick smiled. "You do whatever you think best, Mrs. Knightley. You and your husband are top of the trees for me."

Emma couldn't hold back a grin. "Thank you."

Mr. Mitchell helped Harriet up and escorted them outside, with Dick following.

Emma stopped in the drive. "Would you do me the favor of keeping our discussion private for now? I don't want to start any harmful rumors about . . ."

"About Mr. Barlowe." The farmer nodded. "Never fear, ma'am. Dick and I know how to keep our mouths shut."

"Thank you. I'm very grateful to both of you."

"Goodness," exclaimed Harriet as she and Emma walked down the drive. "I can hardly believe that someone as mild as Mr. Barlowe could be involved in anything so dangerous. I certainly can't imagine him threatening anyone."

"I suppose not," Emma replied.

Still, she would bet a bob that the vicar was involved somehow. There were simply too many coincidences starting to build up.

Could he also be guilty of murder, callously pushing Prudence to her death? Emma thought not. But what if he'd had an accomplice, someone who—according to Dick—might be a local man, as well? Could that mystery person be responsible for Prudence's death?

   Her instincts told her that she was finally on the right track. And if that was the case, Highbury might have more than smugglers lurking in its midst. It just might have a ruthless killer, as well.

Chapter 25

Emma returned to Hartfield to find the front hall stacked with luggage. "Goodness, Simon. What is all this?"

The footman left off sorting the bags and came over to take her outerwear. "Mr. Knightley has just returned from London, ma'am."

"And apparently brought half the city home with him."

"Just Mrs. John Knightley and the children."

Emma stared at him, astonished. "My sister is here?"

"Yes, ma'am. The children are upstairs in the nursery, and Mr. Woodhouse, Mr. Knightley, and Mrs. Knightley are in the drawing room."

What could have brought Isabella back to Hartfield so soon?

She hurried down the hall and into the drawing room to find her loved ones seated in front of the fire, enjoying the contents of a large tea tray. George glanced up, smiled, and came to meet her. Since they'd parted with just a *titch* of irritation between them, stepping into his embrace felt like heaven.

"Are you well, my darling?" he murmured.

"Perfectly." She glanced over his shoulder. "Is everything all right in Brunswick Square?"

"I think so."

Emma reluctantly broke off the embrace and went to greet her sister. "Dearest, what a surprise."

"I hope it's a happy one," said Isabella, returning her hug.

"Silly, of course it is. Father and I were talking just this morning about asking you to return to Hartfield." She smiled. "It's like an answer to a prayer."

"Indeed," said their father. "Although I do hope Isabella and the children did not catch cold on the trip. Carriages can be so drafty."

"George saw to everything," Isabella said. "We had blankets and hot bricks all the way down."

"Yes, we were quite snug," George dryly replied. "All seven of us."

Emma tried not to laugh. Wedged into a carriage with a passel of lively children—one of them a squirmy baby—was hardly the ticket for comfortable travel.

She took a seat as Isabella poured her a cup of tea. "Will John be joining us at some point?"

"I'm afraid he's terribly busy at the moment. In fact, it was he who suggested we return to Highbury. He knew I felt quite dreadful about leaving you and Father in the midst of such an uproar, and he thought you could use my support."

"That was very kind of him."

And most unlike her brother-in-law, who hated being separated from his wife and children.

"As long as you're not too worried about the, er, problems we've been experiencing in Highbury," Emma added.

Isabella shrugged. "Both John and George assured me that both Hartfield and Donwell were perfectly safe, and that I was not to worry about any of it."

When Emma lifted an eyebrow at her husband, he also shrugged. "Despite our recent difficulties, I do think Highbury is safe. And since you could use Isabella's support right now, the suggestion made a great deal of sense."

They might just change their minds about that after Emma filled him in on the events of the last few days.

"We must not look a gift horse in the mouth, Emma," Father said. "We should be very grateful for Isabella's visit. The children will benefit as well, as the country is always better than the city."

Emma smiled. "Of course I'm grateful. You must stay as long as you wish, Isabella."

"I wish you could stay forever," Father wistfully said.

"I think Miss Bates might have something to say about that," Emma wryly replied. "Now, isn't it time for your afternoon nap, Father? Don't forget the Bates ladies and the Westons are coming for dinner. You'll want to be properly rested."

"Dear me, I forgot all about that in the excitement of George and Isabella's arrival."

"I'll go up with you, Father," said Isabella. "I want to check on the children and then take a rest myself."

"Very wise, my dear. Travel is so fatiguing. Perhaps we should have Perry in to look you and the children over, just to be safe. A restorative tonic might be in order."

As they left the room, arm in arm, Father and Isabella debated the merits of restorative tonics versus calming draughts.

Emma turned back to her husband. "I cannot believe John encouraged Isabella to return here without him. Are you sure all is well?"

"It seems to be. I will say that John is quite harried with work, poor fellow, and this business with Larkins has added to it."

"I'm sorry to hear it. I hope, however, you were able to make some progress."

"We were. On John's advice, I hired a barrister with an excellent reputation in criminal defense. Unfortunately, his initial opinion is that the case against Larkins is strong."

"Drat. That's not good."

"John and I did contact a Bow Street Runner, though. A

Mr. Phelps has taken the case, and will focus on tracking down the smuggling gang."

"That, at least, is excellent news." She placed a large piece of walnut cake on a plate and handed it to him. "If we can untangle that knot, we should be able to clear Larkins of both charges."

"Remember, we don't as yet have any clear evidence that the smugglers were behind Prudence's death."

She eyed him with exasperation. "Then the only reasonable conclusion would be that Larkins is guilty of both crimes. Either that or two separate criminals would be trying to frame him."

George took a bite of cake before answering. "Not necessarily. He could be cleared of the charge of smuggling but still be in possession of contraband goods. As we've seen, it's not uncommon for otherwise law-abiding citizens to buy from smugglers. The Crown could easily make the case that the bloody mobcap—and the fact that Larkins harbored feelings for Prudence—are separate and apart from the presence of the contraband tobacco."

"But we know it's not, George," she argued.

"I understand, my dear, but *we* will not be sitting on the jury at the murder trial."

She couldn't help muttering a mildly naughty oath under her breath.

George put down his plate and came to sit next to her. "It's early days. We have hired the best defense, and now Mr. Phelps is on the case. We're doing everything we can to run the smugglers to ground."

"There have actually been developments in that regard, although I don't even know where to begin. It's been rather a fright since you've been gone."

"My dear, you fill me with trepidation." George narrowed his gaze. "You've not been interfering in the investigation, have you?"

She rounded her eyes. "Why would you make that inference?"

"Because I've known you my entire life?"

"Yes, but someone needs to investigate things around here, especially since poor Mr. Clarke was attacked in the churchyard—presumably while looking for smugglers."

George looked stunned. "Was he badly injured?"

"He's recovering, although it was a near thing. If Mr. Barlowe hadn't found him early the next morning, the poor man probably would have frozen to death. He's at the Crown, and Mrs. Stokes has been taking care of him. But I'm sure Mr. Clarke will wish to speak to you himself."

George shook his head. "I can hardly believe it. This is much too close to home, Emma."

"Wait until you hear the next piece of the puzzle."

She then proceeded to tell him about the strange lights in the bell tower, and what she and Miss Bates had discovered.

"You went up into the tower with Miss Bates?" he asked in apparent disbelief.

"I didn't wish to bring her along, but she insisted. In all fairness, she's been surprisingly helpful."

George muttered something under his breath about *angels fearing to tread*.

Emma patted his knee. "There was nothing dangerous about it, unless one counts a ridiculous discussion with Mr. Barlowe as dangerous."

He sighed. "So he caught you snooping."

"Not snooping. Investigating."

"Emma, you know the constable investigates these matters."

"Unfortunately, however, he keeps arriving at the wrong conclusion."

"Emma—"

"George, you must trust me on this. Constable Sharpe is convinced it was a simple robbery, but that's a ridiculous conclusion. And Miss Bates and I agree that Mr. Barlowe is acting very suspiciously, and he's also in possession of what are likely contraband goods. How else could you explain that he has the best French brandy in the village?"

"I cannot," he reluctantly replied.

"And then there were the lights in the bell tower. Perry saw them, and *he* is certainly a reliable witness. Even you must agree with that."

She obviously must have sounded a bit put out because he flashed her a rueful smile as he took her hand.

"Of course you're a reliable witness, and obviously you're a great deal more perceptive and intelligent than Constable Sharpe. But that's not the point."

"You're afraid I'll run myself into trouble. I understand, George, but I've been very careful."

He pressed a quick kiss to her mouth. "All right, I believe you. And I share your concern. I also see a discussion with both Mr. Clarke and Mr. Barlowe in my immediate future."

"That's excellent, but there's more."

His dark eyebrows went up. "Really?"

"Yes. Harriet stopped by this morning with some *quite* alarming information. Oh, and then there's William Cox."

He sighed. "Good Lord. I've only been gone three days, Emma."

She wrinkled her nose in sympathy. "I know. It's a lot to take in, dearest."

As she related the details she'd alluded to, George's expression grew ever more troubled.

"If it was just as William said," Emma finished, "one might conclude that the smugglers were merely passing by Highbury or Donwell on their way to London, and that no one in the parish was involved to any real degree. However, from what Dick Curtis told us, that's probably not the case."

George slowly shook his head. "It's a great shame that Harriet cannot give us the name of her friend."

"I cannot ask her to break her promise. Her friend is very frightened, and one cannot blame her."

George fell to pondering for several moments before rising and pulling her up. "I think a chat with Mr. Barlowe is the first thing in order."

"What, now?"

"No time like the present."

"Do you wish me to go with you, then?"

Her husband regarded her with a sardonic eye. "Can I stop you?"

She smiled. "I suppose you could lock me in our bedroom."

"And you would pick the lock."

As he led her from the room, Emma decided she'd quite like to learn how to pick a lock. Given the events of the past few weeks, such a skill might come in handy.

Mr. Barlowe seemed to crumple before their eyes. Since George had just threatened to haul him in front of a revenue agent, the curate's reaction wasn't surprising.

"I swear, Mr. Knightley," he pleaded, "I had nothing to do with it. The smugglers were using the bell tower for storage long before I arrived in Highbury."

Emma exchanged an astonished glance with George.

"Truly?" she asked Mr. Barlowe.

He bobbed his head like a demented peahen. "I'll tell you everything I know, which isn't really very much. As long as you don't haul me in front of a revenue agent, that is."

What little color remained in his face drained away. Emma didn't think she'd ever seen anyone go so pale before—at least while still alive.

"And please don't tell the bishop," he added. "I'll never get another position."

"Who and what I tell depends entirely on you," George sternly replied.

They were sitting in the main drawing room of the vicarage— a very cold drawing room, since Mr. Barlowe declined to build a fire. Given his initial reluctance to speak with them, he'd probably hoped to freeze them out and send them on their way.

He'd certainly been surprised to see them and had only reluctantly invited them into the vicarage. The curate had initially denied any strange doings in the church's bell tower, while also vowing that he knew nothing about smugglers. It wasn't until George donned his magistrate's persona and threatened him with legal action that the man had cracked.

And thank goodness for that, because Emma was exceedingly tired of being cold. Solving a murder and rousting a smuggling ring in the middle of January was not for the faint of heart.

George speared Mr. Barlowe with a stern gaze. "How do you know the smuggling activity predated your appearance in Highbury?"

"The vicarage cook told me. She said that the vicar before Mr. Elton was the one who started it all."

Yet another unwelcome surprise.

"That would have been Mr. Allen," said Emma, shaking her head. "I cannot believe it. He seemed such a respectable man."

"Did Mr. Elton continue this arrangement?" George asked.

"Cook said he was frightened by the smugglers and did his best to ignore them." Mr. Barlowe shuddered. "Which I can certainly understand. Look what the brutes did to poor Mr. Clarke."

Emma glanced at the decanters and liquor bottles inside the breakfront. "I suppose that accounts for the excellent spirits and tea you have here."

Mr. Barlowe nodded. "Payment in kind for using the bell tower for storage."

"But you said the smugglers had stopped using the bell tower when you arrived in Highbury?" asked George.

The curate's gaze darted about the room, looking anywhere but at them.

"So I had assumed," he finally replied. "I . . . I never saw any signs of activity in the tower or anywhere else in the church. Nor did my cook mention it."

"Come, Mr. Barlowe," Emma said in a skeptical tone. "I saw the marks on the bell tower floor. They looked very much like someone had been dragging about casks. I very much doubt they were from pews stored up there."

George frowned. "What pews? They haven't been replaced in decades."

When Emma raised her eyebrows at the curate, he winced.

"All right, I did that," he admitted. "Or, rather, it was Mrs. Stokes and a few of her men from the Crown Inn."

Emma felt her jaw sag. "Are you suggesting Mrs. Stokes is part of the smuggling ring?"

He flapped his hands. "No, of course not. She has nothing to do with it, as far as I know."

"Then what the devil was she doing in your bell tower?" George demanded.

"I asked her to take what was left. Two casks of spirits were still there when I took up the position in Highbury. I don't know why they were left behind, and I don't care. I just wanted them gone!"

"Because of the increase in the smuggling activity?" George asked.

"Yes, and because of Miss Parr's death. Everyone was asking questions, first about that poor girl and then about the smugglers. I . . . I grew frightened. If anyone thought to look up in the bell tower, they would see the casks and think I was involved."

Emma exchanged another glance with George.

"What does Miss Parr's death have to do with the smugglers?" she asked as calmly as she could manage.

The curate blinked at her question, as if genuinely surprised. "Nothing, as far as I know. Although I suppose that's not right, because Larkins is obviously guilty of both crimes."

Emma scoffed. "That is *not* true."

Mr. Barlowe was obviously recovering, because he bristled at her. "Everyone else seems to think he's guilty."

"Then everyone is exceedingly stupid," she retorted.

George touched her knee in silent warning.

"Mr. Barlowe," he asked, "did you truly hear or see nothing on the night Mr. Clarke was attacked?"

"I did not, sir. My bedroom is on the other side of the house, facing away from the churchyard. It was only by chance that I found him the next morning."

That response, at least, had the ring of truth.

Emma blew out a frustrated sigh. "If the smugglers weren't using the church anymore, why were they up in the bell tower in so visible a fashion?"

George thought for a few moments. "They must have wanted to be visible, to attract Mr. Clarke's attention."

The puzzle piece dropped into place.

"So they could set upon him and make it look like a robbery." Emma huffed in disgust. "Which was the conclusion drawn by Constable Sharpe, naturally."

The curate pressed a hand to his mouth, looking both ill and ill at ease. Emma couldn't shake the sense that the man was still withholding something.

"Mr. Barlowe, why did you ask Mrs. Stokes to remove the casks instead of coming to me?" asked George.

He had the grace to look ashamed. "I know it was very wrong, but I was frightened of what you and others might think. I worried it might affect my position here in Highbury."

"You don't know my husband very well, do you?" Emma dryly responded.

"I don't know anyone here very well, Mrs. Knightley," he stiffly replied.

"Which I would suggest is your fault, sir."

He started to huff when George interrupted him. "So Mrs. Stokes simply agreed to take your request to remove the casks?"

Mr. Barlowe struggled to calm himself. "No, she was most unhappy about it. But I managed to persuade her. I suppose she took pity on me."

George glanced at Emma and rose, extending a hand to help her to her feet.

"Is there anything else you can tell us, Mr. Barlowe?" asked George. "If so, I would strongly advise you to do it now."

The curate came unsteadily to his feet, as if his knees were knocking. "I know nothing else, sir. I promise."

"And I'll hold you to that promise."

Mr. Barlowe morosely trailed them to the front door.

"If you think of anything else at all, send me a note immediately," said George in his best magistrate's voice.

Mr. Barlowe shifted nervously from one foot to the other. "You may be sure of it, sir. You have my word."

Then he ushered George and Emma out the door, banging it behind them.

"I suppose we must cross him off our list of suspects," Emma said with a sigh.

"I never had him on it," George replied. "The man seems frightened of his own shadow, and is certainly too frightened to be a smuggler."

"True. Yet, I cannot help but feel he's withholding something." She grimaced. "I can't quite put my finger on it."

"While Mr. Barlowe is obviously not forthcoming by nature, I believe we put the fear of God into him. I cannot imagine him withholding anything of value at this point."

"I hope you're correct," she said as they started to walk briskly up Vicarage Lane. "By the by, are you thinking we should pop in on Mrs. Stokes?"

Her husband's glance was amused. "How did you know?"

"Unlike Mr. Barlowe, I know you *very* well."

"I'm happy to hear it. And, yes, I feel a visit to Mrs. Stokes is in order. Although I believe her to be innocent of smuggling, I cannot forget her reaction to Mr. Clarke at the inquest. If you recall, she seemed most uncomfortable at the suggestion that some in Highbury might be in receipt of contraband goods."

"I had forgotten that. I hope you're correct that she's not involved."

"I feel certain there's no direct involvement. Still, she might be able to provide us with useful information. Innkeepers often know more about the contraband trade than anyone."

By now they were approaching the Crown Inn. It was quiet at this time of day, as both tradesmen and laborers were still at work. Although a coaching establishment, the Crown never had much traffic in that regard, since Highbury was fairly out of the way.

They stepped inside to see Mrs. Stokes down the hall, behind the high counter that served to check in the occasional guest. She glanced up, clearly surprised to see them.

"Mr. Knightley and Mrs. Knightley, my word," she exclaimed as she came round the counter. "How can I help you?"

A tall, sturdy woman with a deceptively placid manner, Mrs. Stokes was well able to handle the sort of incidents that occurred in a coaching inn and tavern, including dealing with the occasional raucous customer. She became the sole proprietor of the Crown after the death of her husband some years ago, and had a reputation for running a clean, respectable establishment.

"Good afternoon," said George. "My wife and I were hoping to chat with you. Perhaps we could step into your office for a bit more privacy?"

The woman's steady hazel gaze grew wary, but she simply nodded. "This way, if you please."

She led them into a small office behind the counter that held a desk, two wooden chairs, and several shelves neatly stacked with ledgers.

Mrs. Stokes sat down at her desk, and Emma took the other chair. When George closed the door and positioned himself against it, Mrs. Stokes looked dismayed.

"Is something wrong, Mr. Knightley?"

George smiled. "I trust not. But first, may I inquire as to the state of Mr. Clarke's health?"

"He took a dreadful beating and was all but perishing from the cold. His nose was broken, but Mr. Perry thankfully sorted that out. The poor man was bruised from head to toe and knocked unconscious. Dr. Hughes insists he stay in bed for a few more days, at least."

"Is there anything we can do to help?" asked Emma.

"I shouldn't think so, ma'am." The innkeeper cast her a long-suffering look. "Between Mr. Perry and Dr. Hughes, I have quite enough help."

Emma exchanged a sympathetic grimace with her.

"Please tell Mr. Clarke I'll call on him tomorrow," said George, "if he feels well enough for visitors."

"I will, and I think he'll be happy to see you. He's that keen to get back on the job." She let out a little snort. "I half expect him to sneak down into my cellars, looking for contraband."

Emma captured her gaze. "And would he find any?"

Mrs. Stokes blinked. "He would not, Mrs. Knightley. Of that you can be sure."

"Not even two casks from the church bell tower?"

The innkeeper stilled for several long seconds, which the casement clock on the corner of her desk counted down.

Mrs. Stokes finally breathed out a frustrated sigh. "No good deed goes unpunished, I suppose. Mr. Barlowe seemed to forget that particular saying when he was preaching to me about charity toward one's neighbors."

"So you did relieve Mr. Barlowe of his casks," said George.

She reluctantly nodded. "Only because he was so blasted insistent. Begging your pardon, Mrs. Knightley."

"There's no need," Emma replied. "And we truly aren't trying to catch you out, Mrs. Stokes."

"I believe you just did," she ruefully replied.

"I'm hoping this discussion need not go further than this room," said George. "But given the current situation in Highbury, including the attack on Mr. Clarke, we need to verify the circumstances regarding the transfer of the casks to your establishment."

"I'll do my best to answer your questions, Mr. Knightley. I know it's a terrible situation for poor Larkins, and I'd like to help as best I can."

George gave an appreciative nod. "Thank you. Now, Mr. Barlowe told us that the casks were already in the bell tower when he took up his position as curate. And he claimed he had no contact with the smuggling gang since his arrival."

"That's what he told me too, sir."

"Do you believe him?" asked Emma.

Mrs. Stokes nodded. "Mr. Barlowe was scared half out of his wits at the thought of anyone discovering those casks, so he begged me to take them off his hands. He was afraid someone might find them and draw the wrong conclusions."

"And you're truly convinced he has nothing to do with the smugglers?" asked Emma.

"I'd stake a week's worth of receipts on it, Mrs. Knightley. He's too timid, for one thing. And for another, he didn't ask me for a shilling to take those casks. He just wanted them gone."

Emma waggled a hand. "I can't help feeling he's hiding something."

"I think he's just afraid, ma'am," said Mrs. Stokes. "He's worried the smugglers might want to use the church again to store their goods. What happened to Mr. Clarke put the fear of God into him, if you'll pardon the pun."

Emma supposed she had to agree. Mr. Barlowe was not temperamentally suited to dangerous ventures such as smuggling, and for all his odd behaviors he seemed to take his duties as curate very seriously.

"Mrs. Stokes," said George, "I was also wondering if you could shed any light on the charges against Mr. Larkins."

She scoffed. "Larkins is no more guilty of smuggling than I am. The poor man's been set up—by the real smugglers, I reckon."

Emma rewarded her with a smile. "It's good to know that not everyone in town thinks him a criminal."

"Larkins had dinner at the Crown on the night of Prudence's death, did he not?" asked George.

"He did. I told Constable Sharpe that. But Larkins didn't stay late. He wanted to be near the abbey in case he was needed." She grimaced. "I wish he'd stayed longer, so I could have vouched for him."

"How did he seem that night?" asked Emma.

She shrugged. "Quiet and polite, same as he always is."

"Just a few more questions," said George. "Has any information come to your ears about this smuggling gang? Rumors or gossip from either regulars or those passing through?"

"There's gossip aplenty, but it's all nonsense."

She paused for a few seconds, considering them with a shrewd gaze.

"When my husband was alive, he allowed freetraders to use the Crown as storage on their way to London," she added. "He was paid in spirits—top-drawer French brandy and Holland gin, mostly. My Joe were a good man, but we almost came to blows more than a few times over it. Couldn't talk him out of it, though, so I did my best to ignore it."

"That wasn't particularly unusual during those war years," George replied in a sympathetic tone.

Emma leaned forward. "Did you ever meet any of these smugglers?"

"Just once, after my husband died. Six years ago, now. One of the varlets came sniffing around, wanting to keep the same deal." Her expression grew hard. "I sent him off with a stiff word, I can tell you."

"Did you recognize the man, perchance?" asked George.

"Never saw him before, sir. He weren't no local man, that I know. I thought he was a London fellow by his accent."

Emma couldn't help being curious. "What did he look like?"

"I recollect that he was an older man, with a bit of polish to him. Very sure of himself, as if he'd been running a rig for a long time." She huffed out a laugh. "The fool tried to intimidate me. I told him that if he ever showed his face at the Crown again, he'd find the barrel of my pistol shoved in it."

Emma regarded the innkeeper with newfound respect. "How did he take that?"

"He knew I meant it. I never saw him again."

"Thank you, Mrs. Stokes," said George. "You've been very helpful."

The innkeeper escorted them to the front door. "I'll keep my ears open, Mr. Knightley. If I hear anything of value, I'll let you know."

"I appreciate that."

They made their farewells and then turned in the direction of Hartfield.

"What do you think?" Emma asked.

"We confirmed that Barlowe is not a suspect, nor is Mrs. Stokes."

"I'm not sure how that helps."

George glanced down at her. "Does it not strike you as interesting that we have a smuggling gang in the vicinity of Highbury, and yet they've made no attempt in the past six years to enlist the help of the only innkeeper in the village? One would think that would be a natural partnership for any self-respecting smuggling gang."

Emma frowned, her pace involuntarily slowing. "Because they knew there would be no point."

George smiled. "Exactly."

"Dearest, of course! Because it's the same gang as six years ago!"

"Or at least one involving some of the same people."

She squeezed his arm. "George, that's very good."

"I have my moments," he wryly replied.

"You have many good moments. You're quite the smartest man in Surrey. That's why I married you."

He cast her a knowing glance. "That's the *only* reason?"

Emma felt her cheeks grow hot. "Hush, George. We're out in public."

He chuckled.

"You realize what this means," she said.

"Yes, but I'd like your thoughts on the matter."

"It means that the smugglers know a great deal about Highbury and those who live here."

"Yes, they are quite familiar with us, as we had begun to suspect."

Emma's spurt of elation faded as the full implications of that sank in. Someone, perhaps even a local, had a very close eye on Highbury and the people who lived there.

And whoever that was, they weren't afraid to kill to achieve their aims.

Chapter 26

"How tiresome that you must return to London so soon," Emma said as she poured herself another cup of tea. "You're gone so often these days I fear you'll forget what I look like."

George eyed her from across the breakfast table. "Did I forget what you looked like last night?"

She widened her eyes in mock innocence. "Since the lights were out, I cannot say."

He leaned forward, lowering his voice. "Then next time, I suggest we leave a lamp lit. That way you can be sure I haven't forgotten what you look like."

Despite herself, Emma felt a blush rise to her cheeks. "What a thing to say, George. I'm terribly shocked."

He returned to slicing his ham. "You didn't seem shocked last night, my dear. The opposite in fact."

While that was certainly true, it was *quite* another thing to discuss it over the breakfast table.

Fortunately, Henry entered the dining room, sparing Emma the need to take her husband to task.

"Good morning," she said to the boy. "I hope you slept well."

"Yes, thank you. I always sleep well at Donwell. It's ever so much quieter than Hartfield, and I even get my own bed."

As he took the seat next to her, he cast her a puzzled look. "Your cheeks are all red, Auntie. Do you have a fever?"

George tried—and failed—to hide a grin behind his coffee cup.

"Heavens, no," Emma responded, feeling even more warmth flood into her face. "I'm perfectly well."

Henry cast suspicious glances between both of them. "You look just like Mama does when I catch Papa kissing her or talking about adult things." His expression became vaguely alarmed. "You're not going to start kissing each other now, are you?"

George laughed while Emma wrapped an arm around her nephew's shoulder.

"No, but I'm going to kiss you," she said, making a show of smooching him on the cheek.

"Ugh. Adults are silly."

"I think you still like us, despite our silliness," she replied. "And you're enjoying your stay here, yes?"

"I'll say. I hope I can stay with you and Uncle George whenever we come to Highbury."

"Then I'll see what can be arranged with your mama."

They had now been settled at the abbey for the past three days, after Isabella had initially been reluctant to let Henry decamp from Hartfield. The attack on Mr. Clarke had greatly unsettled her, and she'd even thought to return to London. Emma had pointed out that it was Mr. Clarke's work as a revenue agent that had made him a target. Since no one other than him in Highbury was involved with smugglers—at least to any certain knowledge—then no one else should be in danger. With excellent timing, Father had dolefully added that he couldn't bear the thought of Isabella leaving so soon, giving every indication that he would fall into a melancholic state. With George's reassurances that all would be well, Isabella had finally allowed herself to be persuaded to stay. She'd even agreed that Henry could return to the abbey with George and Emma.

Thankfully, the three days had been blessedly quiet. The smugglers had appeared to fade into the night as if they'd never existed, which while good for Highbury was not so good for Larkins. The need to clear his name was ever more urgent, so George was returning to London.

Emma smiled at her nephew. "What would you like for breakfast? I can ring for Harry to bring you coddled eggs."

Henry shook his head. "I already talked to him in the corridor. He said there were still some of Serle's butterscotch scones left in the kitchen, so he's going to bring them up."

"Hmm. I think you should have a slice of ham, too. Your mother wouldn't like it if you only ate sweets for breakfast."

Henry reached for a slice of honey cake. "That's one of the reasons I like staying with you. I can eat nice things for breakfast, instead of gruel or stupid old toast."

The boy did seem to be thriving under their care. Emma thought he might even have gained a pound or two.

"Very well," she agreed. "But don't tell your mother."

Henry rolled his eyes, perfectly communicating that it was an unnecessary admonition.

"George, would you like another cup of coffee?" she asked.

"Thank you, but no. I should be on my way."

Henry frowned. "Where are you going, Uncle George?"

"I must travel to London, but I should return by tomorrow night."

"Are you going to meet with the Bow Street Runner? I wish I could go with you."

Emma raised her eyebrows. "Why is that, Henry?"

"Because I'd like to become a runner someday. I think it would be very exciting."

"I suggest you don't tell your mother of any such ambition." Isabella would faint on the spot.

"I'm not that dumb, Auntie Emma," the boy said with an exasperated sigh.

She ruffled his hair. "You're the opposite of dumb. I think you're the smartest Knightley there is."

He suffered her affections but kept his attention on his uncle. "*Are* you going to meet with the runner?"

When George cast her a quick glance, Emma shrugged. "It's not as if Henry hasn't been exposed to this dreadful situation from the beginning."

"Very true," he replied. "Then, yes. Your father and I are going to meet with the runner. We'll see—"

He paused when Harry entered with a plate of scones. "Here you go, Master Henry. Mrs. Hodges warmed them up for you."

Henry gave the footman a grateful smile before turning back to his uncle. "Do you think the runner will have any information for you about the smugglers or Mr. Larkins?"

"I would expect so," George replied. "Else I'll be travelling all that way for nothing."

Henry shook his head. "Papa would never ask you to come to London for nothing. I hope what they found helps Mr. Larkins."

"As do we all," said Emma.

George glanced at their footman. "Harry, once you're finished there, please tell Jem to saddle my horse. I want to be on the road within the half hour."

Harry, who'd been stacking plates on the sideboard, nodded. "Right away, Mr. Knightley."

He hurried out, leaving the pile of dirty dishes behind. Emma sighed.

"Don't worry," George said with a wry smile. "I'll also be looking to hire additional staff while I'm in London, including another footman and a maid."

"Thank goodness. While Harry does his best, I fear Mrs. Hodges will turn in her notice if we don't hire more help."

"That is indeed a shocking notion. Now, what are you plans for today, my dear?"

She glanced at her nephew. "Henry and I will be going to Hartfield for most of the day. Father wishes me to go over the household accounts with Miss Bates, and the bride-to-be would also like to discuss wedding preparations."

Neither chore was very appealing, but there was no point in further delay, especially since Highbury had turned peaceful once more. She'd run out of promising avenues of investigation, so she might as well turn her mind to family matters.

Even though Emma still viewed her father's upcoming marriage with a degree of trepidation, there was a significant silver lining. The more time she spent at Donwell, the more she grew to appreciate the gracious old pile and to anticipate her new life with George. As much as she loved her father, her life had been circumscribed by his needs. From now on, though, she would be free to concentrate on her own wishes and dreams, fully embarking on her life as a married woman. She could even imagine a new brood of little Knightleys to awaken Donwell from its years-long slumber.

"You have my sympathies," George wryly commented.

"I will rely on Isabella to do most of the planning. She has a great deal more patience with Miss Bates than I do."

Her husband reached a hand across the table to take hers. "You've made great strides with Miss Bates. Your friendship seems stronger than ever."

"She has rather worn me down," Emma drolly admitted.

George stood. "You don't give yourself enough credit, my dear."

Emma also came to her feet. "Thank you. So, you're off, then."

"I just need to fetch a few things from our room, and then I'll meet you in the front hall. One can hope that Harry has communicated my instructions to Jem by now."

"Oh, you eternal optimist," she joked.

He briefly smiled before turning serious. "You're not to worry while I'm gone, Emma. I truly believe there's no danger from the smugglers at this point. They know we're onto them, so coming back to Highbury would simply be too risky. But just to be sure, I've ordered Harry, both our grooms, and our coachman to keep watch over the house tonight—two of them on each shift. You'll be perfectly safe."

Henry scrambled out of his chair. "I'll look after Auntie Emma, sir. You don't need to worry about that."

George smiled. "I know you will."

Emma hugged her nephew. "And you're not to worry about us, either, George. I'm sure the most alarming thing we'll face in the next few days will be talking Miss Bates out of inviting the entire village to the wedding and persuading Father to allow cake to be served. It's bound to be dreadfully boring."

"I'll hold you to that," he said before exiting the room.

Emma jerked awake as someone jostled her shoulder.

"Auntie Emma, wake up!"

She blinked against the flare of a candle inches from her face and fought to focus.

"Henry?" She shot up to a sitting position. "What's wrong? Are you unwell?"

"I'm fine, but please get up right now!"

Her vision cleared to reveal her nephew standing by the bed in his robe and nightcap, jiggling with impatience. The light flickered madly, so she took the candlestick and set it on her bedside table.

"What's wrong?" she asked again.

"There are men in the back garden again, and this time they're right up against the house."

That news drove away any lingering vestiges of sleep. "Are you sure it's not Harry with our coachman or one of the grooms? Don't forget they're supposed to be watching the house."

"It's not them. I saw the men from the window, and none of them belonged to Donwell. They had a cart with them, too."

Emma threw back the blankets. She shivered in the cold night air as she shoved her feet into her slippers and then groped for her robe at the foot of the bed.

"They were going around the corner of the house," Henry added. "So I stuck my head out the window to get a good look. It was like a donkey cart, but without the donkey. They were pulling it."

Alarm flared as Emma grabbed him by the shoulders. "Please tell me no one saw you."

"I was really quiet. I'm sure no one heard me or saw me."

Emma yanked on her robe, fighting a sense of rampant disbelief. Of all the nights for this to happen, with George gone from the house. And where in thunderbolts were Harry and the stable staff while all this was transpiring?

She lit her bedside candle off his. "You're sure you didn't see Harry or one of the grooms?"

"Yes. Maybe he just didn't hear them."

More likely the dratted fellow had fallen asleep in the kitchen. But that was exactly why George had organized the men in watches of two.

"Henry, what woke you?"

"Maybe the cart wheels on the gravel? But after I was awake I had to use the . . ." He trailed off, looking embarrassed.

"The chamber pot?"

He nodded. "When I was finished, that's when I heard more noise."

Emma headed for the door. "I'll go find Harry and the others. I want you to go back in your room and lock the door, understood?"

In the light of his candle, Henry looked like a little ghost in a nightcap. The expression on his face, though, was very human—and very annoyed.

"I'm coming with you, Auntie Emma. I promised Uncle George I would take care of you."

"That's very kind of you, dear, but Uncle George didn't mean—"

"No."

Henry's expression was the spitting image of his father's when John decided to dig in his heels. Even if she managed to persuade her nephew to return to his room, he would simply sneak out a few minutes later and follow her downstairs.

She capitulated. "You're to stay behind me and do everything I tell you to do. Promise?"

"I promise."

As quickly as she could, Emma made her way to the stairs that led to the great hall and peered over the banister. The hall was shrouded in darkness and silence, with no sign of life. She'd expected to see a fire in the hearth or at least a lantern on one of the tables. It seemed clear that no one had been in the hall since she'd gone up to bed some hours ago.

"All right, let's go down and check the kitchen. The men are probably there, since it's the warmest room in the house."

"They probably did fall asleep," Henry commented with marked disapproval.

"I shouldn't be surprised."

At least in Harry's case. But Donwell's coachmen and two grooms were very dependable men. Then again, the abbey was very large, with very thick walls. She supposed it was possible that one could sit in the kitchen and not hear people creeping about outside, though she knew George had impressed upon his men the need to stay alert.

What were the smugglers doing back in Highbury in the first place, and why at Donwell Abbey? Even Mr. Clarke, still recovering from his injuries, had planned to return to Leatherhead, convinced—according to George—that the danger to their village had passed.

Emma led the way down the long gallery toward the service rooms. When they reached the swinging door that led to the kitchen, Emma gingerly pushed it open, wincing at the squeak of its hinges.

"It looks pretty dark down there," Henry whispered.

It did indeed. Either no one was in the kitchen or the watchmen had fallen asleep and the lamps had guttered out.

"Be careful going down the steps," she cautioned.

She trod down the short staircase, Henry drifting in her wake. When she reached the bottom, Emma held her candle up high. Its rays of illumination cast only a faint light over the large space, just enough to show her that the kitchen was empty.

"Blast," she muttered.

Where in the name of St. George was everyone?

"Maybe they're out in the stables," said Henry. "You can see the back of the house better from there."

"If that's the case, then I can only assume they've *all* fallen asleep," she replied, trying to keep the frustration from her voice.

"Or maybe they saw the smugglers and went after them."

She immediately rejected that thought. If that were the case, surely they would have heard some sort of commotion.

A sense of foreboding began to crowd out her frustration.

"Wait here," she told Henry.

She crossed the kitchen and climbed the short flight of stairs to the courtyard and stables. After placing her candle on the step beneath her, she carefully cracked open the unlocked door. Perhaps Harry had already gone out that way.

Cautiously, she opened it a few more inches, enough to get a better view of the stable buildings. She shivered as the cold night air struck her face, but thankfully there was no wind. The silence was distinctly unnerving, although reason told her that was perfectly normal at this time of night.

Even more unnerving was the fact that the stables were completely dark. While the coachman had a small cottage behind the building, the grooms lived in a set of rooms directly above the stables. If the men were keeping watch from there, light should be shining through the upstairs window that looked out over the yard.

Quietly, she retreated down the stairs. Henry waited at the bottom, his features marked with an anxious little frown.

"Are they up there?" he whispered.

She shook her head. Going around him, she went to the fireplace, neatly arranged with various cooking implements and racks, and with a large teakettle hanging from its hook. What was left of the embers was barely smoldering.

"What do we do?" Henry whispered.

Emma took his hand and started back to the kitchen stairs. "Dear, I think you should go up to your room and lock your door."

He dug in his heels, sliding a bit on the kitchen floor. "No."

"Henry—"

"No," he stubbornly said. "You might need me. Besides, I'll just sneak out again and you know it."

Emma blew out an exasperated breath. She did know it. She also knew Isabella would kill her if anything happened to the boy.

Should she venture out to the stables and try to raise help? No, she quickly discarded that notion. Depending on which way the smugglers went once they finished whatever it was they were doing, she might be spotted.

One thing did seem clear. They needed help.

"Let's go wake Mrs. Hodges," she said.

The housekeeper's rooms were just up the stairs, at the head of the corridor that led to the long gallery and the front of the house. Emma glanced up the dead-quiet corridor and then quietly tapped on Mrs. Hodges's door.

"I don't think she heard you," whispered Henry after several moments.

Steeling herself, Emma rapped her knuckles hard on the wood.

In the silence, it sounded as loud as gunshot. Thankfully, she heard movement in the room seconds later. The door opened to reveal Mrs. Hodges, her nightcap slightly askew over her braid, a large knit shawl thrown over her shoulders.

"Mrs. Knightley," she exclaimed, "I thought I was hearing things. What's wrong?" Her gaze darted downward. "Is Master Henry ill?"

"May we come in?"

The housekeeper looked bewildered but quickly moved aside. Emma closed the door behind them.

"Mrs. Hodges, it would appear the smugglers have returned. Unfortunately, no one is watching the house, and I can't find any of the men."

The housekeeper blinked in surprise. "That makes no sense. Harry and—" She gasped. "Wait. The smugglers have returned?"

"I saw them," Henry said. "They went round the side of the house, toward the old cellars."

"Harry and the others were to keep watch from the kitchen," Mrs. Hodges replied.

"But no one has been in the kitchen for some time, and the stables are dark."

Mrs. Hodges grimaced. "That idiot Harry is probably asleep in his bed."

"Even so, that doesn't explain why none of the grooms are on guard. Mrs. Hodges, do you have the keys to the gun cabinet?"

The other woman simply gaped at her.

"I don't want to have to run all the way to the other side of the house and rummage in my husband's desk," Emma impatiently said.

Mrs. Hodges shook herself. "I have a set in my locked drawer."

As she collected the keys, Emma turned to Henry. "Dear, I want you to go up to the servants quarters and see if Harry is in his room. If he is, fetch him down to the kitchen and wait for us there."

He nodded and headed for the door.

"Oh, and if you see anything to alarm you," she added, "I want you to hide, all right?"

"Don't worry about me, Auntie Emma," he stoutly replied before slipping out the door.

"Mrs. Knightley, you're frightening me."

"Something isn't right, Mrs. Hodges." Emma took the keys. "I'm going to assume we're safe in the house, but it's best not to take chances."

They hastened to the old butler's pantry, a few doors down. For the past several years it had served as storage and as the abbey's gun cabinet. Emma hoped she would find a weapon she could manage. When she was seventeen, she'd gone through a phase when she'd become interested in hunting, more to annoy George than anything else. Naturally, he'd not reacted as she'd expected but had instead taught her how to properly load and handle a shotgun. Then when he'd suggested she go shooting with him, she'd balked. Emma had never thought of herself as particularly squeamish, but George's little lesson had taught her otherwise.

Now, though, she could only be grateful he'd taught her something she'd never expected would come in handy.

Emma pushed an old chair out of the way—really, this room needed a *great* deal of work if she were ever to use it as her office—and unlocked the gun cabinet. Mrs. Hodges, now carrying a lamp, held it up to illuminate the contents. A pistol was probably the better choice for their current situation, but she was most familiar with a shotgun. As a weapon, it looked more intimidating—if it came to a confrontation, she hoped intimidation would be all that was required. The notion of actually firing at another person was off-putting, to say the least.

"Shotgun it is, then," she murmured.

As she carefully extracted the weapon from the cabinet, Mrs. Hodges cast her wary glance.

"Mrs. Knightley, are you sure you wish to do this? Might it not be better to try to get help?"

Emma reached back in to retrieve a cartridge, rather amazed that her hands were so steady. Thank goodness, because shaky hands and lethal weapons made for a decidedly poor outcome.

As she loaded the cartridge she couldn't hold back a little snort. "I think you really mean to ask if I can fire this thing."

Mrs. Hodges grimaced. "That too."

"You can be assured that I can."

While it had been some years, no need to alarm the poor woman any further.

As they were leaving the butler's pantry, Henry came running toward them from the front of the house. Emma's heart sank when she saw he was alone.

"Harry isn't in his room," he breathlessly announced. "And his bed hasn't been slept in, either."

Not good. Not good at all.

Mrs. Hodges huffed. "The oaf was probably drinking with the grooms and feel asleep."

A phantom thought began to coalesce in Emma's brain. It was not a happy one, and she devoutly hoped it wasn't true.

If it were, though, it would clarify some of the more troubling questions that had bedeviled them about the smuggling problem.

"I don't think that's what happened," she said.

Mrs. Hodges shook her head. "Why not?"

Emma bent down to meet her nephew eye to eye. She *hated* what she had to do next, but if what she suspected was true, she needed to get Henry away from the abbey. Who knew what those men were capable of?

"Henry, I need your help," she said, "and it's not going to be easy. If it's too much, you must tell me so."

He returned her gaze, as grave as a judge. "I can do whatever it is, Auntie Emma."

"I need you to dress in your warmest clothes and then run to Randalls and fetch help from Mr. Weston. Can you do that?"

Mrs. Hodges gasped, but Henry never even blinked.

"But I'd rather stay here with you," he said. "I can help protect you."

"I know you would. But, Henry, something has obviously happened to the grooms and our coachmen, and we need more help as soon as possible. You must tell Mr. Weston what's happening. He'll know exactly what to do."

With the exception of Mrs. Goddard's school—and Emma doubted the schoolmistress would be of much assistance in facing down smugglers—Randalls was the closest house. It made perfect sense to send Henry there for help, and it would get him safely out of the way.

Emma straightened. "You can run faster than any of us, Henry. Can you do this for me?"

His chin went up in a determined tilt. "Yes."

"Good boy. Go out through the front door and down the main drive. But don't take the path. Go by Donwell Road and then onto Randalls Road."

While cutting across the side lawns and crossing the Langham Path would be quicker, she couldn't risk him running into the smugglers.

He nodded. "I understand."

She ruffled his hair. "Off with you, then."

He flashed her a cheeky grin before pelting off toward the front hall.

Emma drew in a quavering breath, praying that she'd made the right decision. Her conviction was steadily growing that help would be needed before the night was out.

Shotgun under her arm, she headed back to the kitchen. Mrs. Hodges hurried to keep up.

"Mrs. Knightley, I don't understand," she said. "Why don't you let me go to the stables and fetch Edwards and Jem?"

Emma hurried down the stairs into the kitchen. "Because the smugglers might spot you, and because I fear all is not well with our men. The stable is completely dark, and there's no sign of the grooms."

"But that makes no sense."

"I cannot focus on that right now. I have to get a look around the side of the house to see what's going on."

And if she didn't hurry, she'd miss the smugglers altogether.

Mrs. Hodges grabbed her arm, forcing her to a halt. "Mrs. Knightley, you cannot be serious! If we are without protection, then surely the best thing to do is remain inside until those dreadful men leave."

"I'd like nothing better," Emma grimly replied. "But this might be the only chance we get to clear Larkins and put an end to this terrible business. I have no intention of confronting those men, but I do need to see who they are."

Beyond that, she didn't really have much of a plan.

"How will that help, Mrs. Knightley? You won't even know who they are."

Actually, Emma had a fairly good idea that she would know at least one of them.

"Mrs. Hodges, I must do this," she said firmly to end the discussion.

The housekeeper huffed out an exasperated sigh and let her go. "You can't go out dressed like that. You'll catch your death. Please take one of the cloaks and a pair of boots."

Emma hurried up to the stable yard door. After carefully propping the shotgun against the wall, she grabbed one of the woolen cloaks on a peg and flung it around her shoulders. She shed her slippers and put on a pair of sturdy shoes from a rack by the door. They were a little too large, so she laced them as tightly as she could to compensate.

When she straightened up, she saw Mrs. Hodges also donning a cloak.

"What are you doing?" asked Emma.

"I'm going with you."

Before Emma could object, the housekeeper shot up a hand. "And no objections from you, ma'am. Mr. Knightley would have my head if I let you go out there alone."

"I'll only be a few minutes, I promise. Besides, two people might be more visible—and potentially make more noise," Emma cautioned.

Mrs. Hodges muttered something under her breath but nodded a reluctant agreement.

Picking up the shotgun, Emma opened the door and slipped out into the yard. She made her way toward the wing facing the back gardens, sticking close to the house. The night was clear, with not a whisper of a breeze. Thankfully, the slipper moon shed just enough light while allowing her to keep hidden in the shadows.

As she approached the old wing, she could make out a sudden murmur of voices, so she froze. After a few moments, she steeled herself.

It's now or never, old girl.

She edged around the corner of the building. Keeping low, she crept forward a few feet, staying in the shadows. She fetched up by the stairs that led down to the first of the old storage cellars—the one she'd inspected with Harriet and Henry a few weeks ago. Further along the old wing were two other cellars, several dozen feet past this one. One of them was so ancient that it was both unusable and unsafe, and yet near the stairs to that undercroft were three men, illuminated by the light of a partially shuttered lantern. Just as Henry had said, there was a cart, its wheels wrapped in cloth, no doubt to muffle the sound of the cart on the gravel. The cart was fully loaded with small casks containing what she could only assume was alcohol. Two of the men were in the process of roping down their haul while the other peered into the undercroft entrance.

From this distance their features were a blur. Emma had to get closer if she wanted to make them out.

Just as she'd steeled herself to start moving again, another man emerged from the undercroft, a cask on his broad shoulders. He handed off the cask to his mates, who turned and loaded it onto the cart. The broad-shouldered man banged the dust off his gloves and walked around the cart, giving it a quick inspection.

He spoke quietly to the other men, pointing in the direction of the Langham Path. Then he turned and glanced up at the house, as if to determine that all was still quiet.

By the light of that slipper moon, Emma could easily recognize both the set of the man's shoulders and his profile. A breeze kicked up, flapping his greatcoat around his booted legs.

"All right, lads," said Harry, his voice snatched up onto the wind. "That's the last of it, so get on your way."

Chapter 27

I knew it.

Harry had been involved in the wretched scheme all along. Now as she looked back, it made perfect sense. He'd been at Donwell long enough to be above suspicion, and he had played the part of dolt so well that no one would have suspected he had the wit to oversee a smuggling operation.

And then there was Prudence...

Stealthily, she beat a retreat back around the corner and out of sight of the men. If her instincts were correct, and it was hard to fault them given this new development, it would be reasonable to assume that hapless Harry was both a smuggler and a ruthless killer. And now they were trapped in the house with him. She could attempt to sneak over to the stables to secure help from the grooms, but it was likely that Harry had somehow managed to put the men out of commission.

At the thought that he might have *permanently* put them out of commission, Emma's stomach pitched sideways and she had to lean against the wall to catch her breath. Then she heard the quiet murmur of voices and the creak of the cart, and she knew she had little time to waste. Harry would either depart with the smugglers or return to the house. Either way, she and Mrs. Hodges needed to be ready. Help *would* eventually arrive from Randalls. Until it did, they needed to keep Harry under control and then—God willing—hand him off to Mr. Weston and his men.

Emma hastened toward the kitchen. As she tightened her grip on the shotgun, she sent up a prayer of thanks that her husband had taught her how to use the weapon. George would be aghast to see her right now, but his lesson—initially intended to hoist her on her own petard—just might save Mrs. Hodges's life and hers.

As she came around the end of the wing, a pale light filtered into the yard from the kitchen windows. Emma grimaced. It would not be good for Harry *or* the smugglers to see that. George would have undoubtedly counseled her to take Mrs. Hodges and hide upstairs until help arrived. It was certainly the sensible thing to do under the circumstances.

A moment later, she discarded that option. Their best chance of getting a confession out of Harry would be through the element of surprise, both by catching him in the act *and* by holding him at the working end of a shotgun. Otherwise, he might come up with an excuse for his actions, claiming he'd been forced into helping the smugglers, just like Harriet's farmer friend and others had been forced into helping these criminals.

Harry needed to be caught off guard so he would stumble his way into a confession that she hoped would exonerate Larkins.

Glancing up at the still-dark stable apartments one more time, Emma slipped through the kitchen door and closed it quietly behind her. A tense Mrs. Hodges was at the bottom of the steps, holding a formidable-looking rolling pin. Her expression boded ill for any miscreant who dared step foot in her kitchen.

The housekeeper expelled a sigh of relief and lowered her makeshift weapon. "Thank God, Mrs. Knightley. I was beginning to worry you'd fallen afoul of those villains. I was just about to come after you."

"You'd best not put your weapon away just yet."

Emma hurried over to the kitchen table, blowing out her candle and shuttering the lamp. It plunged the kitchen into almost total darkness, but her eyes quickly adjusted and she could still make out the housekeeper's form. She took Mrs. Hodges by the arm and drew her over to stand in the entrance of the pantry.

"Harry is involved in this," Emma said. "He was there with the smugglers. They were bringing up casks from the derelict cellar at the far end of the wing and loading them onto a cart."

"What?" the housekeeper exclaimed.

"Hush," Emma hissed. "He could return any moment."

"Sorry," Mrs. Hodges whispered. "But, Harry? The man's a nincompoop if I ever met one. And I've never seen anything to suggest he's involved in such doings."

Emma thought back to the night when her nephew had first spotted suspicious lights in the garden. When they'd gone to investigate, whom had they found in the kitchen, ostensibly raiding the pantry? That would be Harry, who had a knack for being on the scene when any sort of trouble had occurred. She'd been a blind fool not to see it before now.

"He's not as hapless as he wanted us to believe," Emma replied. "In fact, he seemed to be directing the operation."

Mrs. Hodges sucked in a startled breath. "Lord. Mrs. Knightley, what do you intend to do?"

"If he returns to the kitchen, I intend to confront him and get a confession out of him."

"But you already saw him with the smugglers. What sort of—" The housekeeper broke off, as hideous enlightenment dawned. "He... Prudence? Do you think he could have killed her?"

"It's the only reasonable explanation."

Mrs. Hodges breathed out a quiet moan, but then seemed to

gather herself. "Don't you think it would be best if we waited for Mr. Weston? What if Harry is armed?"

"I saw no evidence that he was. He did, however, appear to be garbed for travel."

Harry had been booted, wearing both a greatcoat and a hat. Was he simply accompanying his men on a run, or did he have something else planned? His escape, perhaps? But why would he feel the need . . .

She shook her head. Of course he was planning his escape. After all, he'd obviously done something to the grooms and Donwell's coachman to render them helpless. There'd be no chance of talking his way out of *that*.

The clock on the kitchen mantle chimed out the hour, startling them both. Mr. Weston should be arriving with reinforcements soon, because Henry would have made it to Randalls by now. Still, it would take some time to rouse the household, get prepared, and then set off to Donwell.

Emma wavered. She and Mrs. Hodges *could* hold off, retreating back to her rooms and hoping for the best.

"Mrs. Knightley, I think I hear him," Mrs. Hodges said in a panicked whisper.

As Emma glanced toward the high kitchen windows, she caught the crunch of footsteps on the gravel path. A shadow passed in front the windows, darker against dark.

Time had run out, and the decision had been made for her. "Mrs. Hodges, I want you to stay behind me."

The housekeeper muttered under her breath but moved into the pantry. Emma positioned herself in the doorway, shotgun up and aimed at the steps leading down from the yard. She was rather amazed at how calm she felt, the gun steady in her grip. Perhaps she was in some sort of shock. If so, she hoped it lasted a little longer.

The door from the yard creaked open and Harry descended the stairs, carrying a lantern. Emma had to resist the impulse to shrink back into the pantry, but thankfully he never looked their way.

After placing the lantern on the mantle, he bent to retrieve logs from the basket and arranged them in the fireplace. Using a spill lit from the lantern's flame, he soon got a fire crackling in the grate. Then he straightened and shrugged out of his greatcoat. As he turned to throw the garment onto a chair, Emma stepped forward, her shotgun aimed squarely at his chest.

Harry froze, coat in hand, his gaze widening with shock.

"Drop it on the floor," Emma ordered in her sternest voice.

If he did have a weapon, it was likely stowed in his coat.

Harry's gaze locked on hers, growing as sharp as a blade, and it sent a chill skating across the back of Emma's neck. Even in the flickering, uneven light, his expression looked positively murderous.

Then he blinked and everything changed. Suddenly he was again the befuddled footman she'd always known.

"Lord, Mrs. Knightley! You scared me right out of my brainbox. Begging your pardon, ma'am, but you shouldn't be sneaking up on a poor fellow in the dead of night. I was like to have a heart attack." Then he frowned. "Why are you pointing a shotgun at me?"

Mrs. Hodges leaned out from behind Emma. "Because you're a lying, smuggling varlet, that's why. For half a shilling, I'd shoot you myself."

His eyes popped even wider. "Smuggling! Me, smuggling? Mrs. H, why ever would you think such a daft thing?"

"Give over, Harry," Emma snapped. "I just saw you out there with those men, unloading casks from the cellar. Now, do what I say and drop your coat on the floor."

He paused for a long moment before grimacing. "I . . . well . . . I'm sorry, Mrs. Knightley. Truly I am. But they made me do it. Honest. They said they'd beat me within an inch of my life if I didn't help them."

She scoffed. "Is that so? And how did they get access to Donwell's cellars in the first place?"

"It was Mr. Larkins, ma'am. I swear it. I didn't know anything about it until those fellows showed up and said I had to help, now that Mr. Larkins was in the pogey."

"If that was the case, why didn't you tell me or Mr. Knightley?"

"I . . . I was afraid I'd lose my job . . . or get arrested by that Sharpe fellow. The smugglers said Mr. Knightley would think it was all me. He would never believe it was Mr. Larkins."

"Because Larkins isn't the smuggler," Emma retorted. "*You* are."

Mrs. Hodges made a disgusted noise. "It's been you all along. Playing the hapless idiot to fool us all."

"But I *am* an idiot, Mrs. H!"

One who was still holding his coat, and he appeared to be inching a hand toward a pocket.

"Harry," Emma said, "if you do not drop the coat, I *will* shoot you. I'm a very good shot, and I will happily put a hole in your shoulder for all the trouble you've caused."

She breathed a sigh of relief when he took her threat to heart and finally dropped the coat on the floor.

He held up his hands in a gesture of surrender. "Please, just let me explain, ma'am. I never saw them fellows until a few weeks ago. That was when they showed up, making all their threats."

"Mrs. Hodges," said Emma. "Would you please open the other lantern so we have more light?"

That would certainly help if she *did* have to shoot him.

Quietly, the housekeeper complied. As more light illuminated the room, Emma stepped out of the pantry doorway and again moved in front of Mrs. Hodges.

"Did they also threaten to hurt our stable staff?" Emma asked him. "Because their absence this evening is quite noticeable."

Something ugly flashed across his features, startling her, but vanishing a moment later.

"They . . . they told me I had to drug our men." His voice took on a whiny pitch. "They gave me laudanum and told me to put it in their ale. I didn't have a choice, Mrs. Knightley. They said they'd kill me if I didn't help them."

Emma narrowed her gaze on him. "And did they also force you to kill Prudence?"

Genuine shock distorted his features, and he took a hasty step forward.

"No, blast you! It wasn't me," he exclaimed. "You've got it all wrong. I would *never* have hurt Prudence. I was going to marry her."

Now it was Emma's turn to be shocked—again. Harry had clearly dropped all pretenses now, putting aside the fool. He looked genuinely outraged by her accusation.

"Then if you didn't kill her," she asked, "who did?"

"I'm afraid it was me," said a voice from behind her. "And I'm also afraid that if you don't lower your shotgun, Mrs. Knightley, I might have to kill you, too."

Emma's brain seemed to stumble over itself. What in God's name was happening here?

"Or I suppose I could just kill Mrs. Hodges," said the man in a bizarrely casual drawl. "That will serve just as well, I should think."

A choked exclamation from Mrs. Hodges had Emma quickly lowering her weapon. Then she turned to confront Guy Plumtree. He was garbed in a stylish greatcoat, a mildly regretful expression on his attractive features. He was holding the business end of a pistol aimed at Mrs. Hodges, standing not more than five feet behind her.

"I . . . I didn't hear him come in," the housekeeper stammered.

Neither had Emma. She'd been too busy interrogating

Harry to hear the door from the stable yard open or feel the chill that had entered the room with Guy's entrance.

While she felt the chill now, she suspected that had more to do with fear than the temperature of the room.

"You killed Prudence?" she finally managed. "But why? You didn't even—" She broke off with a grimace. "Of course. You're part of this blasted smuggling ring."

Guy waved an admonishing finger. "Such language from a lady. Mr. Knightley would be terribly shocked."

"Mr. Knightley will see you hang," retorted Mrs. Hodges.

"It's about time you showed up," griped Harry. "But now we've got a right mess on our hands, thanks to you killing poor Pru."

Guy shrugged. "If I hadn't killed the girl, she would have gone to Mr. Knightley and revealed all. Obviously, I couldn't allow that to happen."

"I told you I'd take care of it," Harry gritted out. "She would have listened to me. She always did."

Guy made an impatient sound. "We've been over this countless times, Harry. I made the decision, and I stand by it. Now, get the gun from Mrs. Knightley before she does something foolish."

Despite the danger, Emma couldn't help herself. "Like shooting you?"

Guy actually laughed. "I doubt you have it in you, ma'am. Although I will say you did seem quite determined to shoot Harry. Not that I blame you. I've been tempted to shoot him a few times, myself."

"Bastard," Harry muttered.

Emma mentally blinked, taking note of the animosity between the partners in crime. Perhaps at some point she could use that against them, at least until help arrived.

And where *was* that help? Mr. Weston and his men should have arrived by now.

"Harry, the gun," Guy sharply said.

The footman stalked around the table and jerked the shotgun from her hands.

"You and Mrs. Hodges, sit yourselves down at the table," he barked.

"*Please* sit down at the table," Guy corrected. "There's no need to be rude."

Emma stared at him in disbelief. "You're holding a pistol on us."

He shrugged. "A necessity until we can figure out what to do with you. Now, please do sit, ladies."

Emma and Mrs. Hodges pulled out chairs from the kitchen table and sat next to each other.

"I don't have to figure out what I'm doing," Harry said as he leaned the shotgun up against the fireplace. He swiped up his greatcoat and shrugged back into it. "I'm done with it all. I've got all the blunt I need, so you won't be seeing me again."

Guy scoffed. "Your father won't like that, I'd wager."

"I don't care what that hellhound thinks. I've done more than enough for him, what with spending two years in this moldy old pile, always at his beck and call."

Emma gaped at him. "You've been operating out of Donwell Abbey for two years?"

"That's no business of yours," he snapped.

"Harry, your lack of manners is truly appalling," Guy said as he moved around to the opposite side of the table.

He pulled out a chair and took a seat across from them, his pistol now trained on Emma.

"Of course it's your business, ma'am," he said in a genial tone. "To answer your question, Harry took the job at Donwell Abbey to oversee his father's smuggling operations in this part of Surrey. One must give Mr. Trotman a great deal of credit for setting up and maintaining such a successful venture for so many years." He glanced at Harry. "I'm sure he'll be most disappointed to hear you won't be following in his footsteps."

Emma gasped as illumination struck. "Harry's father was the one who stored his contraband at the Crown Inn. He had an arrangement with Mr. Stokes."

Guy nodded. "Very perceptive of you, Mrs. Knightley. It was apparently a lucrative arrangement for all involved. Unfortunately, Mrs. Stokes put an end to it when her dear husband shuffled off this mortal coil."

Emma stared at him, doing her best to ignore the weapon pointed right at her chest. She simply had to keep him talking until Mr. Weston and his men arrived.

"And what about the church?" she asked. "And Mr. Barlowe? What is his part in all of this?"

"Dear, silly Barlowe," responded Guy with a snort. "He has no involvement at all in this, Mrs. Knightley. Our merry band of smugglers ceased using the bell tower as our principal depot almost a year ago." He leaned forward, as if sharing a secret. "We found a much better place to hide them, much more out of the way."

She blinked. "Donwell Abbey. After my husband moved to Hartfield."

"A clever lady, indeed," he replied in an admiring tone. "Yes, we needed something more secure. Given the minimal staff at the abbey—not to mention the fact that Harry was already living here—it made for the perfect depot along our route. Until Prudence was about to ruin everything like the silly girl that she was. She gave me no choice, really."

"God help us," whispered Mrs. Hodges.

Emma forced down the queasy sensation gripping her throat. "But how did Prudence find out about all this in the first place?"

Guy gestured at Harry. "Blame him. He was courting the girl and couldn't keep his fool mouth shut."

Harry cast him a murderous glare. "Prudence and me was

going to get married good and proper. But you had to ruin it, didn't you? *You* killed her and made a mess of everything."

"You were the one who ruined it, dear fellow. I know you and Prudence had your little plans to run away up north, but unfortunately for you the girl was honest—a character flaw you should have anticipated."

Emma was still trying to absorb this astounding revelation. It was difficult to do with a pistol aimed at one's heart. "But Harry denied being involved with Prudence."

The footman barely spared her a glance. "Her father would never have approved, so we kept it secret."

"And no wonder," exclaimed an outraged Mrs. Hodges. "Since you're a common criminal."

"Shut your gob, you old fool." Then Harry narrowed his gaze on Guy. "And you shut your gob, too. You'll get us hanged, you will."

Guy pondered that comment for a few moments, as if working through to some sort of conclusion. "At this point, I should think you'd have realized it doesn't matter what I tell them."

A deadly stillness settled over Emma. She had to swallow twice before she could reply. "Because you're going to kill us."

Mrs. Hodges gasped and covered her mouth.

Guy actually had the nerve to look regretful. "I'm afraid so. I'm simply trying to decide the best way. Shooting you would be messy, and one never knows what evidence might be left behind. Take Prudence, for instance. I believed I'd thought of everything in that particular scenario, and yet here we are."

The man was obviously *quite* mad—and as deadly as an adder.

"You could simply leave," she managed to reply. "Like Harry suggested."

The footman gave a sharp nod. "She's right. Tie them up and let's be gone. I've no taste for killing women."

Guy's features suddenly drained of anything approaching humanity. "And let them trumpet to the world that I'm the one who murdered Prudence? I think not. Nor do I have any intention of living a life on the run. I'm not a lowly footman or the son of a criminal, Harry. I have an inheritance and a future, and I've no intention of giving either of them up."

Emma could barely speak past the horror that threatened to close her throat. "You're a monster."

His chilling gaze settled on her. "Perhaps, or perhaps I'm merely determined to finally live my life as I see fit, once my father passes, that is."

"Poor Squire Plumtree," whispered Mrs. Hodges.

Soon-to-be dead Squire Plumtree, Emma feared. "You'll never get away with it."

He gave a bizarrely casual shrug. "Of course I will. With you and Mrs. Hodges out of the way and Harry in the wind, no one will suspect me of a thing. I'm only the ne'er-do-well son of Squire Plumtree, perfectly pleasant and perfectly harmless. I've been very careful. Only Harry knows who I am."

Keep him talking.

"Not Mr. Barlowe?" she asked.

"That fool doesn't suspect a thing," he contemptuously replied. "I only befriended him to keep an eye on that blasted church for any lingering problems. And he *did* provide me with quite a handy alibi at the party. We spent most of the evening together, you see. Wouldn't even occur to Barlowe to think about me disappearing for half an hour or so." He paused, and then glanced at Harry. "Ah, I think I have it."

His accomplice looked confused. "Have what?"

"How to get rid of them. A fire will do nicely. These old piles, you know, they catch fire all the time. We'll just cosh the two of them over the head, move them to the great hall, and then set it alight. All that lovely old wood should do the trick."

Under the table, Mrs. Hodges grabbed Emma's hand with trembling fingers. Even Harry looked horrified.

"I ain't coshing them over the head *or* setting a fire," he protested.

"You will," Guy responded in a threatening tone.

Emma cast about desperately for something to—

Yes!

"You're wrong," she blurted out. "There is someone who can identify you. He recognized your voice, and it's only a matter of time until he realizes it's you."

Guy shot Harry a startled glance.

"Don't look at me," said the footman. "Haven't a clue what she's yammering about."

"Then I do believe you're bluffing, Mrs. Knightley," said Guy.

She lifted a defiant chin. "I'm not. And there's also Henry, my nephew."

Her captor frowned. "What about him?"

Harry muttered a curse. "I forgot about him. He's staying here at the abbey. But I ain't killing no kid, either."

"You couldn't even if you wanted to," Emma retorted. "When I realized we were in danger, I sent him off to the Westons to fetch help."

"That tears it." Harry picked up the shotgun. "Plumtree, you can do what you like, but I'm leaving."

"Don't be a fool," his accomplice contemptuously replied. "If she *had* sent the boy to Randalls, Weston would surely be here by now."

That, unfortunately, was true. Emma very much feared something dreadful had happened to Henry on the way to Randalls. That thought scared her more than Guy's weapon.

"Don't care," snapped Harry.

"Go up to his room and see if he's there," Guy ordered.

"Bugger you."

Guy shoved up out of his chair and jabbed a finger at Harry as they began to hotly debate how to proceed. In the process, Guy let the hand holding the pistol drop to his side.

Emma leaned toward Mrs. Hodges.

"Prepare to run for the stable yard," she whispered.

The housekeeper threw her a startled glance but then squeezed her hand before letting go.

As the confrontation between the two men escalated into shouting, Emma steeled herself to do what she must. Guy had given her an idea. It was a terrible one, but it just might save their lives.

"Now," she murmured to Mrs. Hodges.

Emma then scrambled to her feet, grabbed the lantern off the table, and hurled it directly at Guy. It just missed and smashed into the window behind him. The glass shattered and oil spewed onto the window curtains, setting them ablaze.

Emma heard Guy curse, but she and Mrs. Hodges were already halfway across the kitchen. Mrs. Hodges suddenly veered sideways—with astonishing fleetness of foot for a woman her age—and fled up the stairs to the stable yard. Emma ran straight for the steps back to the main house, half expecting the blast of a pistol at any second.

Her foot hit the bottom stair and she surged upward, three steps at a time. She pushed through the swinging door but then slipped on the top step, her too-large boots tripping her up. Recovering, she scrambled out into the corridor, running as fast as she dared. If she fell, Guy would catch her. Even now she could hear footsteps pounding behind her.

"Stop, or I'll shoot," he roared.

Emma would rather take her chances getting shot than getting burned up in a fire. She ran as hard as she could, turning from the service corridor into the long gallery. If she could just reach the great hall—

Boom.

A bust of a Knightley ancestor exploded. She flinched when a shard of stone struck the side of her head, and she went down hard on one knee. Gasping for breath, she pushed herself up, only to freeze when she felt the pistol barrel press against her shoulder.

"I have you, Mrs. Knightley. There's no point in trying to escape."

Guy's voice chilled her to the very marrow. Still, she had no intention of cowering on the floor, waiting to be murdered.

Then a thought darted into her head. He couldn't shoot her, could he? He'd already fired the pistol.

She sucked in a calming breath. "May I at least stand?"

For several seconds, as long as eternity, she heard only his breathing.

Then he withdrew the barrel from her shoulder.

"Please do stand, Mrs. Knightley. I should hate for you to be made uncomfortable," he calmly said.

Lunatic.

She took her time getting up, darting a quick look around for a possible weapon to use. There was that hideous bust of Julius Caesar on the pedestal just over there. Perhaps—

"Turn around, please," said Guy, as she heard a thump.

When she turned, her heart plummeted right down to the cellar. The villain had discarded the spent pistol, tossing it to the floor. Now he held a lethal-looking knife in his hand.

Even in the shadows of the long gallery, she could see the gleam in his eyes.

"Just so, ma'am," he said. "I am still armed. And I assure you that you won't be able to outrun me."

Surely he could *not* be that stupid.

"Surely you cannot be that stupid," she said, ignoring the manic thud of her heart.

He shrugged with an eerie nonchalance. "I will do what I must."

"Mr. Plumtree, if you're as clever as you say you are, I suggest you be on your way. Help *will* arrive—"

Were those voices drifting up from the kitchen?

Yes!

She mustered a smile. "Ah. It seems help has finally arrived."

The sound of distant shouts echoed along the corridor, confirming that hope.

Guy muttered a *quite* foul curse. "You would appear to be correct, ma'am."

"You might want to flee," she helpfully said. "Might I suggest the front door? You have my word I won't try to stop you."

Not while he was holding her at knifepoint, at any rate.

"Oh, I'm going," he snarled. "And you're coming with me."

"What?" She started to back away, almost tripping over her dratted boots.

"I have no intention of getting caught, and you will certainly prove useful as a hostage."

He advanced on her, but she continued to scramble backward.

"Stop that," he snapped, grabbing for her.

From behind him, a tall figure quietly loomed from the dark, then lunged and smashed something into the back of Guy's skull.

The wretch crumpled to the floor at Emma's feet.

Stunned, she stood there for a moment, gaping down at him. Then she looked up. The tall, greatcoated figure resolved into Mr. Weston, pointing a shotgun at Guy.

"Is that what you hit him with?" she asked.

"Yes, the butt of my gun. The blasted villain's lucky I didn't shoot him, but I was afraid to take the risk of some of the shot hitting you." He stepped forward. "Are you all right, dear?"

She sank into a conveniently situated armchair. "Yes, he . . . he didn't hurt me."

"Thank God. Forgive me, Emma. I should have been here sooner."

"You arrived just in time." She glanced down at the unconscious Guy. "I don't think you need to keep your gun on him, though. It sounded like you split his head open."

Mr. Weston scowled. "Better for everyone if I did. Gave me the shock of my life when Mrs. Hodges told me Guy Plumtree was pursuing you through the house like a blasted madman."

"Is Mrs. Hodges all right?"

When he nodded, Emma sagged with relief.

"She and my footmen are putting out the fire," he said. "Ah, here's my fellow now. Everything all right, Sam?"

The man who joined them was Randalls's senior footman. "Yes, sir. The fire is out. It was just the curtains. We got them down in quick order, and Mrs. Hodges is giving them a good soak."

"Thank heavens." Emma managed a smile. "I was worried I would burn the place down, but I couldn't think what else to do."

"Brilliant thinking on your part, my dear," replied Mr. Weston. He handed his shotgun to Sam. "Keep an eye on this villain in case he wakes up. I'll send one of the other men up with a rope to secure him until Constable Sharpe arrives."

Even though Emma felt ridiculously unsteady, she forced herself to stand. Mr. Weston hurried over to help her.

"Take my arm." He frowned as he finally registered what she was wearing. "That's quite the odd rig. Best be careful with those boots, Emma. They're much too big on you."

"Yes, I know," she dryly replied. "I take it my terribly brave nephew arrived at Randalls in good order."

"Mostly," he said. "Poor lad thought to take a shortcut across our back lawn and had a bit of a fall."

Emma jerked to a halt. "Is he all right? Please tell me that he's all right!"

She'd never forgive herself if Henry were injured.

Mr. Weston patted her hand. "He's fine. Twisted his ankle, but he managed to keep going."

She breathed out a shaky sigh. "I suppose that's why it took so long for you to arrive."

"Yes, and it took Henry a bit of time to get the story out,

too. Poor lad was all wound up by the time he reached Randalls. Then I had to get the men up and organized."

"But you're sure Henry's all right?"

He started her back down the corridor. "It's just a little sprain, Emma. My wife was bustling him right upstairs into a hot bath by the time we were heading out. He's a brave lad. You should be proud of him."

Her eyes stung with tears of relief and pride in her nephew's courage and fortitude.

"Thank goodness," she said. "Isabella would murder me if anything had happened to Henry."

"Let's not have any more talk of murder. We've had quite enough of that around here."

Emma couldn't agree more.

They pushed through the service door and started down the stairs. The odor of smoke assaulted her nose, making her sneeze.

Mr. Weston eyed her with vague alarm. "I hope you're not catching a chill. Your father would be very displeased."

She had to swallow a hysterical impulse to laugh. A possible chill would be the least of her father's worries. Emma couldn't even begin to think how she would explain the evening's events to him.

"I'm fine. It's just the smoke." She eyed the kitchen. "This poor room is not fine, however."

The kitchen was rather a disaster. There were scorch marks all around the window frame and on the brick wall, and the curtains were a sodden heap on the wet floor. Still, it could have been much worse.

After all, Guy had threatened to burn the abbey down, with her and Mrs. Hodges in it.

The housekeeper came hurrying in from the stable yard a moment later.

"Mrs. Knightley, thank God," she exclaimed, rushing up to her. "I was so afraid!"

Emma grimaced at the housekeeper's dirty face and soot-smudged cloak. "Oh dear. Are you all right?"

"It's just a little dirt and smoke, ma'am. Did you get the villain, Mr. Weston?"

He nodded. "Plumtree won't be giving us any more trouble. What about the grooms and your coachmen? Have they come to harm?"

"I don't think so, sir," the housekeeper replied. "But they're still out cold. Apparently, Harry put plenty of laudanum in their ale."

"Unbelievable," Emma said, disgusted. "I should have guessed it was Harry much sooner than I did."

Mrs. Hodges sighed. "I blame myself. He fair pulled the wool over my eyes."

"He pulled the wool over everyone's eyes," Mr. Weston dryly commented. "Quite the clever fellow."

"Where is Harry?" asked Emma.

Mrs. Hodges held up her hands. "Disappeared. He all but knocked me over in his haste to be gone. It seems he had no intention of getting caught."

Emma shrugged. "Or of murdering us, so at least that's one point in his favor."

"I take it he murdered that poor girl, though," said Mr. Weston.

"No, that was Guy," Emma replied.

Mr. Weston looked astonished. "I cannot believe it. Although I suppose I must, seeing he was holding you at knifepoint."

"He fooled all of us," she said. "I only hope his father isn't involved in any of this."

Mr. Weston shook his head. "Not Squire Plumtree. The man's as good as they come. This will ruin him, though, poor fellow. I say, Emma, perhaps—"

He was interrupted when Constable Sharpe barreled in from the stable yard.

"What's all this I hear about smugglers?" he barked.

Then his jaw dropped as he took in the mess around them.

"Good evening, Constable Sharpe," Emma politely said. "Or is it good morning? I hardly know. But how kind of you to join us. Better late than never, I suppose."

Mr. Weston started to laugh but covered it up with a cough.

Constable Sharpe stared at her and then shook his head, looking—if she didn't miss her guess—more than a trifle annoyed.

"Mrs. Knightley," he pronounced in a dour tone. "Why am I not surprised you're in the middle of this?"

Chapter 28

"Father, would you like a cup of tea?" Emma asked. "I'm sure it won't be long now. George and John should be home from Guildford any moment."

Her father emitted a doleful sigh. "I don't know that I have the stomach for tea, my dear. To know that they must visit that vile prison harrows me to the bone. Prisons are such unhealthy places, and on top of that they must ride home in this dreadful weather."

"I'm sure they'll be careful," she soothingly replied. "Don't forget they took the carriage, so they'll be protected from the weather."

Father looked even more alarmed. "But Emma, James and the horses! It's such a long way to travel from Highbury to Guildford. James will not be happy."

"They travelled in John's carriage, remember?" she patiently replied. "John's coachman and horses are quite used to longer trips."

"That's true, Father," Isabella said from the sofa where she sat with Henry. "Highbury is much closer to Guildford than it is to London."

"If you say so, my dear. Nevertheless, I will not be easy until George and John are back here and we can put this murder business behind us. I have not been able to sleep these past two nights, knowing that a ruthless killer had been wandering the halls of Donwell Abbey. Thank goodness he didn't find you, Emma, and that our dear little Henry was able to escape his clutches."

"Yes, very lucky," Emma replied.

She exchanged a furtive glance with her sister. In describing the dramatic events at Donwell, Emma had been deliberately vague, particularly regarding Guy Plumtree's threat to shoot her. After Isabella had recovered from her shock on first hearing of the events—a shock that had required Emma to deploy both smelling salts and sherry—she had readily agreed that the goriest details should be withheld from their father. Of course, all would eventually come out at the murder trial, but that was a worry for another day.

Isabella had reacted quite differently when it came to her son, however. Much to Henry's mortification, his mother had torn a strip off Emma for placing the boy in danger, and then she had dramatically vowed to never again let Henry out of her sight. It had required Mrs. Weston's intervention to soothe Isabella's rattled nerves and, when he'd arrived at Hartfield the next day, John's robust defense of his son as a brave little chap who'd saved the day.

Miss Bates, sitting on the settee with Mrs. Weston, raised a hesitant hand.

"Perhaps Mr. Woodhouse would prefer a ratafia, Mrs. Knightley," she said. "Naturally, Hartfield's tea is superior to anything one could imagine—although of course the tea at Randalls is excellent, too, Mrs. Weston. One could never say anything less. But a nice glass of ratafia might be just the thing to calm Mr. Woodhouse's nerves. I've also been quite unsettled by these dreadful events and would not be averse to a small glass as well."

Mr. Weston, who'd retreated to a corner of Hartfield's drawing room to read a letter from his son, put it aside and rose to his feet.

"Capital idea, Miss Bates," he said. "A little glass of something sounds just the thing. I'll be happy to fetch and carry for you and Mr. Woodhouse."

"And perhaps pour a brandy for yourself while you're at it?" his wife wryly asked.

"Can't blame me, my dear," he mildly countered. "All this waiting around is getting on my poor nerves, too."

Emma cast him a wry smile. "I doubt that anything rattles your nerves, sir."

The fact that he'd rolled up Guy Plumtree while hardly batting an eyelash was proof of that, as was his steady presence in the aftermath of both the fire and Guy's arrest. As Emma could have predicted, Constable Sharpe had been less than helpful in dealing with a chaotic situation, so Mr. Weston's calm demeanor had been invaluable.

He shook his head. "I beg to differ, my dear. When I came upon that blasted Plumtree fellow in the long gallery, holding a—"

Mr. Weston broke off when Isabella jumped to her feet, almost knocking over the small tea table in front of her.

"I think I'll have a brandy, too," she exclaimed. "Emma, would you like one?"

Emma had to bite her lip to keep from laughing. Isabella loathed brandy.

"I'd prefer a sherry," she managed to reply.

"Good, I'll help fetch everyone's drink."

Isabella promptly seized Mr. Weston's arm and dragged him off to the sideboard, no doubt reminding him in urgent whispers that Father was *not* to hear the details of Emma's near escape.

Mr. Woodhouse frowned. "I didn't know that Isabella partook of brandy. In fact, I don't think I've ever seen her drink it."

"Perhaps it's a newly acquired taste," Emma said.

"Mama drinks brandy all the time at home," Henry put in. "She says it helps her sleep."

Emma blinked at that unexpected revelation. "Does she now? Well, good for her."

Father peered at her. "Emma, why is everyone acting so strangely? I do not approve."

Thankfully, she was spared a reply when she heard voices out in the hall. A moment later, the door opened and George and John entered the room.

Emma hurried to meet them. "Finally! We were wondering if you'd ever return."

George greeted her with a smile and an encompassing embrace. He'd been deeply shaken by her near-fatal encounter three nights ago, even though she'd done her best to assure him that she'd suffered no lasting ill effects. As she'd expected, her dear husband had blamed himself for not being there to protect her, as well as for failing to see that Harry was the snake in their little garden all along. It had taken a concerted effort on Emma's part to assure him that she was perfectly well. George had responded *quite* passionately, with the happy result of proving that all her various parts were still in excellent working order.

He dropped a quick kiss on the top of her head. "I apologize for the delay. The interview with Plumtree took longer than expected but was fruitful." He glanced at his brother, who'd gone to greet his wife and son. "Thanks to John."

"Of course, we want to hear all about it," Emma said. "But first, come sit and have tea and something to eat."

"John and I supped at an inn in Guildford before we returned."

Father shook his head in disapproval "One should avoid inns whenever possible, George. Mr. Perry often reminds us that they're very unhealthy places to eat. It would have been better if you'd waited until you returned to Hartfield."

John, who'd settled next to his son on the sofa, glanced over with a sardonic expression. "Actually, the jailer offered to feed us, but George and I decided an inn would provide a more pleasant atmosphere and better food."

Father stared at him, obviously struck dumb at the notion of eating prison food.

Isabella hastened over, handing the poor old dear a glass. "Here's your ratafia, Father. By the by, I'm sure John was only teasing."

"I wasn't," John replied in his usual blunt manner. "And the food at the inn was rather good, thanks to George. Poor fellow has spent quite a bit of time in Guildford this last year, what with the murders and such. So now he knows all the best places to eat."

"George," exclaimed Father, extremely perturbed, "I cannot believe you frequent unknown inns in so reckless a manner. Who knows what sorts of contagion you might be exposed to in such establishments?"

Emma directed a warning glance at her brother-in-law, daring him to contradict what she was about to say. "John is *undoubtedly* teasing, Father. Now, please tell us what happened, George. We've been on tenterhooks all day. Were you able to secure Larkins's release from prison?"

George nodded. "We were, thanks to Mr. Clarke. Constable Sharpe was still inclined to hold Larkins on smuggling charges, but Clarke is satisfied that he was an innocent victim in all this. We were able to bring Larkins home with us. He's now safely back at Donwell and most happy to be there." He smiled at Emma. "He's especially grateful to you, my dear, and will be presenting his thanks to you in person."

"He would have been most welcome to join us tonight," she replied. "If anyone deserves to be feted, it's poor Larkins."

"I did make that offer, but I suspect he's feeling overwhelmed at the moment and in need of some peace and quiet. Mrs. Hodges has him well in hand, though. She will see to his comfort."

"Dear Mr. Larkins," exclaimed Miss Bates. "What a terrible trial for him. One quite wishes to throw him a party to make up for his dreadful experience."

Emma was done with parties for a good while.

"And Mrs. Knightley also deserves to be feted," added Miss Bates, beaming at her. "You have been so brave through all of this—a true Joan of Arc, or... or even a female St. George, slaying dragons. Your courage at the abbey that dreadful night! You're an inspiration to all of us."

Mr. Woodhouse held up his hands. "I beg you, my dear Hetty, do not encourage her. I do not approve of this new habit of investigating murders—or smuggling, for that matter."

"Father, it's not as if I go looking for murders to investigate," Emma protested.

"I'm quite sure her investigating days are now over," George firmly said. "Isn't that right, my dear?"

She rounded her eyes at him. "Of course, dearest. And it's not as if I was investigating in the conventional sense. Miss Bates and I simply happened to stumble upon the occasional clue, now and again."

"Mrs. Knightley, you do not do yourself justice," said Miss Bates. "You would make a splendid investigator. Except women aren't supposed to be investigators, are they? I find it all rather confusing, because Mrs. Knightley is so much better at it than Constable Sharpe."

Emma made a point of avoiding her husband's ironic eye. "Thank you, ma'am. However, I believe the true hero in all of this is Henry. He was very brave in running to get Mr. Weston's help."

Isabella shuddered. "Yes, and he injured himself in the process. I still can barely sleep at night, thinking of him all alone in the cold and the dark."

Henry rolled his eyes. "It was only a sprain, Mama, and I got up right away. It was stupid of me to fall in the first place."

John hugged his son. "Nonsense, my boy. You were very brave, and we're all very proud of you."

"Indeed we are," said George with a smile.

"I missed all the exciting bits, though," Henry said. "Back at the abbey."

"And a good thing, too." Isabella glanced at the watch pinned to her waist. "Now, I think it's time for you to be in bed, dear. It's quite late."

"But I want to hear all about the dastardly Guy," the boy protested.

"You most decidedly do not," his mother firmly replied. "John, tell Henry it's time to go to bed."

"Your mama's right, my boy. Say good night to everyone and then it's off to bed."

Henry rolled his eyes and protested a bit more, but at his father's prodding dutifully exchanged hugs with his grandfather and then Emma.

"I'll tell you all about it later," she whispered to him as she returned his embrace.

Her nephew beamed at her, and then let his father lead him off without further complaint.

After handing his son over to a waiting footman, John returned to sit next to Isabella.

"Now that Henry is safely out of the way," said Emma, "please don't keep us in suspense any longer. What did the evil Guy have to say for himself?"

George, who'd fetched himself a brandy, settled into the chair next to Emma. "Quite a bit, as it turned out. Between Plumtree's testimony and the information supplied by the runner we hired, we now have what I think is a faithful and mostly complete picture of events."

"I'm surprised to hear that," Emma said. "I was convinced that Plumtree would try to blame everything on Harry or refuse to talk. Did he actually admit to killing Prudence?"

"He did."

She frowned. "But wouldn't that send him straight to the gallows? How could that be in his best interest?"

George nodded toward his brother. "John came up with a very effective strategy that had the effect of loosening Plumtree's tongue."

Isabella gazed adoringly at her husband. "I've always said that John is quite the most clever barrister in London."

John flashed his wife a smile as he affectionately took her hand. "It was nothing, my dear, really."

"Dearest, you are being much too modest, as you always are."

As happy as Emma was to see Isabella and John restored to their usual state of domestic bliss, she was anxious to hear what this strategy actually was.

"So, what did you suggest?" she asked with a hint of impatience.

John tore his gaze away from his wife. "What? Oh, I suggested to Plumtree that he wasn't in his right mind when he murdered Prudence, and that such might be a useful defense at trial. Under the Criminal Lunatics Bill, one can escape the gallows if found to be of unsound mind while committing the crime."

Miss Bates scrunched up her face. "I suppose that makes sense. No sane person could throw that poor girl out the window. Prudence was so terribly kind and sweet."

"But do you think a court would truly find him insane?" asked Emma. "He struck me as exceedingly calculating. And he certainly was sane enough to fool the rest of us."

And yet, there'd been a coldness and cruelty about him that had been distinctly unnerving. It had crossed her mind in those terrible moments that night that he'd lost his grip on reality.

John shrugged. "It's a high bar, I'll admit, but it's the only chance he's got. I offered to help his father find a barrister skilled in such cases in exchange for talking to us."

Emma sighed. "Poor Squire Plumtree. You saw him today, as well?"

"We did," George replied in a grim tone. "The poor fellow is devastated, and he blames himself. By neglecting his duties at Plumtree Manor, he allowed his son to come to such a state."

Mr. Weston scoffed. "Nonsense. I had to send Frank away as a child, and he's a capital fellow. Guy's simply a villain who deserves all the punishment coming to him."

"Did he tell you how he killed Prudence?" Emma asked her husband.

It was the *how* that she still found so perplexing.

"Perhaps it's best to start at the beginning," George replied. "With the smugglers, and how they ended up at Donwell in the first place."

"Harry explained that," Emma pointed out. "They needed a safer place to store their goods. When you decamped to Hartfield, that gave them the opportunity they were looking for."

Father flapped an agitated hand. "And a good thing George moved to Hartfield. It would have been dreadful if he'd been forced to live at Donwell with smugglers coming and going at all hours of the night. Who knows what they might have done to him."

"Father, it was George's move to Hartfield . . ." Emma shook her head. "Never mind. Go on, dearest."

"Harry was only one spoke in the wheel," George continued. "An important one, but the history of this particular gang goes back further than Harry's role in it. Thanks to Mr. Weston's quick thinking, we were able to identify one of their most important depots along the route to London—an inn from which they'd been operating for some years."

Mr. Weston waved a self-deprecating hand. "Just an old military tactic, old fellow. Divide and conquer."

"It worked," George said. "Directing two of your footmen to follow the smugglers on that last run from Donwell was a bit of genius."

"How brave of those footmen! And how wise of you, Mr. Weston," exclaimed Miss Bates. "Were those terrible smugglers captured?"

"They were," Mr. Weston replied. "The smugglers holed themselves up for the day at the inn, thinking themselves safe. My lads alerted the local authorities, who caught the blighters dead to rights."

"Once Mr. Weston alerted me about that," said George, "I notified Mr. Clarke. Events moved quickly after that."

That was certainly true. The first thing Emma had done after Constable Sharpe arrested Guy Plumtree that dreadful night was to pen an urgent note to George. At first light, one of Hartfield's grooms had set off for John's house in Brunswick Square. George and John had arrived back in Highbury by midafternoon and, after reassuring themselves that their respective family members were all well, had launched into the investigation. The past three days had been a flurry of activity involving meetings with lawmen, runners, and revenue agents. Fortunately, most of that had taken place at Donwell, sparing Father and Isabella constant disruptions to their peace.

"Poor Mr. Clarke," said Miss Bates with a sigh. "To be called from his sickbed to deal with such a dreadful situation."

"He's recovered fairly well," George replied. "And he's

happy to see the resolution of this case. The Trotman Gang has been operating in these parts for years along the roads up from the coast, and it has now been thoroughly dismantled."

Emma blinked. "Trotman. As in . . ."

"Harry Trotman," George dryly replied. "Donwell's footman."

Emma sighed. "Right under our noses the entire time."

"Good heavens," exclaimed Mrs. Weston. "That must mean Harry wasn't simply doing this on the side, in addition to his duties."

George nodded. "He was an integral part of the gang founded by his father, Stanley Trotman. Their base of operations was a tavern that Trotman owned on the outskirts of London."

"The same gang that used the Crown Inn as a depot when Mr. Stokes was alive," noted Emma.

"Yes. The Crown was a convenient waystop, but Trotman was forced to adjust the route when Mrs. Stokes turned them away. While they continued to use our church on occasion, for the most part they reduced their activity in and around Highbury."

Emma frowned. "I don't entirely understand what Harry was doing in the mix. Guy mentioned that Harry's father wished him to oversee the route in Surrey, but why a footman at Donwell?"

"According to Mrs. Trotman, it was her husband's idea."

"Wait, there's a *Mrs.* Trotman?" exclaimed Mrs. Weston. "How did you find out about her?"

John set down his brandy and took up the narrative. "That was down to Phelps, our runner. As you know, he's been working the case from the London end of things. His investigations led him to a tavern in Hampstead, which he then put under observation. Once the smugglers coming from Donwell were apprehended and Mr. Clarke sent word they were part of the Trotman Gang, Stevens put together a force of runners to raid the tavern and arrested Trotman and his accomplices."

Miss Bates pressed her hands to her cheeks. "Gracious! This all sounds like something out of a novel."

"An exceedingly bad novel," Father huffed. "The Trotmans appear to be the most unsavory sort of persons."

"Criminals generally are," John sardonically noted.

Emma waved an impatient hand. "May we get back to Mrs. Trotman? What was her role in all of this?"

"She was a very useful witness, as it turned out," said George. "Once her husband was under lock and key, she was quite happy to speak with Phelps."

"Why would she give testimony against her own husband and son?" Emma asked.

George hesitated. "Let me just say that the Stanley Trotman was neither an affectionate husband nor loving father. Mrs. Trotman had wished to escape from under his thumb for some time—as did Harry, apparently."

"And yet Harry was doing his father's bidding," she responded.

"Somewhat reluctantly, as it turns out. It was Stanley Trotman's idea to place Harry at Donwell as a footman. From there, Harry would oversee the smuggling ring in this part of Surrey and look for potential places to store their contraband. As customs enforcement became more effective, the gang was forced to alter their route on a fairly regular basis."

"If that's the case," Emma said, "it was a stroke of good luck for them to get Harry placed at Donwell."

"Unfortunately," George dryly replied. "About three years ago, I placed an ad for additional staff in one of the London gazettes. Stanley Trotman happened to see the ad and ordered his son to apply for a job as footman."

Emma shook her head. "But how did Harry *get* the job? He'd obviously never been a footman."

"Trotman fabricated the references, quite adroitly I might

add, since they fooled both me and Larkins. Harry also seemed a pleasant, biddable fellow, and he certainly had the physical qualifications for the position."

"Must have been a doddle for him," observed Mr. Weston. "With most of the abbey shut up, the fellow didn't have the heaviest of duties."

"He did not," George replied. "Which also gave him time to attend to his more nefarious activities."

Mrs. Weston blew out a disgusted breath. "He always seemed such a pleasant fellow, if not very bright."

Emma raised her eyebrows at her husband. "I suspect his dim behavior was all an act."

George nodded. "He was obviously much smarter than we thought, given his ability to pull off his deception for as long as he did."

Emma couldn't help feeling disgust for her lamentable lack of acumen. "How embarrassing that none of us ever noticed."

"Quite mortifying. You can be sure I'll be paying much greater attention to such matters in the future."

"As will Larkins, I'm sure," she replied. "Speaking of Larkins, I'm assuming it was Harry who framed him. But why was that even necessary? After all, Prudence's death had been declared an accident. At that point, no one suspected Harry of anything."

"It was Plumtree's idea, although Harry was the one who planted the evidence in Larkins's cottage," replied George. "As you've all obviously surmised by now, Harry and his men had begun using Donwell's old cellars to store contraband. Donwell was not one of their regular depots, but it served as a convenient backup when they had any difficulties with their regular routes."

Mr. Weston frowned. "Taking quite the risk, if you ask me, since you're the local magistrate."

"True, but once I moved to Hartfield, Harry was able to utilize Donwell to an even greater extent. The fact that Larkins lived just off the estate made it an easy target, as did having the undercroft and the abandoned cellars."

Emma thoughtfully tapped her chin. "But Donwell then became much less attractive once we decided to move back on a permanent basis. I understand all that. Still, why the need to frame Larkins?"

"Both Plumtree and Harry were concerned that Larkins was becoming suspicious about the cellars," George replied. "You'll recall that you observed that at least one of the cellars was in rather good condition. And Harriet noticed an odd smell when she inspected it with you, did she not?"

Emma grimaced. "She thought it smelled like tobacco. I thought it was just musty from disuse."

"Harriet was correct. They'd been using that particular cellar to store contraband tobacco."

"Which they removed on the night little Henry first saw them in the garden," Emma said. "George, when I found that package on the day of the skating party, was it deliberately left there?"

"I'll admit I didn't think to ask Guy that particular question, but it would make sense if they did—as evidence that would eventually lead to Larkins. Harry also knew Larkins was increasingly unhappy with his performance and would soon be recommending that he be let go. Since Mrs. Hodges would no doubt support that recommendation, Harry and Guy concluded that Larkins needed to be removed."

"One cannot help but be shocked by such cruelty," said Mrs. Weston. "To torment a good man like Larkins is beyond the pale."

Mr. Weston patted her hand. "The villains will pay, my dear. You may be sure of it."

Emma grimaced. "It seems like a lot of trouble to go through, since Donwell's usefulness was coming to an end. I'm afraid I don't entirely understand their reasoning, George."

"Plumtree and Harry still had need of Donwell on occasion, and they were willing to take the risk in the short term. As a location to store contraband, it was above suspicion."

"So they framed Larkins to remove any impediment to their villainous plans."

"Yes." George cast her a wry smile. "And they just might have gotten away with it if not for you, my dear. You were quite dogged in your pursuit of the truth."

"George, we all knew Larkins was innocent." She wrinkled her nose at him. "And I take it you mean I made rather a nuisance of myself."

"Mrs. Knightley, I must disagree," Miss Bates protested. "You were a true heroine in defending poor Mr. Larkins. Why, Athena herself couldn't have been more successful in restoring justice to Highbury."

Emma had to bite back a smile at the notion of herself as an avenging goddess. "You give me too much credit and not enough to yourself, ma'am. You were exceedingly helpful throughout this entire ordeal."

The little spinster blushed with pleasure.

"Very true," said Father, clearly much struck. "Quite heroic. But I do hope you both will refrain from such heroics in the future. It is exceedingly hard on my nerves."

"I'm sure nothing like this will happen again," Isabella said in a soothing tone.

"That's what Emma said the last time," her father gloomily replied.

True enough.

"How did Harry manage to acquire Prudence's mobcap and pink ribbon?" asked Mrs. Weston. "Those particular items more than anything convinced the coroner's jury that Larkins had murdered her."

"That and the fact that Larkins had been in love with the girl," added Mr. Weston.

Emma held up a restraining hand. "Which none of us will *ever* mention again. As for the mobcap and ribbons, Harry was the one we sent up to secure Prudence's room after . . ." She glanced at her father, who was still looking decidedly unsettled. "After the event."

"That and the fact that he and Prudence were secretly betrothed," said George.

Emma nodded. "Harry did seem genuinely distressed when she died. I don't think he feigned that emotion."

"If you'll recall, Prudence's father and brothers suspected that she was seeing someone."

Emma sighed, feeling dreadfully sad for the girl. "Initially, I wondered if Harry had feelings for her, but he swore up and down that he had a sweetheart back in London. He was very convincing."

"He had to be," said George.

Miss Bates fluttered a hand. "I don't understand why they needed to keep it a secret. No one even knew Harry was a smuggler."

"Plumtree insisted," George replied. "He felt knowledge of their relationship would attract too much attention—mostly from me, but obviously from the other servants, as well."

"Harry also told us that Prudence's family would not have approved," Emma interjected.

George nodded. "I'm not surprised, given how protective they were of the girl. It did not meet with Mr. Trotman's approval either, according to his wife. But Harry was set on leaving the smuggling game behind and moving to Yorkshire, where he and Prudence intended to open an inn. Mrs. Trotman also wished to join them there, to escape from her husband."

"I assume Harry was going to use his ill-gotten gains to fund this new life?" Emma asked.

George nodded. "Yes."

"Was Prudence aware of the source of his funds?"

"Not at first," he replied. "According to Plumtree, Harry managed to keep it secret from her for several weeks."

"But she eventually found out," Emma concluded.

"And became quite upset. She insisted that if Harry wished to marry her, he needed to cease his smuggling activities immediately. He promised that he would, although he had no intention of doing so until his business at Donwell was concluded. As you can imagine, that turn of events made Plumtree very nervous. He thought Harry was a fool for getting involved with Prudence in the first place."

John let out a disgusted snort. "The blighter made that pretty clear. I was tempted to darken his daylights when he started talking about the poor girl. Personally, I hope the judge sees through this lunacy nonsense and sends the man straight to the gallows."

"John, you must refrain from using such rough language around the ladies," Father said with disapproval. "It will offend their delicate sensibilities."

Since her brother-in-law responded to that paternal reprimand with a scowl, obviously readying a sharp retort, Emma hastily intervened.

"I will assume that Prudence discovered that Harry had not, in fact, given up smuggling," she said to George.

"Indeed. She found out that Harry and Guy were going to carry out a run the night of the betrothal party at Donwell."

Mr. Weston made a disgusted noise. "The night of the party? What absolute nerve. I don't know how you can relate this all so calmly, Knightley. It's outrageous."

"I never said it wasn't," George replied. "However, it was quite a clever move on their part. They intended to use the commotion as a distraction to cover the removal of tobacco from the cellar. I understand from Mr. Clarke that it's not an uncommon tactic to use such events to do so."

Now it all became clear.

"Prudence and Harry fought before the party, didn't they?" asked Emma. "That's what she was *truly* upset about, not—"

She mentally winced, recalling her suspicion that William Cox had been the cause of the girl's upset.

"That's what she was upset about," she rather lamely concluded.

George's gaze held an ironic glint since he obviously knew what she was thinking. Thankfully, he merely nodded.

"Yes. Prudence threatened to come to me and expose the entire scheme if Harry went ahead with the plan. He promised her that it would be his final run, because then they would have the funds they needed to start their new life."

Emma couldn't help but recall how distressed Prudence had been that night. "I wonder if she still intended to go to you, regardless."

"She *was* very upset when we saw her in the corridor," commented Mrs. Weston.

"We cannot know," George replied. "What we do know is that Plumtree was not reassured by Harry's insistence that he could manage Prudence. He decided, obviously without Harry's knowledge, that Prudence needed to be silenced."

Miss Bates dabbed her eyes with a handkerchief, clearly overcome. "That poor, poor girl. And when I think of how many pleasant conversations I had with Guy over the years . . . why, it's almost impossible to believe."

"I for one never trusted the Plumtrees," said Father in a severe tone. "The squire is much too bluff and blustering for my comfort."

"He's a good man for all that," Mrs. Weston gently corrected. "One cannot help but feel for him."

"And his son is the opposite of blustering," Emma noted. "He's the proverbial snake in the garden. But, George, we saw Prudence's room and there was no evidence of a struggle. How did Guy manage to avoid it?"

"Ah, that was because he dosed her with one hundred proof spirits."

"Good Lord!" exclaimed Mr. Weston. "That's awful."

"I don't understand," Emma said with a frown. "What does that mean?"

"One never drinks any spirit—brandy, port, or gin—in a pure distillation," Mr. Weston replied. "It's always watered down in order to make it palatable and safe. If one were to drink one hundred percent alcohol, one could become insensible very quickly. If one drank enough, it could even be lethal."

Emma pressed a hand to her stomach, feeling slightly queasy. "It was Guy who filched the decanter of sherry from the drawing room, wasn't it? He doctored it with spirits and fed it to Prudence, knowing it would render her unconscious—or even kill her."

"Correct," George replied. "Plumtree followed Prudence up to her room, ostensibly to persuade her to support Harry. In reality, of course, he had a different goal in mind."

Mrs. Weston grimaced. "How utterly wicked. But I wonder how he persuaded Prudence to drink such a dreadful concoction? She never imbibed spirits, according to those who knew her."

"Unfortunately, her unfamiliarity with spirits probably worked against her, since she might not have recognized how strong it was. And Plumtree did state she was exceedingly upset—quite agitated, in fact. He convinced her that a glass of sherry would settle her nerves, so they could then talk and find an agreeable solution to the problem." George's expression became even grimmer. "His powers of persuasion were successful. Once Prudence drank a glass of the doctored spirits, it probably took mere minutes before she was incapacitated—or at least unable to defend herself."

A heavy silence fell over the room. Emma struggled to keep her emotions at bay—fury at the ugliness of it all, and sorrow for a young life so callously snuffed out.

John stirred first and put his arm around Isabella. "Are you all right, my dear? It's an ugly tale."

Isabella drew in a quavering breath. "I . . . I think so. But what a dreadful man. One can hardly believe it of him."

At this point, Emma could almost believe Guy was indeed a lunatic. That a young man with so many advantages could do what he did defied all rational explanation.

"Harry *was* genuinely upset that night," she said again. "He must truly have been fond of Prudence."

"Not fond enough to take action against his accomplice," George replied. "But Plumtree did admit that Harry was furious with him."

Mr. Weston let out a disgusted snort. "Likely because it threatened to bring the whole rig down around their ears."

"There is that," admitted George.

Emma curled her hands into fists and knocked them together in frustration. "But *why*, George? Why was Guy involved with this in the first place? He's the son of a wealthy squire, for heaven's sake. How did he become mixed up with a criminal gang?"

"Bad seed from the start, I'd say," opined Mr. Weston.

"That's not much of an explanation, dear," replied his wife.

"Good enough for me."

Miss Bates shook her head. "I agree with Mrs. Knightley. It seems impossible that Guy could be a smuggler, much less a ruthless . . ." She stopped on a sigh.

"From what we could gather, it initially started off as a lark," said George. "Plumtree met Harry quite by chance one day in—"

Emma put up a hand. "Let me guess. A tavern in Leatherhead."

"Yes. As you know, Plumtree never had the opportunity to attend university, and was kept close at home by his parents. He greatly chafed against the restrictions they placed on him and was drawn to smuggling as a grand adventure. He came to enjoy it—so much so that he allowed Trotman to use Plumtree Manor as a depot along the route to London."

"Good heavens," exclaimed Mrs. Weston.

"Bad seed," Mr. Weston tersely noted.

Emma frowned. "George, if the smugglers were able to use Plumtree Manor as a depot, then why Donwell, too?"

"You raise an excellent point, my dear. But ask yourself what changed in Guy Plumtree's life in the last year."

She thought for a moment. "His mother died and Squire Plumtree decided to spend most of his time at Plumtree Manor, rather than London."

"Exactly. While his father was absent for much of the time, Plumtree was able to use an abandoned barn to store the contraband. Once his father returned to the manor, that became impossible. It was Plumtree's suggestion that he and Harry transfer the operation to Donwell—which lined up nicely with my removal to Hartfield."

Emma shook her head. "Guy Plumtree is quite the evil genius for one so young."

"The entire situation is a disgrace," huffed Father. "I do not approve of those Plumtrees, Emma. I do hope we will never have to see any of them in the future."

"No one approves of Guy Plumtree, dear," she replied. "And I doubt the squire will wish to show his face in Highbury ever again."

"He should have kept a better eye on his son," Father sternly said. "I do hope John will never allow my grandchildren to run about unsupervised in such a manner."

"I should think not," John huffily replied. "And I take exception to the very suggestion that—"

Isabella jumped to her feet. "Dearest, your glass is empty. Let me fetch you another brandy."

She snatched the glass—which was not empty—from her husband's hand and hurried to the breakfront. Emma could sympathize with her sister's reaction. It felt as if they'd spent the entire evening dodging one exploding shell of a surprise after another.

"George, I'm sure you and John are exhausted from this awful day," she said. "But it's a relief to finally know what happened."

"I imagine there will be more information revealed at the trial," he replied. "Phelps, our runner, will also be writing up a full report for me." He reached over and gently pressed her arm. "You do realize you'll have to testify at the trial."

She sighed. "I suppose there's no avoiding it."

Father gasped. "George, I do *not* approve of Emma participating in trials. She seems to do quite too many of them. Courtrooms are always so unhealthy. Either they are too drafty or the air is very bad."

"Yes, dear, it's very inconvenient," replied Emma in a consoling voice. "But George will take care of everything."

"The trial won't commence for some weeks," said her husband. "In the meantime, I suggest we all try to resume our normal lives."

Mr. Weston lifted his glass in salute. "Hear, hear. I've had quite enough of smugglers and madmen running about dear old Highbury."

Miss Bates raised a timid hand. "I do have one more question, Mr. Knightley. If it's not too much trouble."

George smiled at her. "Of course not, ma'am."

"I was wondering about poor Mr. Barlowe. He is innocent in all of this, is he not?"

"He is. Plumtree curried our vicar's friendship simply to keep an eye on him, since the church had been used by the smuggling gang—a fact that Mr. Barlowe knew."

Emma had completely forgotten about their vicar. "That reminds me. What about the lights in the bell tower some weeks back? Before the casks were removed and Mr. Clarke was attacked?"

"That, strangely enough, *was* Barlowe and Plumtree," George replied. "As he considered Plumtree a friend, Barlowe took the risk of showing him the casks, and asked for his help in removing them. Plumtree took great pleasure in refusing the request, piously claiming that he couldn't involve himself in criminal activities. Barlowe then asked Mrs. Stokes to help him with his predicament, which she kindly, if ill-advisedly, did."

Mrs. Weston tsked. "How disgraceful to treat Mr. Barlowe in so shabby a fashion."

"At least he didn't murder the vicar," Mr. Weston sardonically replied.

"No more murders in Highbury," Emma's father said in a surprisingly stern tone. "I forbid it."

Emma smiled at him. "I agree completely, Father. From now on, we will only have happy events."

"Like your wedding, dear sir," added Mrs. Weston with a smile.

Miss Bates clasped her hands together. "Oh, Mrs. Weston, one finds it hard to think happy thoughts after such a dreadful time. However will we manage a wedding?"

"You're not to worry," Emma stoutly said. "It will be just the antidote to all this dreariness."

To think that she was now actually looking forward to the event, and it had only taken solving a murder and breaking up a smuggling ring to effect the change.

Father's anxious expression eased into a tentative smile. "I suppose we must begin making plans immediately, if such is the case." Then he held up a minatory finger and wagged it at Emma. "But, my dear, while you and Miss Bates should certainly plan whatever you wish, I insist there be no more investigations of nefarious activities, and *no cake*."